Ride On

FAITH ERIN HICKS

Colors by KELLY FITZPATRICK

First Second
NEW YORK

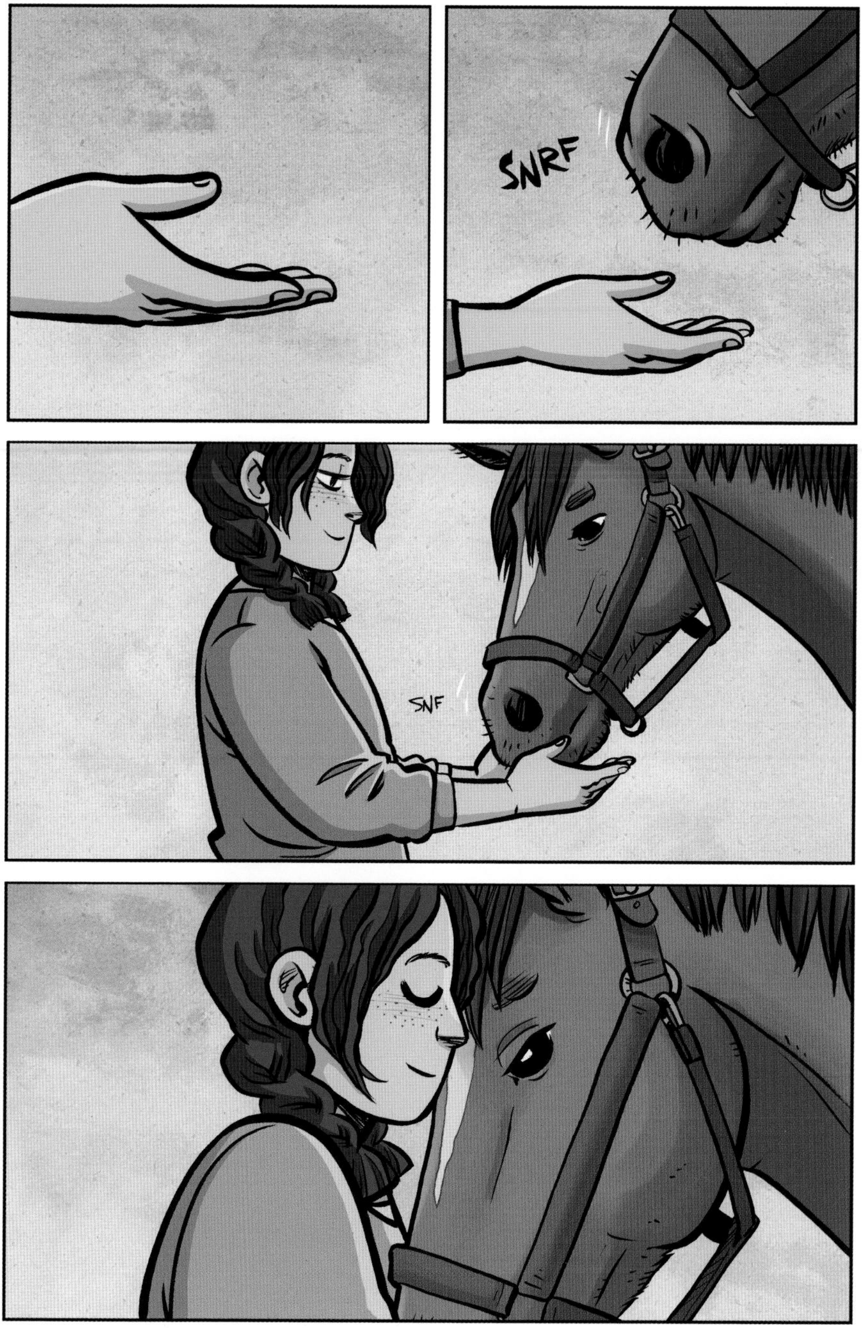
SNRF
SNF

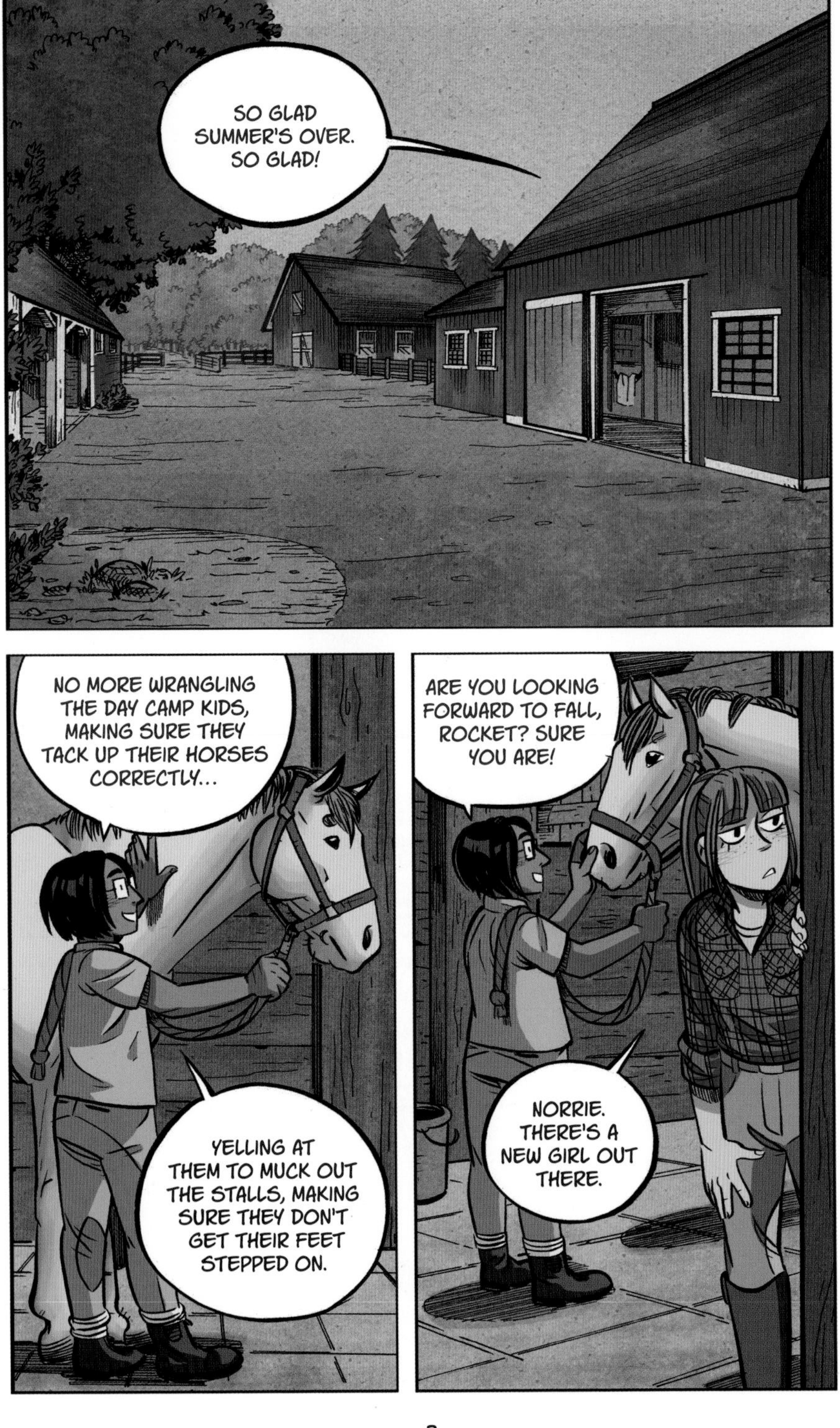
SO GLAD SUMMER'S OVER. SO GLAD!
NO MORE WRANGLING THE DAY CAMP KIDS, MAKING SURE THEY TACK UP THEIR HORSES CORRECTLY...
YELLING AT THEM TO MUCK OUT THE STALLS, MAKING SURE THEY DON'T GET THEIR FEET STEPPED ON.
ARE YOU LOOKING FORWARD TO FALL, ROCKET? SURE YOU ARE!
NORRIE. THERE'S A NEW GIRL OUT THERE.

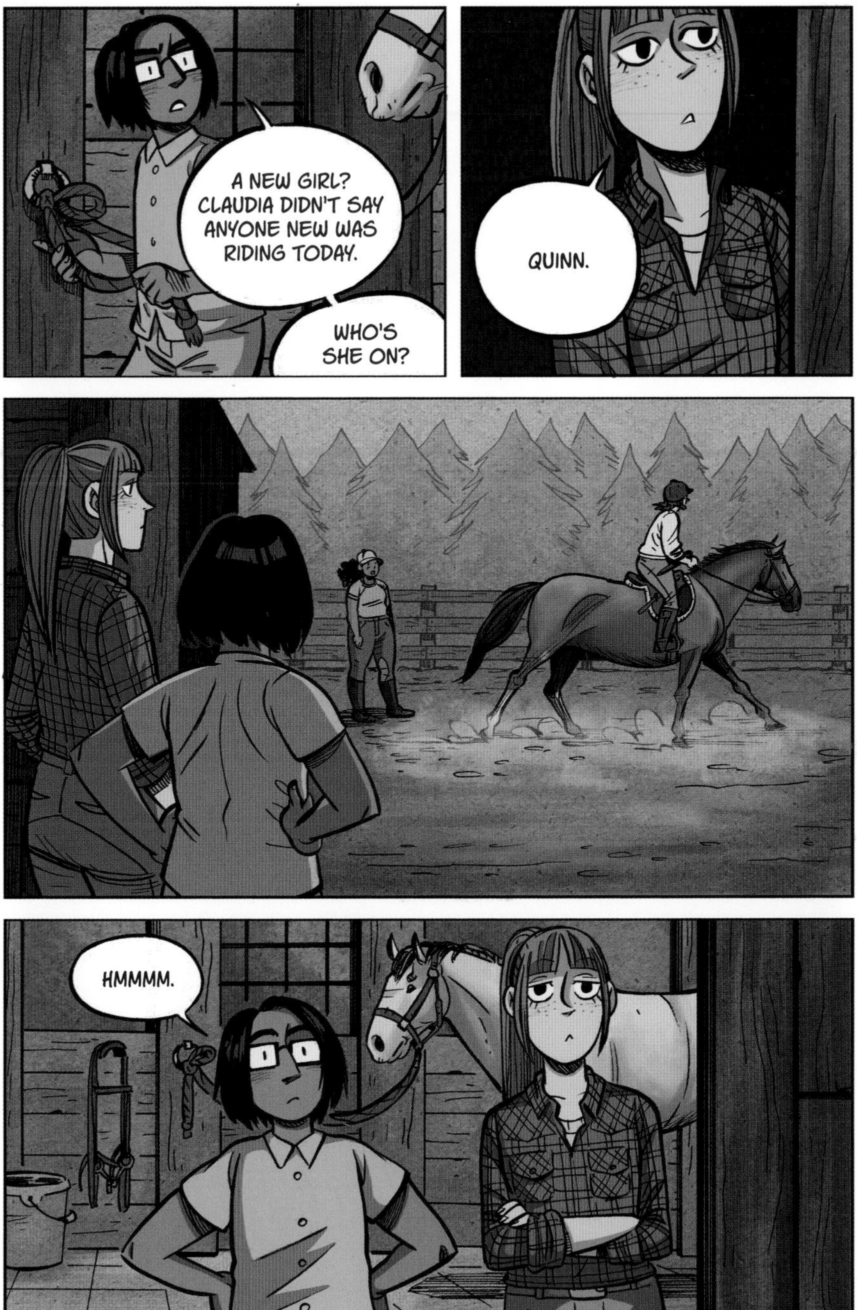
A NEW GIRL? CLAUDIA DIDN'T SAY ANYONE NEW WAS RIDING TODAY.
WHO'S SHE ON?
QUINN.
HMMMM.

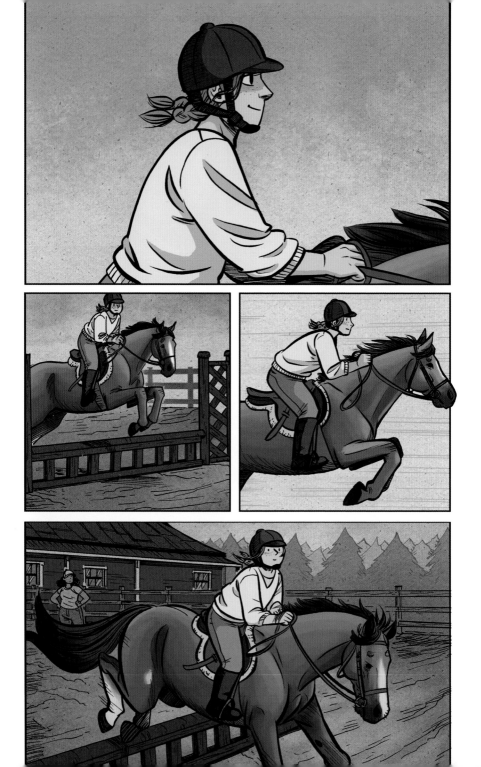

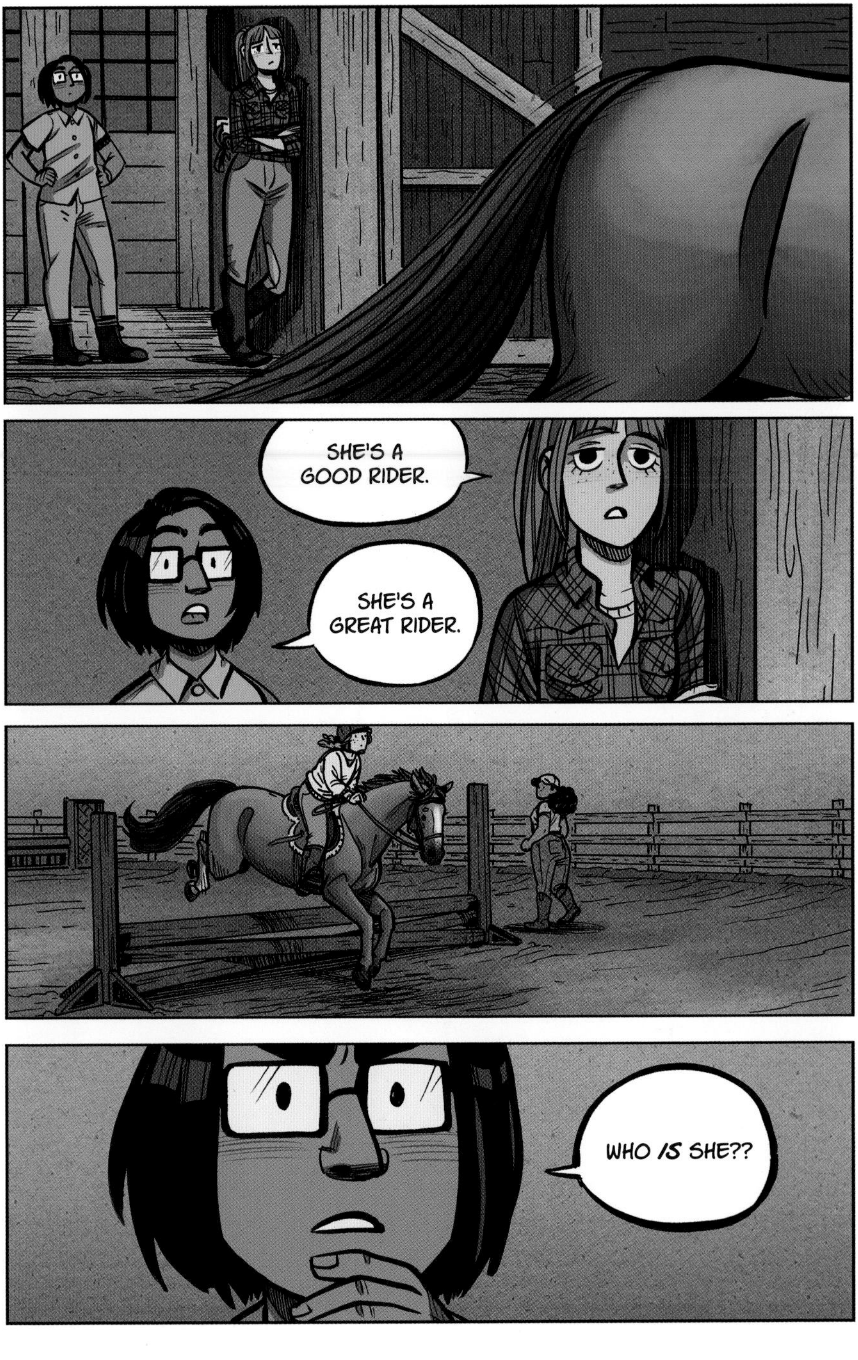
SHE'S A GOOD RIDER.
SHE'S A GREAT RIDER.
WHO *IS* SHE??

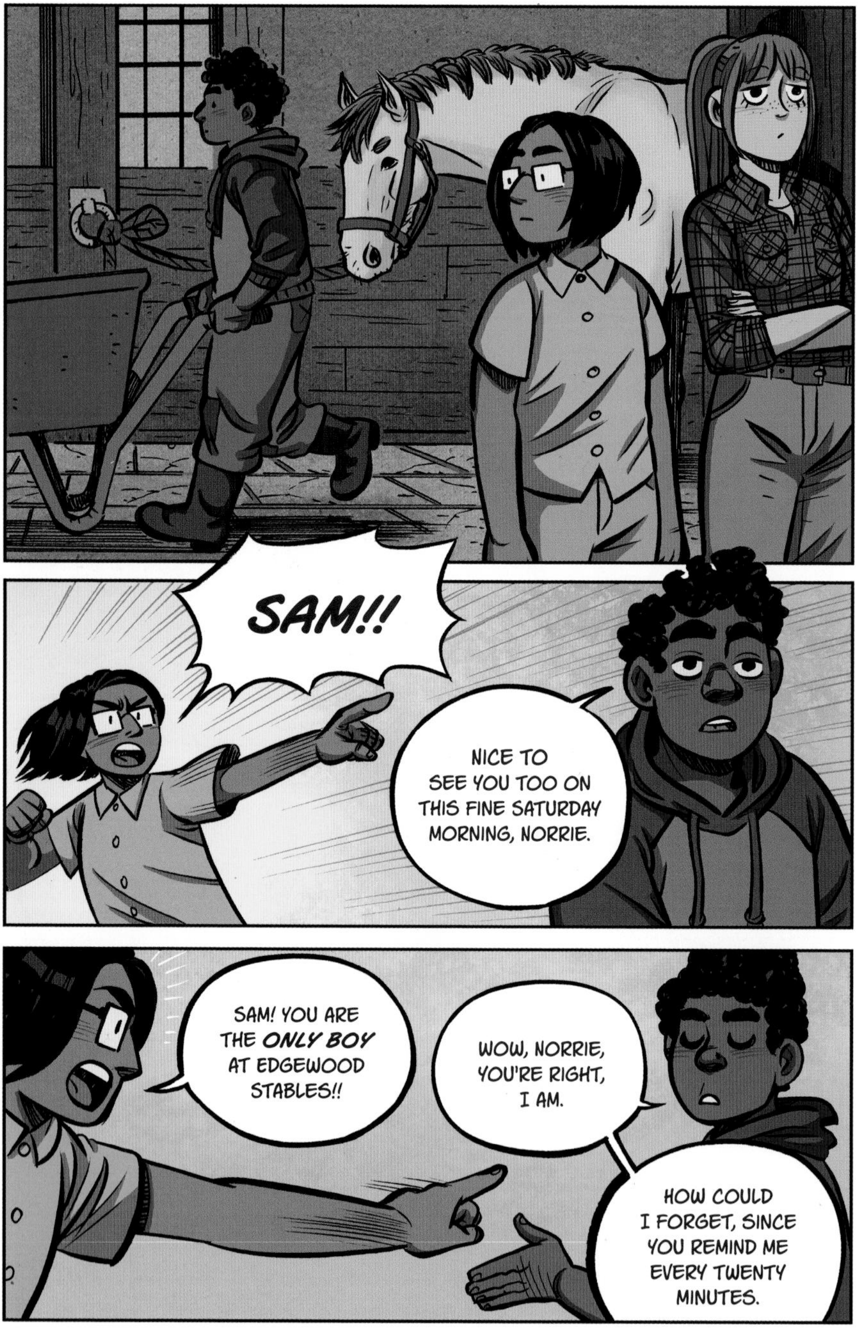
SAM!!
NICE TO SEE YOU TOO ON THIS FINE SATURDAY MORNING, NORRIE.
SAM! YOU ARE THE *ONLY BOY* AT EDGEWOOD STABLES!!
WOW, NORRIE, YOU'RE RIGHT, I AM.
HOW COULD I FORGET, SINCE YOU REMIND ME EVERY TWENTY MINUTES.

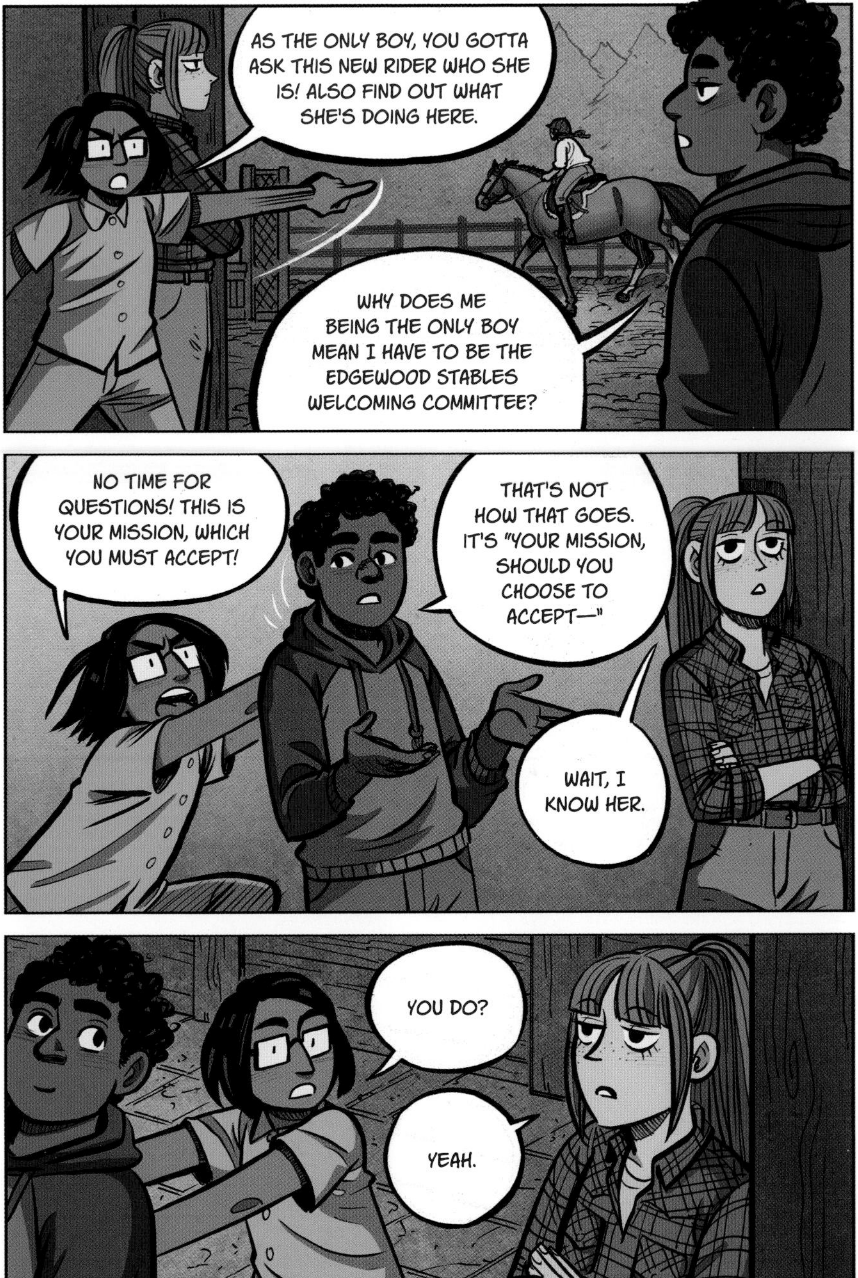
AS THE ONLY BOY, YOU GOTTA ASK THIS NEW RIDER WHO SHE IS! ALSO FIND OUT WHAT SHE'S DOING HERE.
WHY DOES ME BEING THE ONLY BOY MEAN I HAVE TO BE THE EDGEWOOD STABLES WELCOMING COMMITTEE?
NO TIME FOR QUESTIONS! THIS IS YOUR MISSION, WHICH YOU MUST ACCEPT!
THAT'S NOT HOW THAT GOES. IT'S "YOUR MISSION, SHOULD YOU CHOOSE TO ACCEPT—"
WAIT, I KNOW HER.
YOU DO?
YEAH.

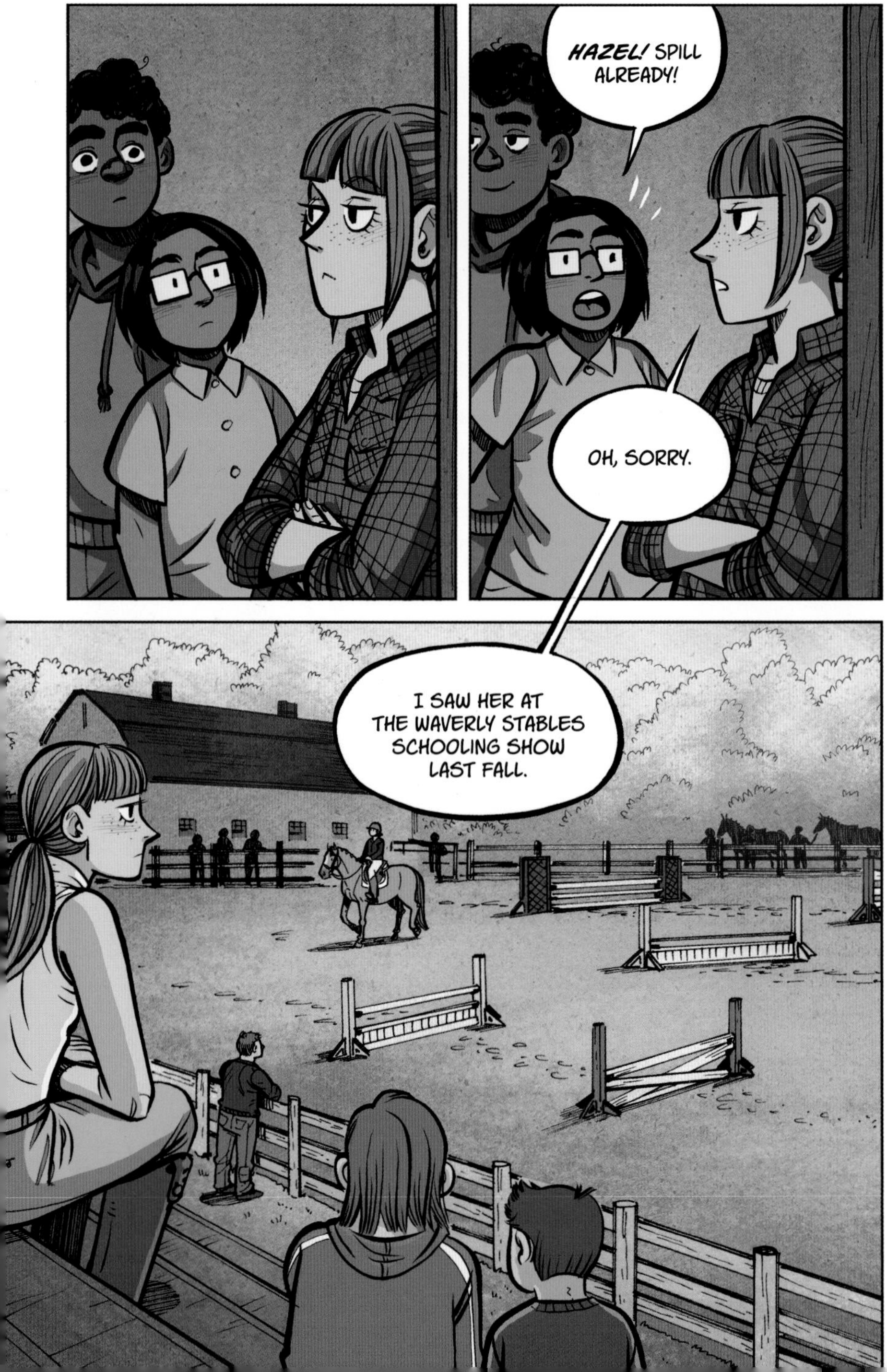
HAZEL! SPILL ALREADY!
OH, SORRY.
I SAW HER AT THE WAVERLY STABLES SCHOOLING SHOW LAST FALL.

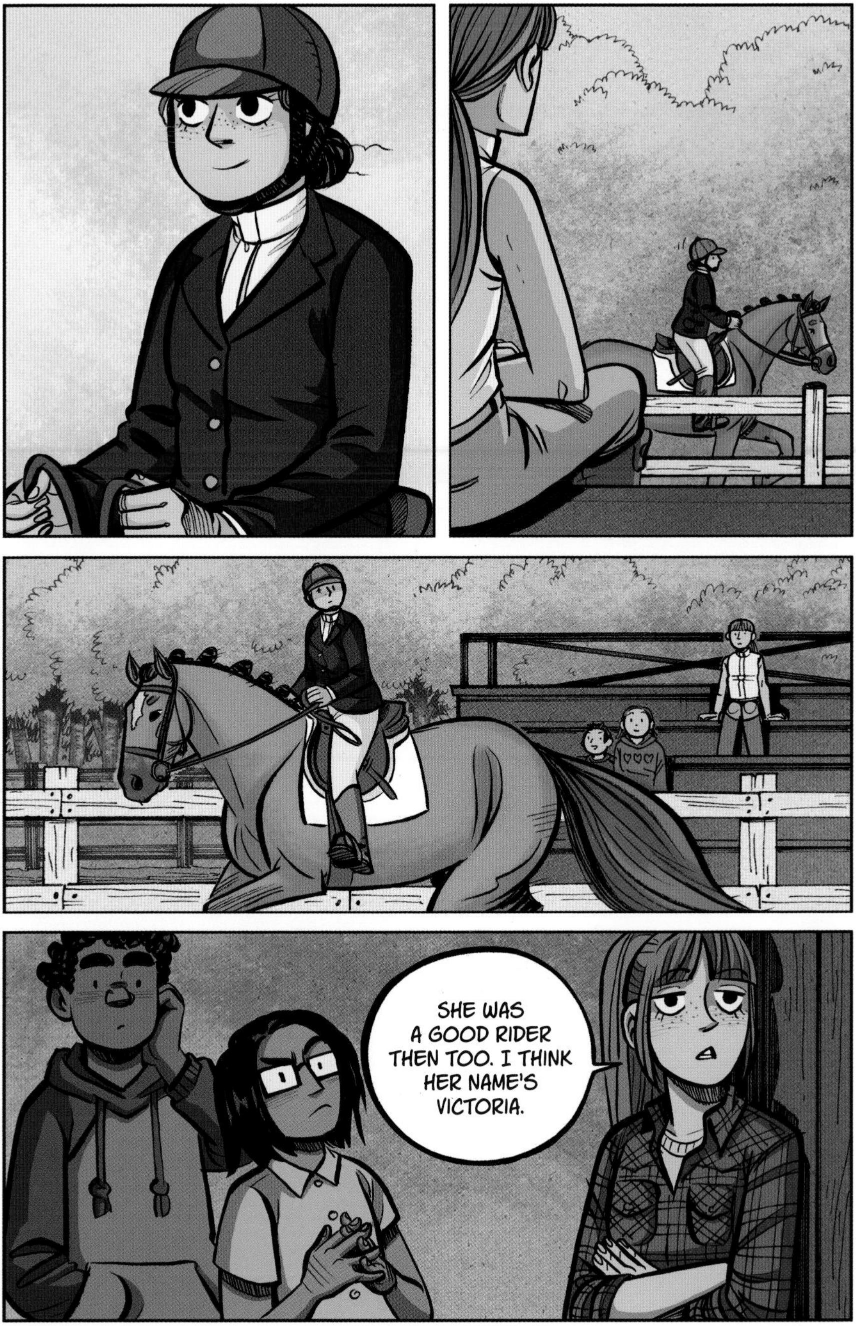
SHE WAS A GOOD RIDER THEN TOO. I THINK HER NAME'S VICTORIA.

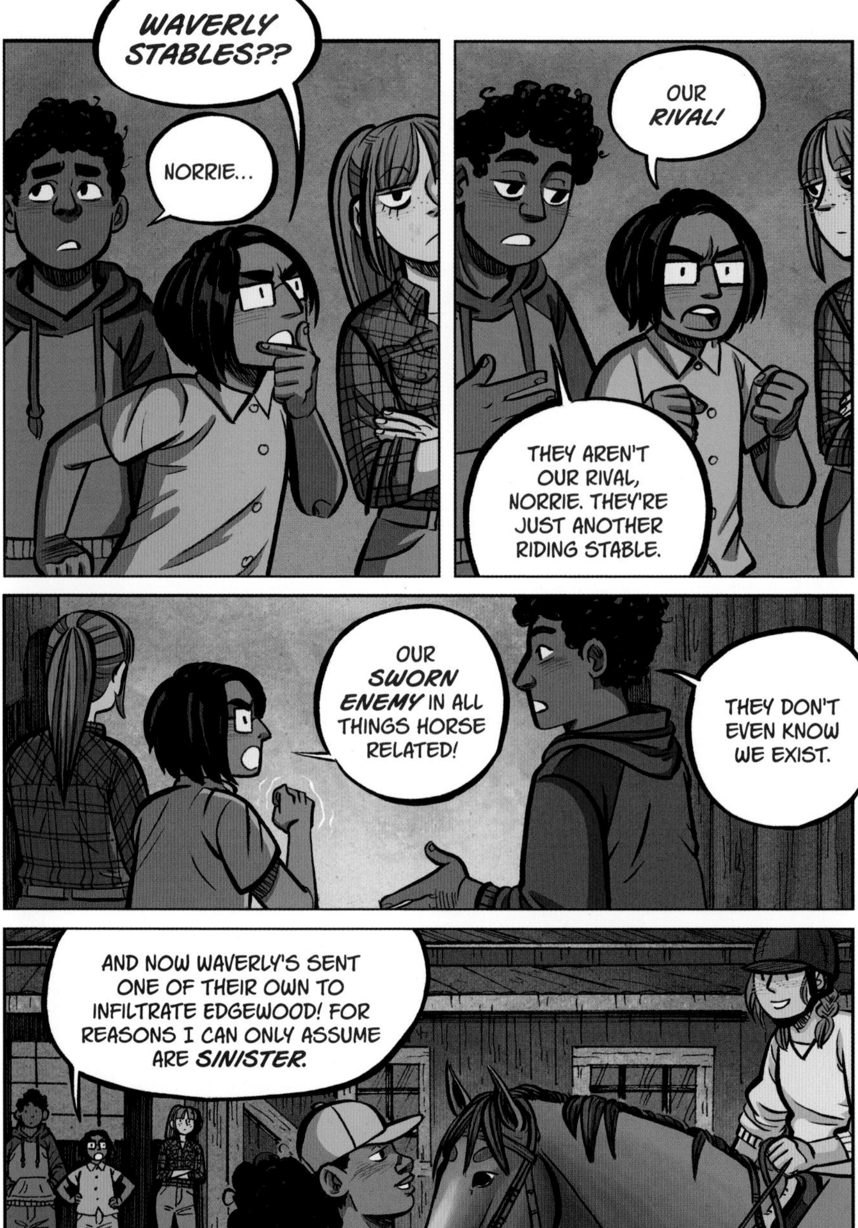
WAVERLY STABLES??
NORRIE...
OUR RIVAL!
THEY AREN'T OUR RIVAL, NORRIE. THEY'RE JUST ANOTHER RIDING STABLE.
OUR SWORN ENEMY IN ALL THINGS HORSE RELATED!
THEY DON'T EVEN KNOW WE EXIST.
AND NOW WAVERLY'S SENT ONE OF THEIR OWN TO INFILTRATE EDGEWOOD! FOR REASONS I CAN ONLY ASSUME ARE SINISTER.

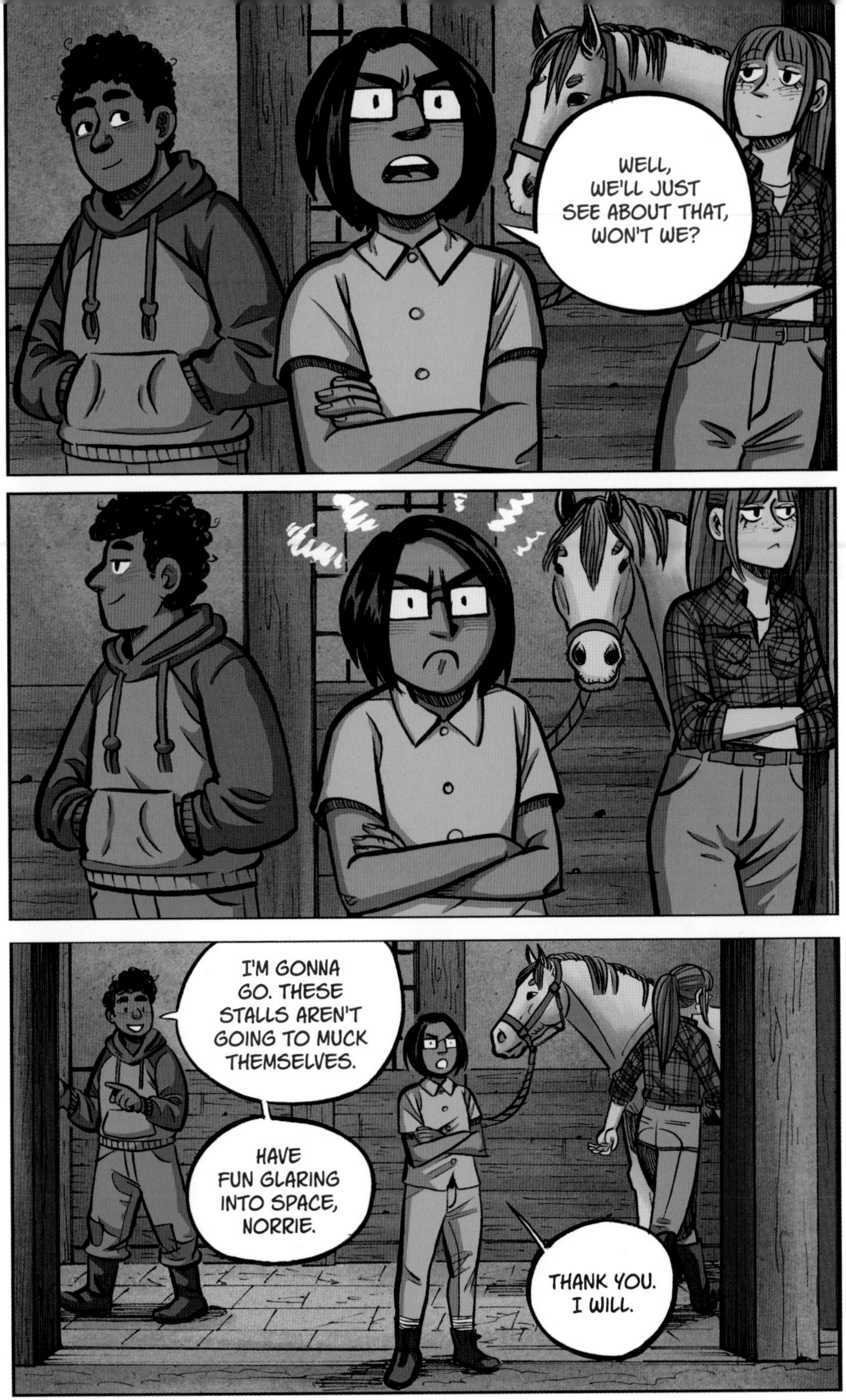
WELL, WE'LL JUST SEE ABOUT THAT, WON'T WE?
I'M GONNA GO. THESE STALLS AREN'T GOING TO MUCK THEMSELVES.
HAVE FUN GLARING INTO SPACE, NORRIE.
THANK YOU. I WILL.

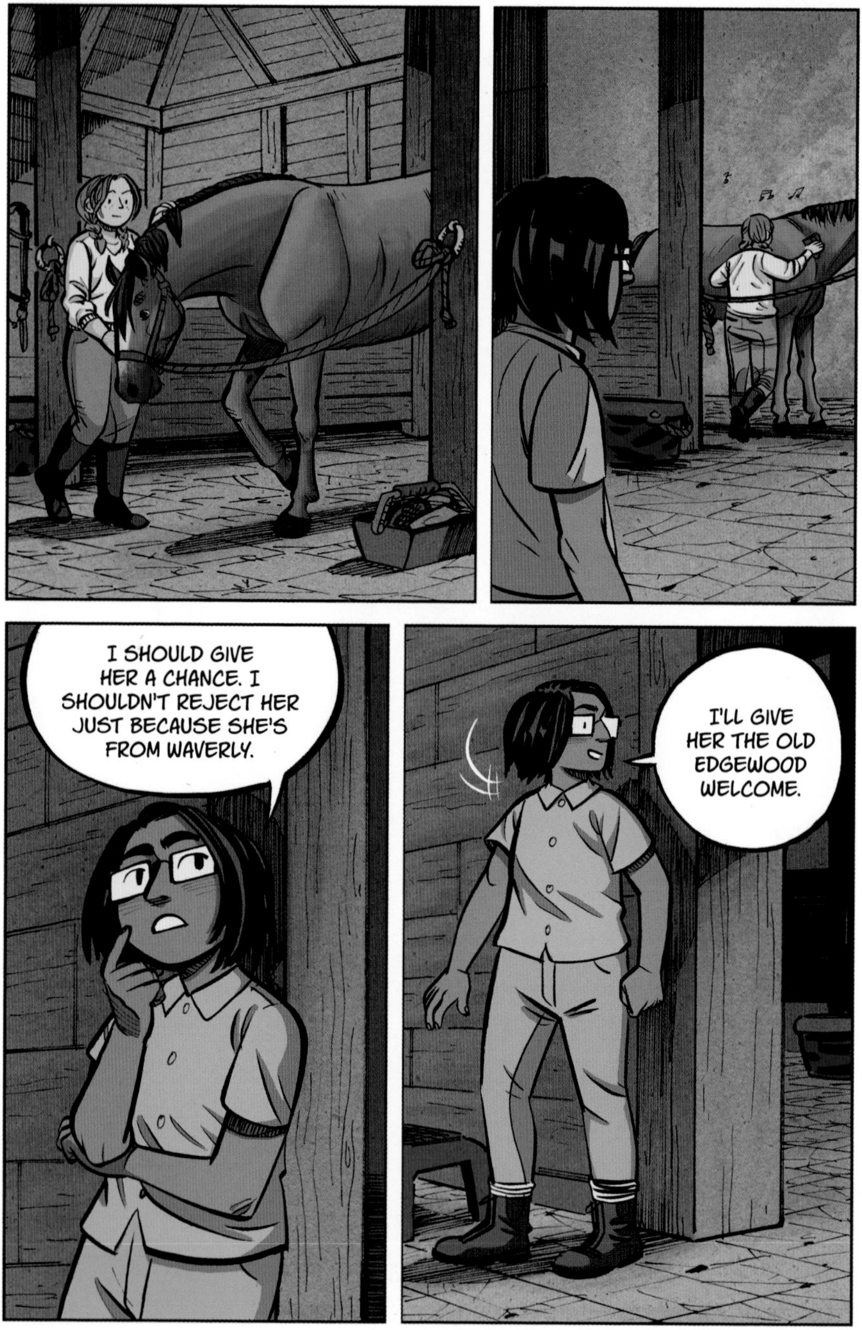
I SHOULD GIVE HER A CHANCE. I SHOULDN'T REJECT HER JUST BECAUSE SHE'S FROM WAVERLY.
I'LL GIVE HER THE OLD EDGEWOOD WELCOME.

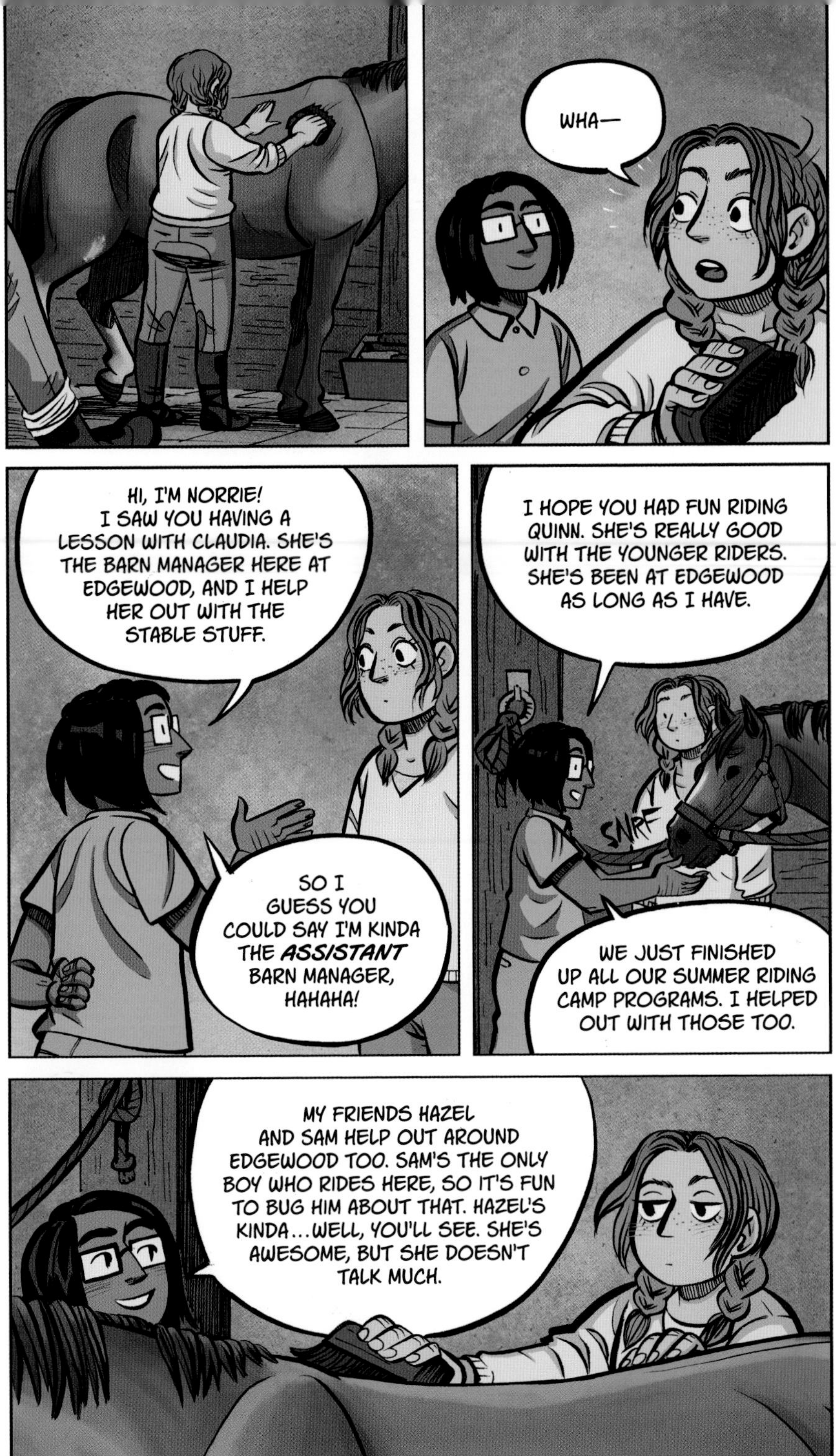
WHA—
HI, I'M NORRIE! I SAW YOU HAVING A LESSON WITH CLAUDIA. SHE'S THE BARN MANAGER HERE AT EDGEWOOD, AND I HELP HER OUT WITH THE STABLE STUFF.
SO I GUESS YOU COULD SAY I'M KINDA THE *ASSISTANT* BARN MANAGER, HAHAHA!
I HOPE YOU HAD FUN RIDING QUINN. SHE'S REALLY GOOD WITH THE YOUNGER RIDERS. SHE'S BEEN AT EDGEWOOD AS LONG AS I HAVE.
SNRF
WE JUST FINISHED UP ALL OUR SUMMER RIDING CAMP PROGRAMS. I HELPED OUT WITH THOSE TOO.
MY FRIENDS HAZEL AND SAM HELP OUT AROUND EDGEWOOD TOO. SAM'S THE ONLY BOY WHO RIDES HERE, SO IT'S FUN TO BUG HIM ABOUT THAT. HAZEL'S KINDA…WELL, YOU'LL SEE. SHE'S AWESOME, BUT SHE DOESN'T TALK MUCH.

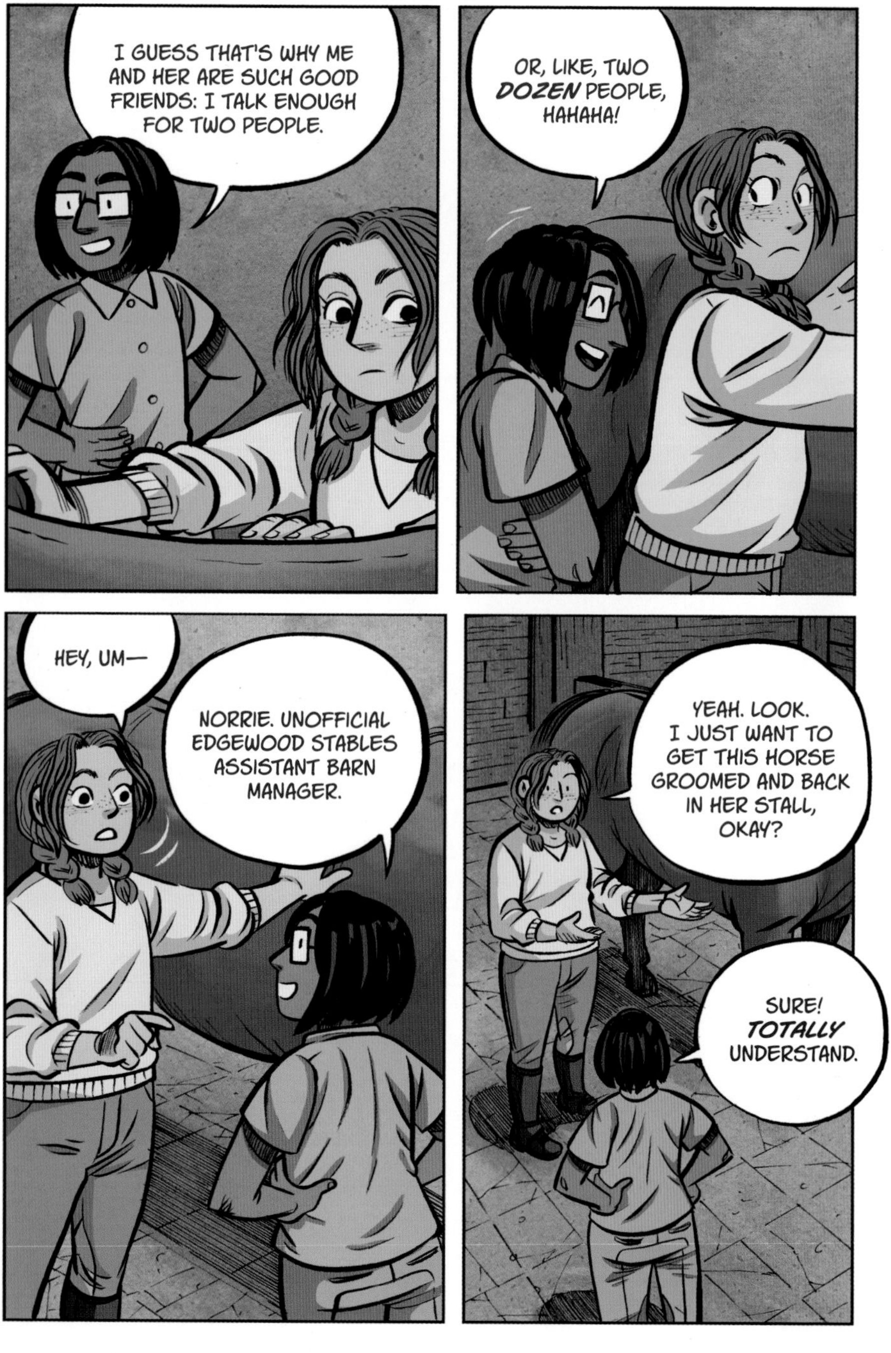
I GUESS THAT'S WHY ME AND HER ARE SUCH GOOD FRIENDS: I TALK ENOUGH FOR TWO PEOPLE.
OR, LIKE, TWO *DOZEN* PEOPLE, HAHAHA!
HEY, UM—
NORRIE. UNOFFICIAL EDGEWOOD STABLES ASSISTANT BARN MANAGER.
YEAH. LOOK. I JUST WANT TO GET THIS HORSE GROOMED AND BACK IN HER STALL, OKAY?
SURE! *TOTALLY* UNDERSTAND.

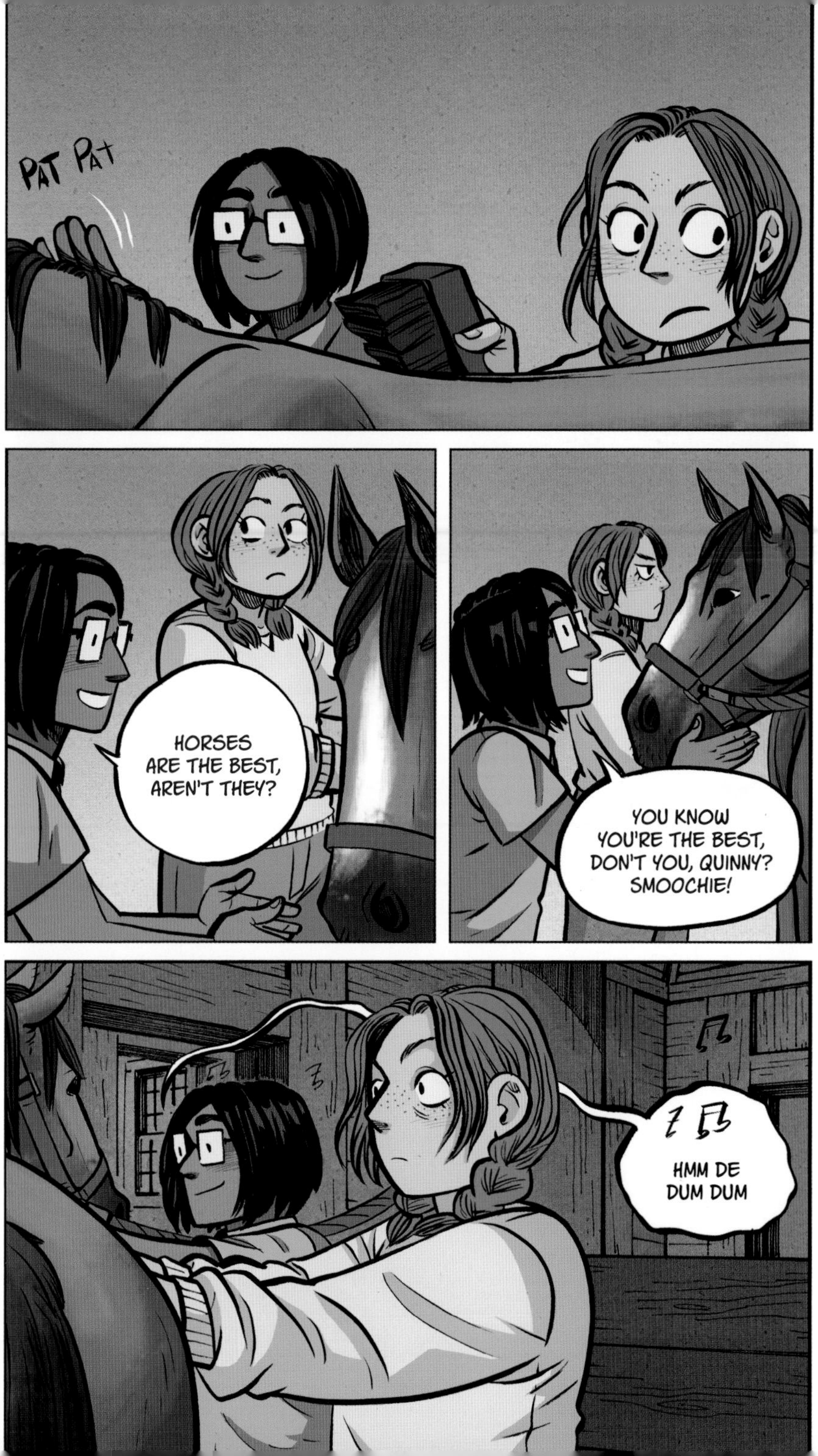
PAT PAT
HORSES ARE THE BEST, AREN'T THEY?
YOU KNOW YOU'RE THE BEST, DON'T YOU, QUINNY? SMOOCHIE!
HMM DE DUM DUM

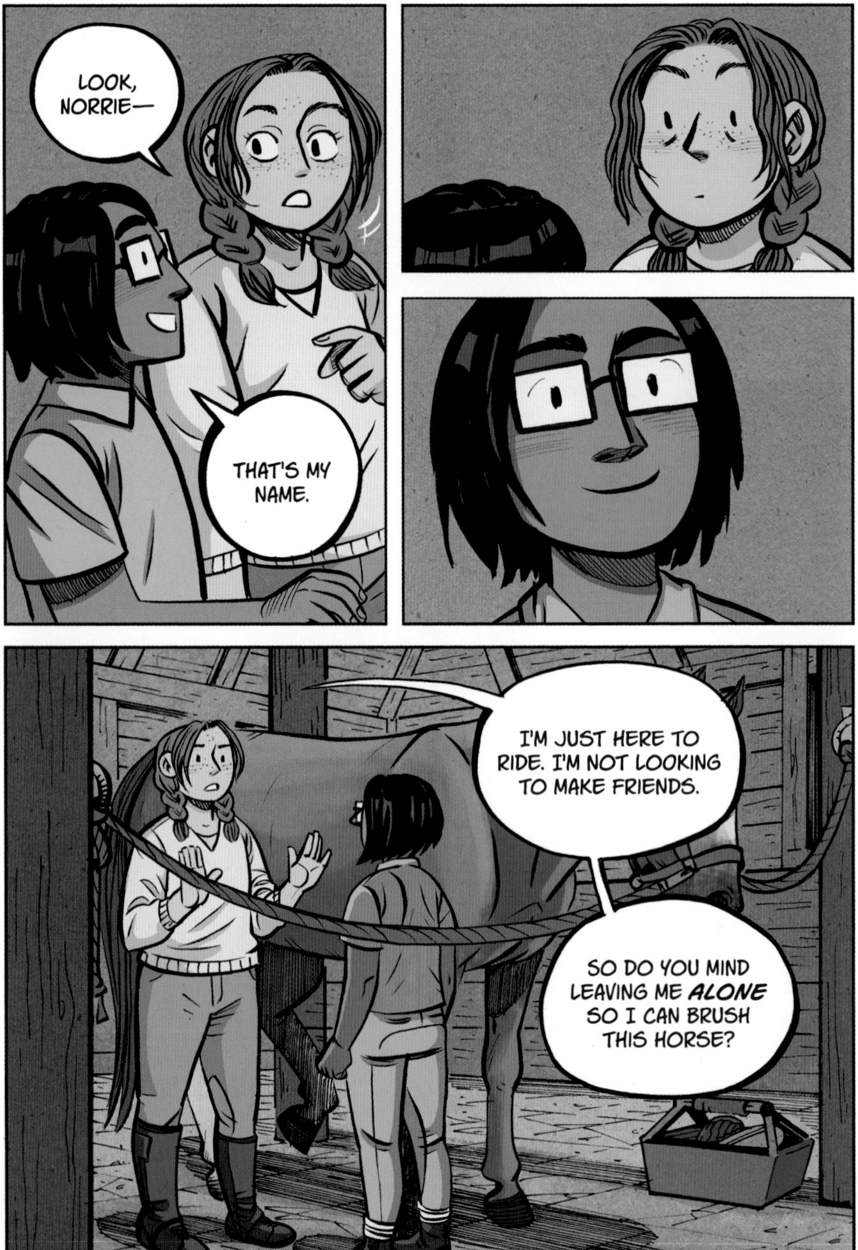
LOOK, NORRIE—
THAT'S MY NAME.
I'M JUST HERE TO RIDE. I'M NOT LOOKING TO MAKE FRIENDS.
SO DO YOU MIND LEAVING ME ALONE SO I CAN BRUSH THIS HORSE?

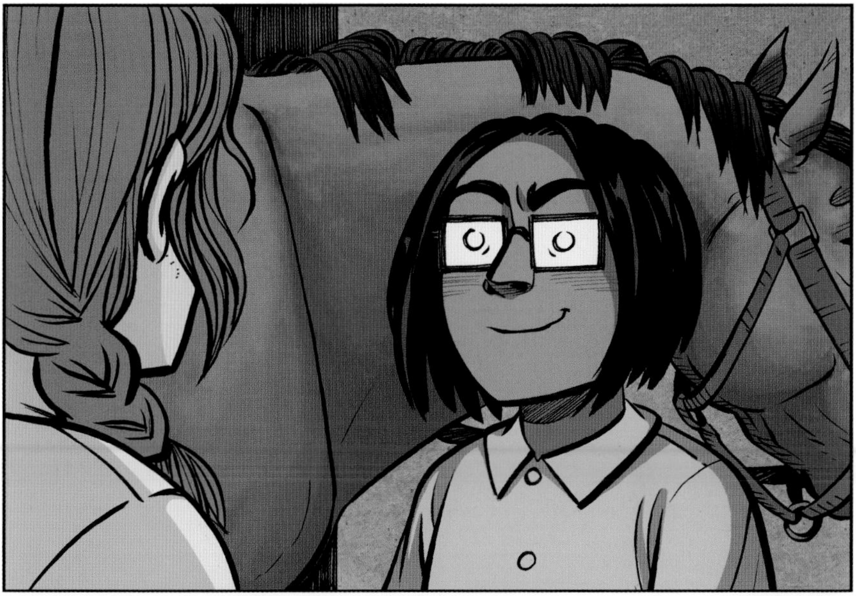

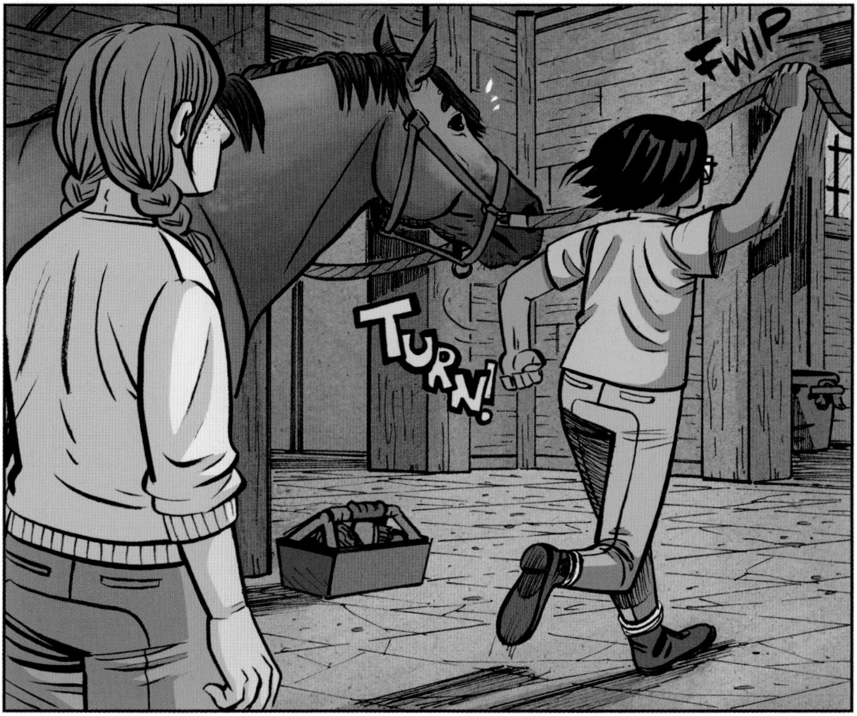
FWIP
TURN!

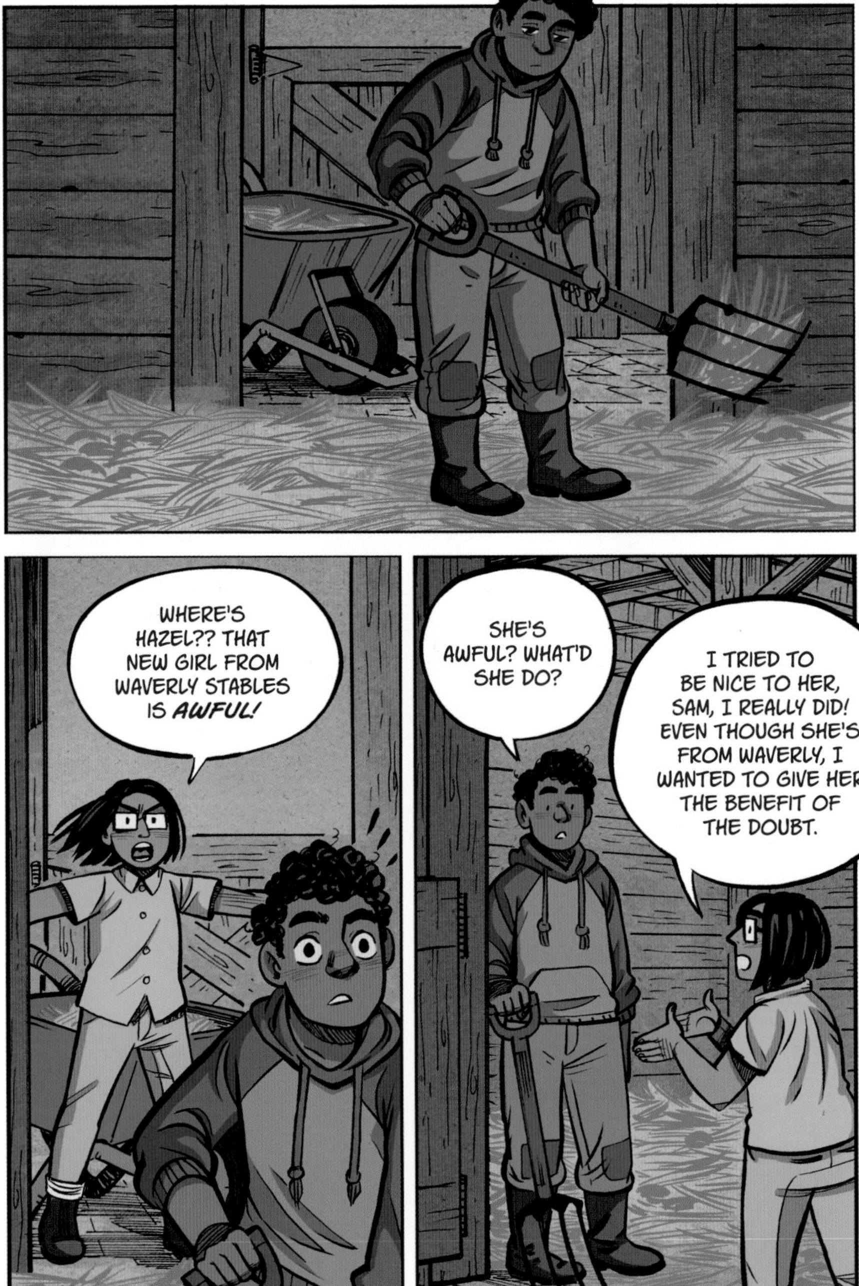
WHERE'S HAZEL?? THAT NEW GIRL FROM WAVERLY STABLES IS **AWFUL!**
SHE'S AWFUL? WHAT'D SHE DO?
I TRIED TO BE NICE TO HER, SAM, I REALLY DID! EVEN THOUGH SHE'S FROM WAVERLY, I WANTED TO GIVE HER THE BENEFIT OF THE DOUBT.

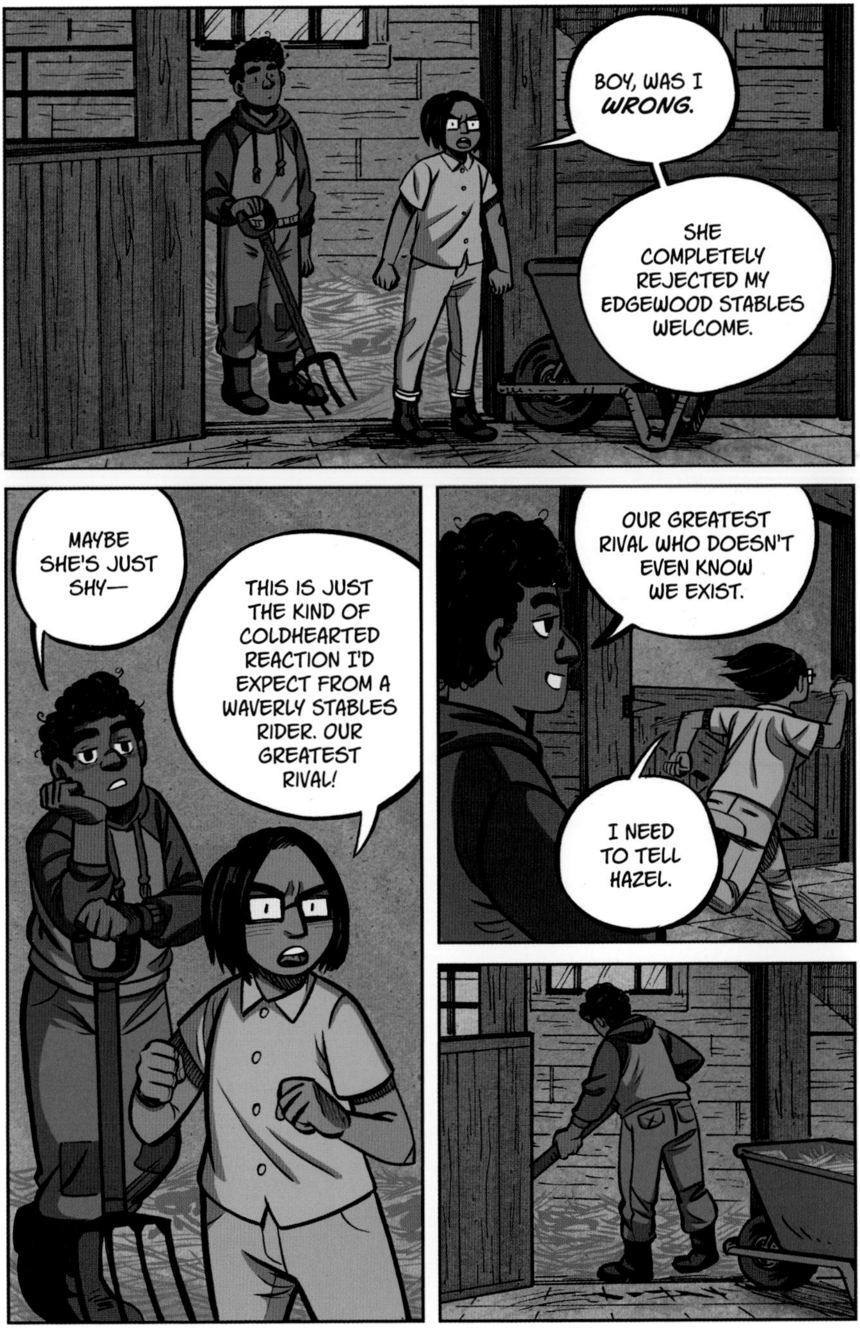
BOY, WAS I *WRONG.*
SHE COMPLETELY REJECTED MY EDGEWOOD STABLES WELCOME.
MAYBE SHE'S JUST SHY—
THIS IS JUST THE KIND OF COLDHEARTED REACTION I'D EXPECT FROM A WAVERLY STABLES RIDER. OUR GREATEST RIVAL!
OUR GREATEST RIVAL WHO DOESN'T EVEN KNOW WE EXIST.
I NEED TO TELL HAZEL.

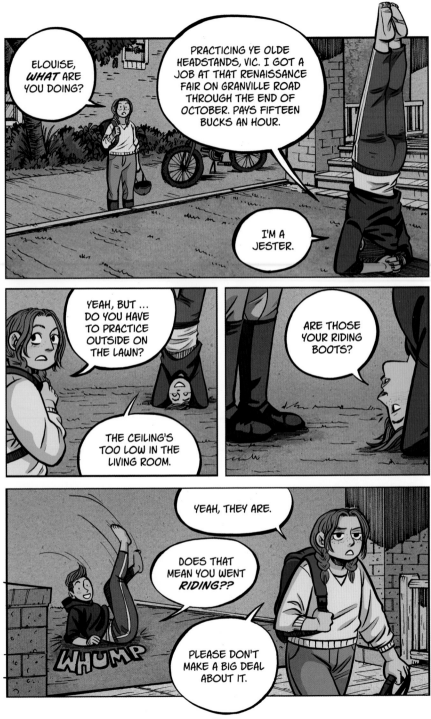

ELOUISE, *WHAT* ARE YOU DOING?

PRACTICING YE OLDE HEADSTANDS, VIC. I GOT A JOB AT THAT RENAISSANCE FAIR ON GRANVILLE ROAD THROUGH THE END OF OCTOBER. PAYS FIFTEEN BUCKS AN HOUR.

I'M A JESTER.

YEAH, BUT ... DO YOU HAVE TO PRACTICE OUTSIDE ON THE LAWN?

THE CEILING'S TOO LOW IN THE LIVING ROOM.

ARE THOSE YOUR RIDING BOOTS?

YEAH, THEY ARE.

DOES THAT MEAN YOU WENT *RIDING??*

PLEASE DON'T MAKE A BIG DEAL ABOUT IT.

WHUMP

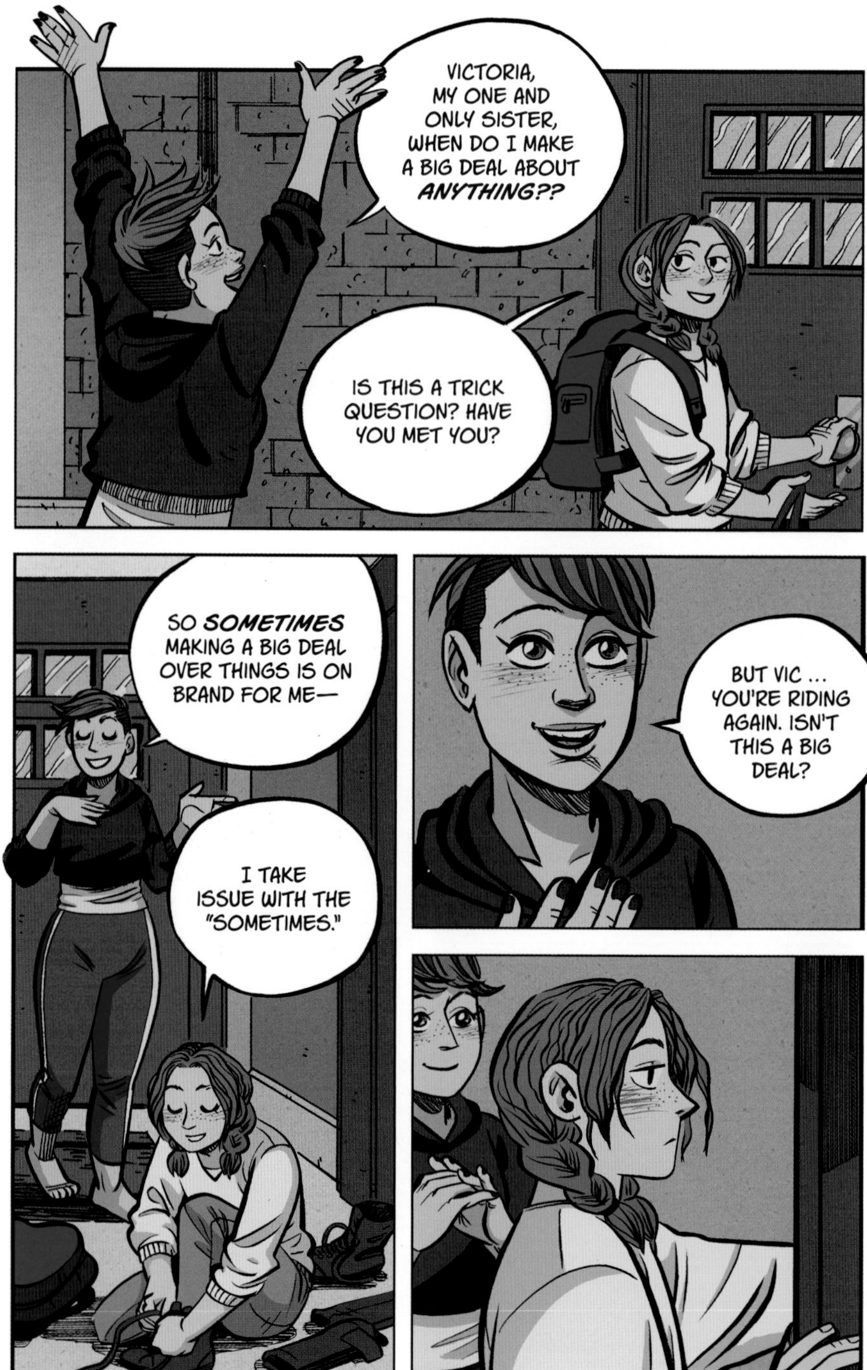
VICTORIA, MY ONE AND ONLY SISTER, WHEN DO I MAKE A BIG DEAL ABOUT *ANYTHING??*
IS THIS A TRICK QUESTION? HAVE YOU MET YOU?
SO *SOMETIMES* MAKING A BIG DEAL OVER THINGS IS ON BRAND FOR ME—
I TAKE ISSUE WITH THE "SOMETIMES."
BUT VIC ... YOU'RE RIDING AGAIN. ISN'T THIS A BIG DEAL?

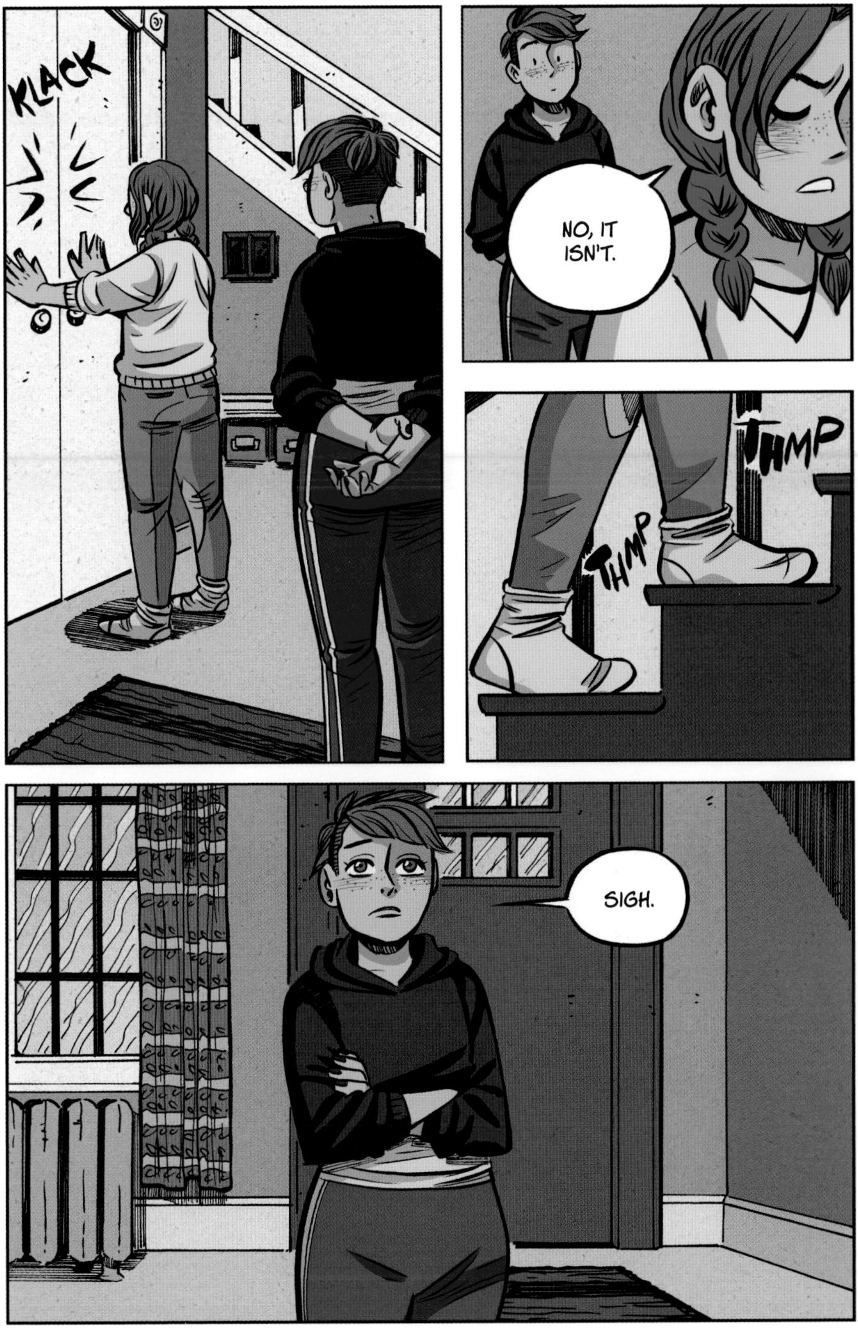
KLACK
NO, IT ISN'T.
THMP
THMP
SIGH.

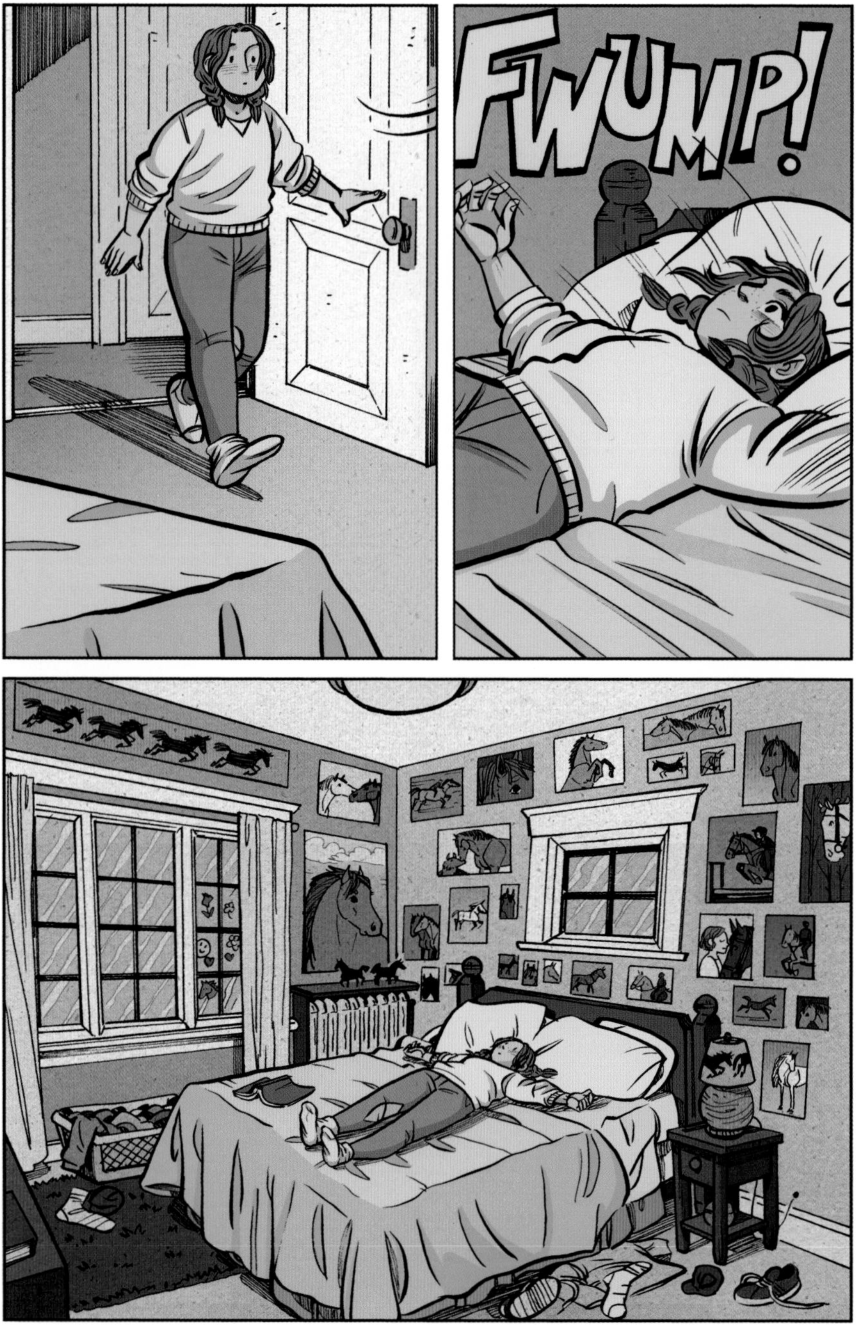
FWUMP!

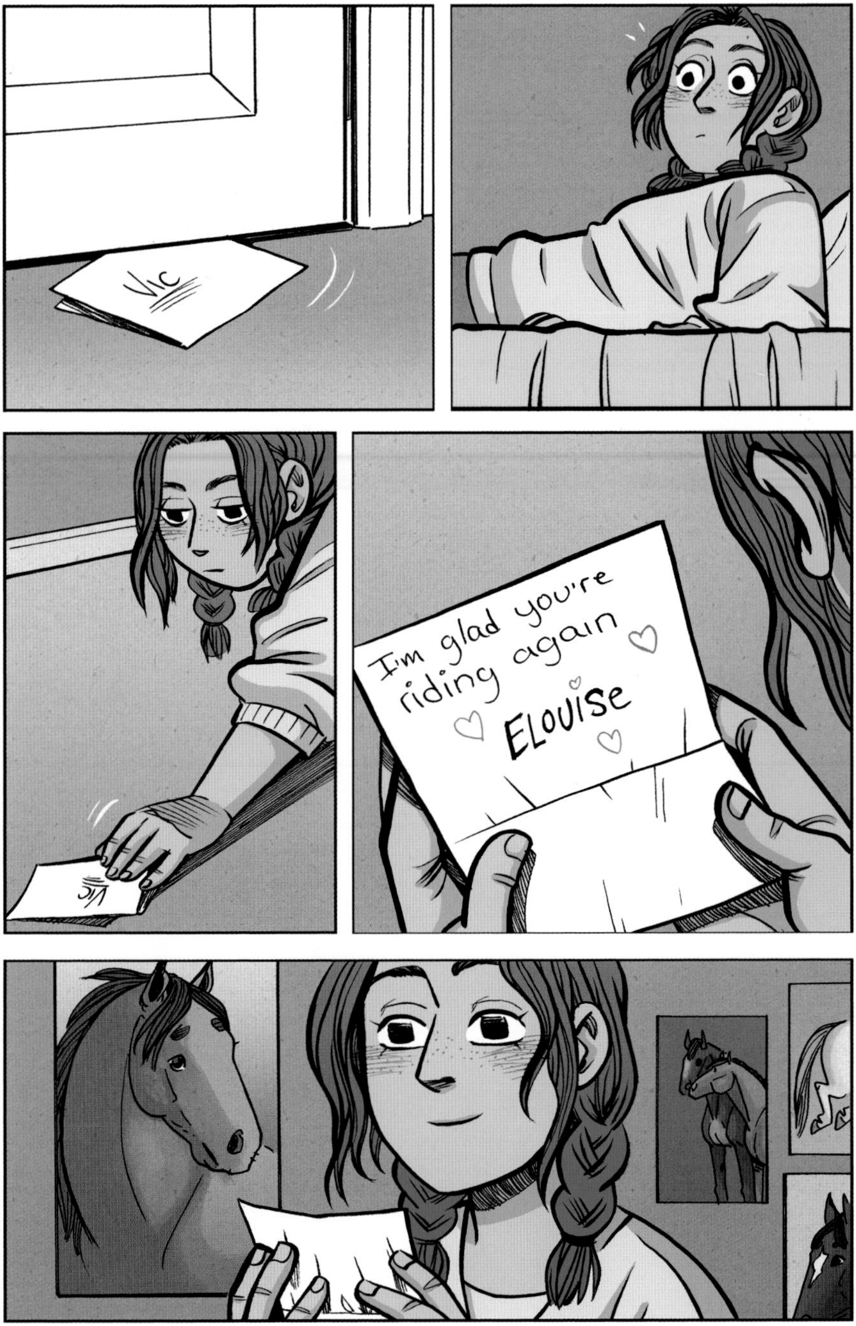
Vic
Vic
I'm glad you're riding again
ELOUISE

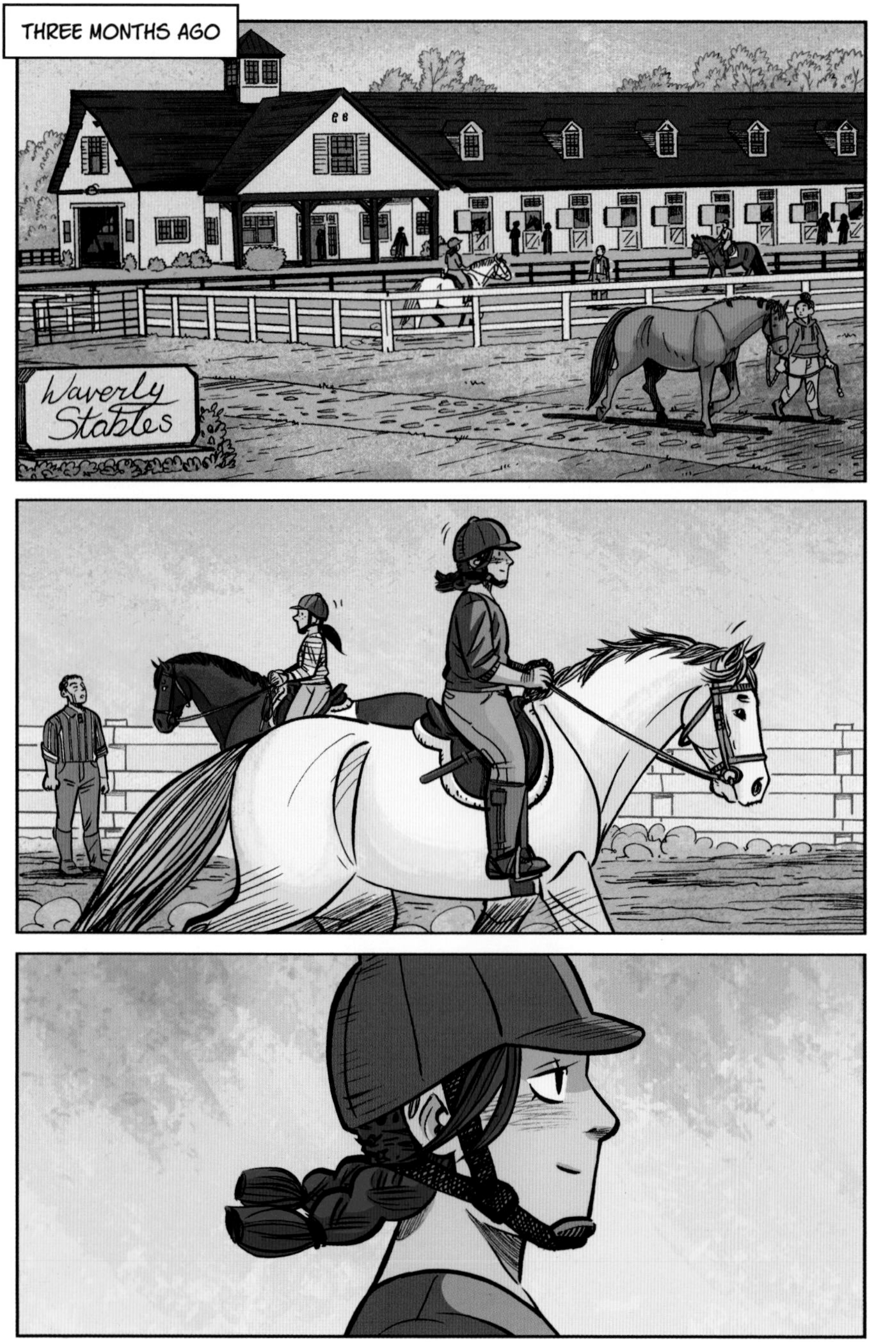
THREE MONTHS AGO
Waverly Stables

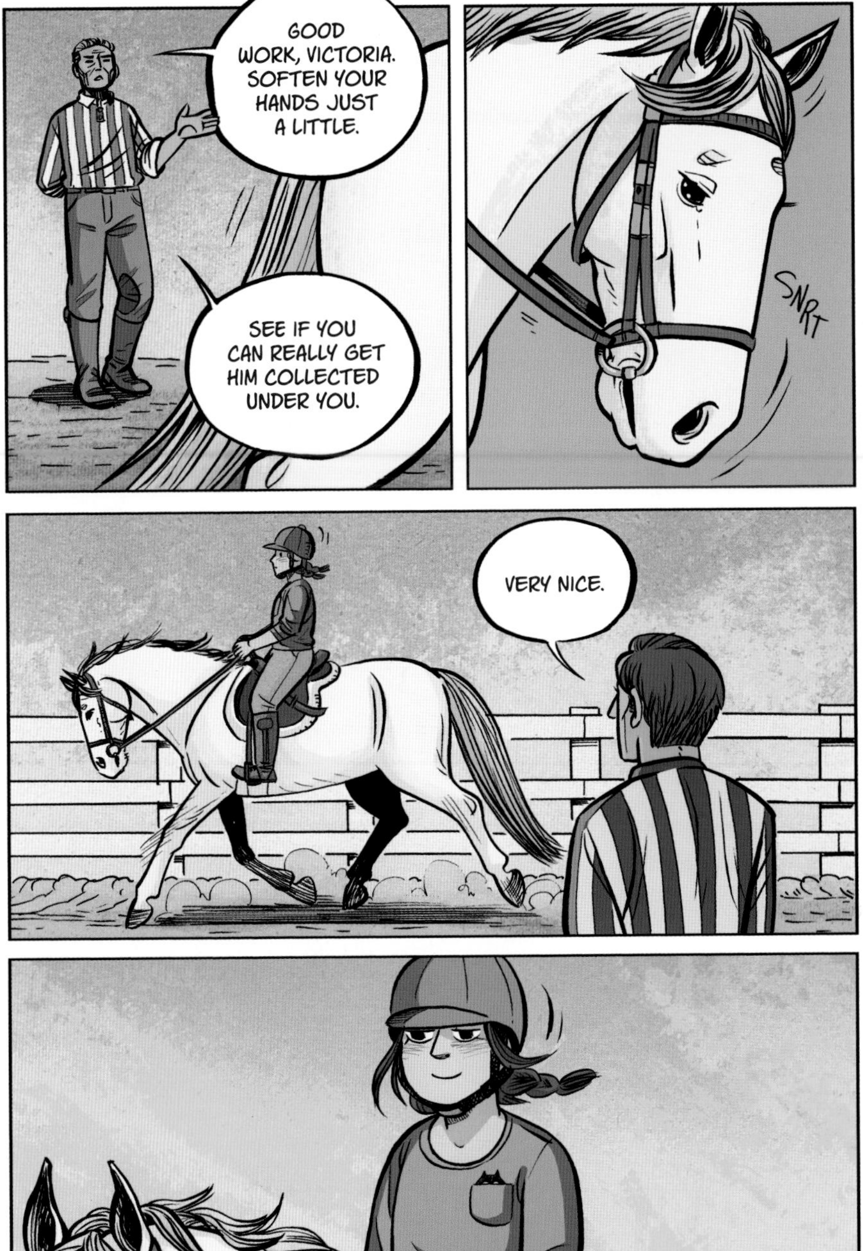
GOOD WORK, VICTORIA. SOFTEN YOUR HANDS JUST A LITTLE.
SEE IF YOU CAN REALLY GET HIM COLLECTED UNDER YOU.
SNRT
VERY NICE.

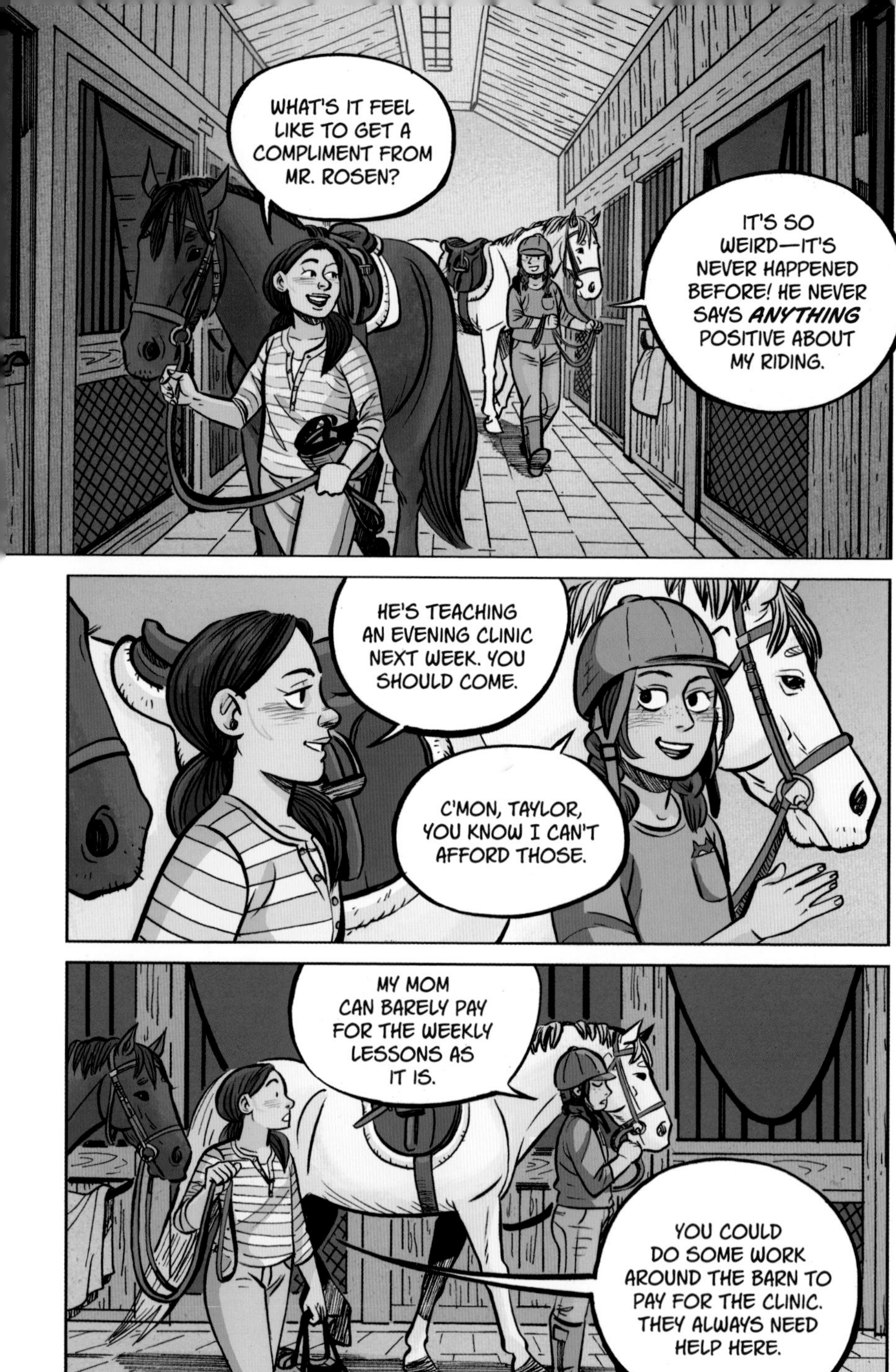

WHAT'S IT FEEL LIKE TO GET A COMPLIMENT FROM MR. ROSEN?
IT'S SO WEIRD—IT'S NEVER HAPPENED BEFORE! HE NEVER SAYS *ANYTHING* POSITIVE ABOUT MY RIDING.
HE'S TEACHING AN EVENING CLINIC NEXT WEEK. YOU SHOULD COME.
C'MON, TAYLOR, YOU KNOW I CAN'T AFFORD THOSE.
MY MOM CAN BARELY PAY FOR THE WEEKLY LESSONS AS IT IS.
YOU COULD DO SOME WORK AROUND THE BARN TO PAY FOR THE CLINIC. THEY ALWAYS NEED HELP HERE.

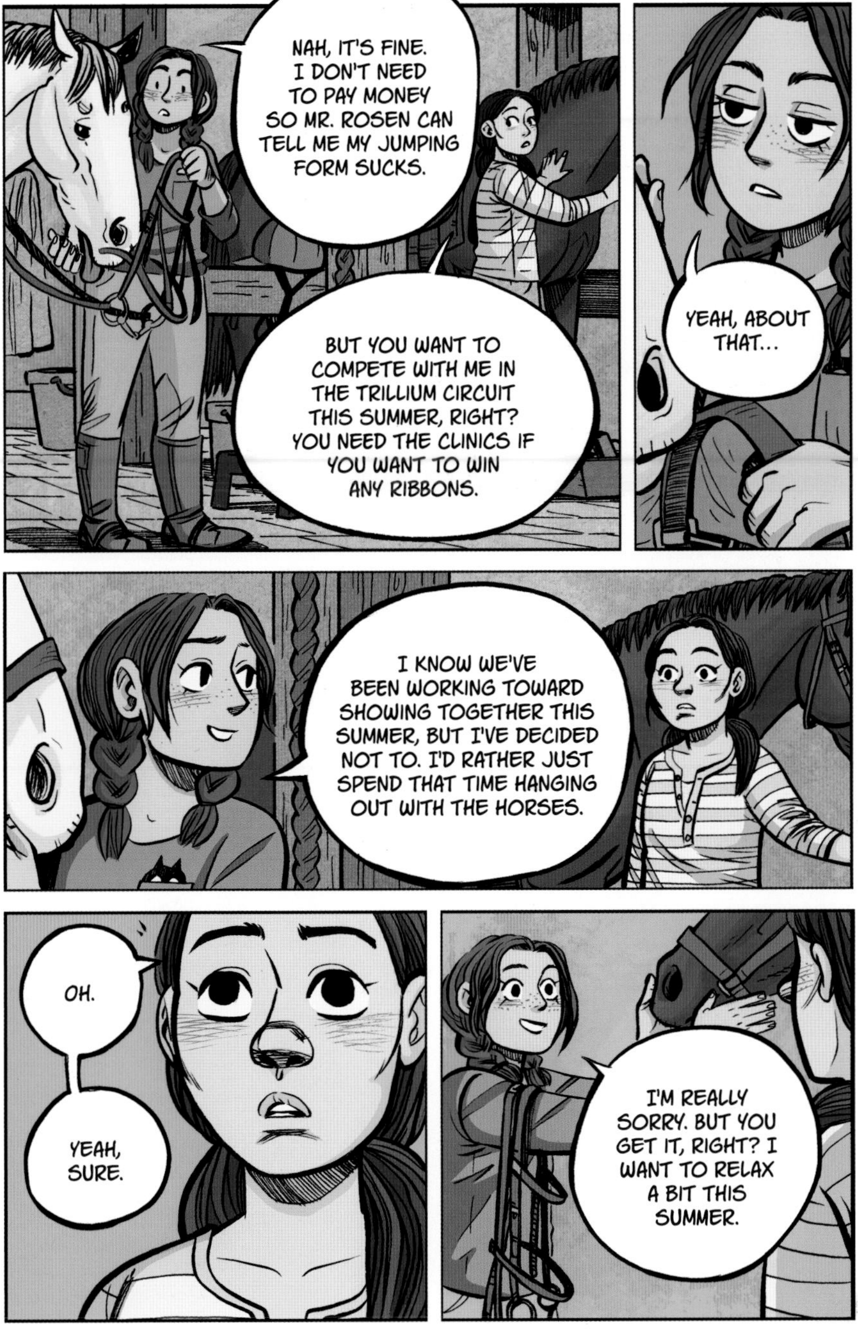
NAH, IT'S FINE. I DON'T NEED TO PAY MONEY SO MR. ROSEN CAN TELL ME MY JUMPING FORM SUCKS.
BUT YOU WANT TO COMPETE WITH ME IN THE TRILLIUM CIRCUIT THIS SUMMER, RIGHT? YOU NEED THE CLINICS IF YOU WANT TO WIN ANY RIBBONS.
YEAH, ABOUT THAT...
I KNOW WE'VE BEEN WORKING TOWARD SHOWING TOGETHER THIS SUMMER, BUT I'VE DECIDED NOT TO. I'D RATHER JUST SPEND THAT TIME HANGING OUT WITH THE HORSES.
OH.
YEAH, SURE.
I'M REALLY SORRY. BUT YOU GET IT, RIGHT? I WANT TO RELAX A BIT THIS SUMMER.

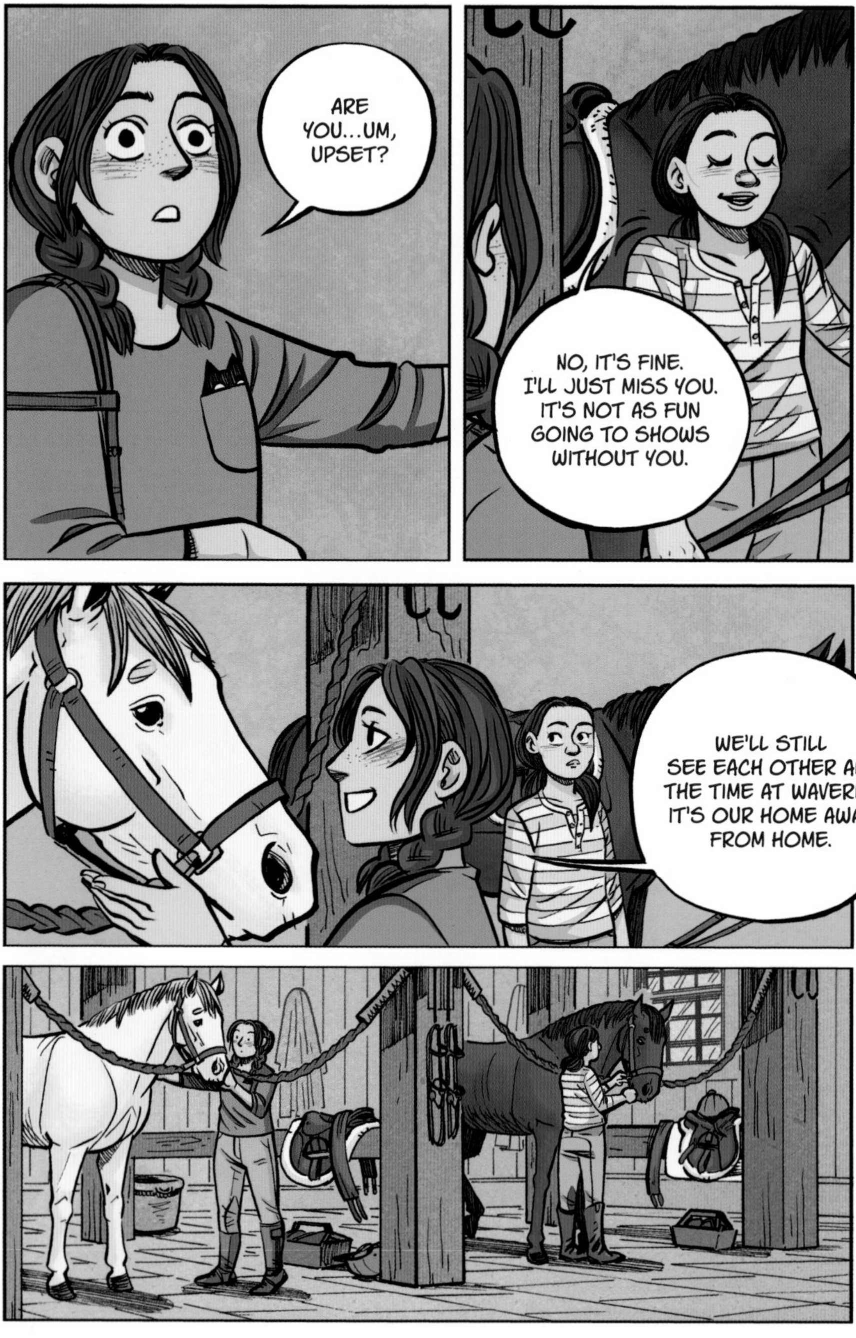
ARE YOU...UM, UPSET?
NO, IT'S FINE. I'LL JUST MISS YOU. IT'S NOT AS FUN GOING TO SHOWS WITHOUT YOU.
WE'LL STILL SEE EACH OTHER ALL THE TIME AT WAVERLY. IT'S OUR HOME AWAY FROM HOME.

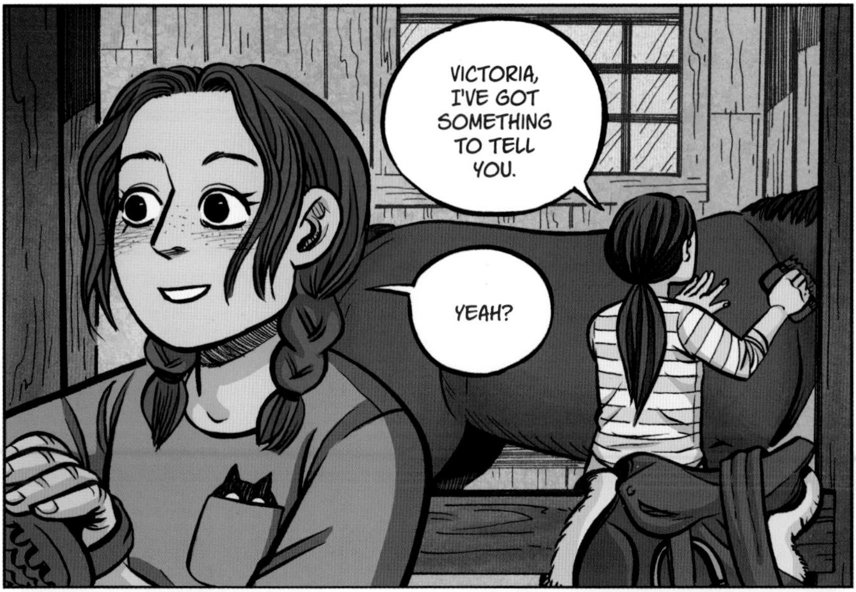
VICTORIA, I'VE GOT SOMETHING TO TELL YOU.
YEAH?

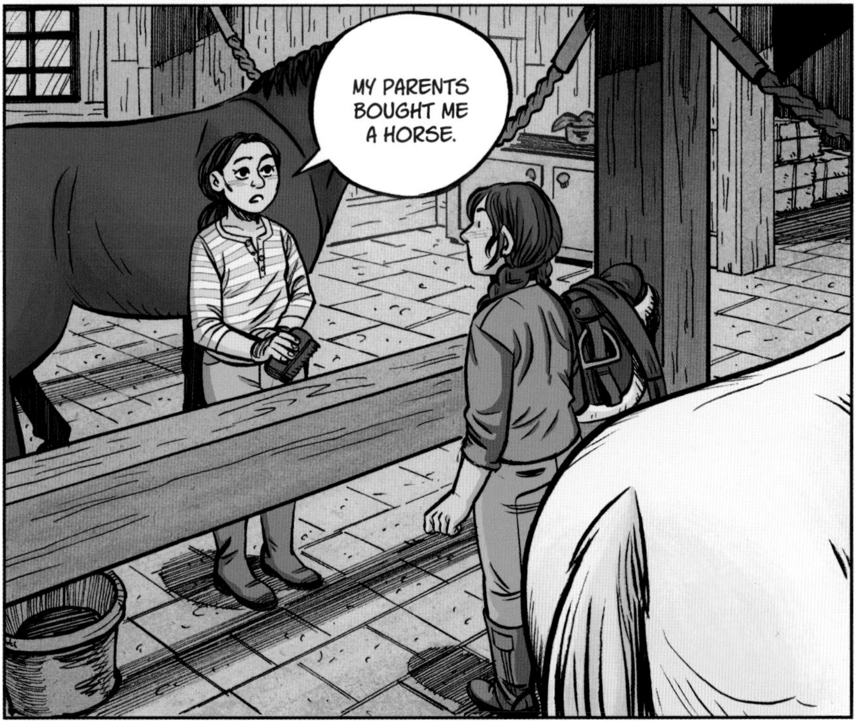
MY PARENTS BOUGHT ME A HORSE.

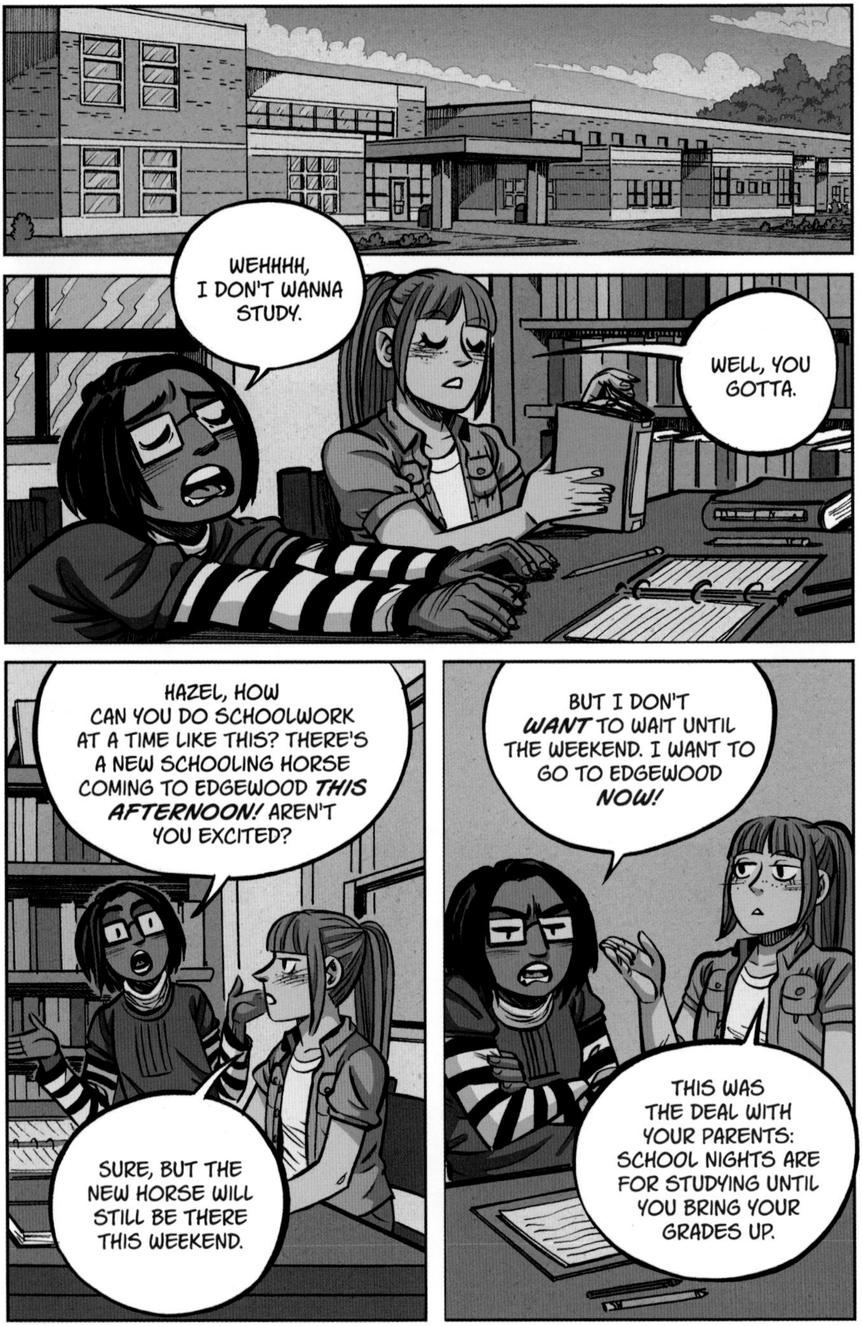
WEHHHH, I DON'T WANNA STUDY.
WELL, YOU GOTTA.
HAZEL, HOW CAN YOU DO SCHOOLWORK AT A TIME LIKE THIS? THERE'S A NEW SCHOOLING HORSE COMING TO EDGEWOOD *THIS AFTERNOON!* AREN'T YOU EXCITED?
SURE, BUT THE NEW HORSE WILL STILL BE THERE THIS WEEKEND.
BUT I DON'T *WANT* TO WAIT UNTIL THE WEEKEND. I WANT TO GO TO EDGEWOOD *NOW!*
THIS WAS THE DEAL WITH YOUR PARENTS: SCHOOL NIGHTS ARE FOR STUDYING UNTIL YOU BRING YOUR GRADES UP.

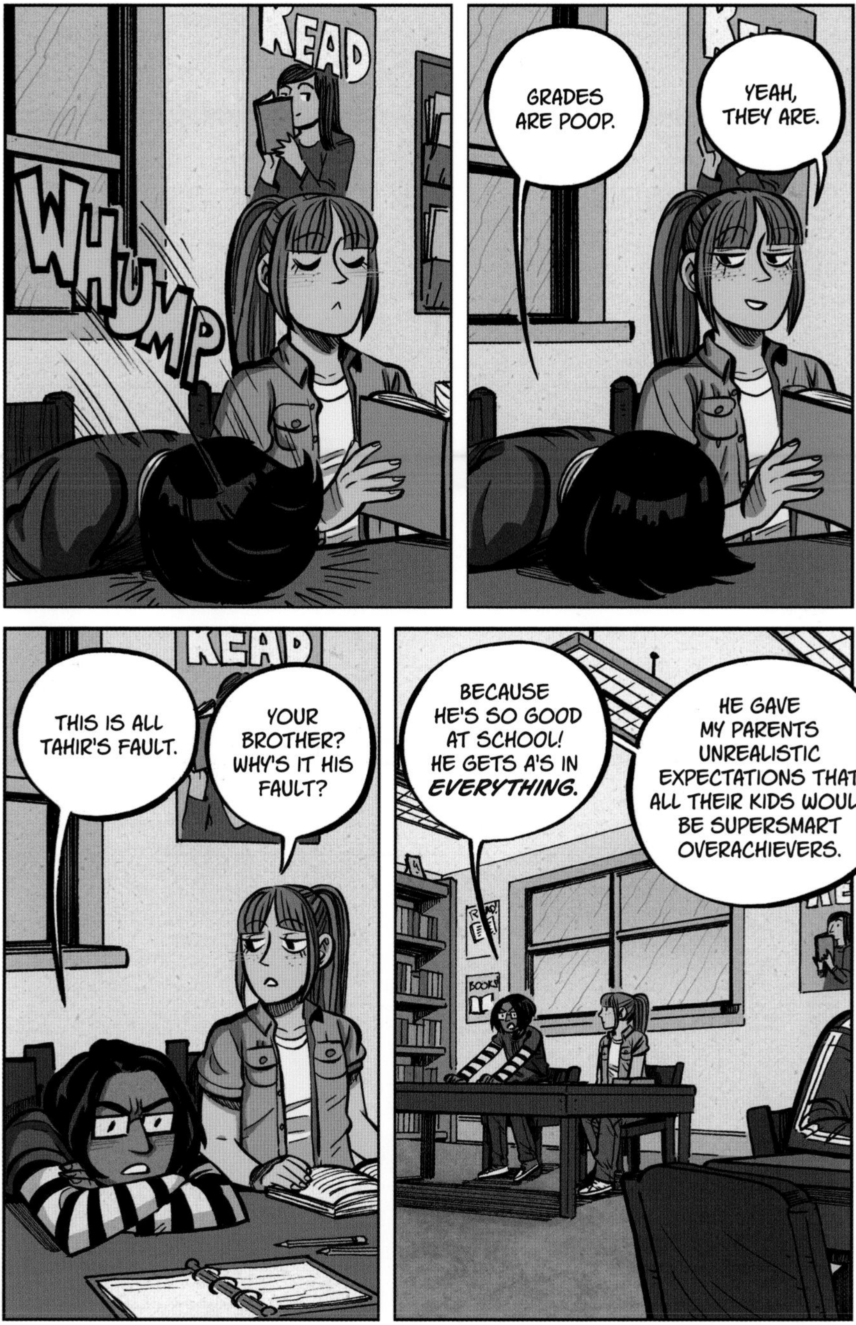
READ
WHUMP
GRADES ARE POOP.
YEAH, THEY ARE.
READ
THIS IS ALL TAHIR'S FAULT.
YOUR BROTHER? WHY'S IT HIS FAULT?
BECAUSE HE'S SO GOOD AT SCHOOL! HE GETS A'S IN *EVERYTHING*.
HE GAVE MY PARENTS UNREALISTIC EXPECTATIONS THAT ALL THEIR KIDS WOULD BE SUPERSMART OVERACHIEVERS.
BOOKS

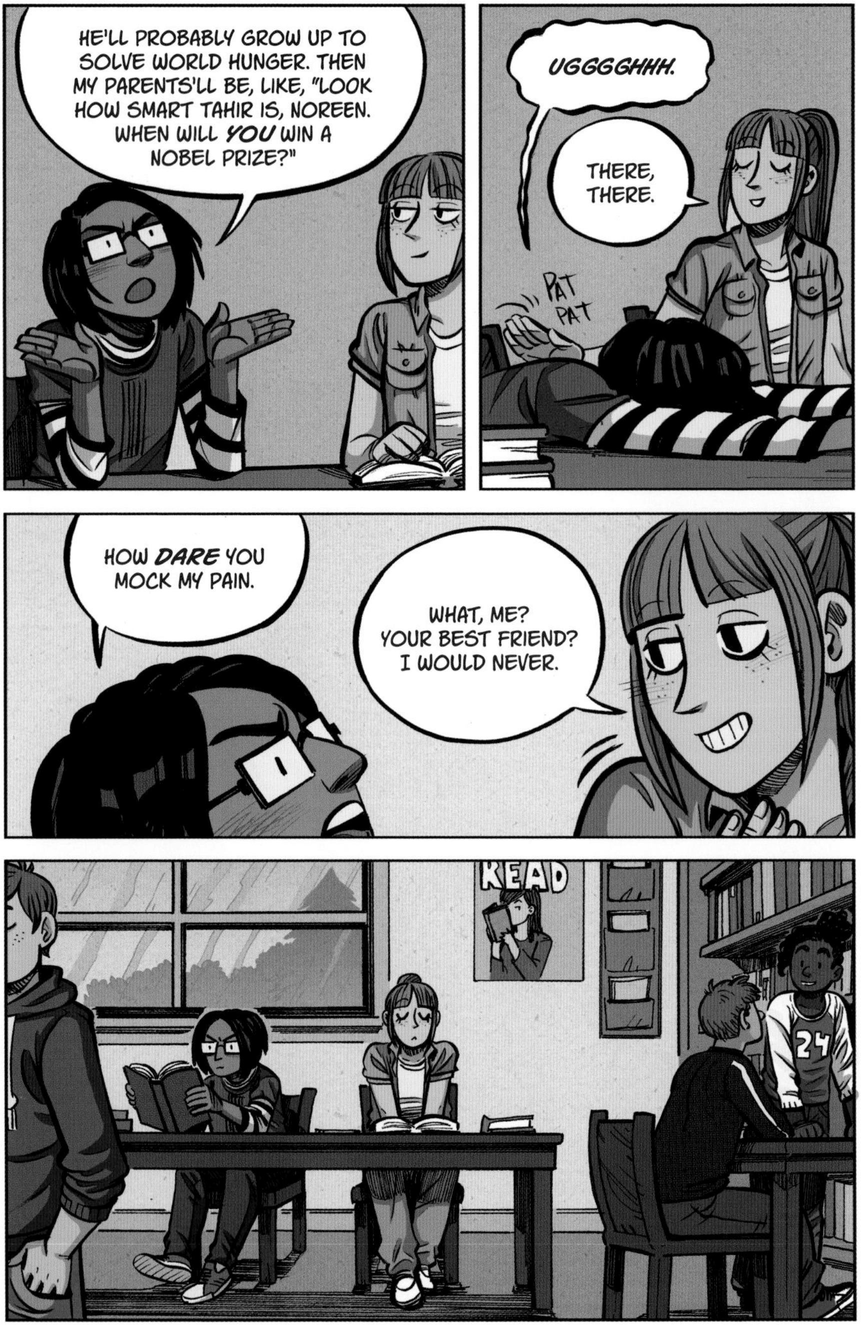
HE'LL PROBABLY GROW UP TO SOLVE WORLD HUNGER. THEN MY PARENTS'LL BE, LIKE, "LOOK HOW SMART TAHIR IS, NOREEN. WHEN WILL *YOU* WIN A NOBEL PRIZE?"
UGGGGHHH.
THERE, THERE.
PAT PAT
HOW *DARE* YOU MOCK MY PAIN.
WHAT, ME? YOUR BEST FRIEND? I WOULD NEVER.
READ
24

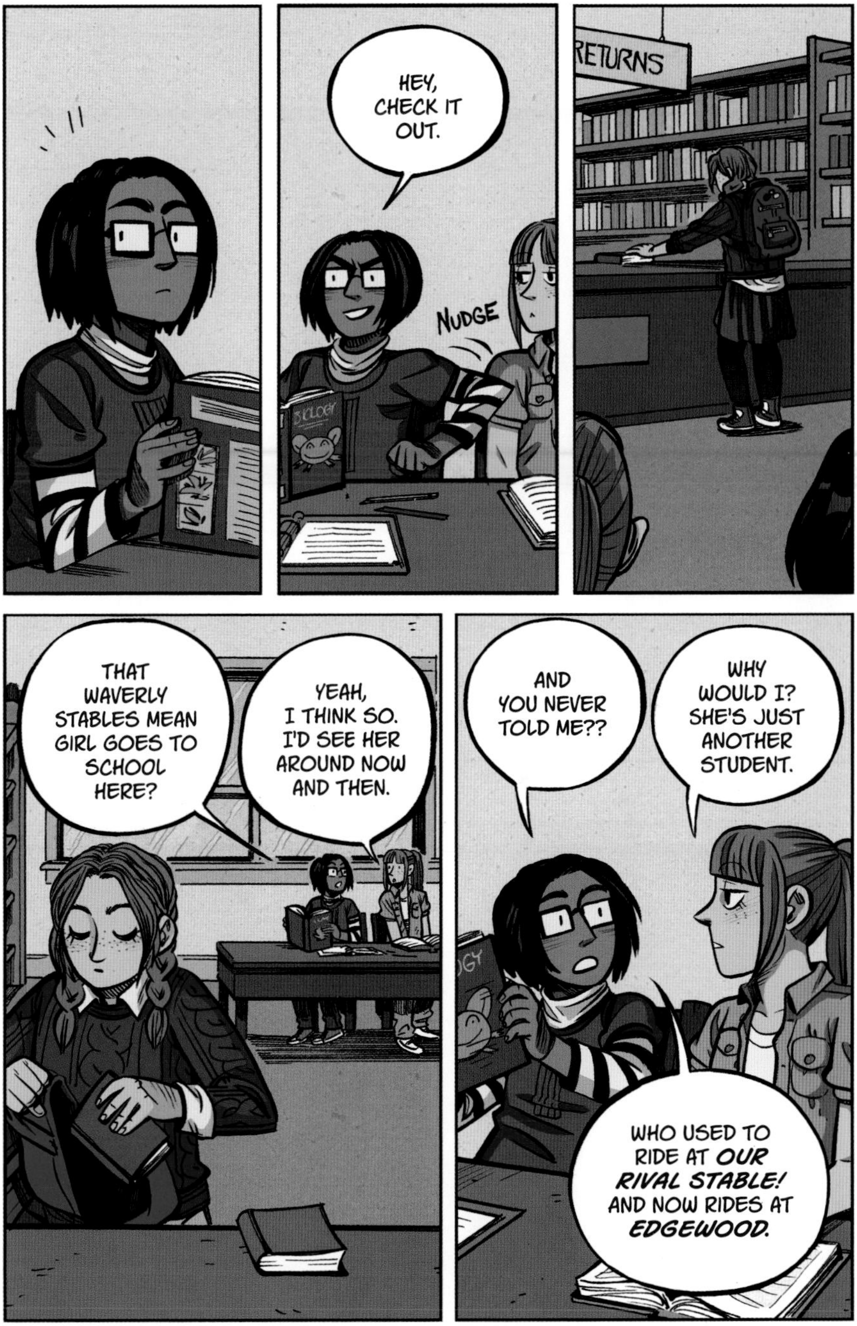
HEY, CHECK IT OUT.
NUDGE
RETURNS
THAT WAVERLY STABLES MEAN GIRL GOES TO SCHOOL HERE?
YEAH, I THINK SO. I'D SEE HER AROUND NOW AND THEN.
AND YOU NEVER TOLD ME??
WHY WOULD I? SHE'S JUST ANOTHER STUDENT.
WHO USED TO RIDE AT OUR RIVAL STABLE! AND NOW RIDES AT EDGEWOOD.

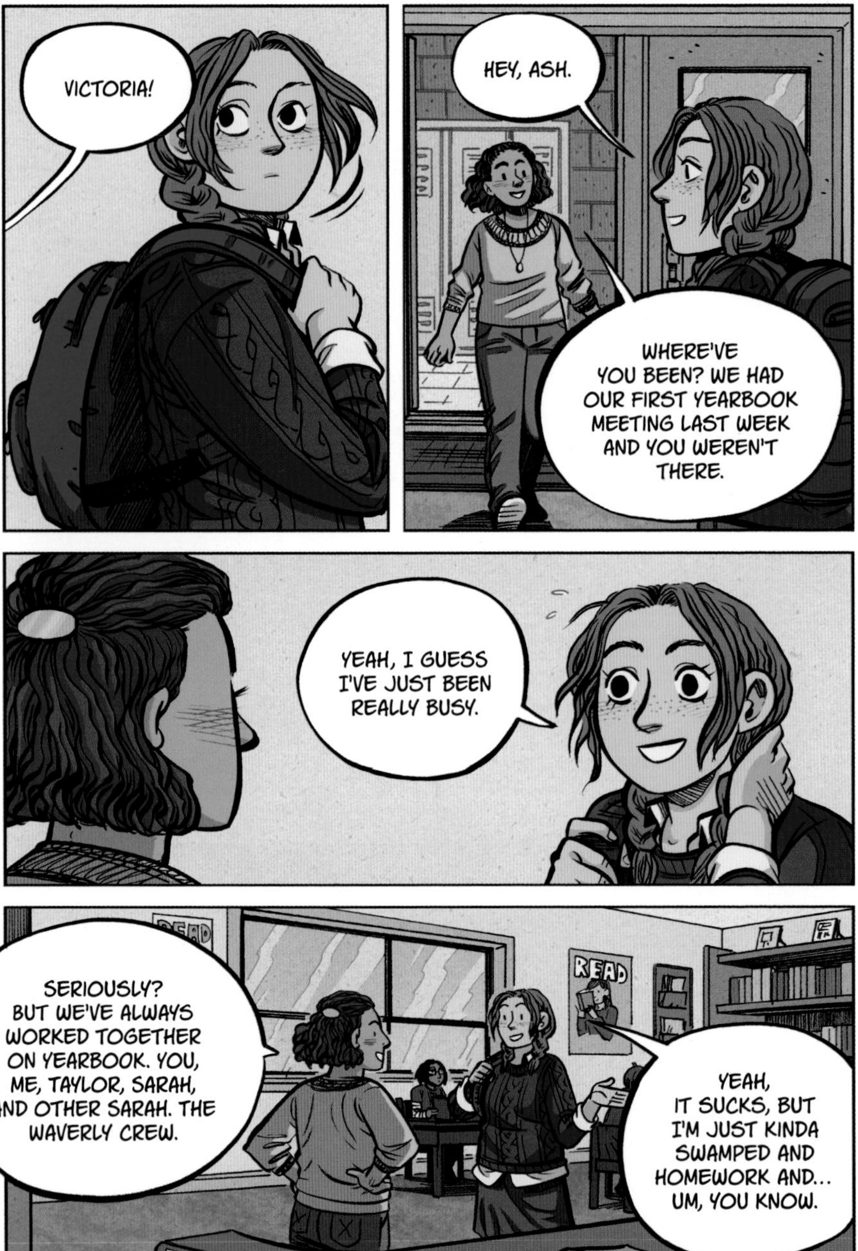
VICTORIA!
HEY, ASH.
WHERE'VE YOU BEEN? WE HAD OUR FIRST YEARBOOK MEETING LAST WEEK AND YOU WEREN'T THERE.
YEAH, I GUESS I'VE JUST BEEN REALLY BUSY.
SERIOUSLY? BUT WE'VE ALWAYS WORKED TOGETHER ON YEARBOOK. YOU, ME, TAYLOR, SARAH, AND OTHER SARAH. THE WAVERLY CREW.
YEAH, IT SUCKS, BUT I'M JUST KINDA SWAMPED AND HOMEWORK AND... UM, YOU KNOW.
READ
READ

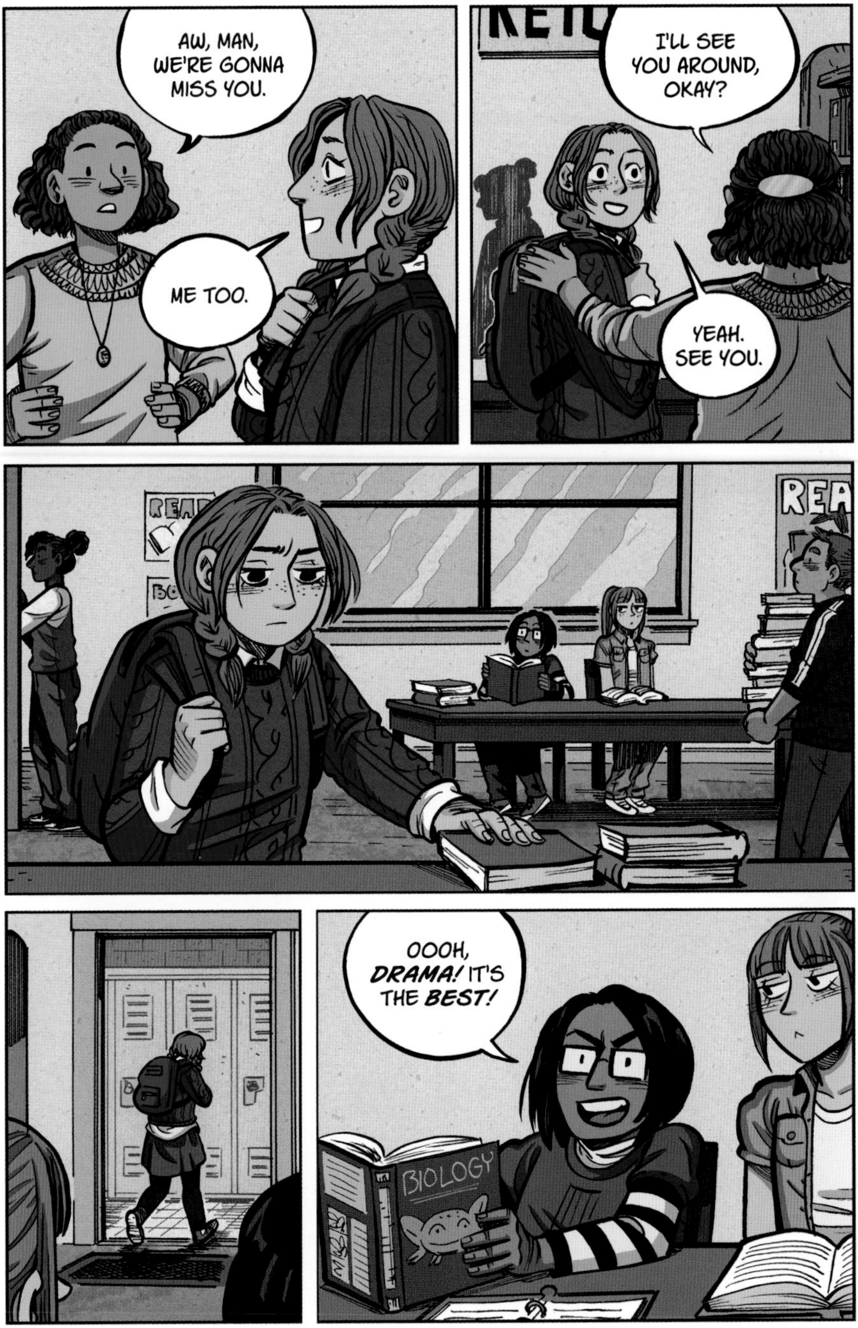
AW, MAN, WE'RE GONNA MISS YOU.
ME TOO.
I'LL SEE YOU AROUND, OKAY?
YEAH. SEE YOU.
OOOH, **DRAMA!** IT'S THE **BEST!**
BIOLOGY

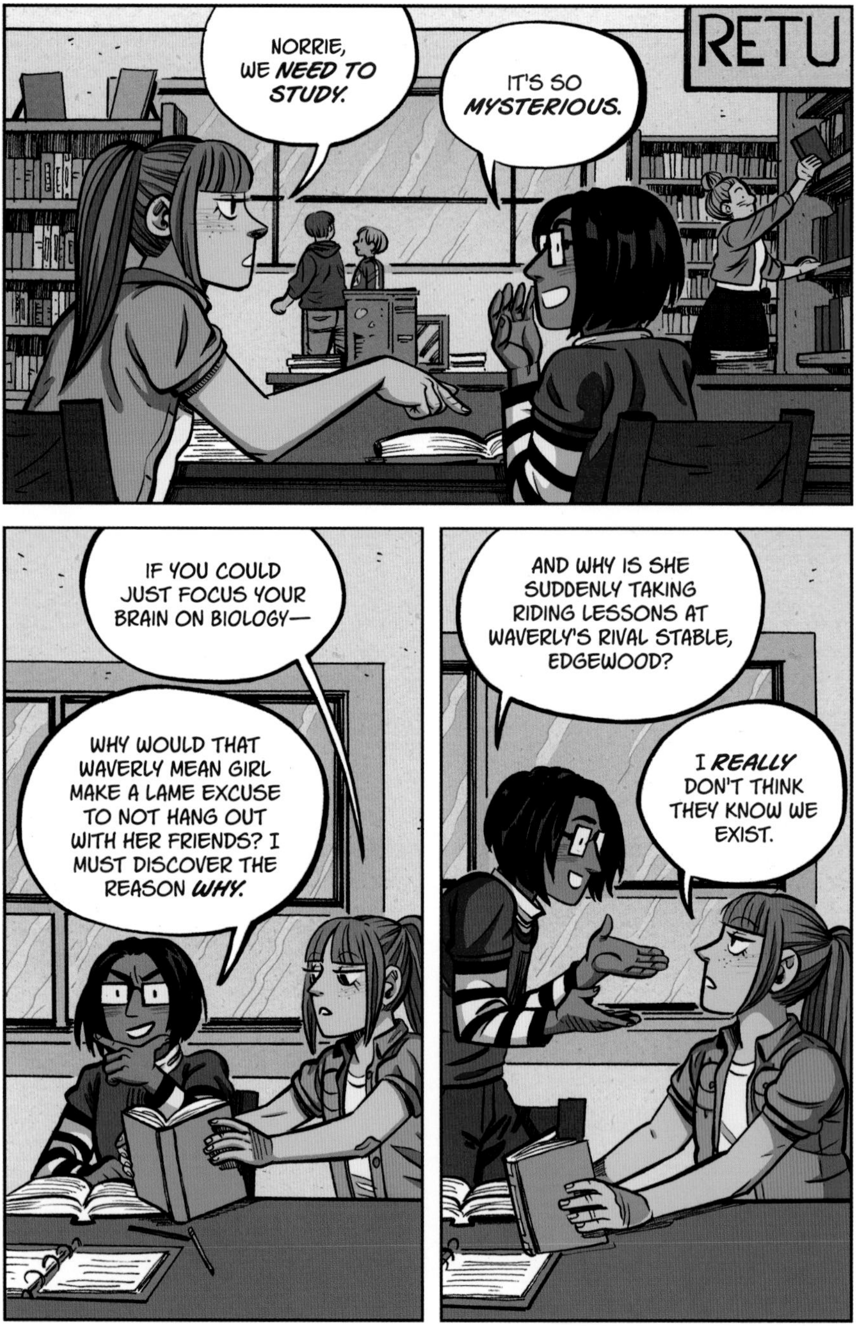
RETU
NORRIE, WE NEED TO STUDY.
IT'S SO MYSTERIOUS.
IF YOU COULD JUST FOCUS YOUR BRAIN ON BIOLOGY—
WHY WOULD THAT WAVERLY MEAN GIRL MAKE A LAME EXCUSE TO NOT HANG OUT WITH HER FRIENDS? I MUST DISCOVER THE REASON WHY.
AND WHY IS SHE SUDDENLY TAKING RIDING LESSONS AT WAVERLY'S RIVAL STABLE, EDGEWOOD?
I REALLY DON'T THINK THEY KNOW WE EXIST.

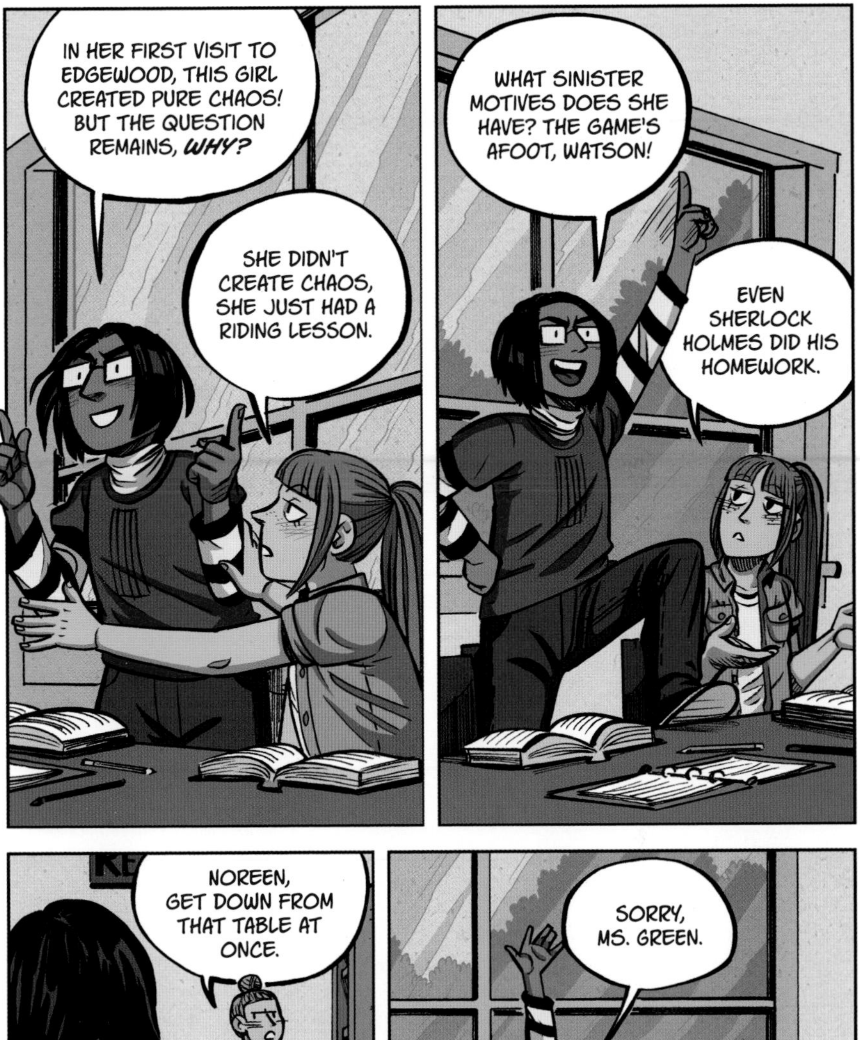
IN HER FIRST VISIT TO EDGEWOOD, THIS GIRL CREATED PURE CHAOS! BUT THE QUESTION REMAINS, *WHY?*
SHE DIDN'T CREATE CHAOS, SHE JUST HAD A RIDING LESSON.
WHAT SINISTER MOTIVES DOES SHE HAVE? THE GAME'S AFOOT, WATSON!
EVEN SHERLOCK HOLMES DID HIS HOMEWORK.
NOREEN, GET DOWN FROM THAT TABLE AT ONCE.
SORRY, MS. GREEN.

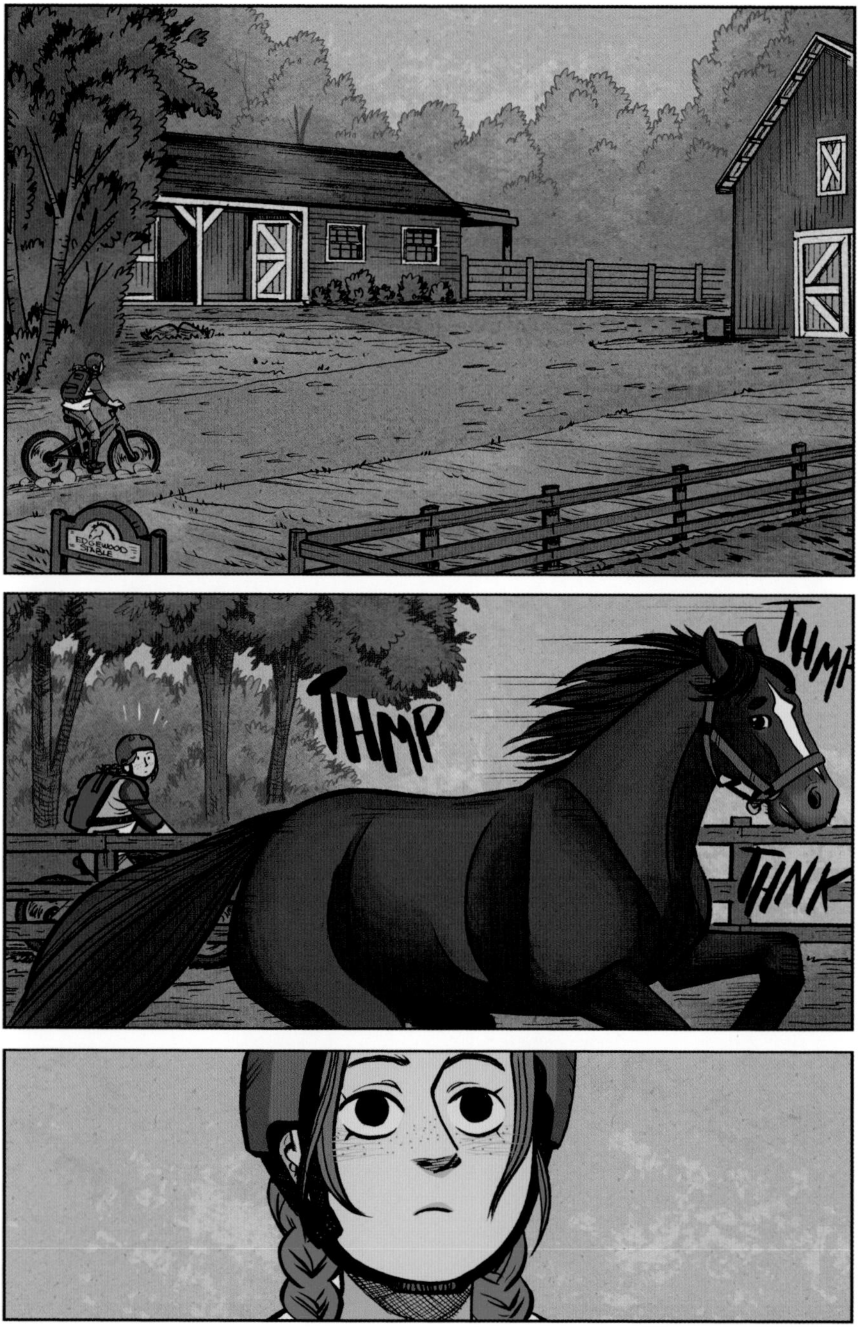
EDGEWOOD STABLE
THMP
THMP
THNK

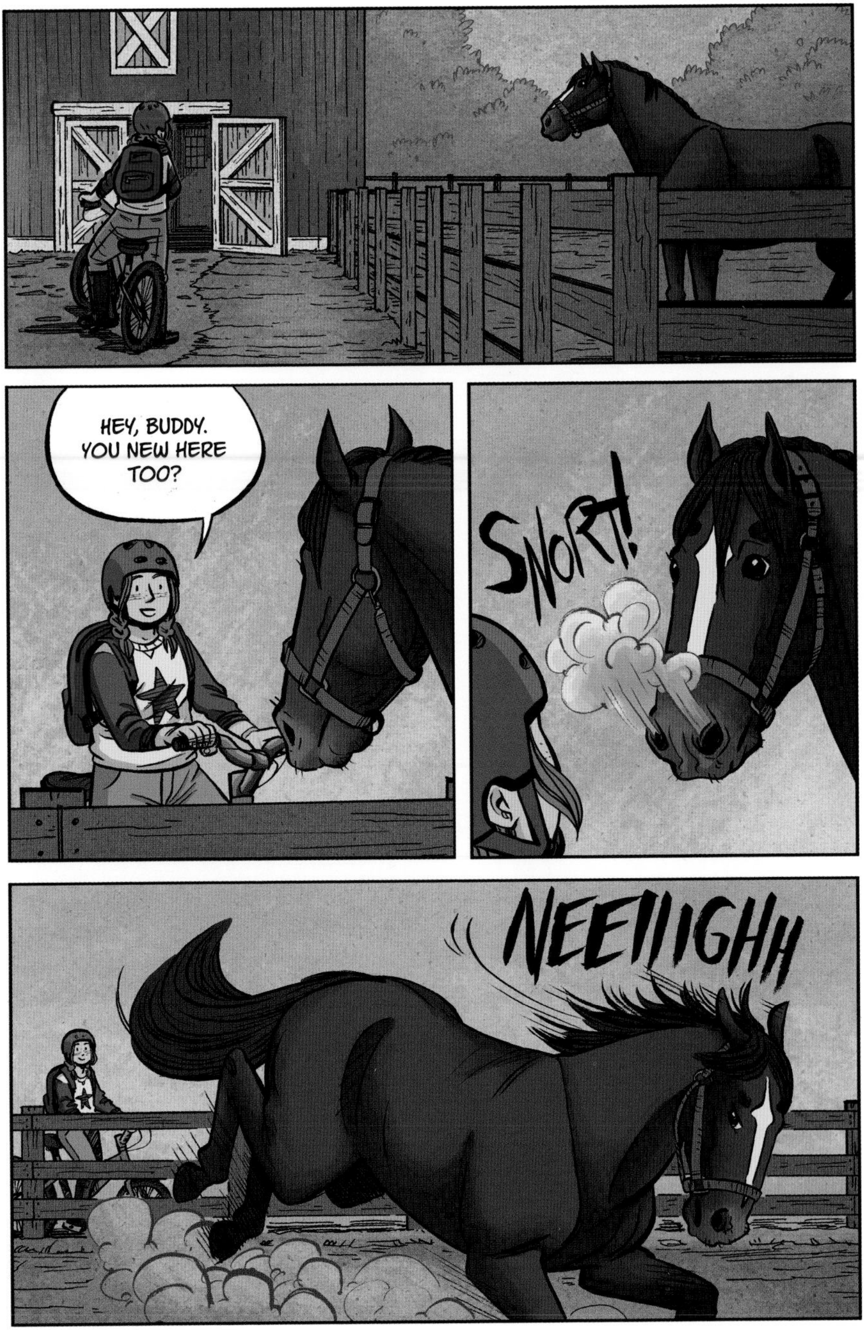
HEY, BUDDY. YOU NEW HERE TOO?
SNORT!
NEEIIIGHH

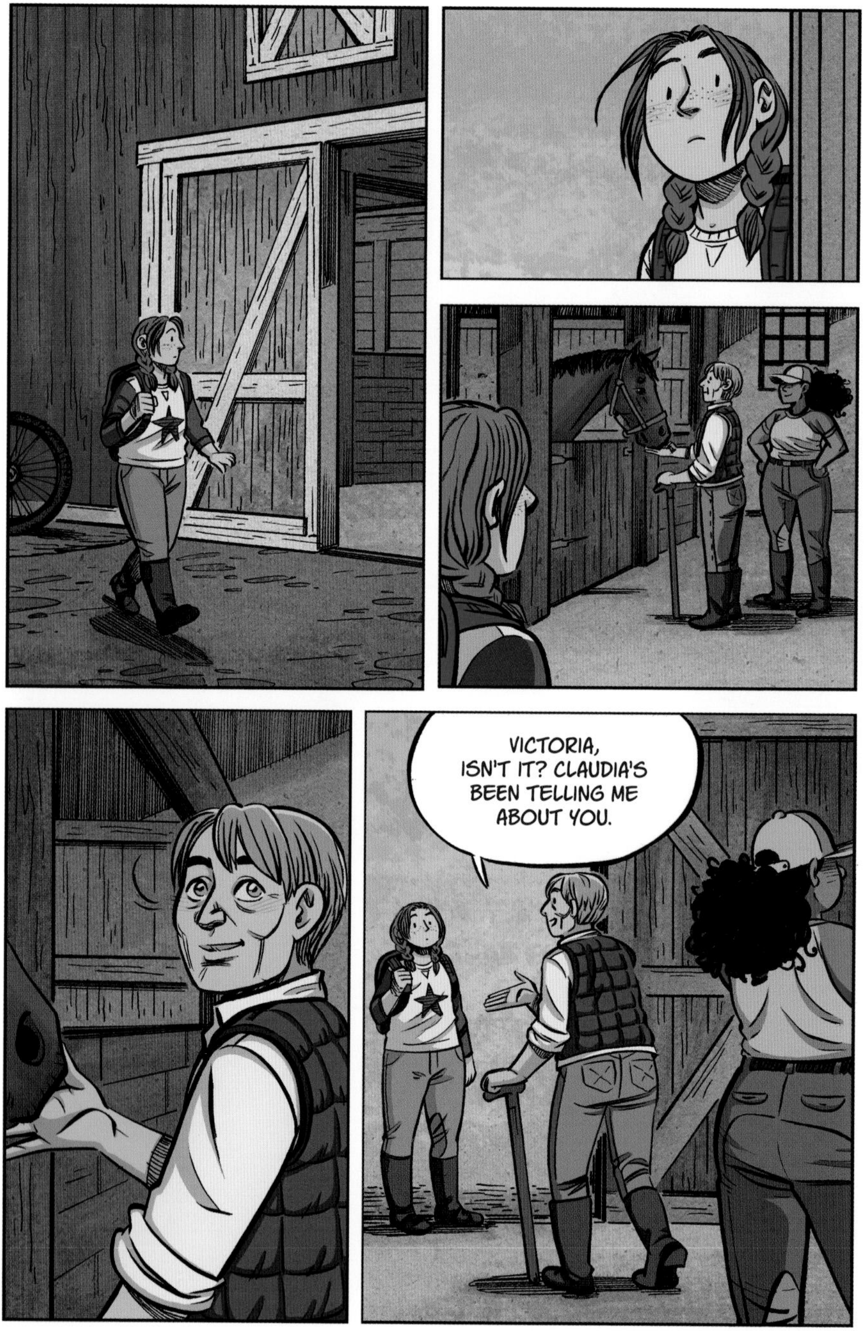
VICTORIA, ISN'T IT? CLAUDIA'S BEEN TELLING ME ABOUT YOU.

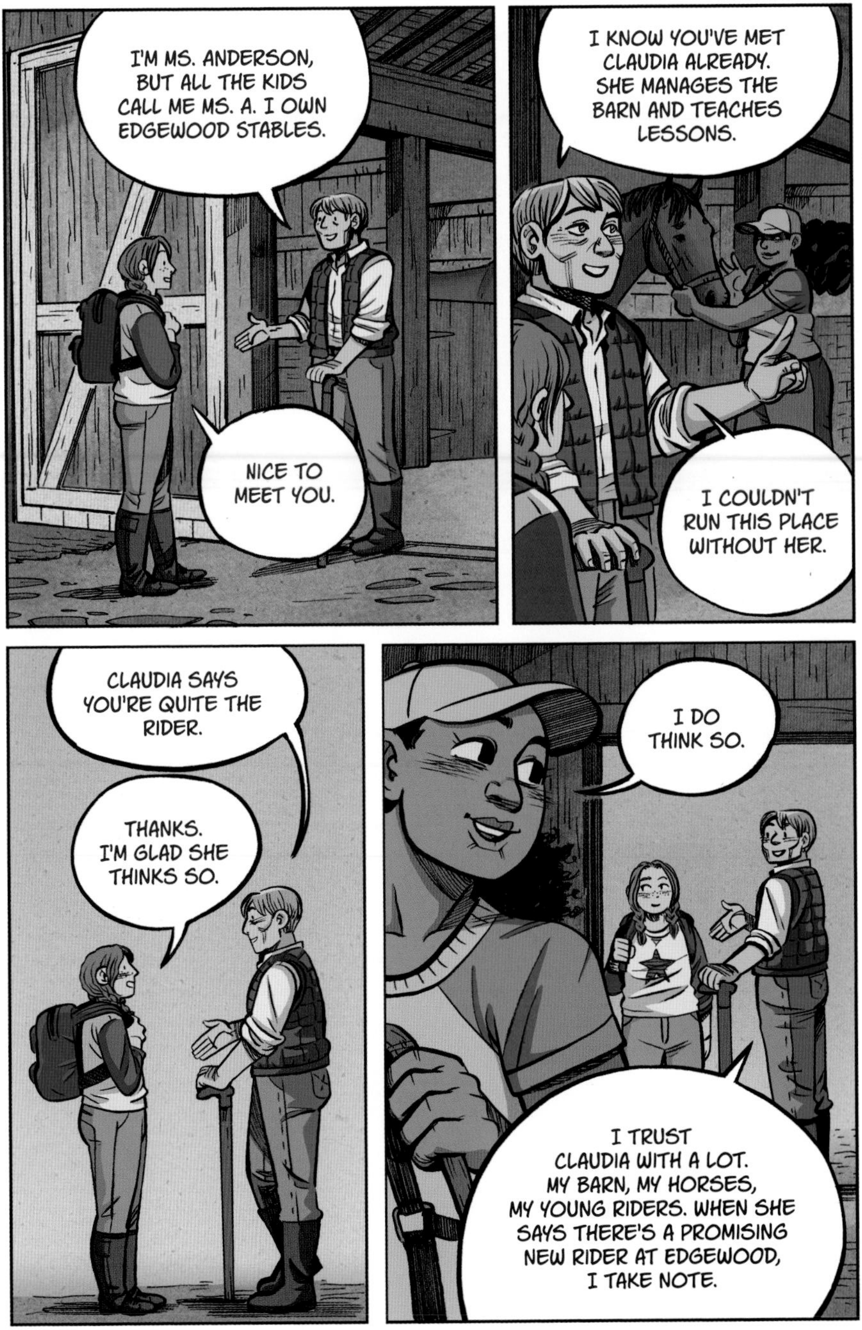

I'M MS. ANDERSON, BUT ALL THE KIDS CALL ME MS. A. I OWN EDGEWOOD STABLES.
NICE TO MEET YOU.
I KNOW YOU'VE MET CLAUDIA ALREADY. SHE MANAGES THE BARN AND TEACHES LESSONS.
I COULDN'T RUN THIS PLACE WITHOUT HER.
CLAUDIA SAYS YOU'RE QUITE THE RIDER.
THANKS. I'M GLAD SHE THINKS SO.
I DO THINK SO.
I TRUST CLAUDIA WITH A LOT. MY BARN, MY HORSES, MY YOUNG RIDERS. WHEN SHE SAYS THERE'S A PROMISING NEW RIDER AT EDGEWOOD, I TAKE NOTE.

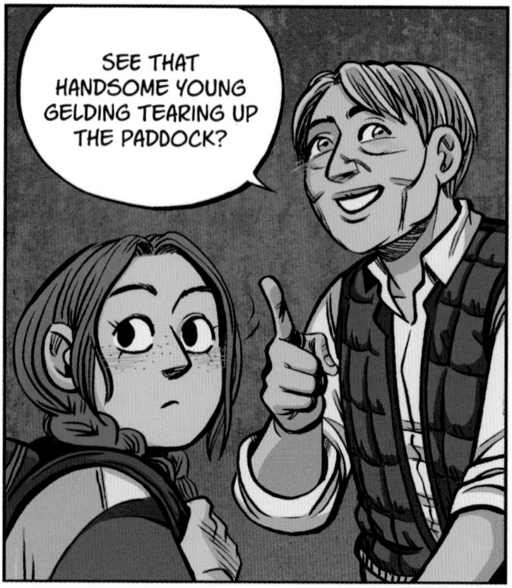
SEE THAT HANDSOME YOUNG GELDING TEARING UP THE PADDOCK?

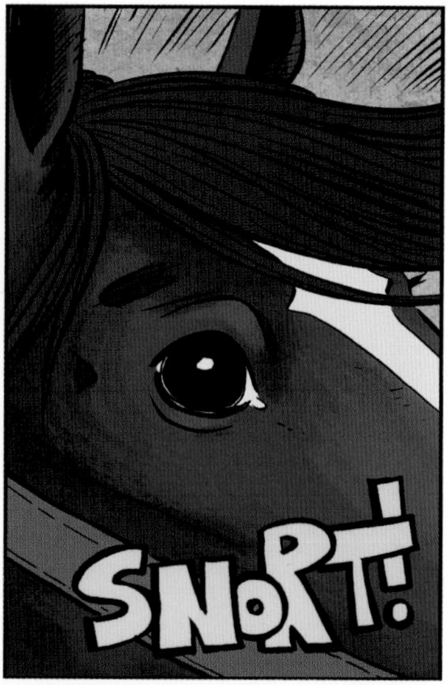
SNORT!

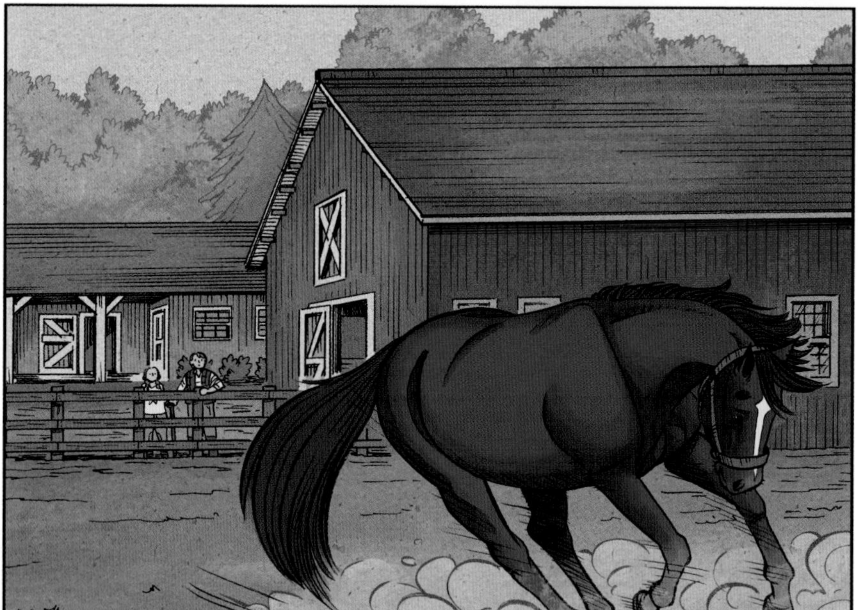

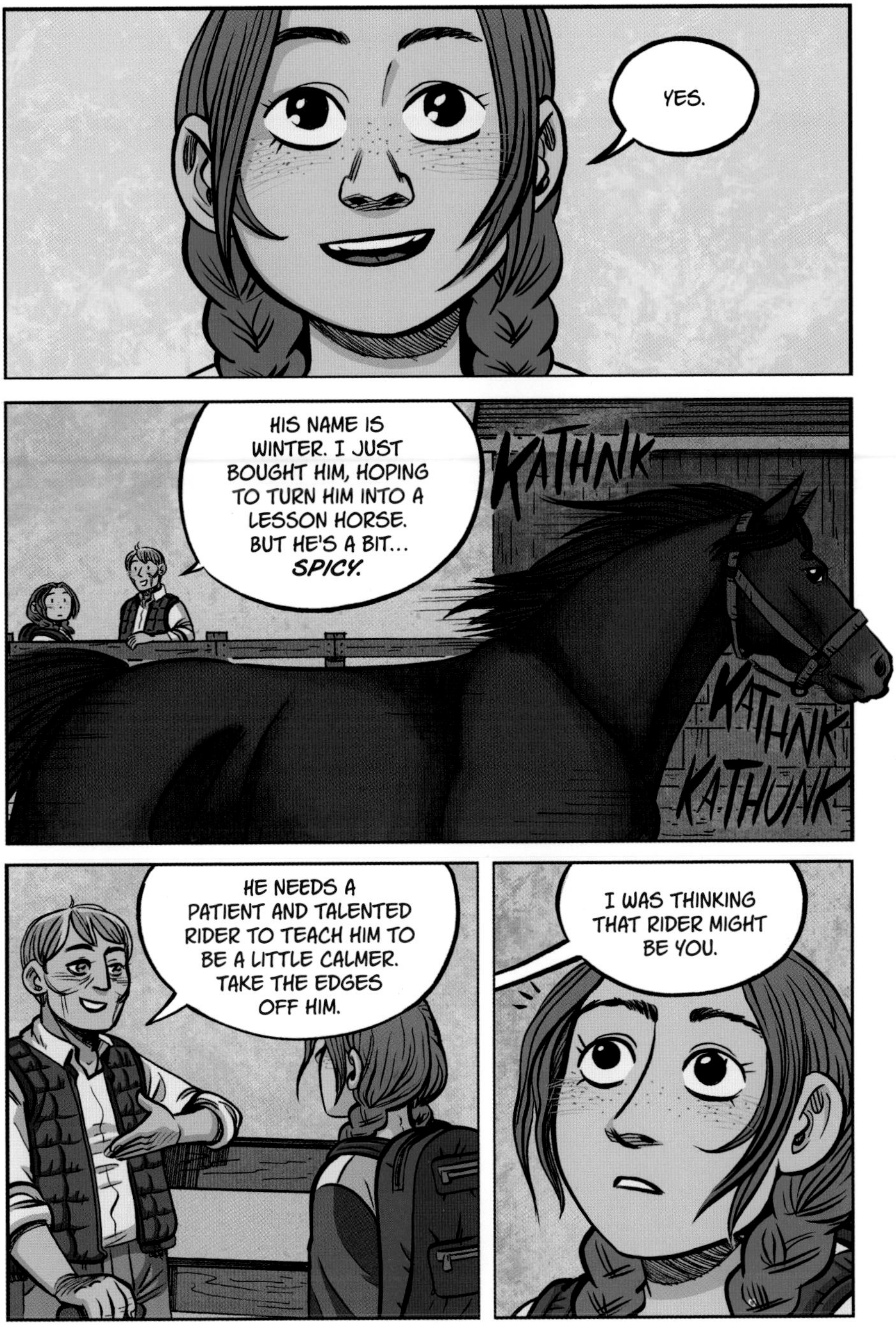
YES.
HIS NAME IS WINTER. I JUST BOUGHT HIM, HOPING TO TURN HIM INTO A LESSON HORSE. BUT HE'S A BIT... SPICY.
KATHNK
KATHNK
KATHUNK
HE NEEDS A PATIENT AND TALENTED RIDER TO TEACH HIM TO BE A LITTLE CALMER. TAKE THE EDGES OFF HIM.
I WAS THINKING THAT RIDER MIGHT BE YOU.

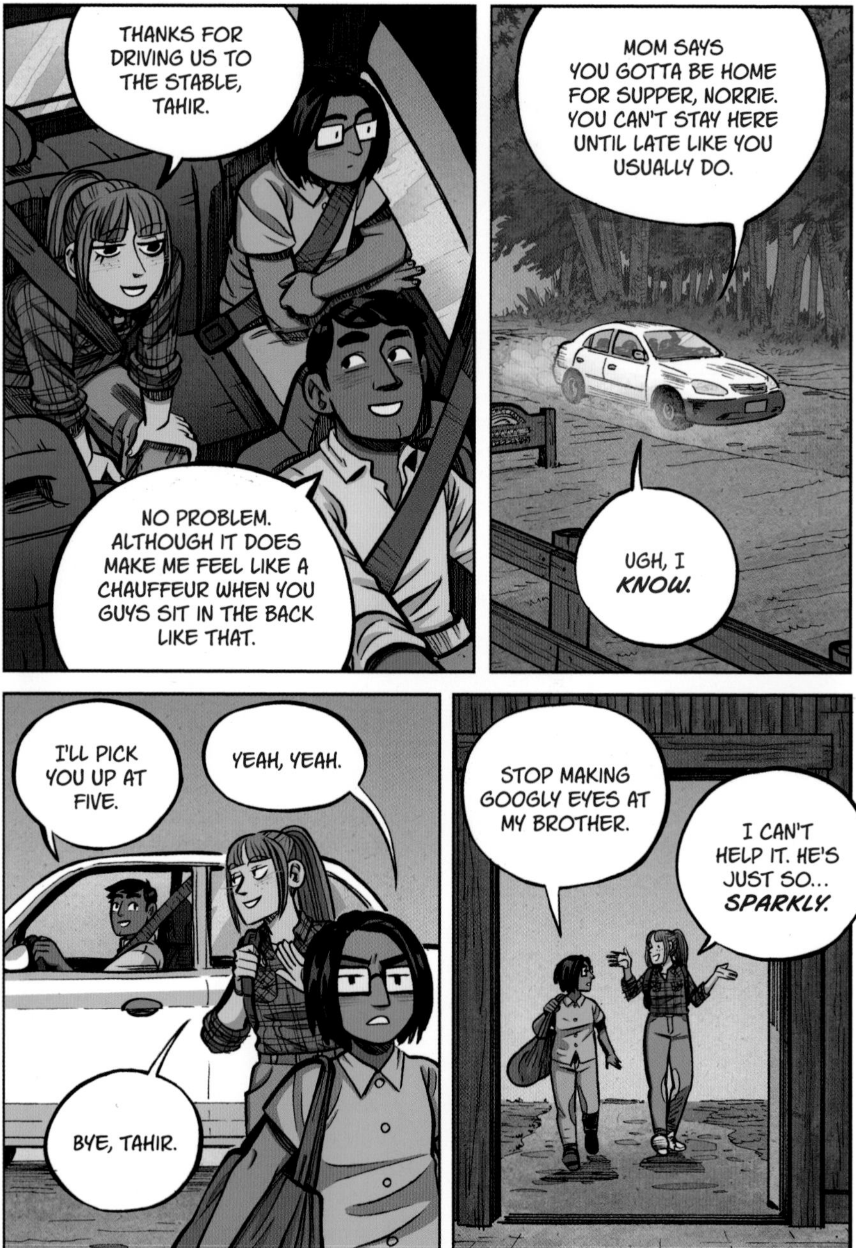

THANKS FOR DRIVING US TO THE STABLE, TAHIR.
NO PROBLEM. ALTHOUGH IT DOES MAKE ME FEEL LIKE A CHAUFFEUR WHEN YOU GUYS SIT IN THE BACK LIKE THAT.
MOM SAYS YOU GOTTA BE HOME FOR SUPPER, NORRIE. YOU CAN'T STAY HERE UNTIL LATE LIKE YOU USUALLY DO.
UGH, I *KNOW.*
I'LL PICK YOU UP AT FIVE.
YEAH, YEAH.
BYE, TAHIR.
STOP MAKING GOOGLY EYES AT MY BROTHER.
I CAN'T HELP IT. HE'S JUST SO... ***SPARKLY.***

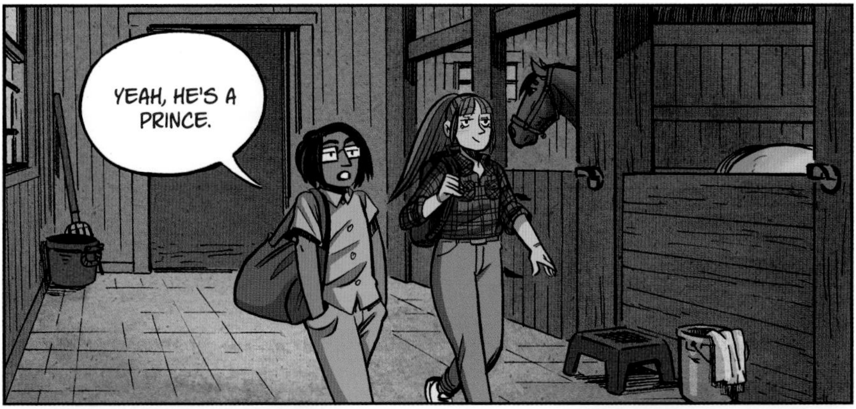
YEAH, HE'S A PRINCE.

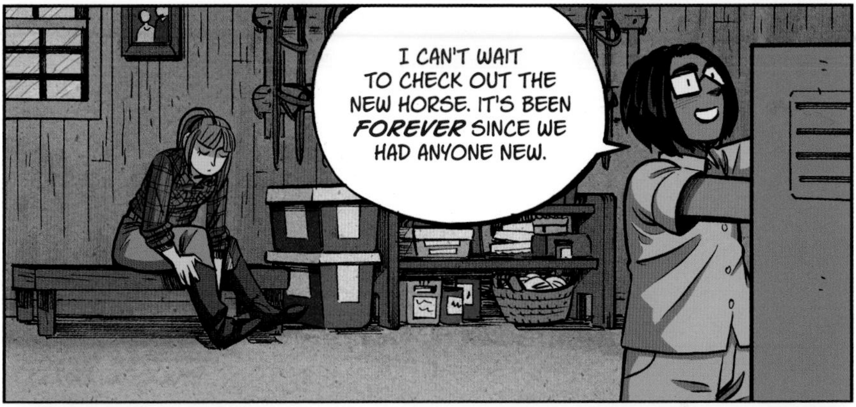
I CAN'T WAIT TO CHECK OUT THE NEW HORSE. IT'S BEEN ***FOREVER*** SINCE WE HAD ANYONE NEW.

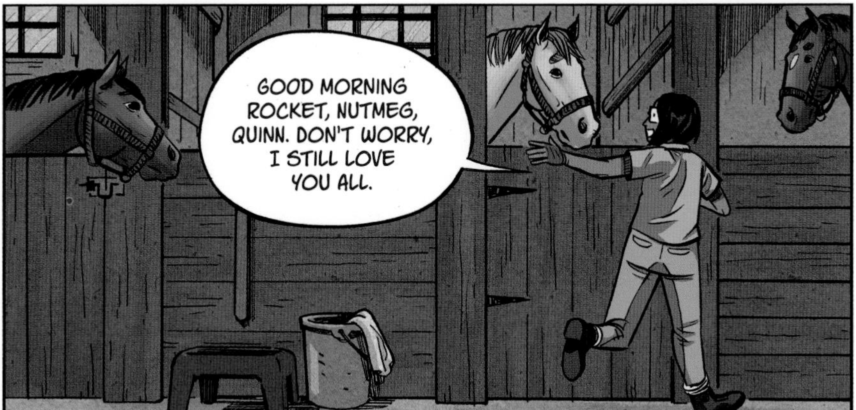
GOOD MORNING ROCKET, NUTMEG, QUINN. DON'T WORRY, I STILL LOVE YOU ALL.

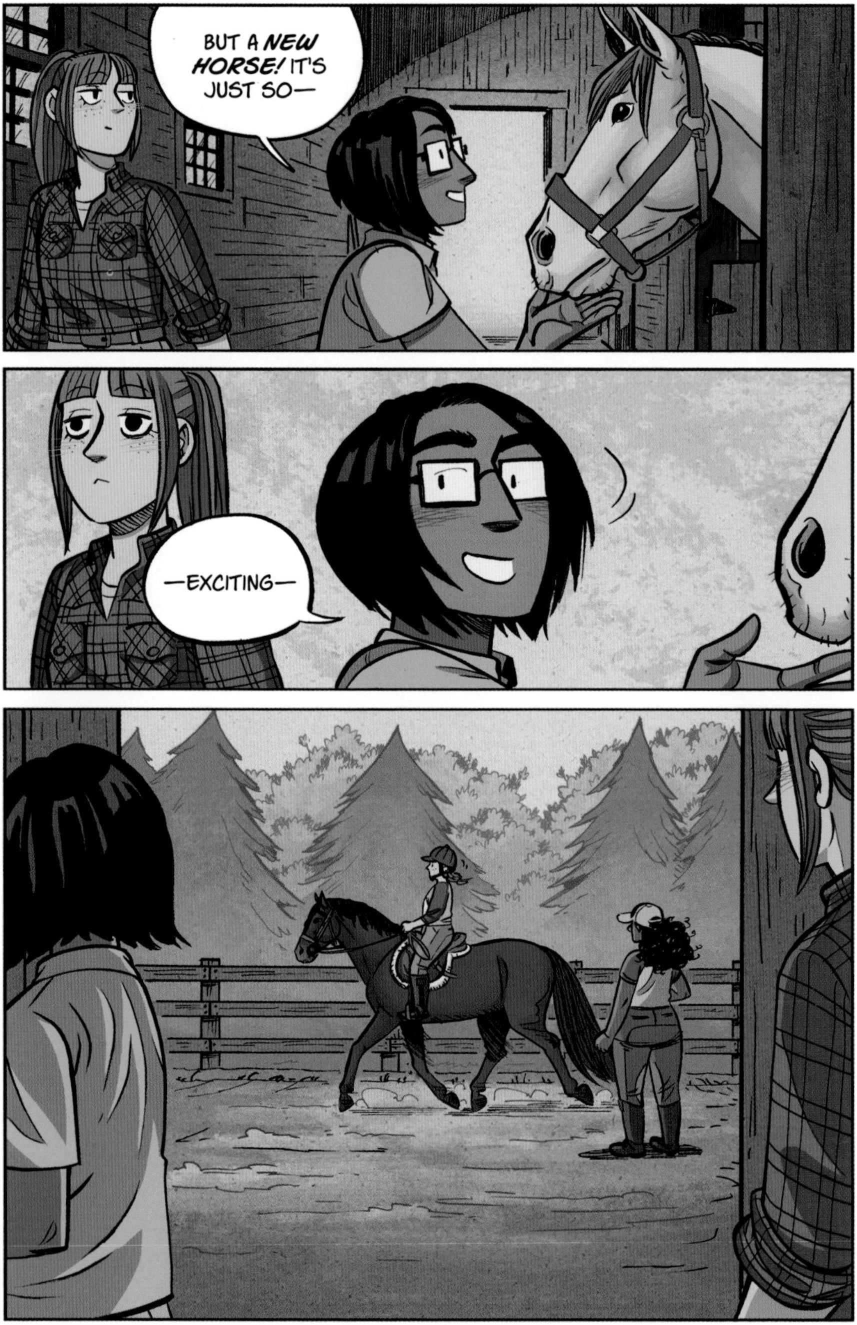

BUT A *NEW HORSE!* IT'S JUST SO—
—EXCITING—

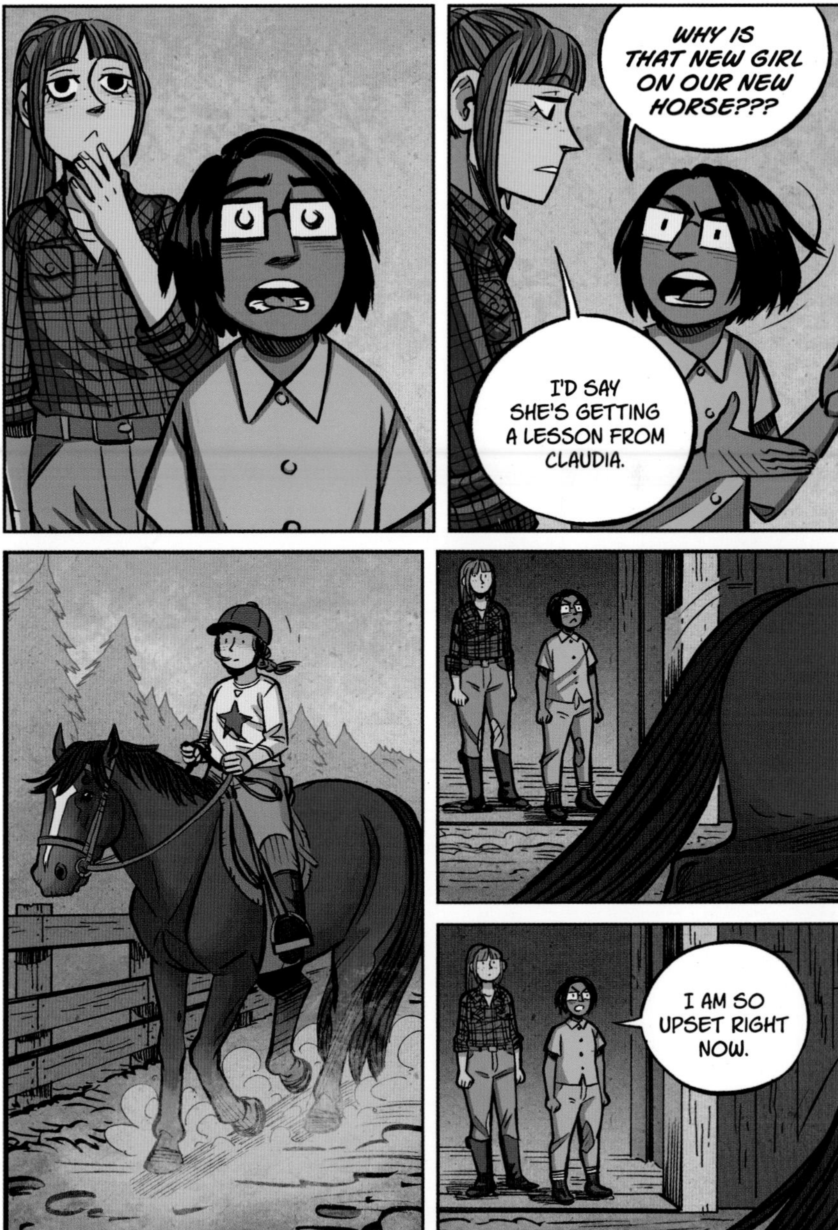
WHY IS THAT NEW GIRL ON OUR NEW HORSE???
I'D SAY SHE'S GETTING A LESSON FROM CLAUDIA.
I AM SO UPSET RIGHT NOW.

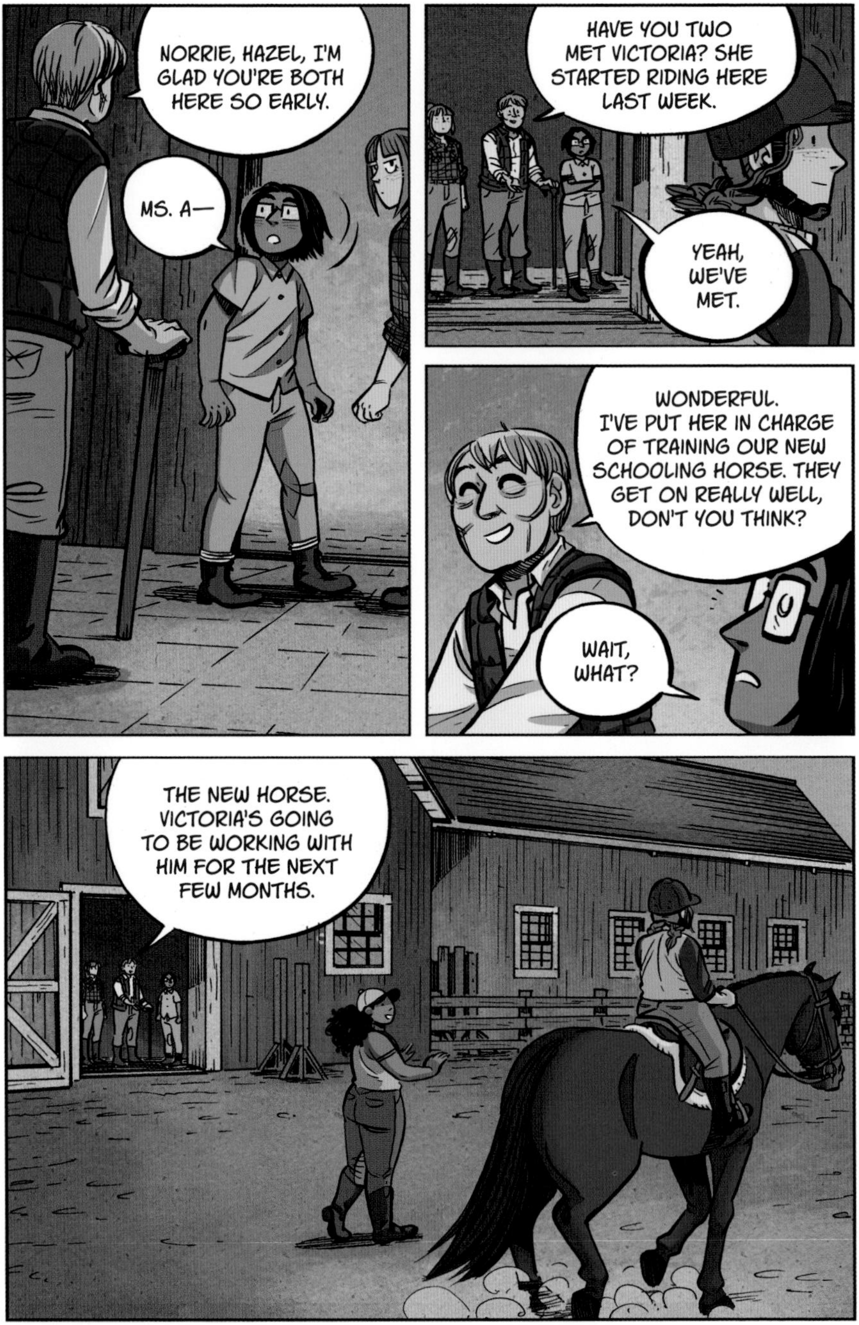
NORRIE, HAZEL, I'M GLAD YOU'RE BOTH HERE SO EARLY.
MS. A—
HAVE YOU TWO MET VICTORIA? SHE STARTED RIDING HERE LAST WEEK.
YEAH, WE'VE MET.
WONDERFUL. I'VE PUT HER IN CHARGE OF TRAINING OUR NEW SCHOOLING HORSE. THEY GET ON REALLY WELL, DON'T YOU THINK?
WAIT, WHAT?
THE NEW HORSE. VICTORIA'S GOING TO BE WORKING WITH HIM FOR THE NEXT FEW MONTHS.

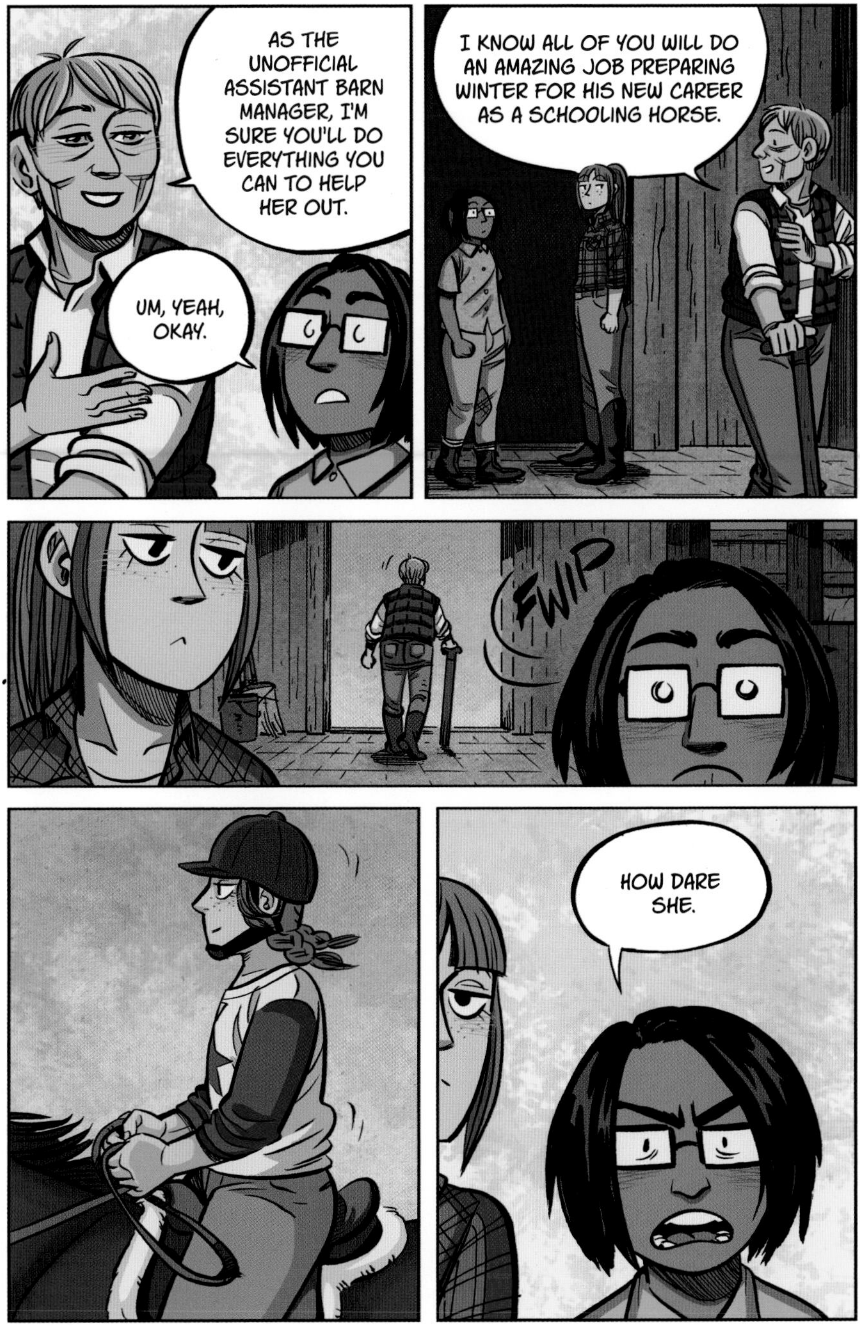
AS THE UNOFFICIAL ASSISTANT BARN MANAGER, I'M SURE YOU'LL DO EVERYTHING YOU CAN TO HELP HER OUT.
UM, YEAH, OKAY.
I KNOW ALL OF YOU WILL DO AN AMAZING JOB PREPARING WINTER FOR HIS NEW CAREER AS A SCHOOLING HORSE.
FWIP
HOW DARE SHE.

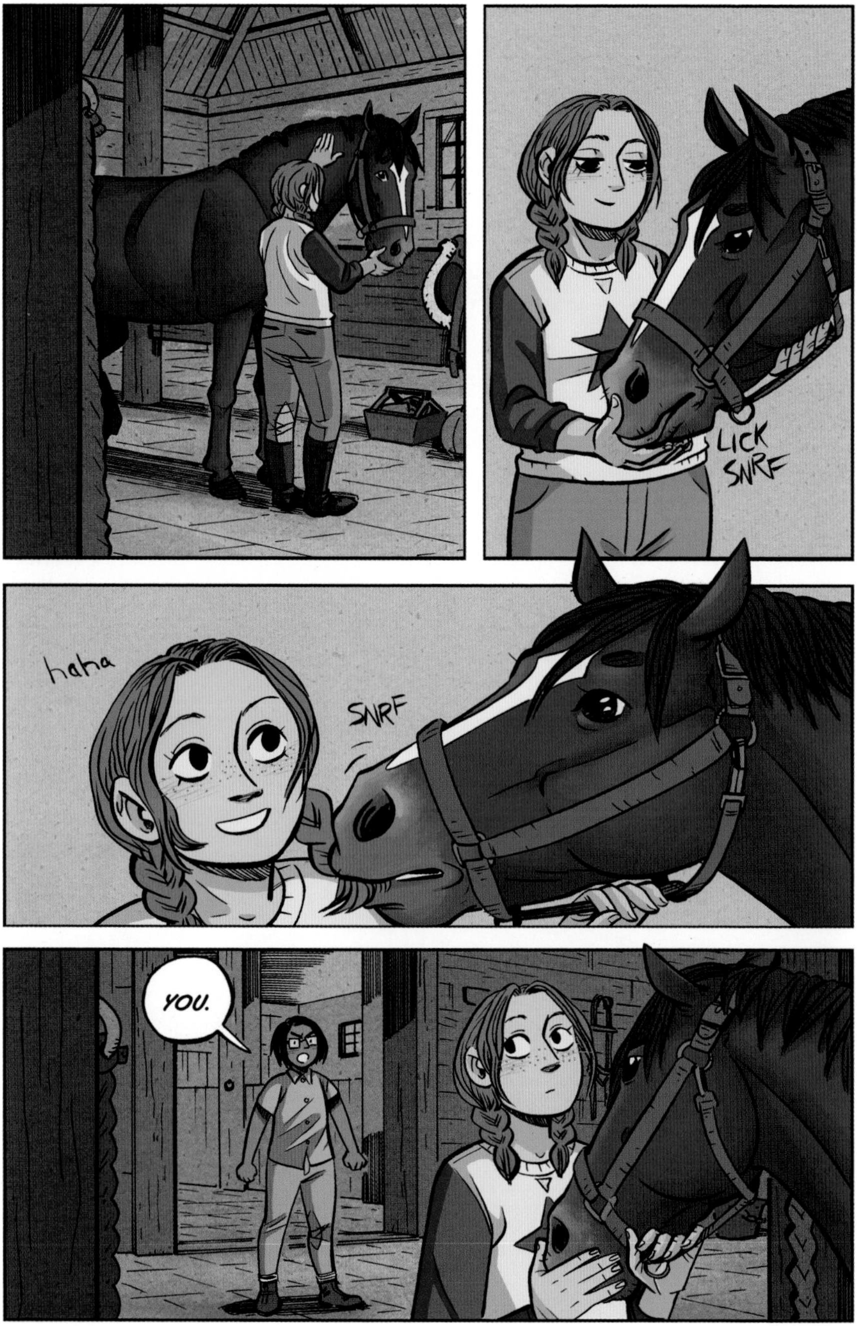
LICK
SNRF
haha
SNRF
YOU.

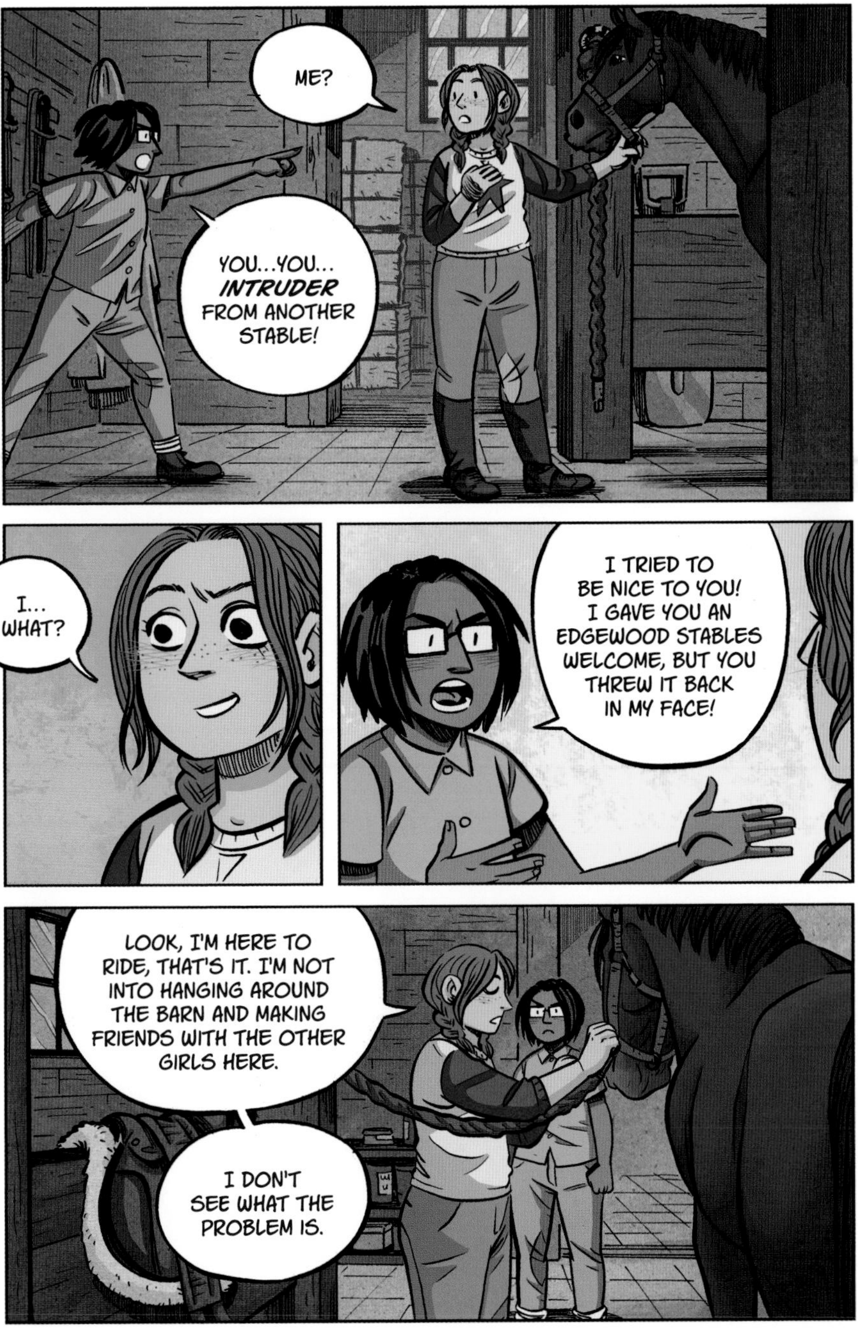
ME?
YOU...YOU... ***INTRUDER*** FROM ANOTHER STABLE!
I... WHAT?
I TRIED TO BE NICE TO YOU! I GAVE YOU AN EDGEWOOD STABLES WELCOME, BUT YOU THREW IT BACK IN MY FACE!
LOOK, I'M HERE TO RIDE, THAT'S IT. I'M NOT INTO HANGING AROUND THE BARN AND MAKING FRIENDS WITH THE OTHER GIRLS HERE.
I DON'T SEE WHAT THE PROBLEM IS.

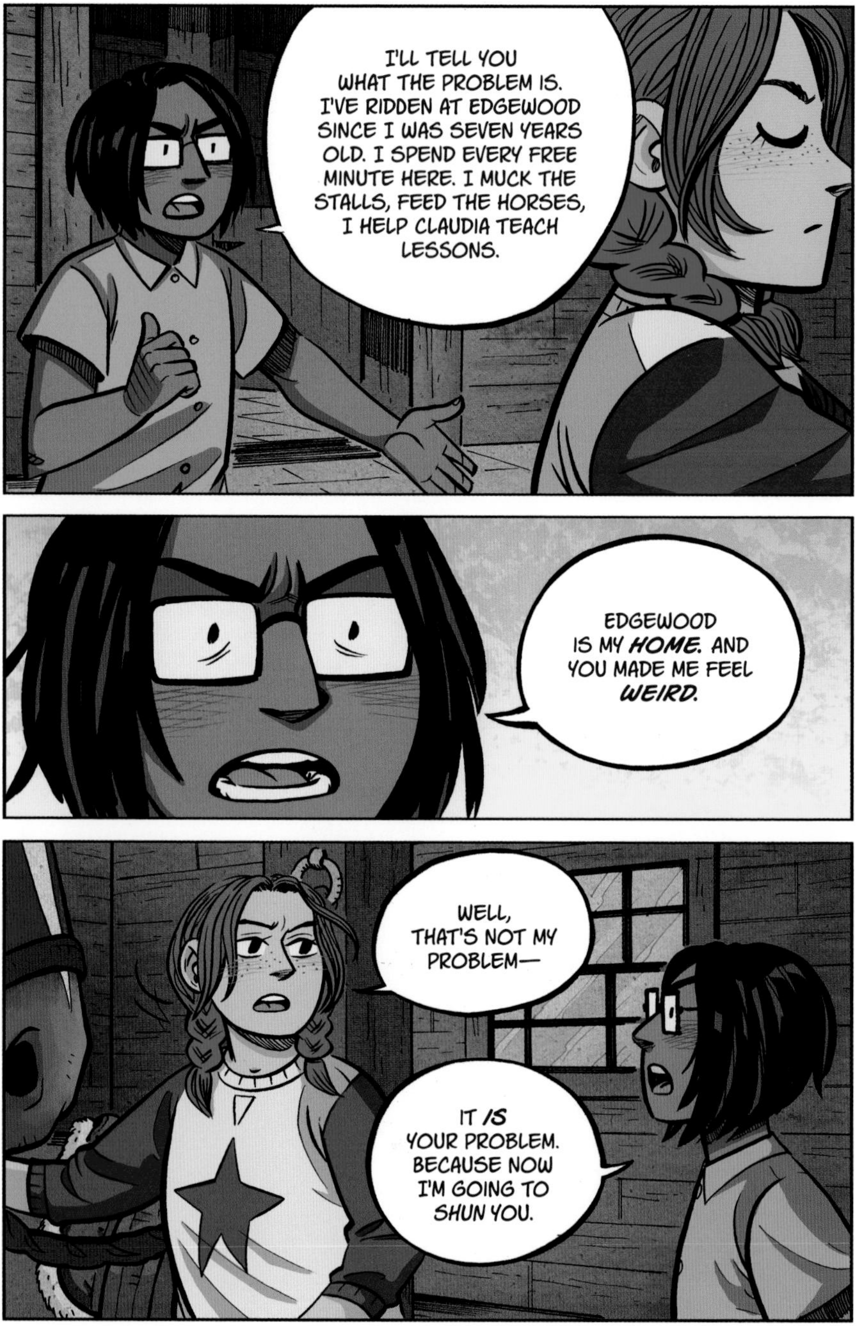
I'LL TELL YOU WHAT THE PROBLEM IS. I'VE RIDDEN AT EDGEWOOD SINCE I WAS SEVEN YEARS OLD. I SPEND EVERY FREE MINUTE HERE. I MUCK THE STALLS, FEED THE HORSES, I HELP CLAUDIA TEACH LESSONS.
EDGEWOOD IS MY *HOME*. AND YOU MADE ME FEEL *WEIRD*.
WELL, THAT'S NOT MY PROBLEM—
IT *IS* YOUR PROBLEM. BECAUSE NOW I'M GOING TO SHUN YOU.

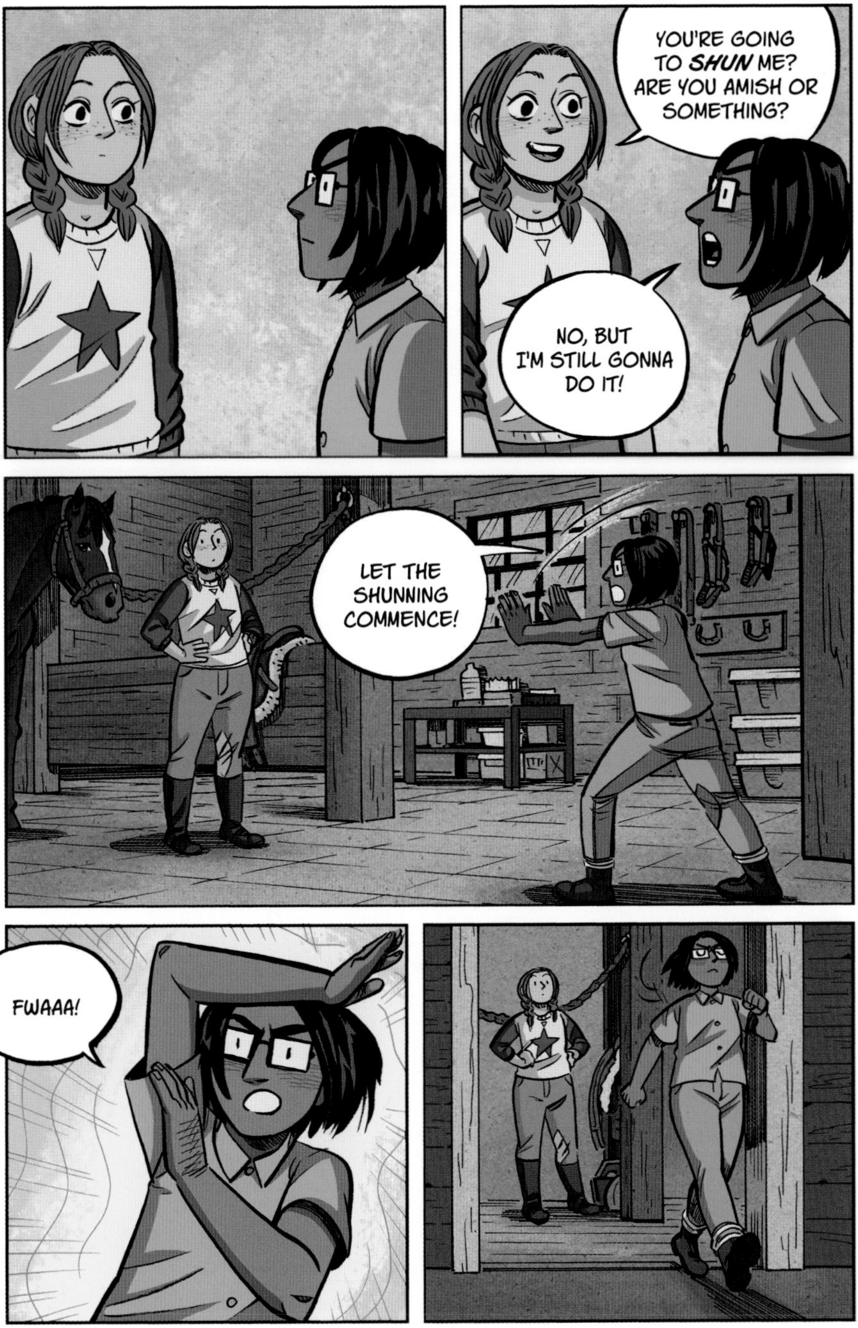
YOU'RE GOING TO SHUN ME? ARE YOU AMISH OR SOMETHING?
NO, BUT I'M STILL GONNA DO IT!
LET THE SHUNNING COMMENCE!
FWAAA!

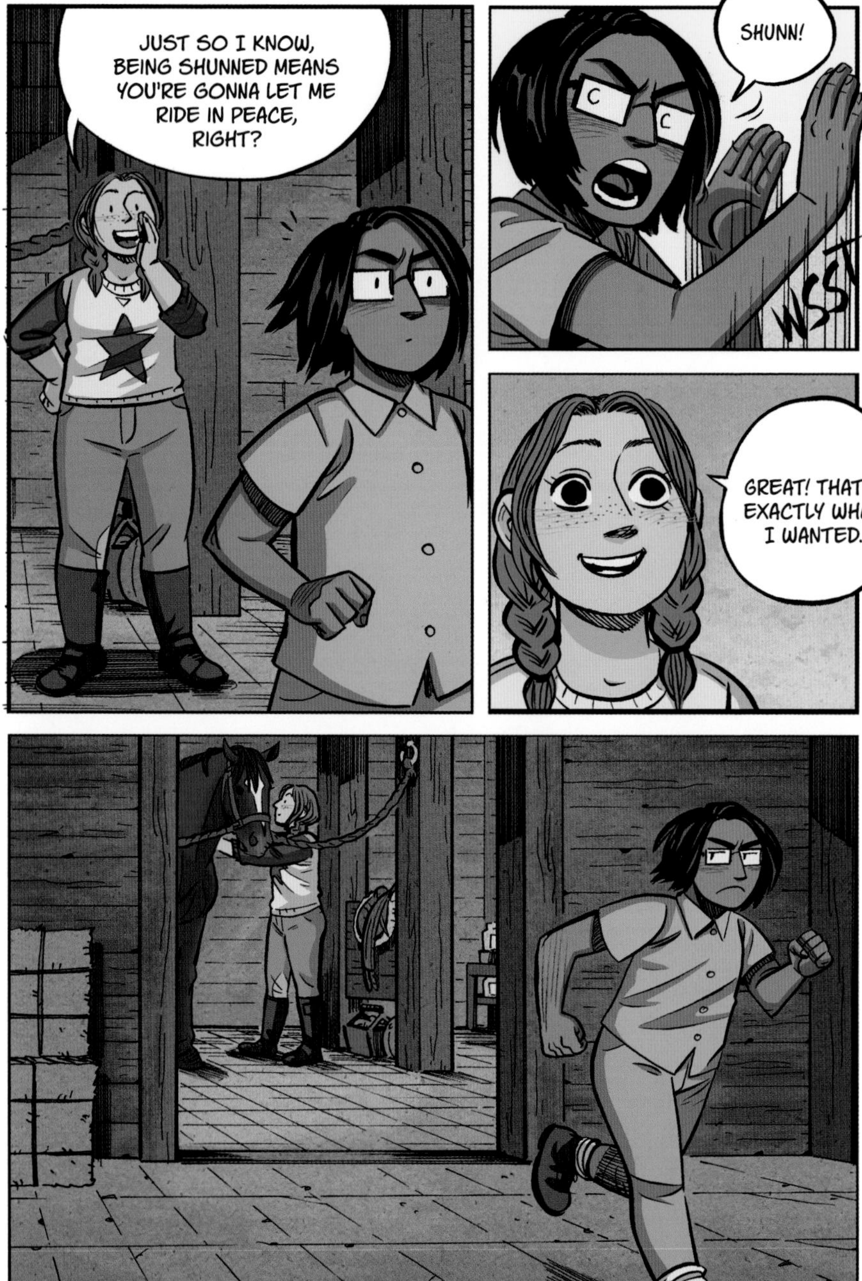
JUST SO I KNOW, BEING SHUNNED MEANS YOU'RE GONNA LET ME RIDE IN PEACE, RIGHT?
SHUNN!
WSST
GREAT! THAT'S EXACTLY WHAT I WANTED.

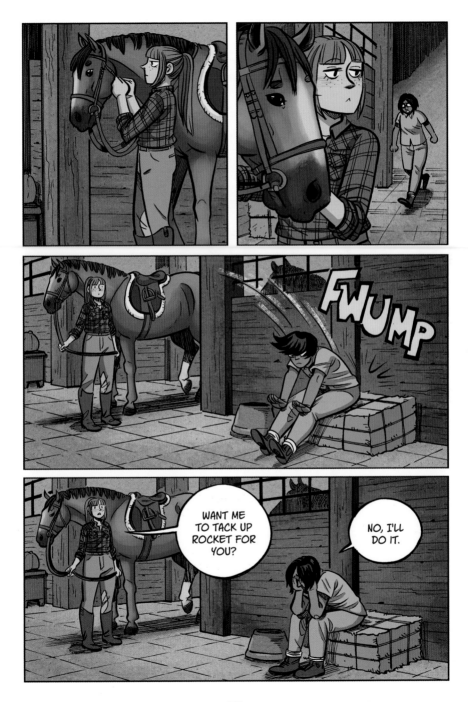

FWUMP

WANT ME TO TACK UP ROCKET FOR YOU?

NO, I'LL DO IT.

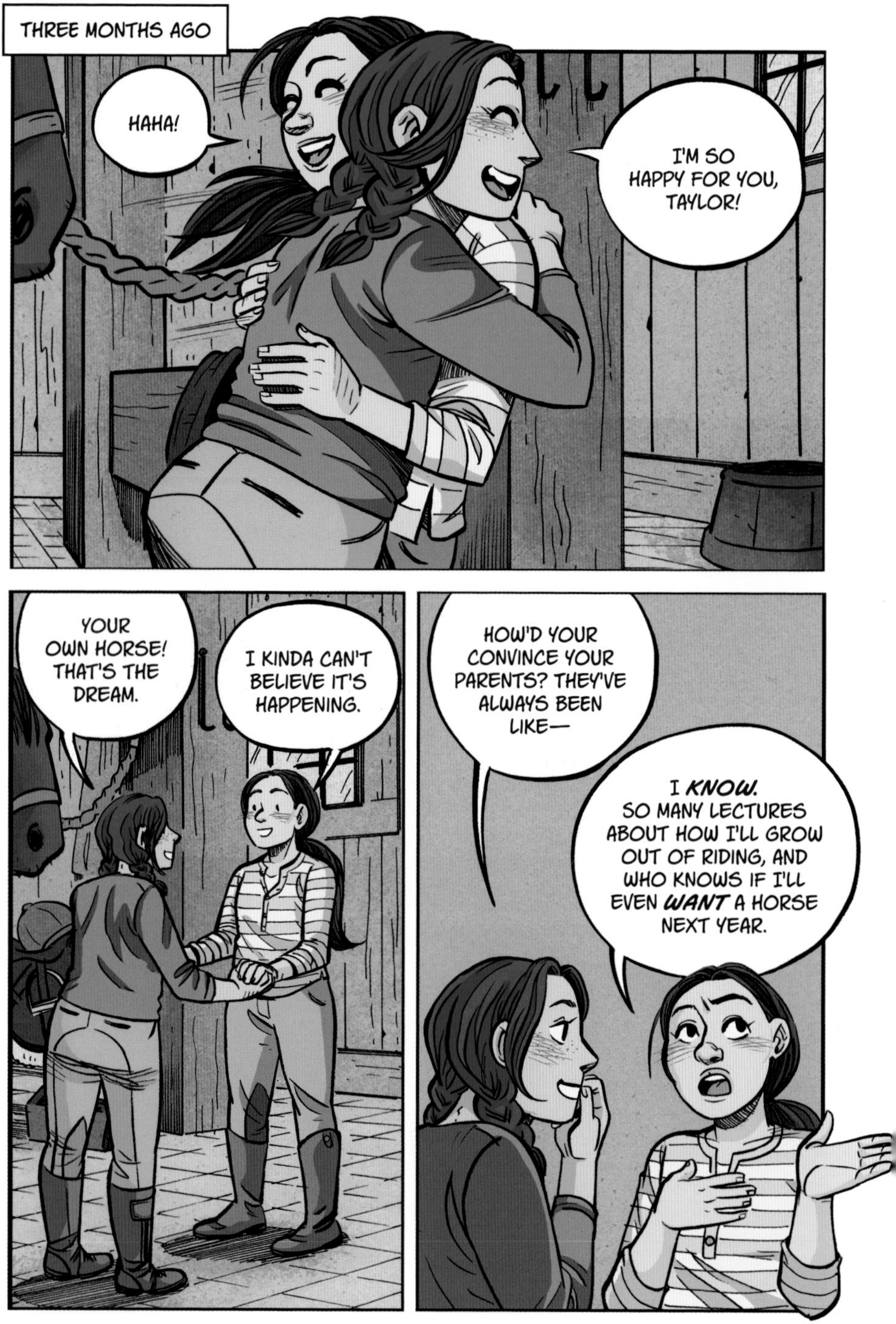
THREE MONTHS AGO
HAHA!
I'M SO HAPPY FOR YOU, TAYLOR!
YOUR OWN HORSE! THAT'S THE DREAM.
I KINDA CAN'T BELIEVE IT'S HAPPENING.
HOW'D YOUR CONVINCE YOUR PARENTS? THEY'VE ALWAYS BEEN LIKE—
I *KNOW.* SO MANY LECTURES ABOUT HOW I'LL GROW OUT OF RIDING, AND WHO KNOWS IF I'LL EVEN *WANT* A HORSE NEXT YEAR.

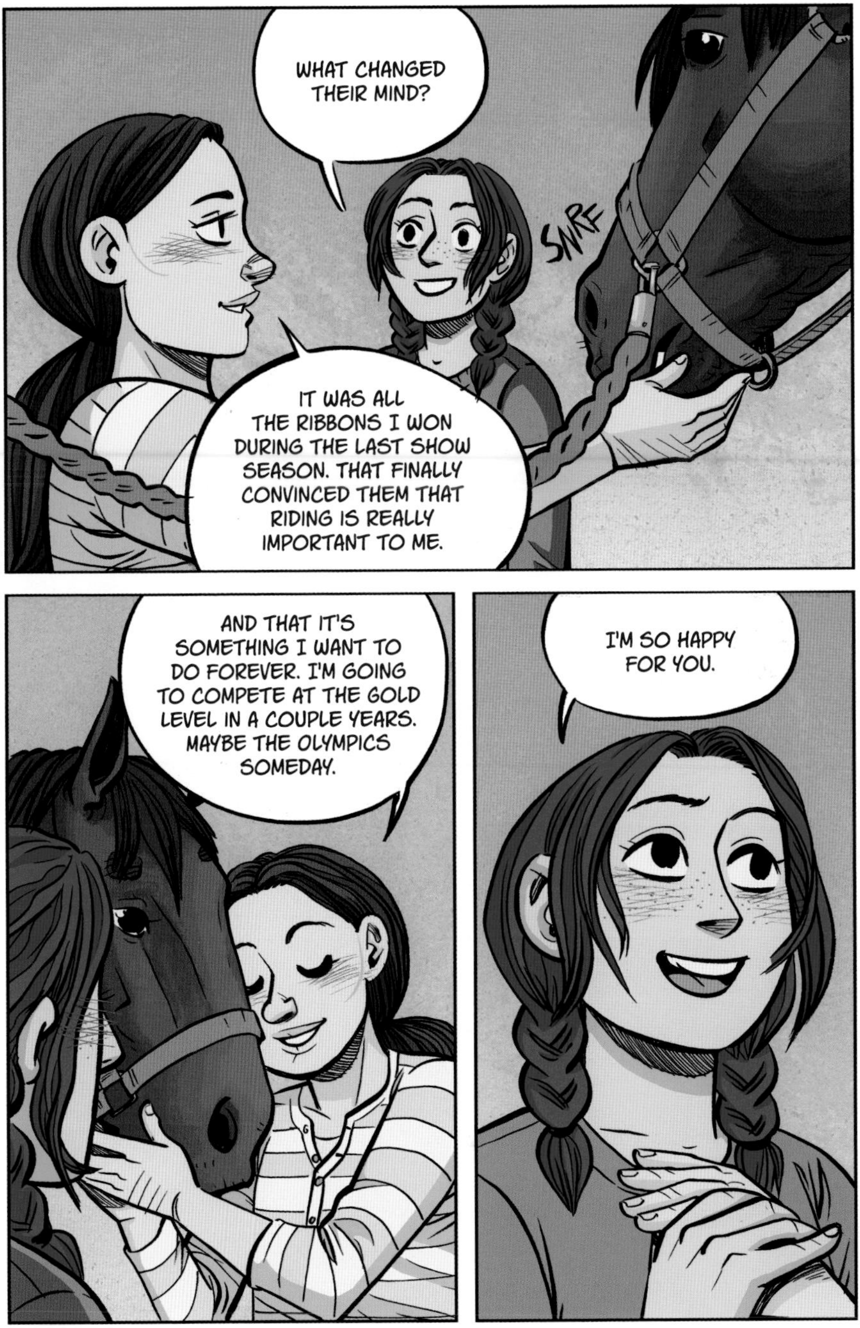
WHAT CHANGED THEIR MIND?
SNRF
IT WAS ALL THE RIBBONS I WON DURING THE LAST SHOW SEASON. THAT FINALLY CONVINCED THEM THAT RIDING IS REALLY IMPORTANT TO ME.
AND THAT IT'S SOMETHING I WANT TO DO FOREVER. I'M GOING TO COMPETE AT THE GOLD LEVEL IN A COUPLE YEARS. MAYBE THE OLYMPICS SOMEDAY.
I'M SO HAPPY FOR YOU.

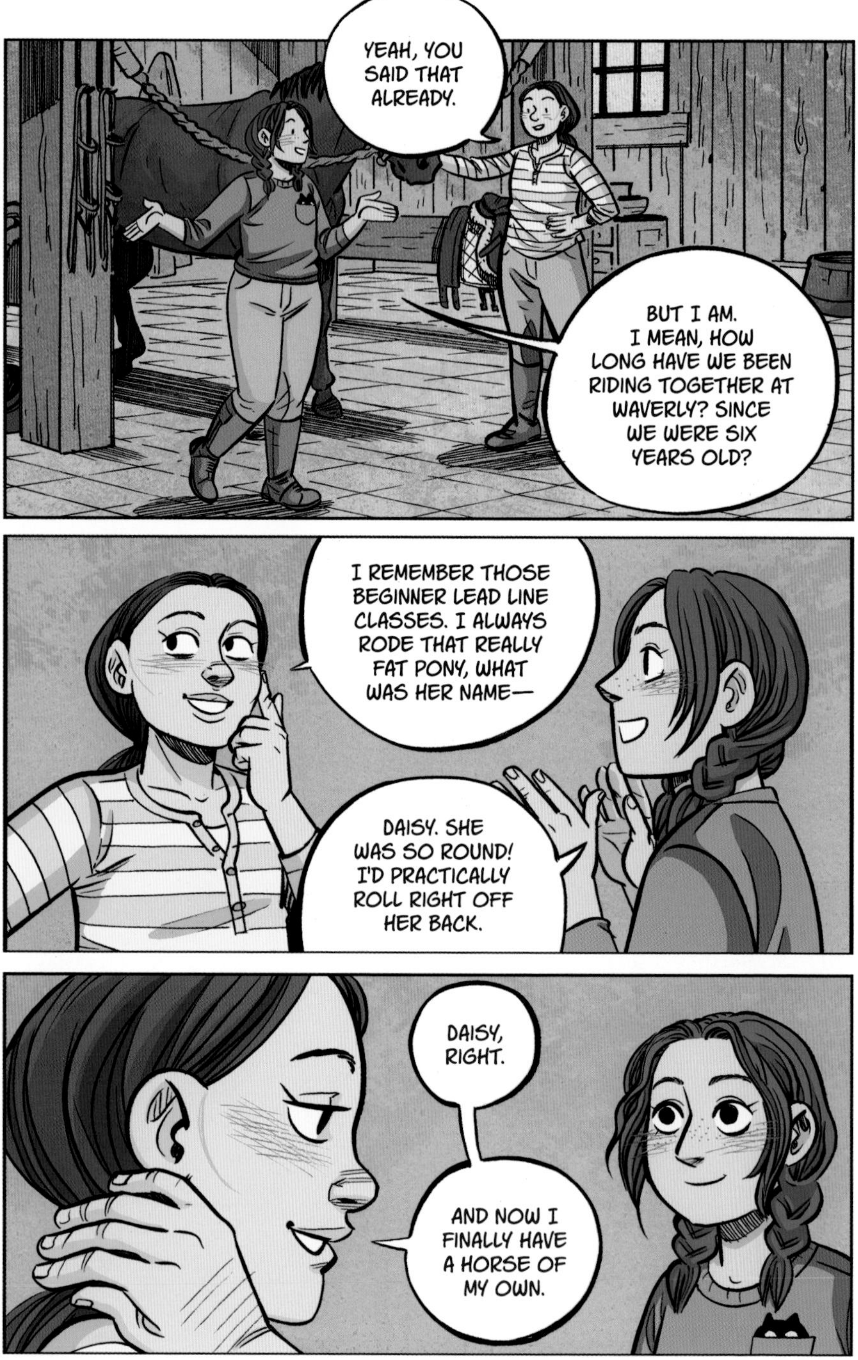
YEAH, YOU SAID THAT ALREADY.
BUT I AM. I MEAN, HOW LONG HAVE WE BEEN RIDING TOGETHER AT WAVERLY? SINCE WE WERE SIX YEARS OLD?
I REMEMBER THOSE BEGINNER LEAD LINE CLASSES. I ALWAYS RODE THAT REALLY FAT PONY, WHAT WAS HER NAME—
DAISY. SHE WAS SO ROUND! I'D PRACTICALLY ROLL RIGHT OFF HER BACK.
DAISY, RIGHT.
AND NOW I FINALLY HAVE A HORSE OF MY OWN.

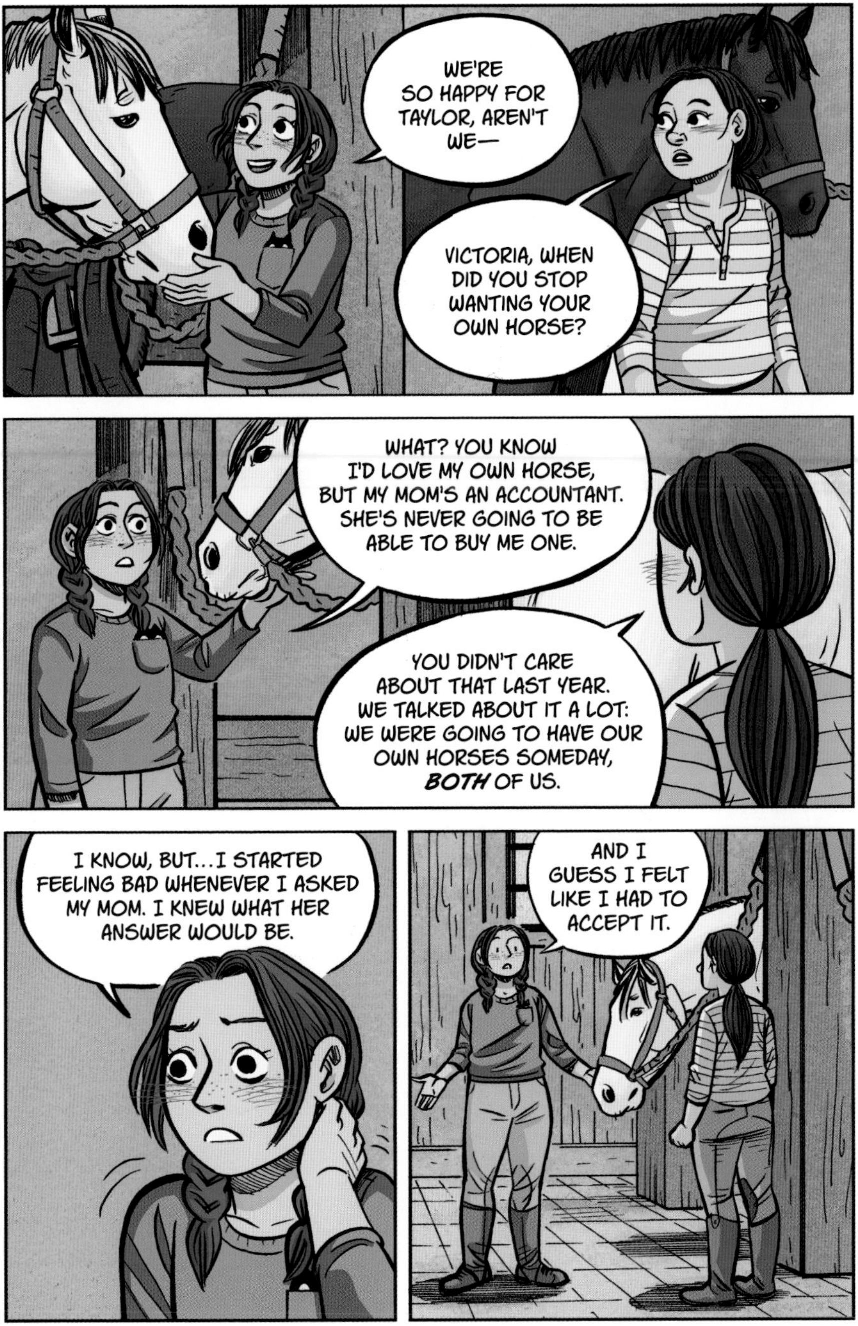
WE'RE SO HAPPY FOR TAYLOR, AREN'T WE—
VICTORIA, WHEN DID YOU STOP WANTING YOUR OWN HORSE?
WHAT? YOU KNOW I'D LOVE MY OWN HORSE, BUT MY MOM'S AN ACCOUNTANT. SHE'S NEVER GOING TO BE ABLE TO BUY ME ONE.
YOU DIDN'T CARE ABOUT THAT LAST YEAR. WE TALKED ABOUT IT A LOT: WE WERE GOING TO HAVE OUR OWN HORSES SOMEDAY, ***BOTH*** OF US.
I KNOW, BUT...I STARTED FEELING BAD WHENEVER I ASKED MY MOM. I KNEW WHAT HER ANSWER WOULD BE.
AND I GUESS I FELT LIKE I HAD TO ACCEPT IT.

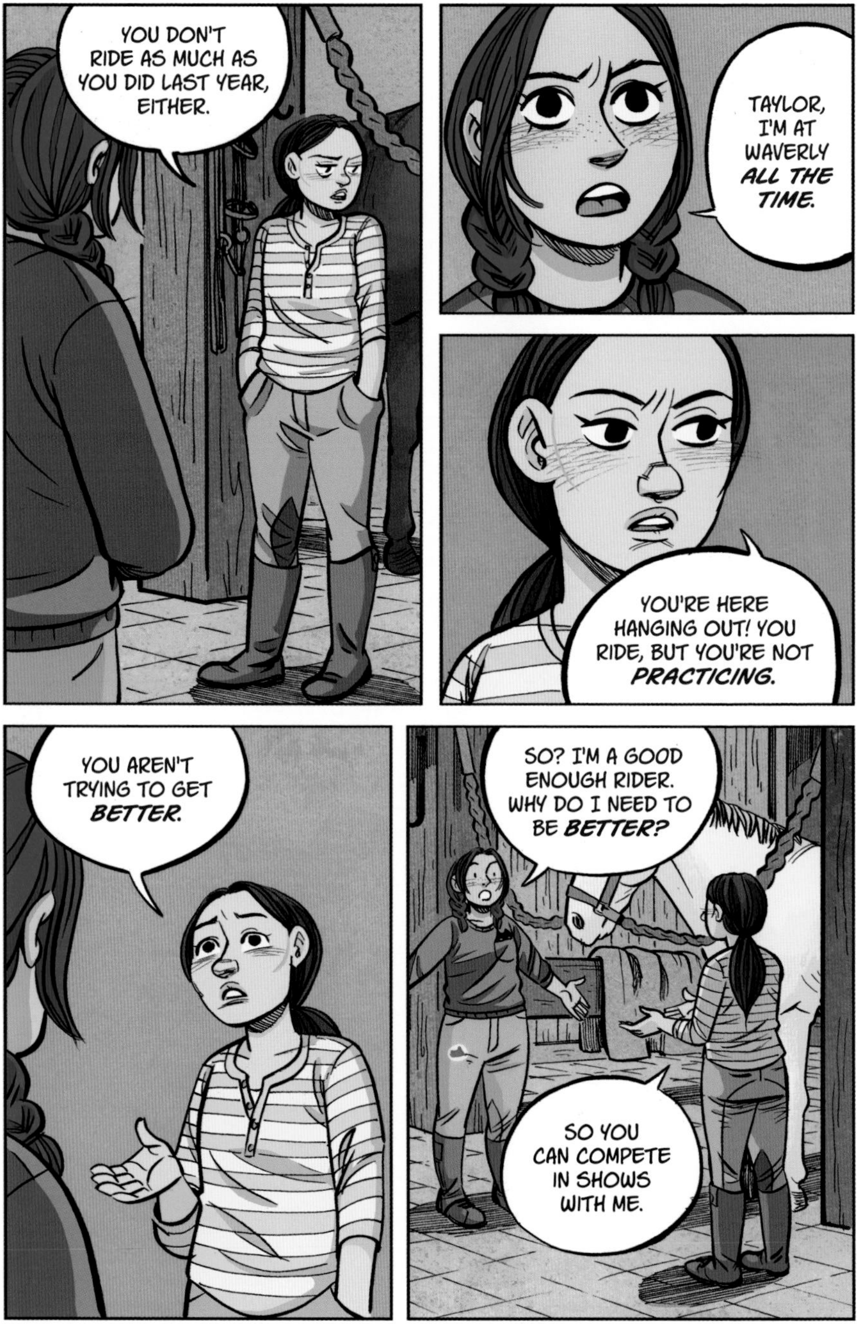
YOU DON'T RIDE AS MUCH AS YOU DID LAST YEAR, EITHER.
TAYLOR, I'M AT WAVERLY *ALL THE TIME.*
YOU'RE HERE HANGING OUT! YOU RIDE, BUT YOU'RE NOT *PRACTICING.*
YOU AREN'T TRYING TO GET *BETTER.*
SO? I'M A GOOD ENOUGH RIDER. WHY DO I NEED TO BE *BETTER?*
SO YOU CAN COMPETE IN SHOWS WITH ME.

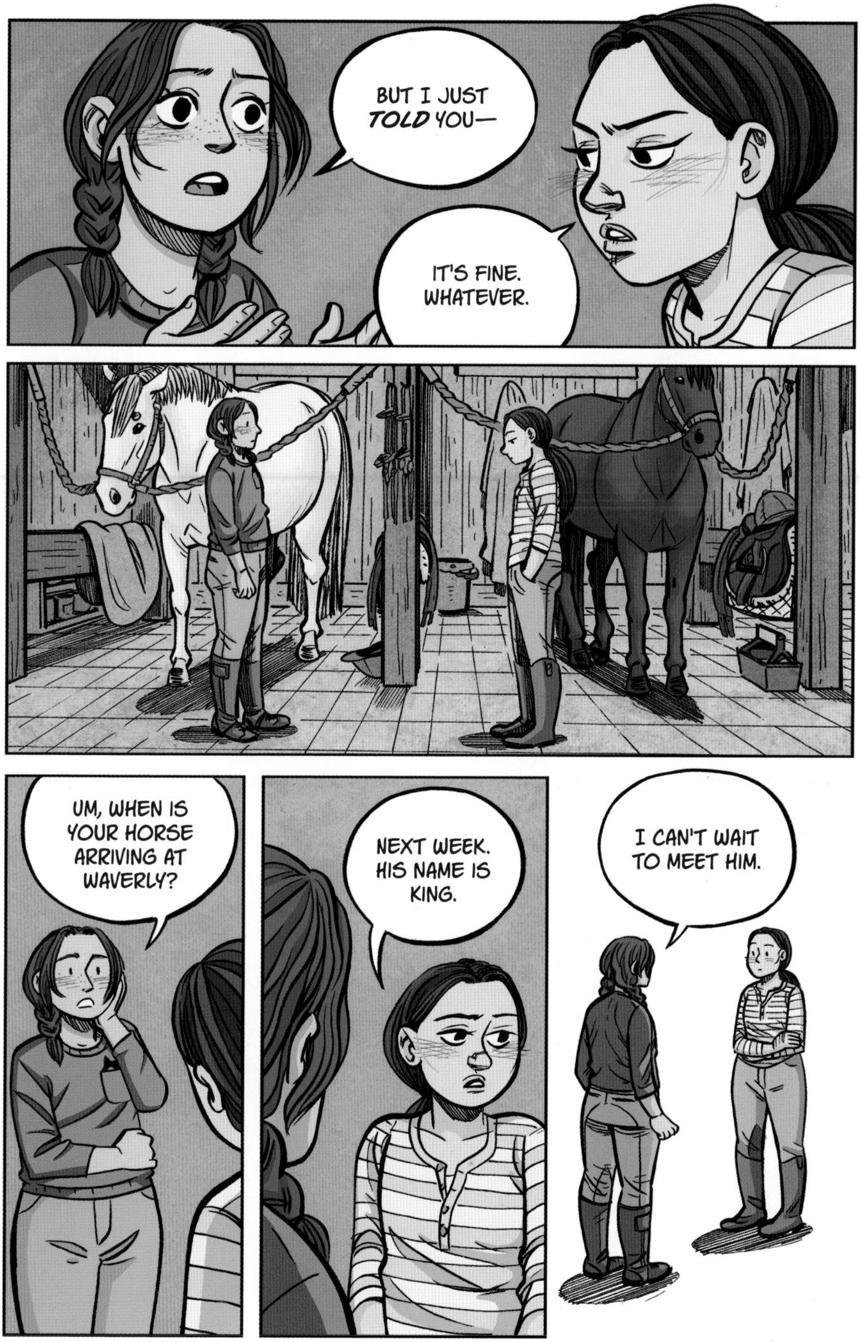
BUT I JUST *TOLD* YOU—
IT'S FINE. WHATEVER.
UM, WHEN IS YOUR HORSE ARRIVING AT WAVERLY?
NEXT WEEK. HIS NAME IS KING.
I CAN'T WAIT TO MEET HIM.

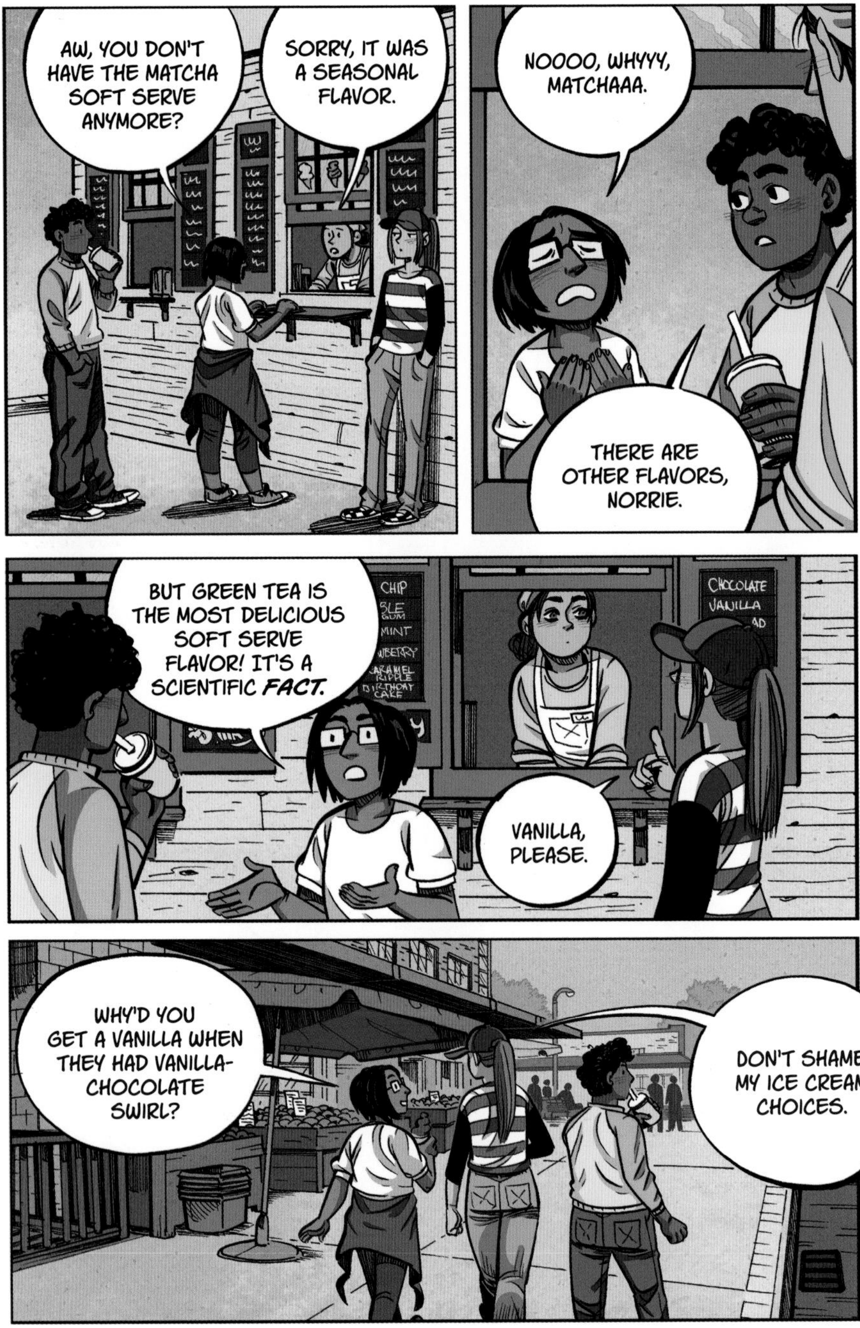
AW, YOU DON'T HAVE THE MATCHA SOFT SERVE ANYMORE?
SORRY, IT WAS A SEASONAL FLAVOR.
NOOOO, WHYYY, MATCHAAA.
THERE ARE OTHER FLAVORS, NORRIE.
BUT GREEN TEA IS THE MOST DELICIOUS SOFT SERVE FLAVOR! IT'S A SCIENTIFIC ***FACT.***
CHIP
MINT
CARAMEL RIPPLE
BIRTHDAY CAKE
CHOCOLATE
VANILLA
VANILLA, PLEASE.
WHY'D YOU GET A VANILLA WHEN THEY HAD VANILLA-CHOCOLATE SWIRL?
DON'T SHAME MY ICE CREAM CHOICES.

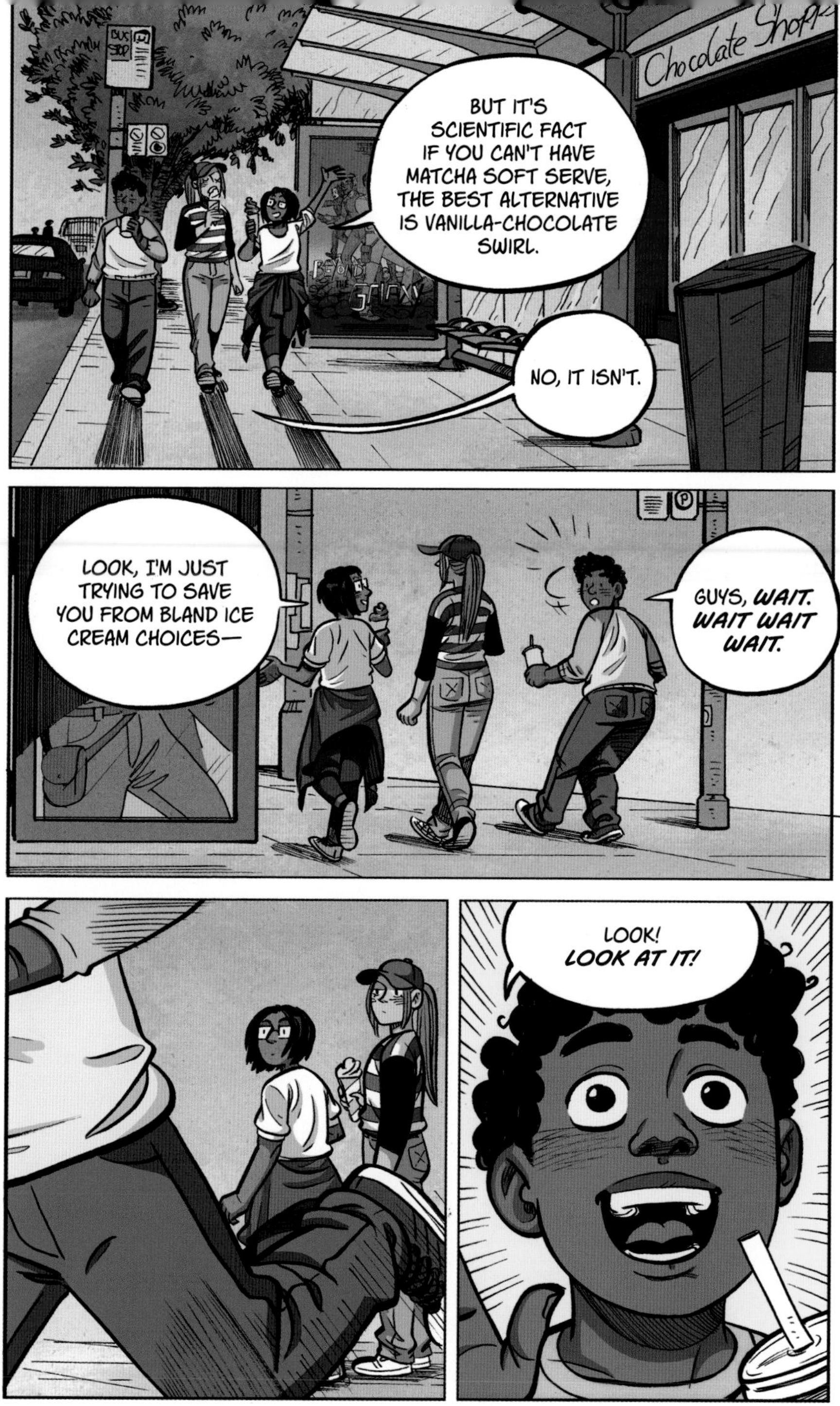
Chocolate Shop
BUS STOP
BEYOND THE GALAXY
BUT IT'S SCIENTIFIC FACT IF YOU CAN'T HAVE MATCHA SOFT SERVE, THE BEST ALTERNATIVE IS VANILLA-CHOCOLATE SWIRL.
NO, IT ISN'T.
LOOK, I'M JUST TRYING TO SAVE YOU FROM BLAND ICE CREAM CHOICES—
GUYS, *WAIT. WAIT WAIT WAIT.*
LOOK! *LOOK AT IT!*

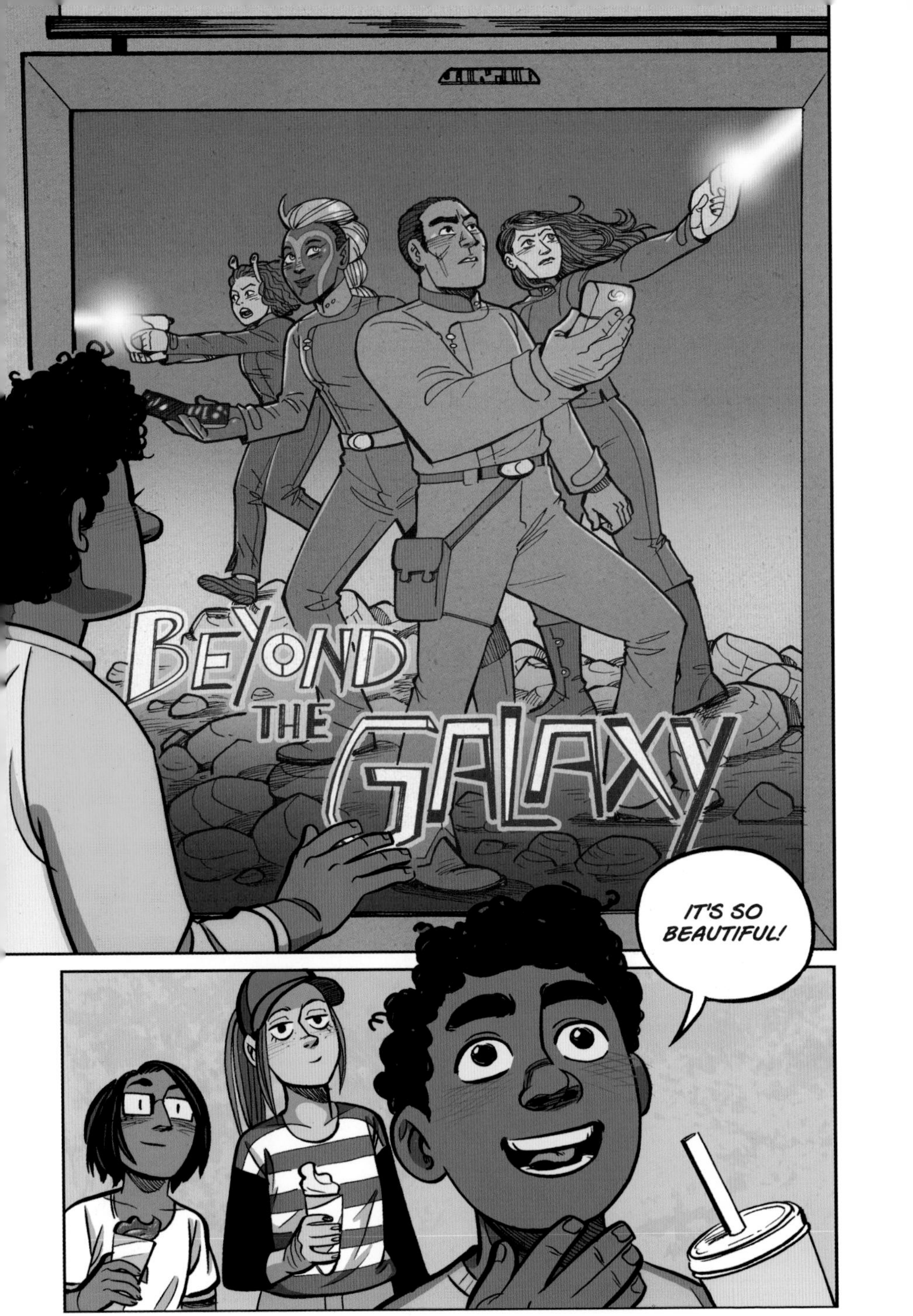
BEYOND THE GALAXY
IT'S SO BEAUTIFUL!

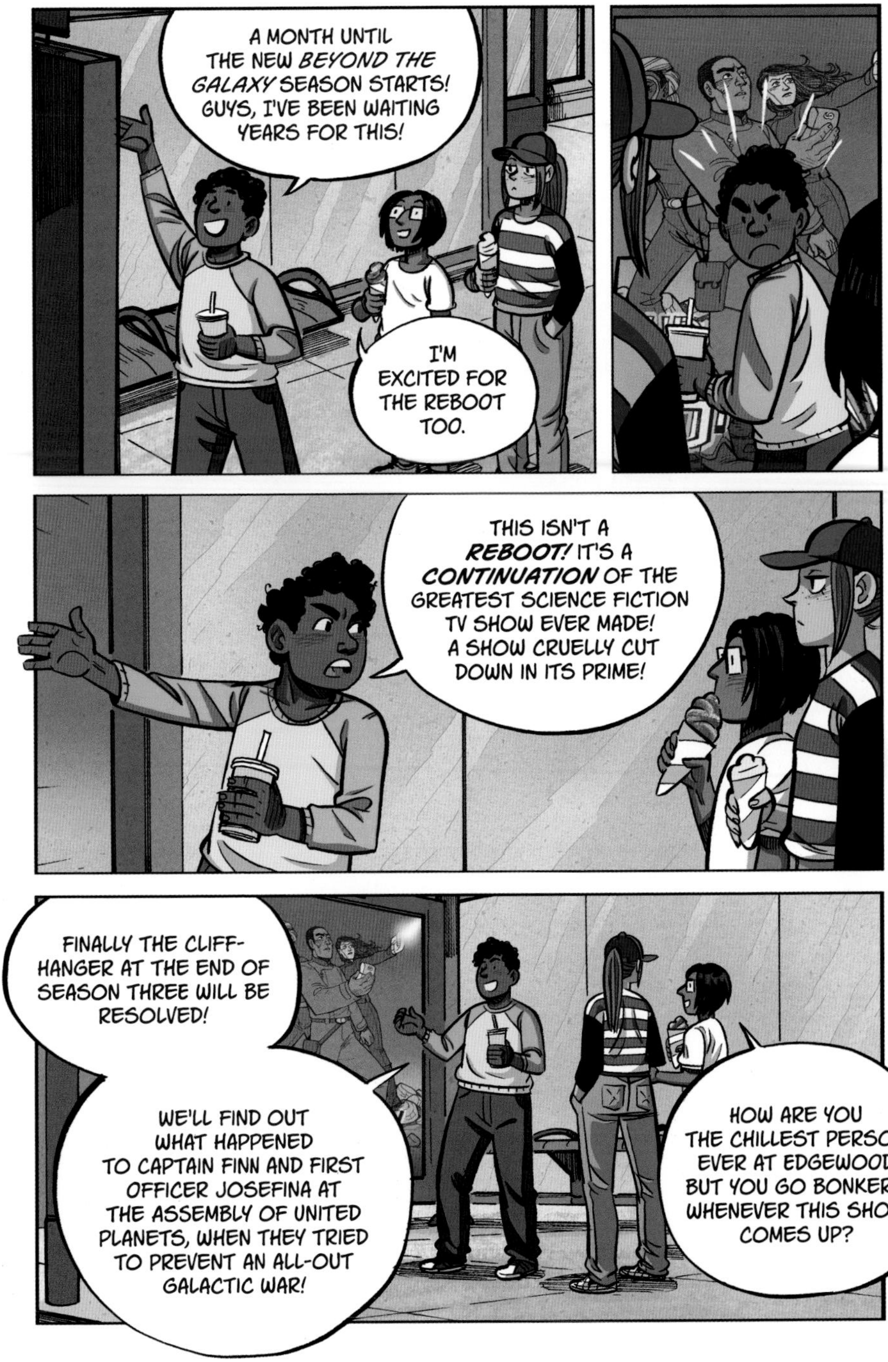
A MONTH UNTIL THE NEW *BEYOND THE GALAXY* SEASON STARTS! GUYS, I'VE BEEN WAITING YEARS FOR THIS!
I'M EXCITED FOR THE REBOOT TOO.
THIS ISN'T A ***REBOOT!*** IT'S A ***CONTINUATION*** OF THE GREATEST SCIENCE FICTION TV SHOW EVER MADE! A SHOW CRUELLY CUT DOWN IN ITS PRIME!
FINALLY THE CLIFF-HANGER AT THE END OF SEASON THREE WILL BE RESOLVED!
WE'LL FIND OUT WHAT HAPPENED TO CAPTAIN FINN AND FIRST OFFICER JOSEFINA AT THE ASSEMBLY OF UNITED PLANETS, WHEN THEY TRIED TO PREVENT AN ALL-OUT GALACTIC WAR!
HOW ARE YOU THE CHILLEST PERSON EVER AT EDGEWOOD BUT YOU GO BONKERS WHENEVER THIS SHOW COMES UP?

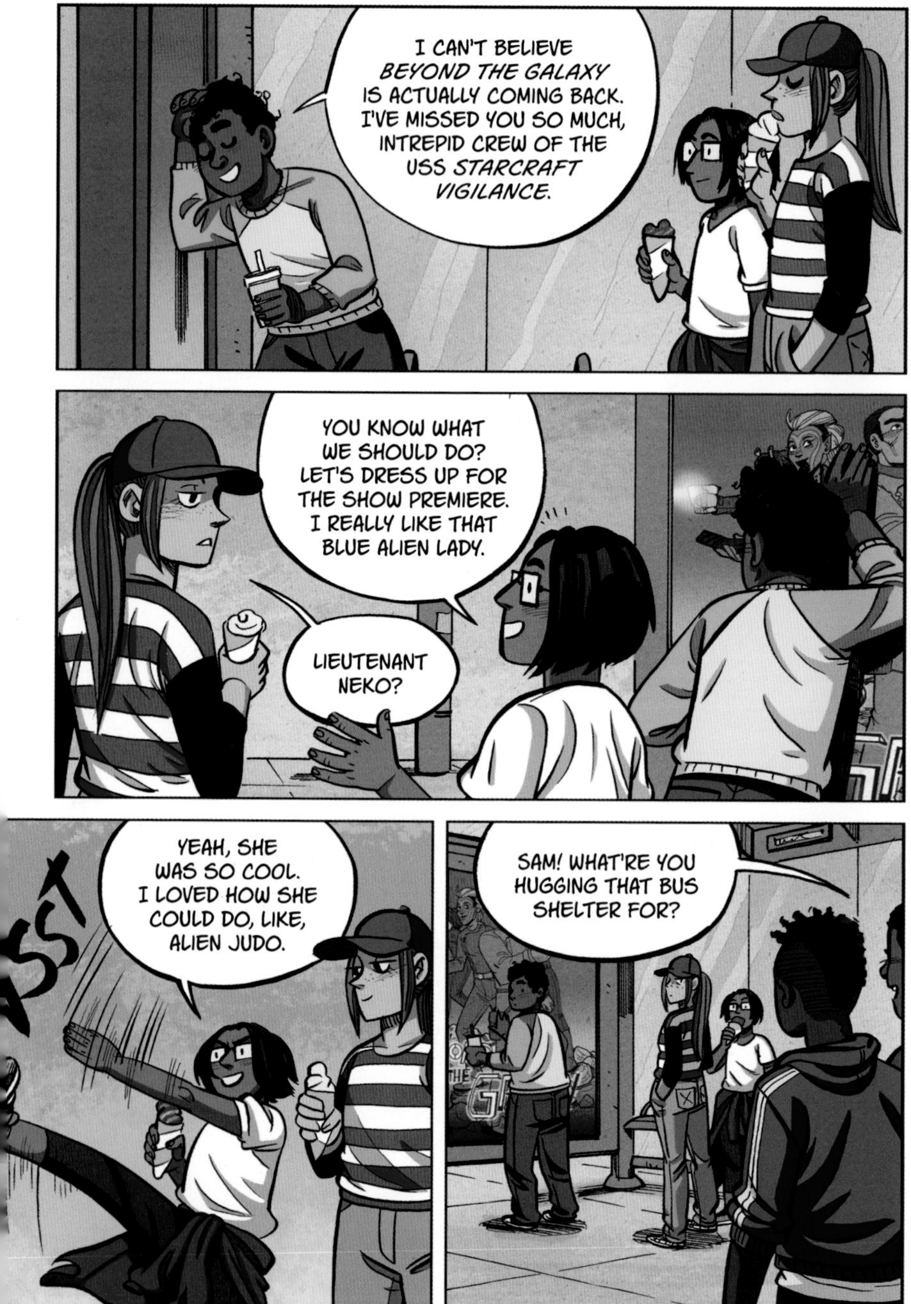
I CAN'T BELIEVE *BEYOND THE GALAXY* IS ACTUALLY COMING BACK. I'VE MISSED YOU SO MUCH, INTREPID CREW OF THE USS *STARCRAFT VIGILANCE*.
YOU KNOW WHAT WE SHOULD DO? LET'S DRESS UP FOR THE SHOW PREMIERE. I REALLY LIKE THAT BLUE ALIEN LADY.
LIEUTENANT NEKO?
YEAH, SHE WAS SO COOL. I LOVED HOW SHE COULD DO, LIKE, ALIEN JUDO.
SST
SAM! WHAT'RE YOU HUGGING THAT BUS SHELTER FOR?

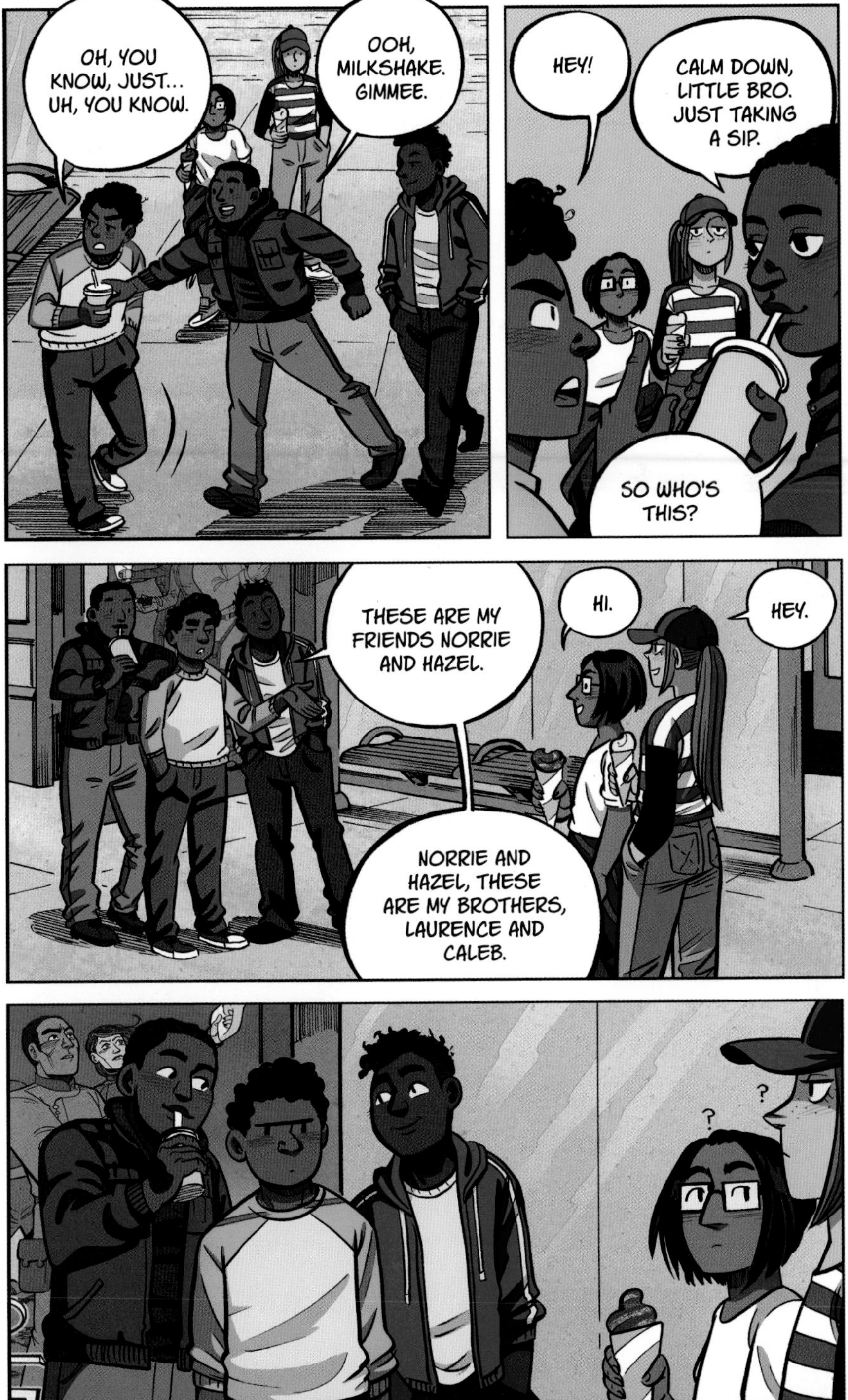
OH, YOU KNOW, JUST... UH, YOU KNOW.
OOH, MILKSHAKE. GIMMEE.
HEY!
CALM DOWN, LITTLE BRO. JUST TAKING A SIP.
SO WHO'S THIS?
THESE ARE MY FRIENDS NORRIE AND HAZEL.
HI.
HEY.
NORRIE AND HAZEL, THESE ARE MY BROTHERS, LAURENCE AND CALEB.
?
?

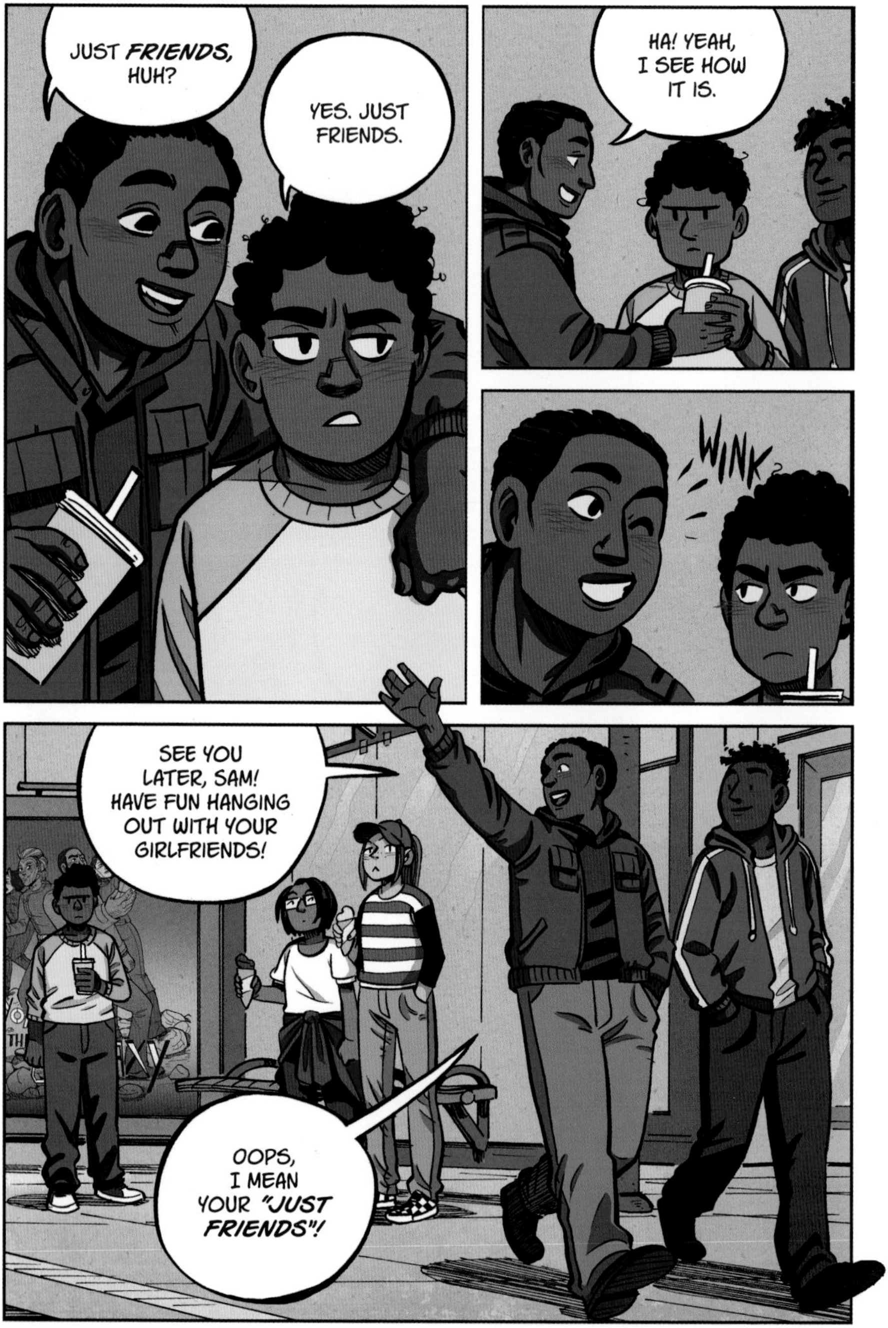
JUST FRIENDS, HUH?
YES. JUST FRIENDS.
HA! YEAH, I SEE HOW IT IS.
WINK
SEE YOU LATER, SAM! HAVE FUN HANGING OUT WITH YOUR GIRLFRIENDS!
OOPS, I MEAN YOUR "JUST FRIENDS"!

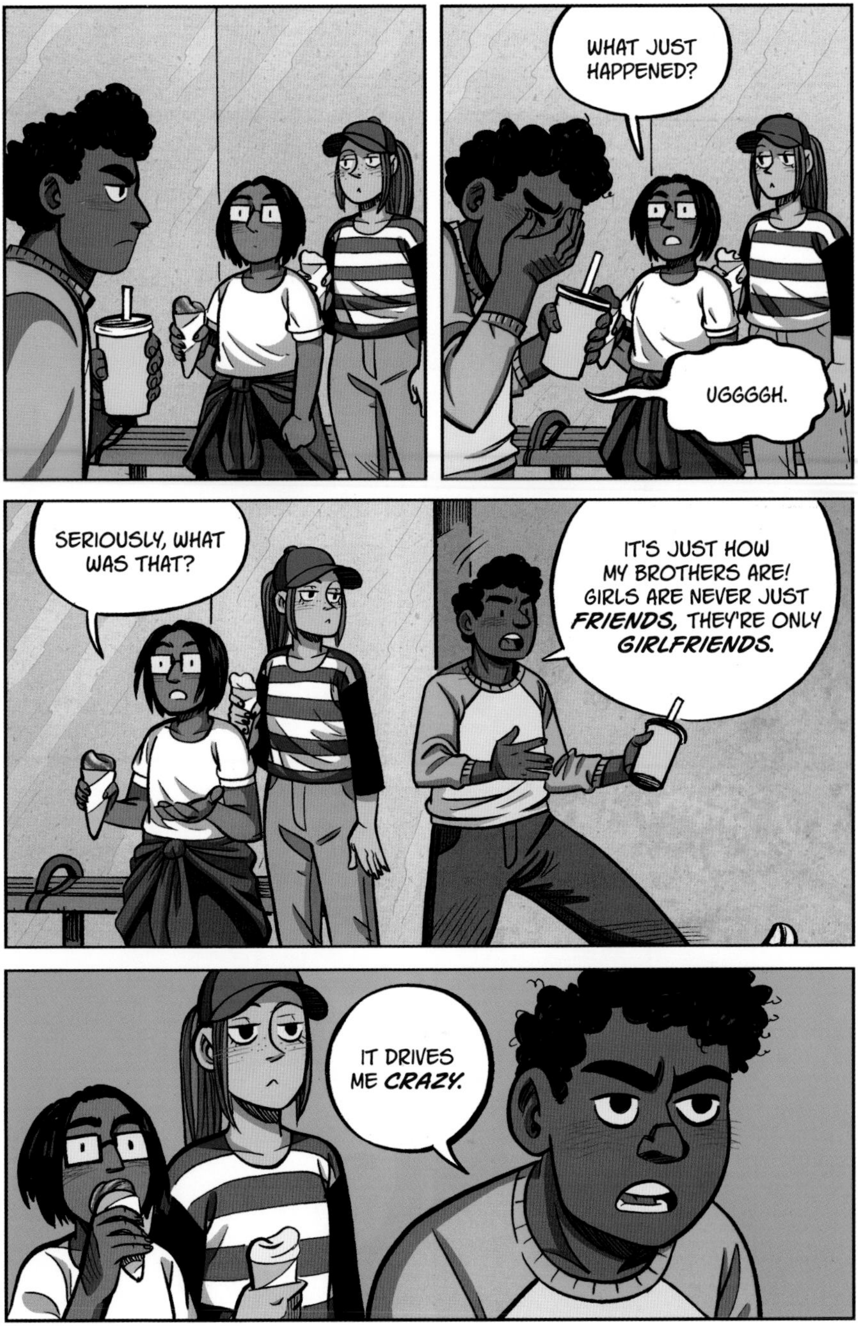
WHAT JUST HAPPENED?
UGGGGH.
SERIOUSLY, WHAT WAS THAT?
IT'S JUST HOW MY BROTHERS ARE! GIRLS ARE NEVER JUST *FRIENDS,* THEY'RE ONLY *GIRLFRIENDS.*
IT DRIVES ME *CRAZY.*

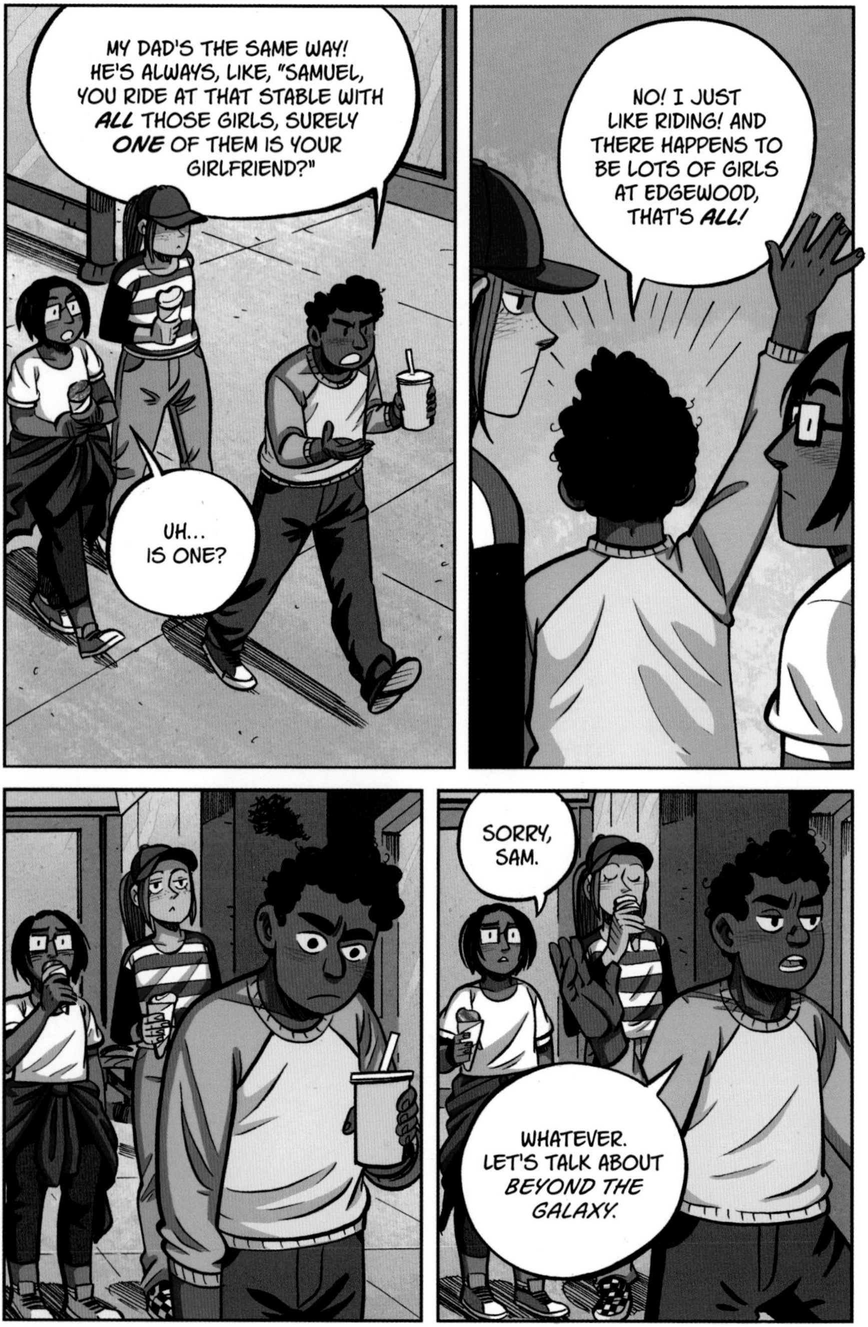
MY DAD'S THE SAME WAY! HE'S ALWAYS, LIKE, "SAMUEL, YOU RIDE AT THAT STABLE WITH ***ALL*** THOSE GIRLS, SURELY ***ONE*** OF THEM IS YOUR GIRLFRIEND?"
UH... IS ONE?
NO! I JUST LIKE RIDING! AND THERE HAPPENS TO BE LOTS OF GIRLS AT EDGEWOOD, THAT'S ***ALL!***
SORRY, SAM.
WHATEVER. LET'S TALK ABOUT *BEYOND THE GALAXY.*

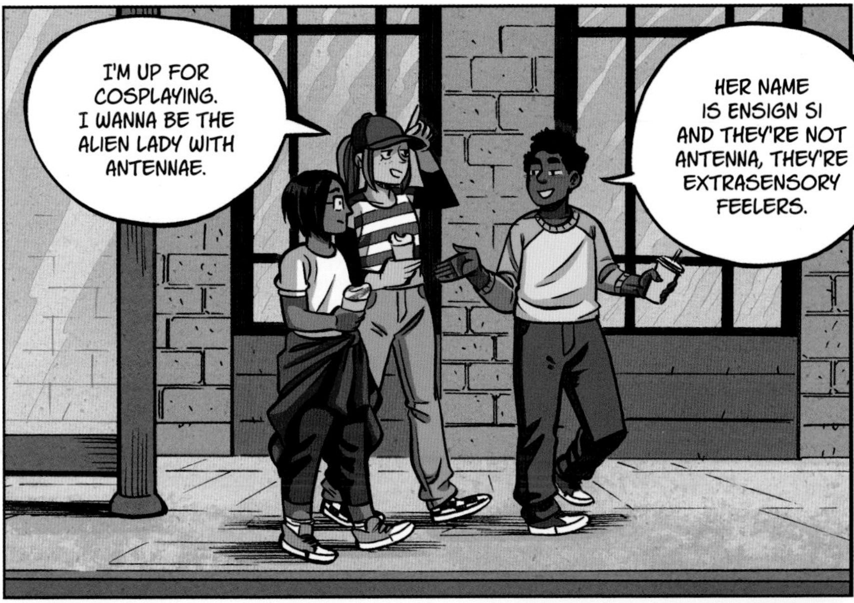
I'M UP FOR COSPLAYING. I WANNA BE THE ALIEN LADY WITH ANTENNAE.
HER NAME IS ENSIGN SI AND THEY'RE NOT ANTENNA, THEY'RE EXTRASENSORY FEELERS.

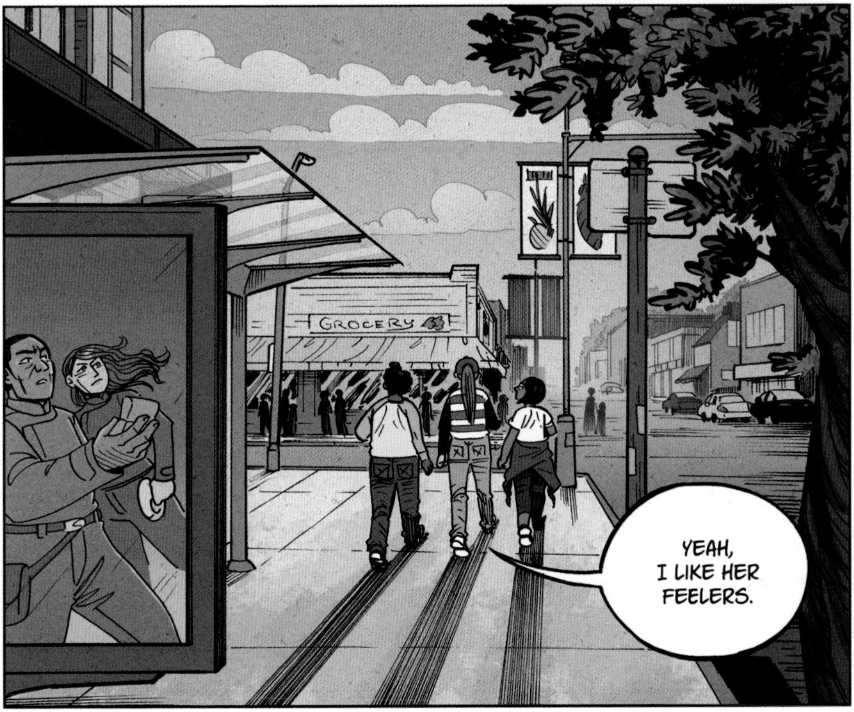
GROCERY
YEAH, I LIKE HER FEELERS.

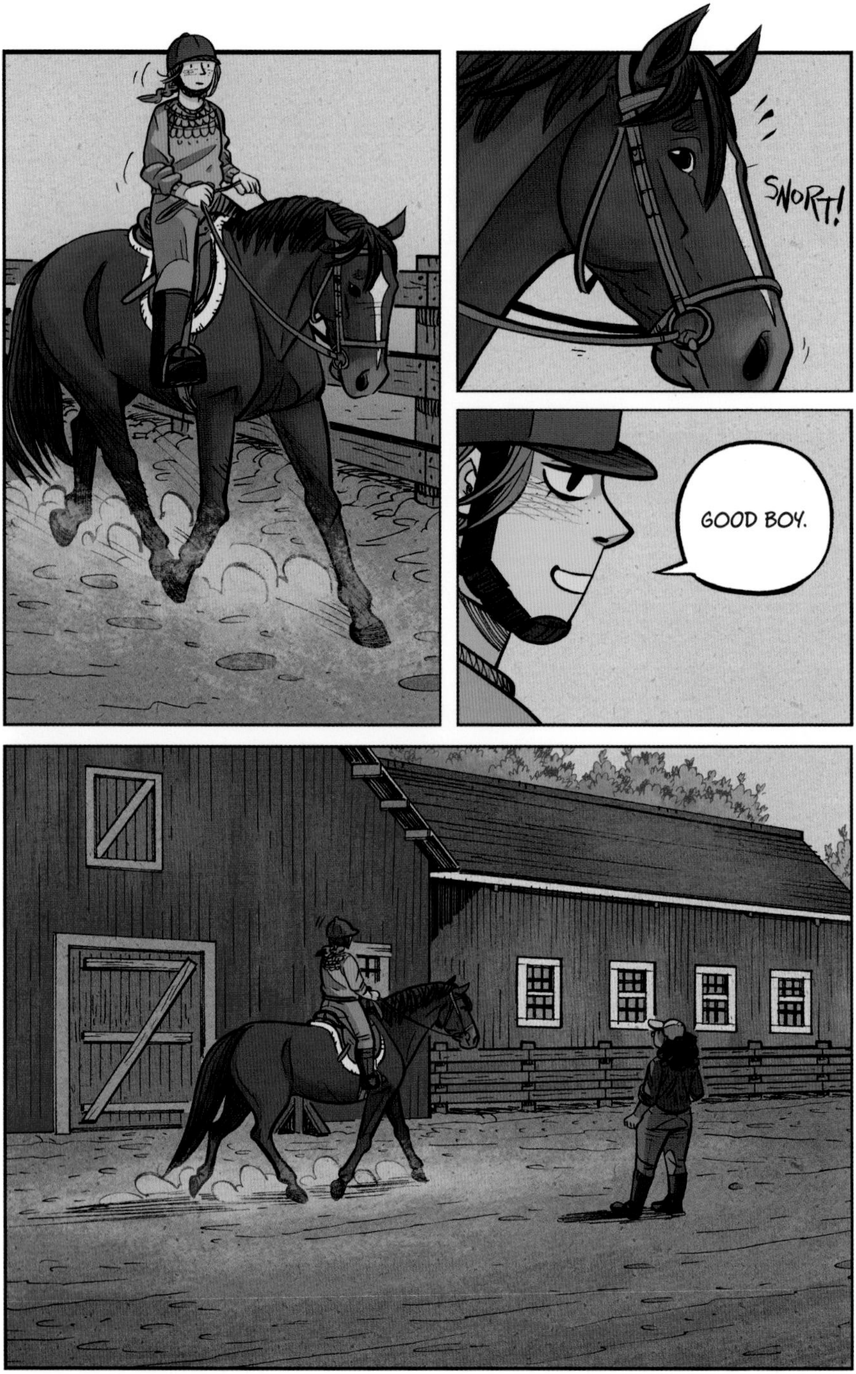
SNORT!
GOOD BOY.

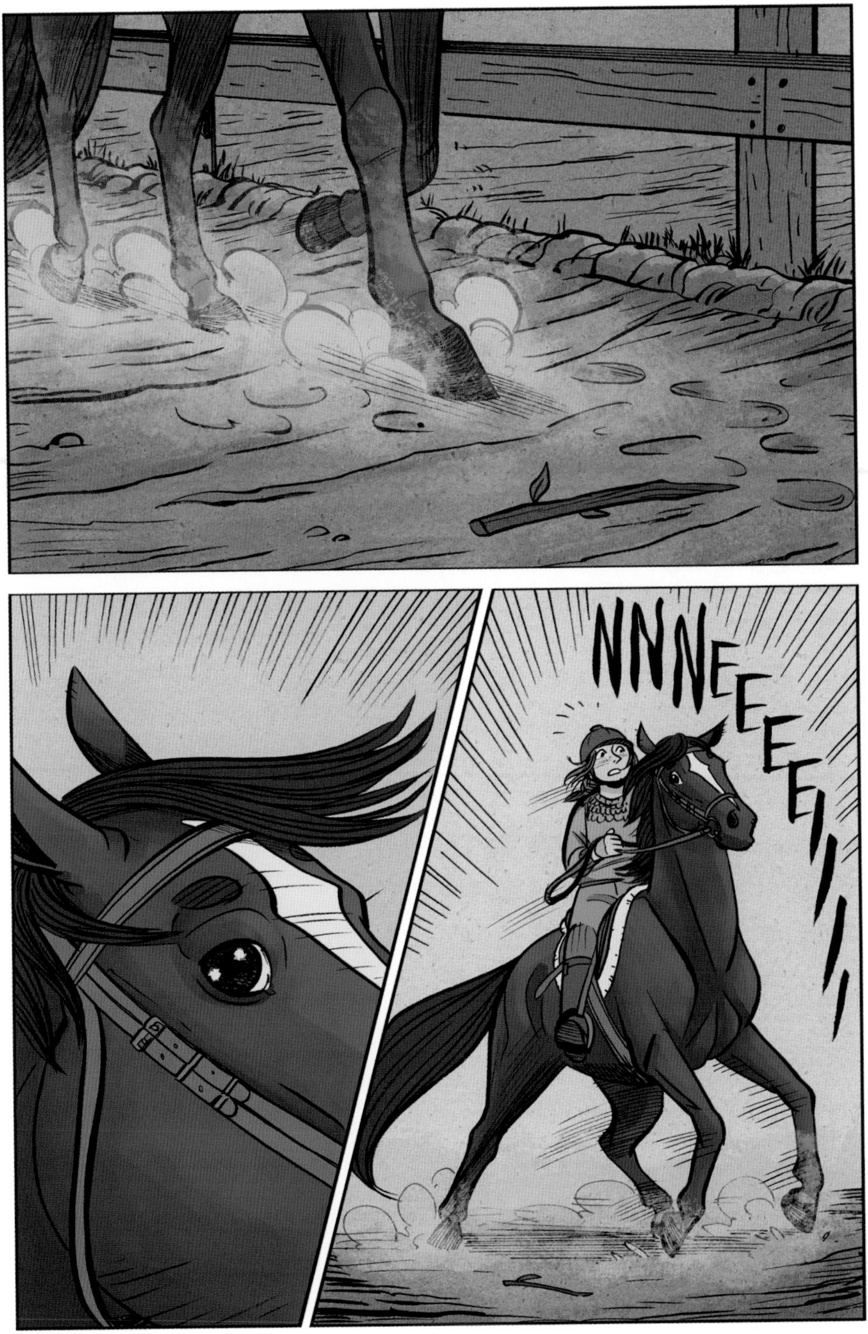
NNNEEEEEIIIII

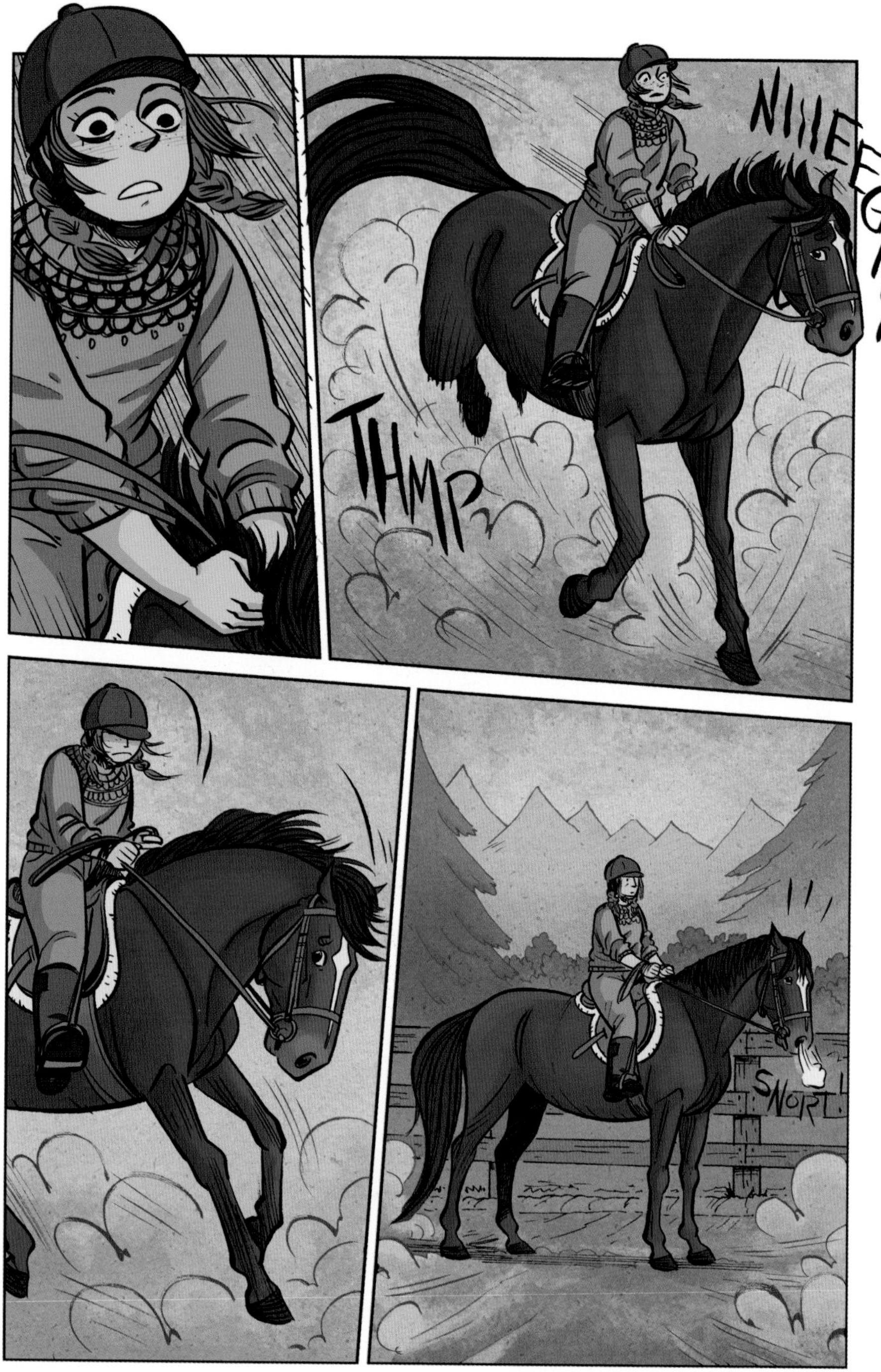
NIIIEEGHH
THMP
SNORT

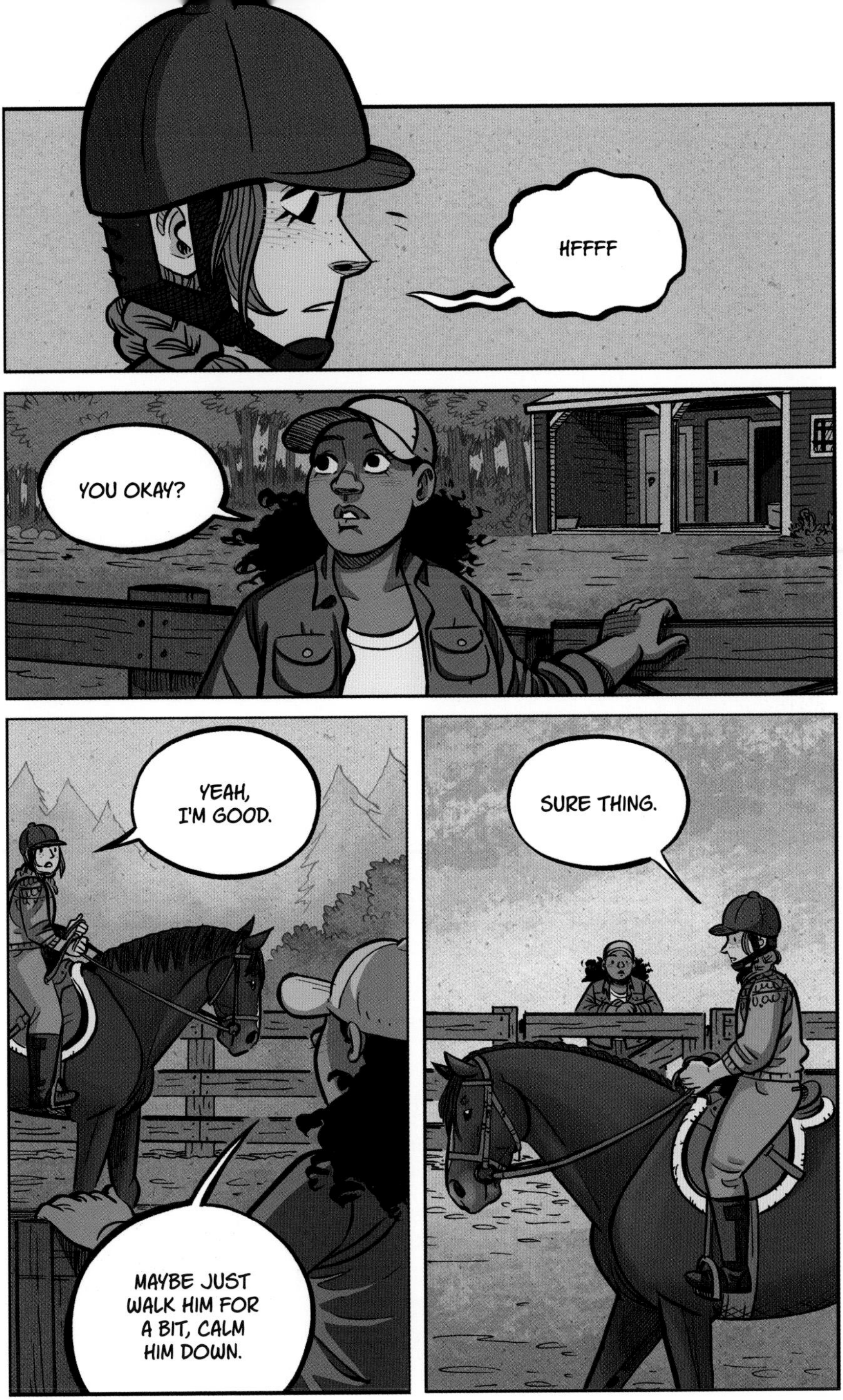
HFFFF
YOU OKAY?
YEAH, I'M GOOD.
MAYBE JUST WALK HIM FOR A BIT, CALM HIM DOWN.
SURE THING.

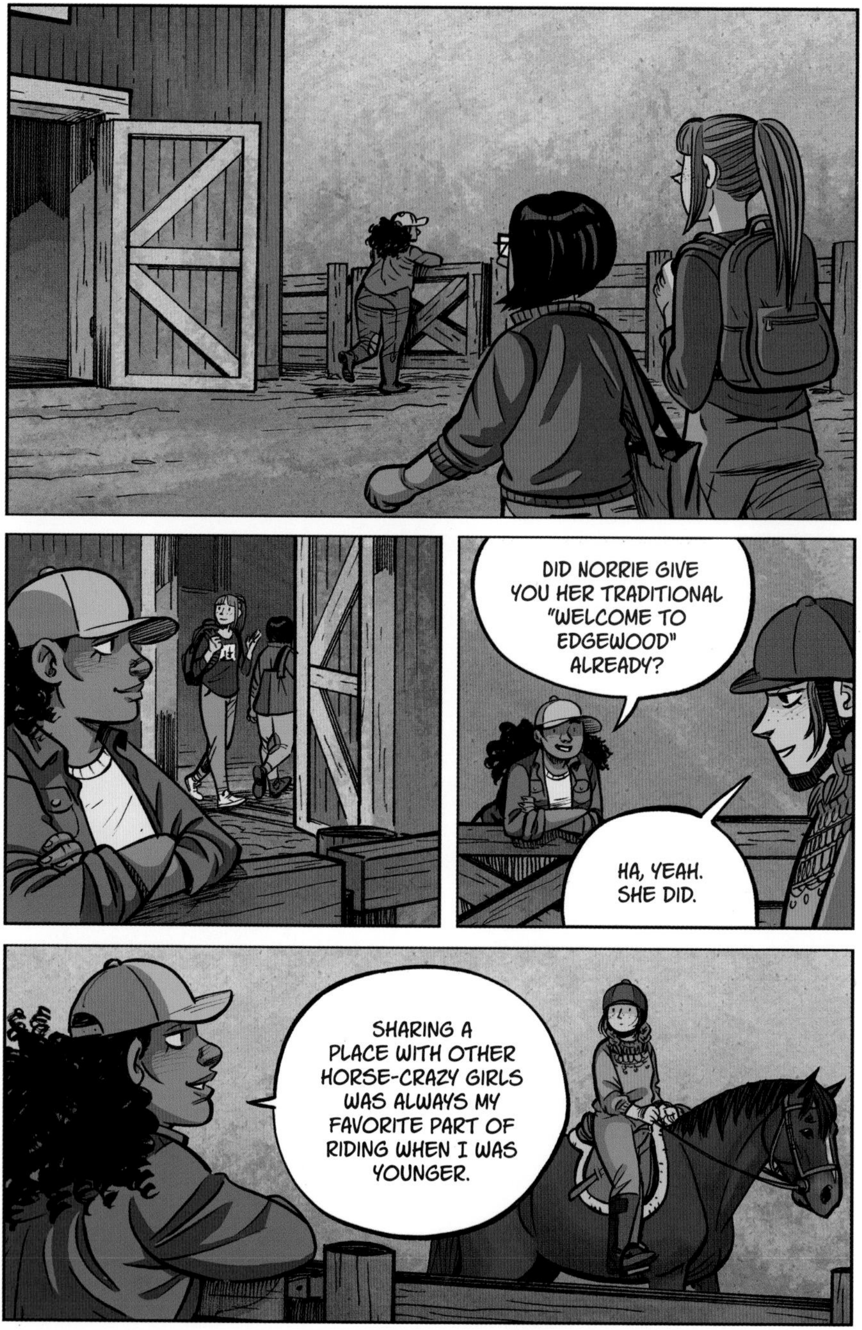
DID NORRIE GIVE YOU HER TRADITIONAL "WELCOME TO EDGEWOOD" ALREADY?
HA, YEAH. SHE DID.
SHARING A PLACE WITH OTHER HORSE-CRAZY GIRLS WAS ALWAYS MY FAVORITE PART OF RIDING WHEN I WAS YOUNGER.

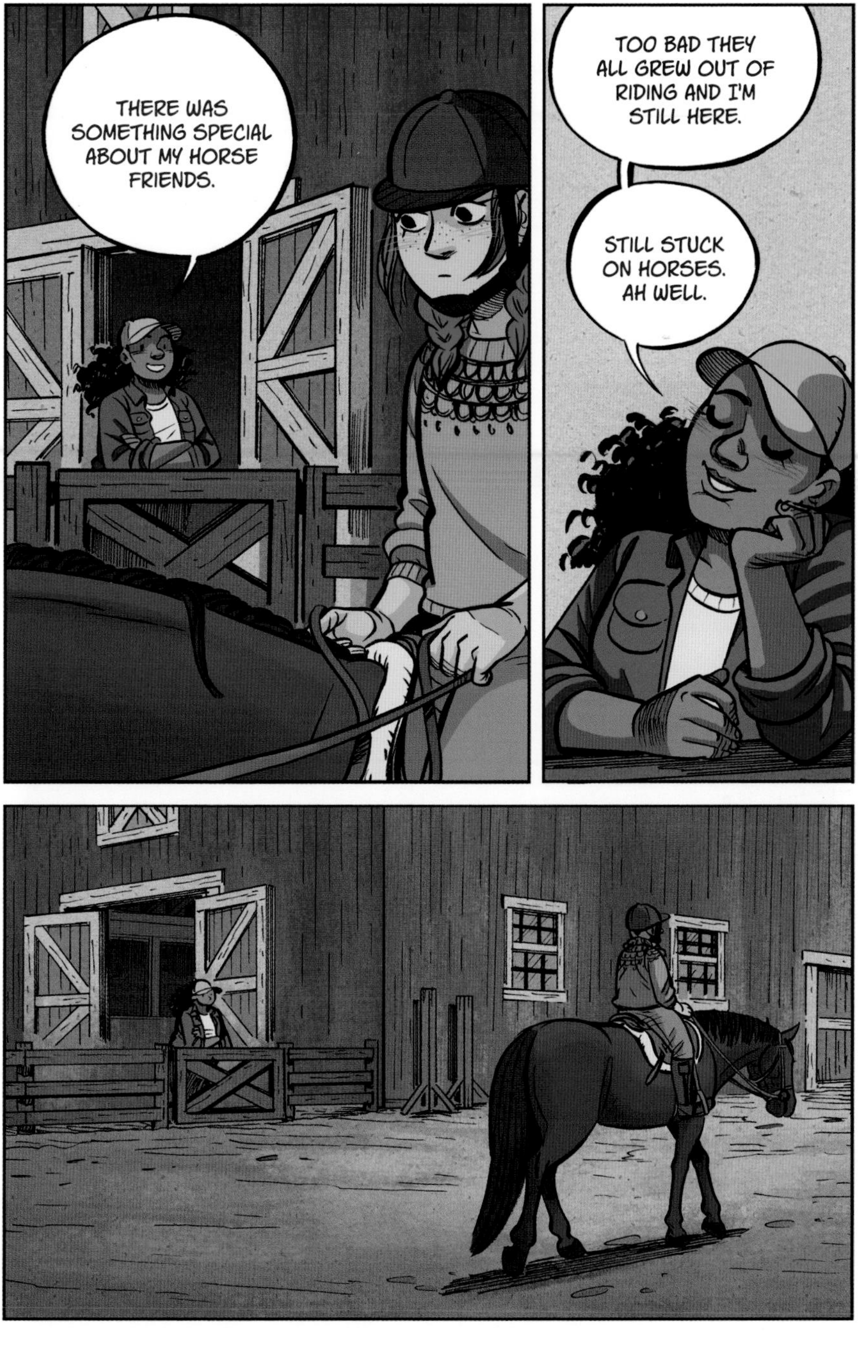
THERE WAS SOMETHING SPECIAL ABOUT MY HORSE FRIENDS.
TOO BAD THEY ALL GREW OUT OF RIDING AND I'M STILL HERE.
STILL STUCK ON HORSES. AH WELL.

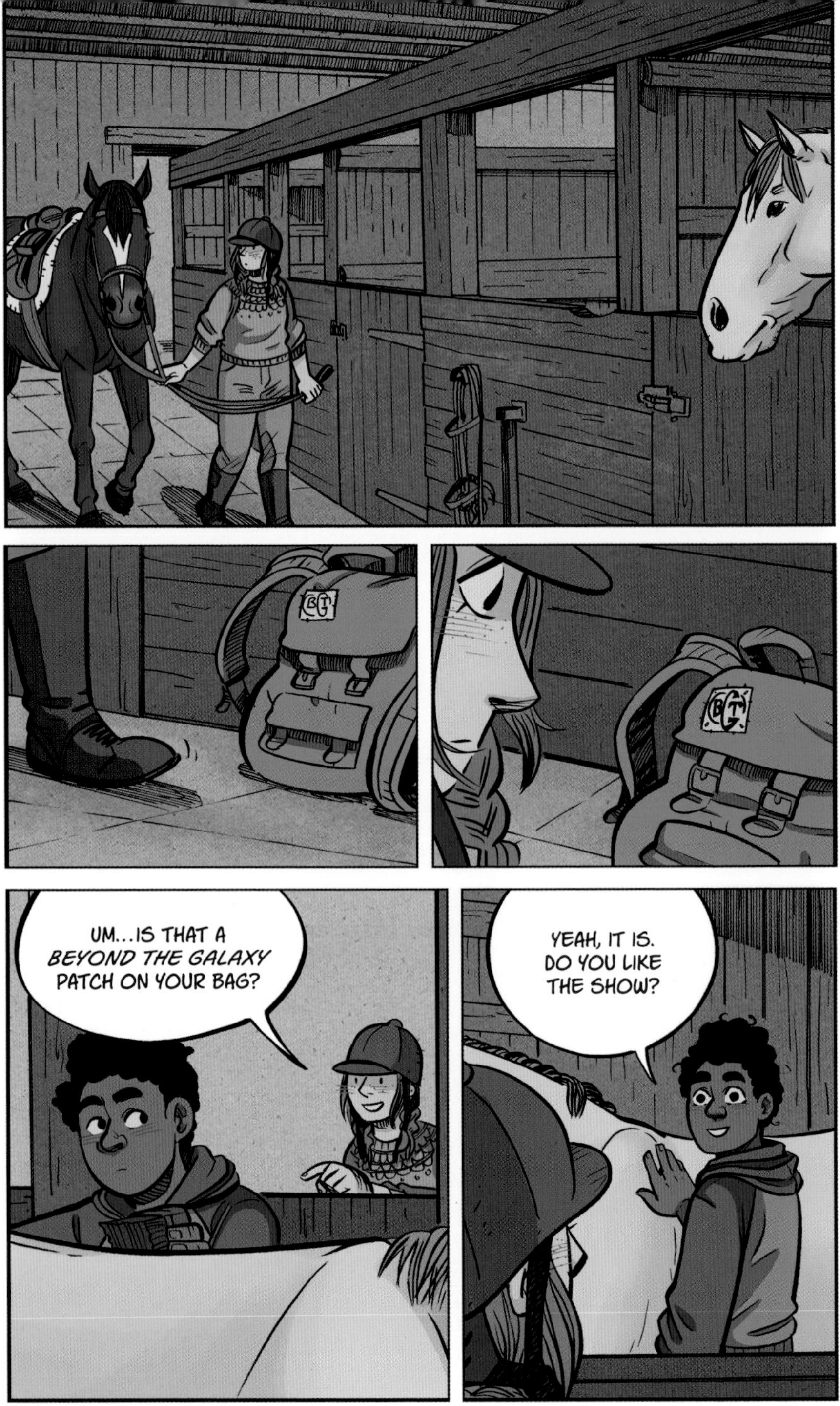
UM...IS THAT A *BEYOND THE GALAXY* PATCH ON YOUR BAG?
YEAH, IT IS. DO YOU LIKE THE SHOW?

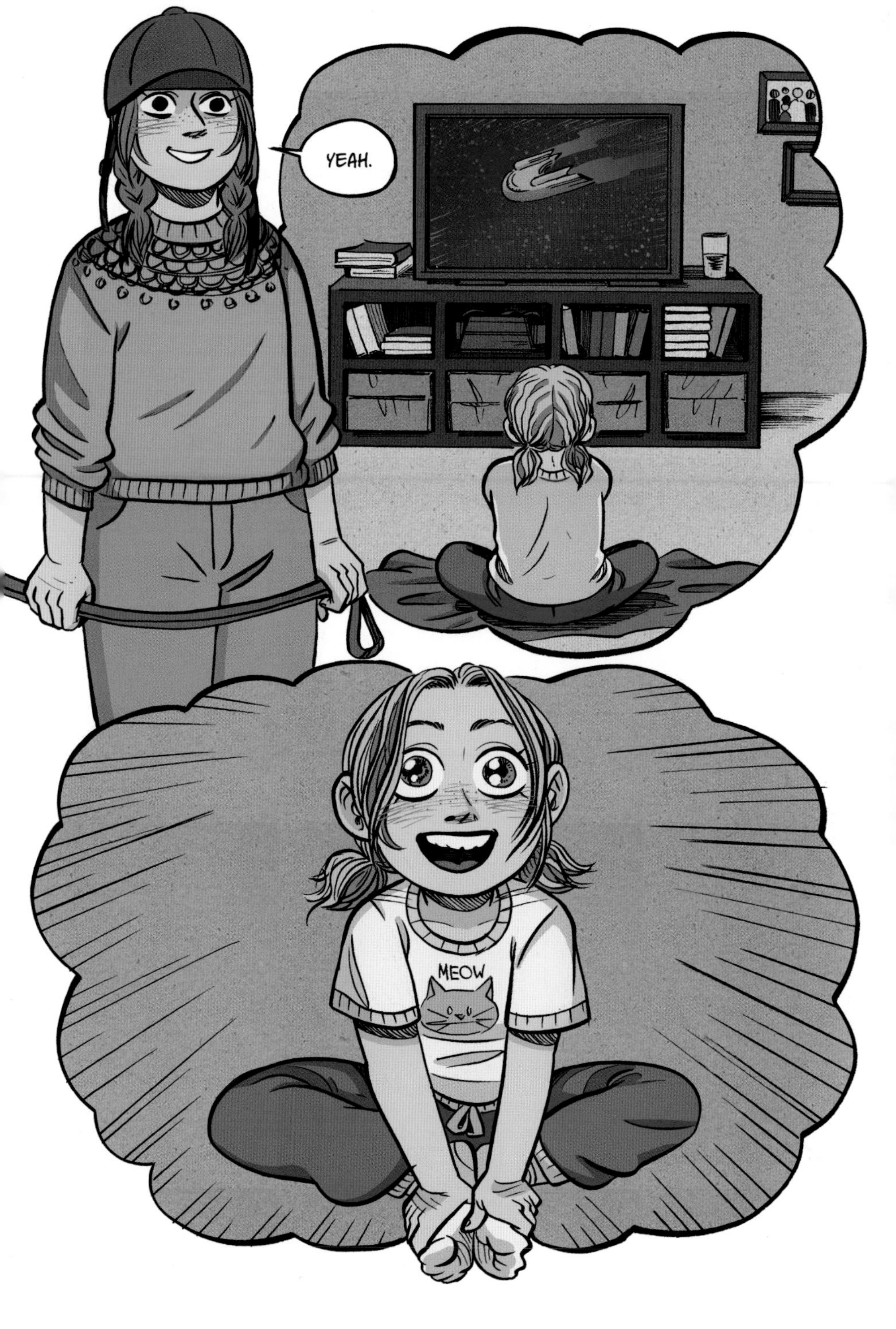
YEAH.
MEOW

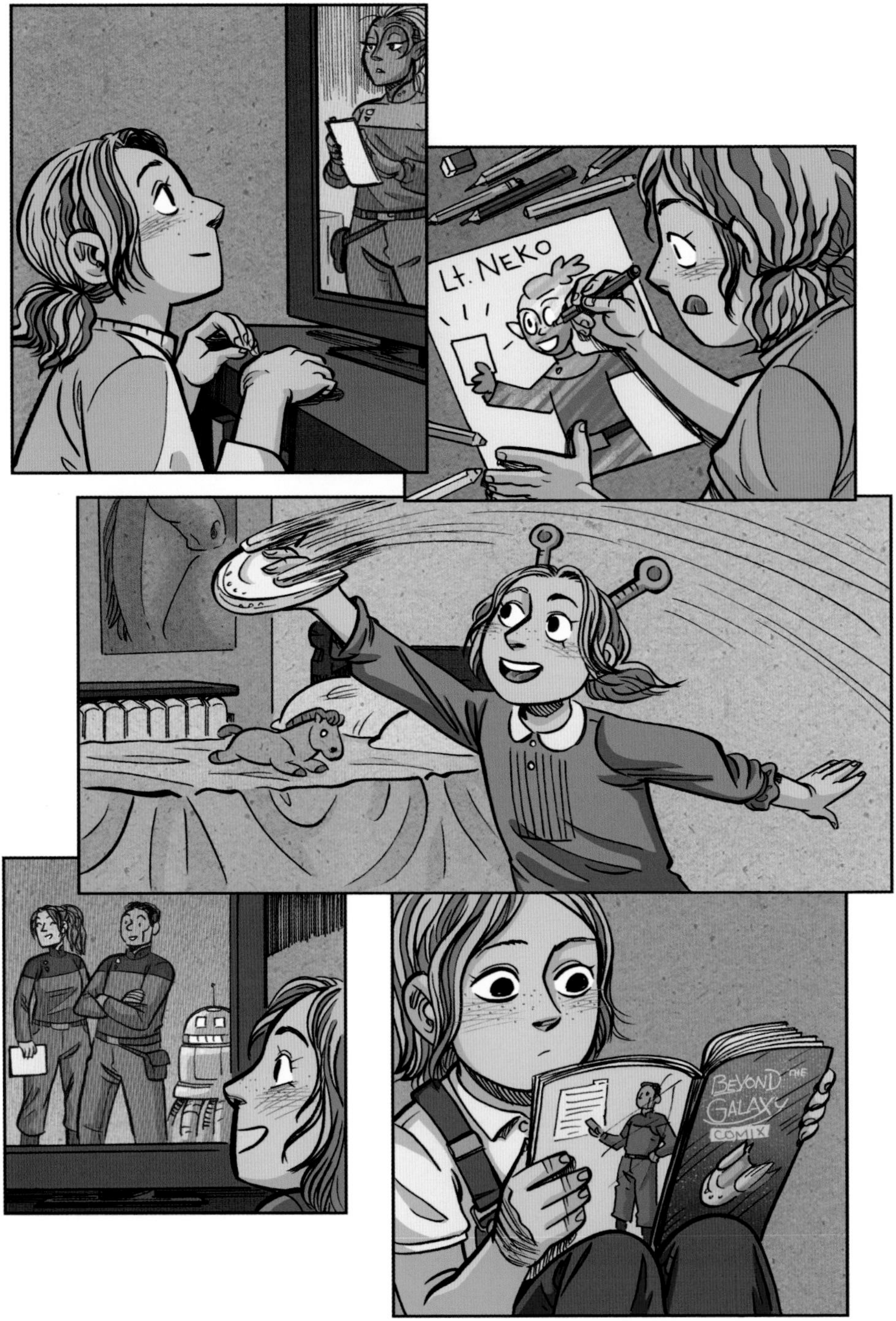

Lt. NEKO
BEYOND THE GALAXY
COMIX

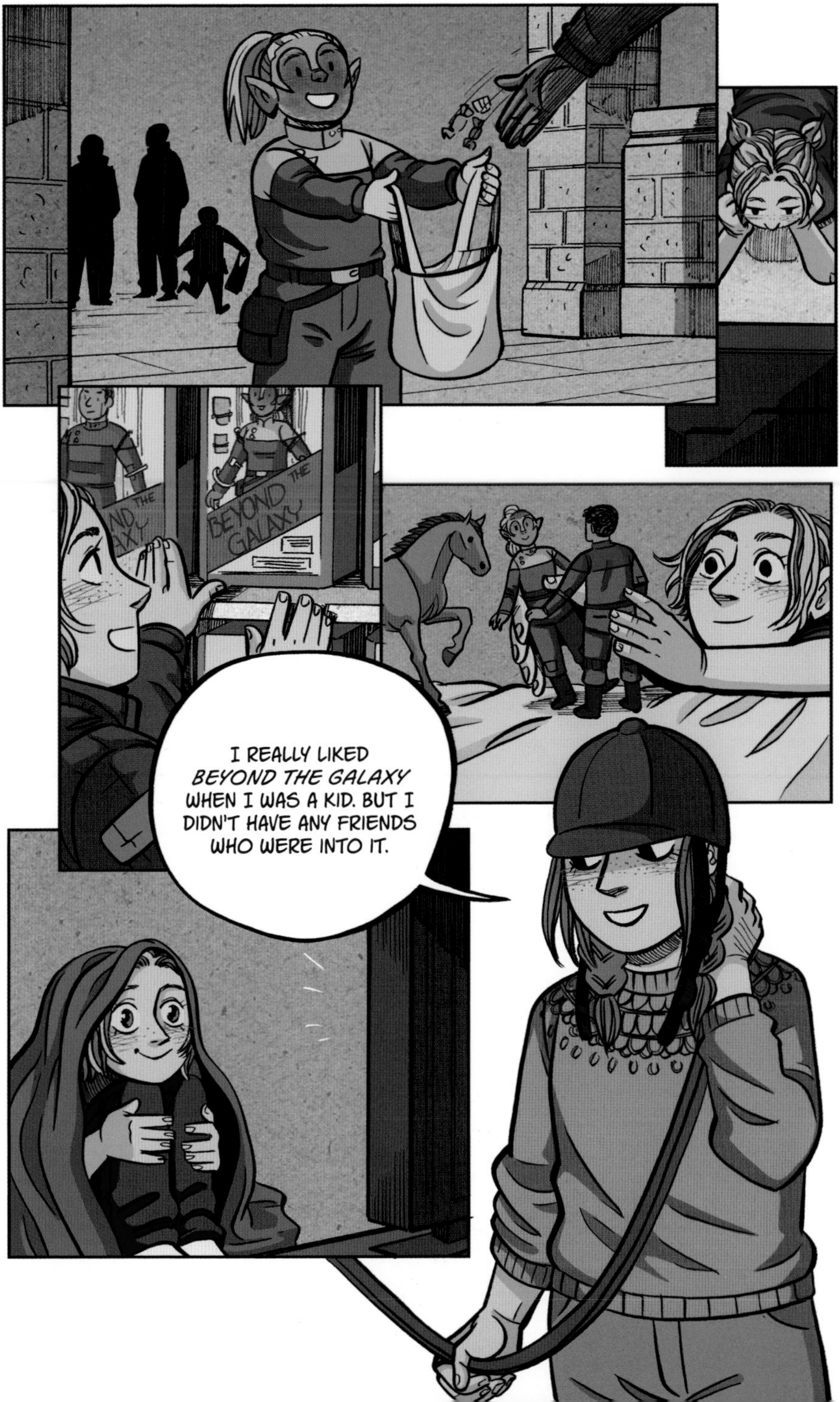
BEYOND THE GALAXY
I REALLY LIKED *BEYOND THE GALAXY* WHEN I WAS A KID. BUT I DIDN'T HAVE ANY FRIENDS WHO WERE INTO IT.

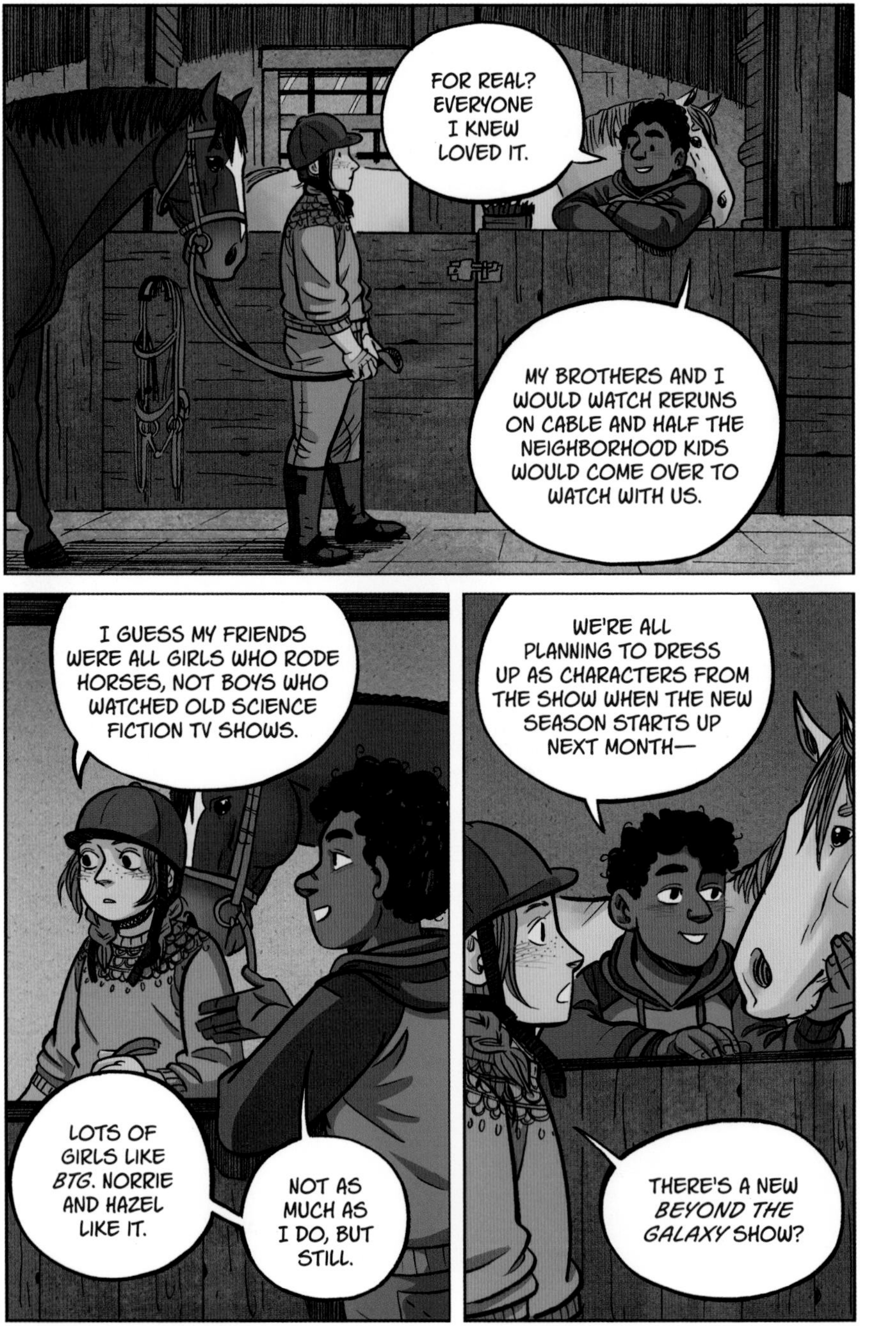
FOR REAL? EVERYONE I KNEW LOVED IT.
MY BROTHERS AND I WOULD WATCH RERUNS ON CABLE AND HALF THE NEIGHBORHOOD KIDS WOULD COME OVER TO WATCH WITH US.
I GUESS MY FRIENDS WERE ALL GIRLS WHO RODE HORSES, NOT BOYS WHO WATCHED OLD SCIENCE FICTION TV SHOWS.
LOTS OF GIRLS LIKE *BTG*. NORRIE AND HAZEL LIKE IT.
NOT AS MUCH AS I DO, BUT STILL.
WE'RE ALL PLANNING TO DRESS UP AS CHARACTERS FROM THE SHOW WHEN THE NEW SEASON STARTS UP NEXT MONTH—
THERE'S A NEW *BEYOND THE GALAXY* SHOW?

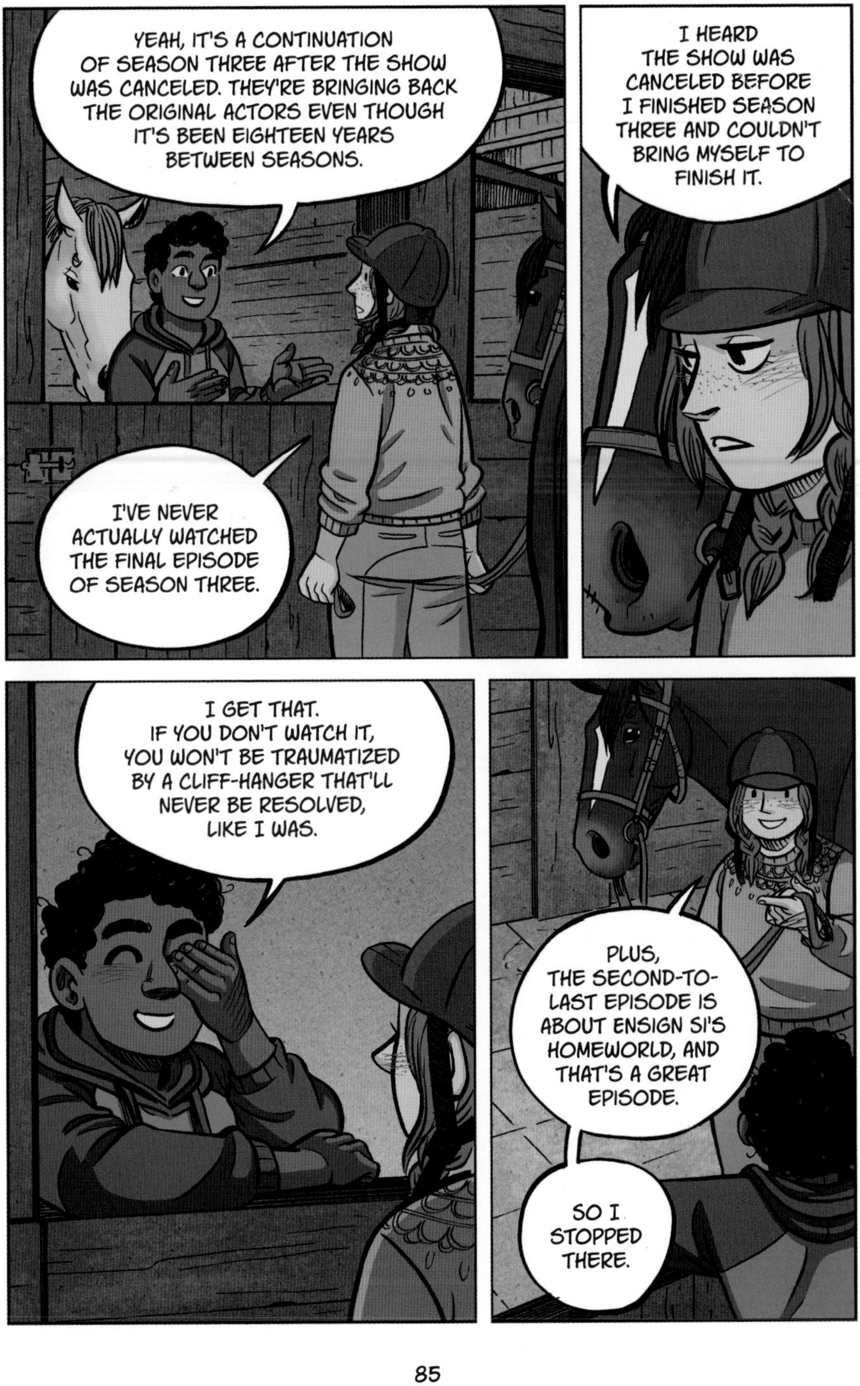

YEAH, IT'S A CONTINUATION OF SEASON THREE AFTER THE SHOW WAS CANCELED. THEY'RE BRINGING BACK THE ORIGINAL ACTORS EVEN THOUGH IT'S BEEN EIGHTEEN YEARS BETWEEN SEASONS.
I'VE NEVER ACTUALLY WATCHED THE FINAL EPISODE OF SEASON THREE.
I HEARD THE SHOW WAS CANCELED BEFORE I FINISHED SEASON THREE AND COULDN'T BRING MYSELF TO FINISH IT.
I GET THAT. IF YOU DON'T WATCH IT, YOU WON'T BE TRAUMATIZED BY A CLIFF-HANGER THAT'LL NEVER BE RESOLVED, LIKE I WAS.
PLUS, THE SECOND-TO-LAST EPISODE IS ABOUT ENSIGN SI'S HOMEWORLD, AND THAT'S A GREAT EPISODE.
SO I STOPPED THERE.

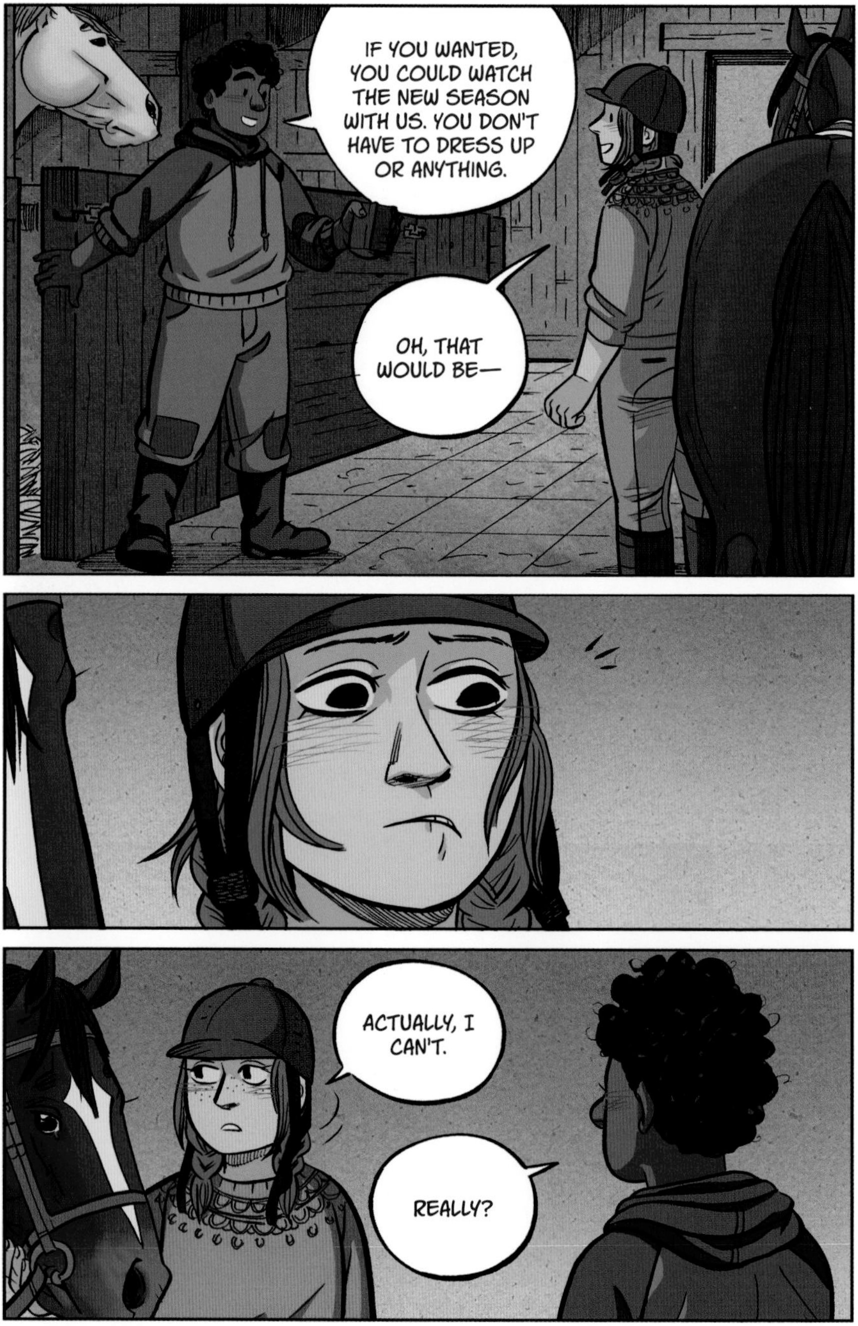
IF YOU WANTED, YOU COULD WATCH THE NEW SEASON WITH US. YOU DON'T HAVE TO DRESS UP OR ANYTHING.
OH, THAT WOULD BE—
ACTUALLY, I CAN'T.
REALLY?

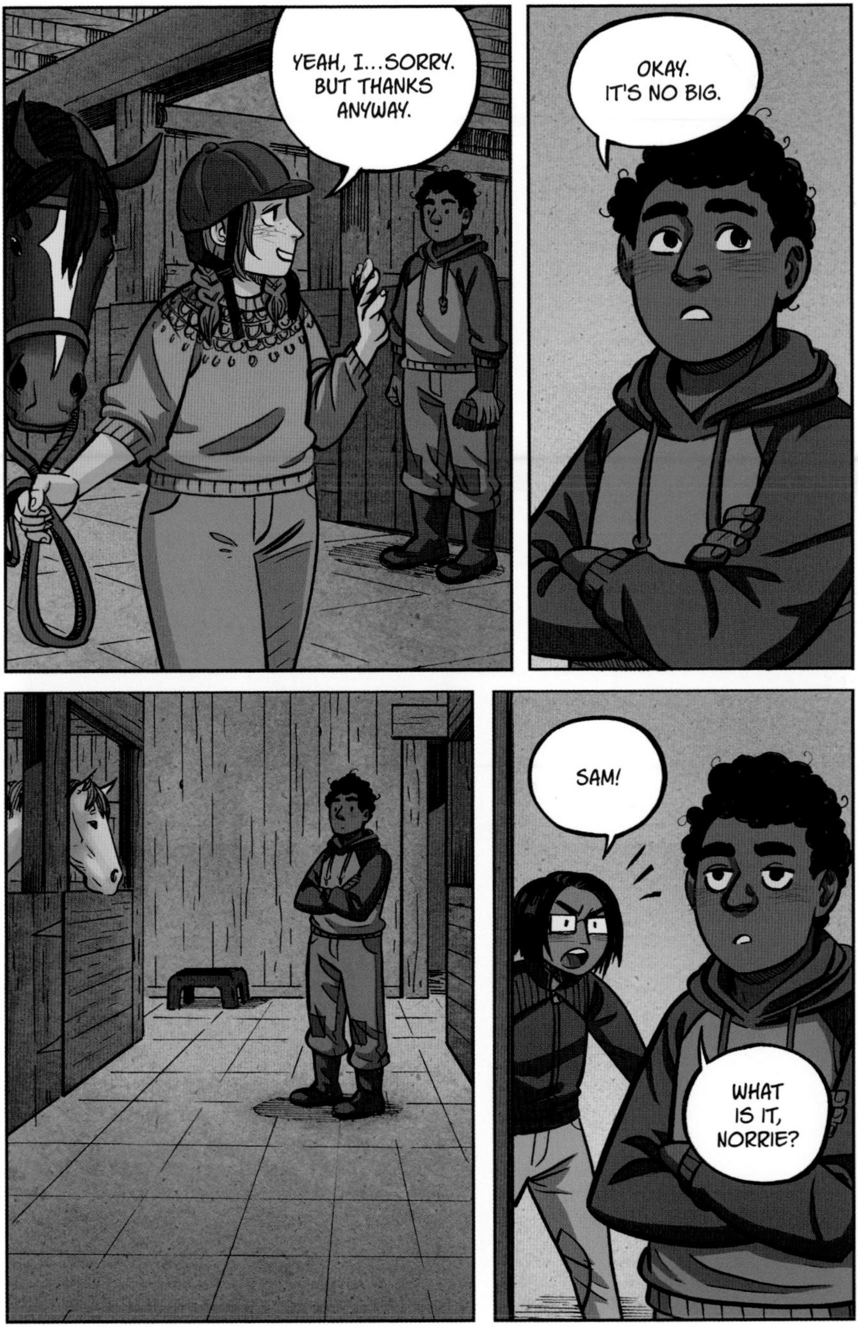
YEAH, I...SORRY. BUT THANKS ANYWAY.
OKAY. IT'S NO BIG.
SAM!
WHAT IS IT, NORRIE?

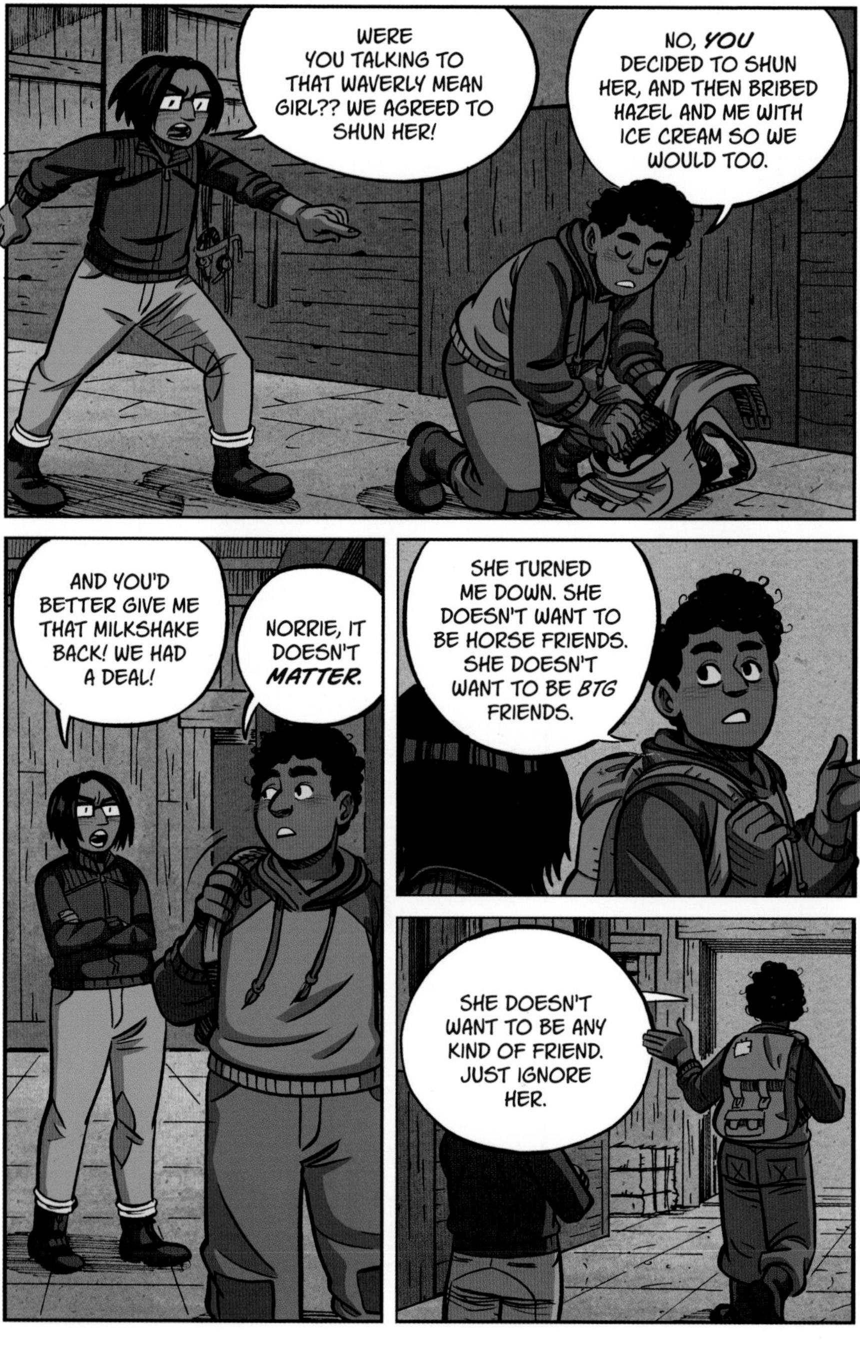
WERE YOU TALKING TO THAT WAVERLY MEAN GIRL?? WE AGREED TO SHUN HER!
NO, *YOU* DECIDED TO SHUN HER, AND THEN BRIBED HAZEL AND ME WITH ICE CREAM SO WE WOULD TOO.
AND YOU'D BETTER GIVE ME THAT MILKSHAKE BACK! WE HAD A DEAL!
NORRIE, IT DOESN'T *MATTER*.
SHE TURNED ME DOWN. SHE DOESN'T WANT TO BE HORSE FRIENDS. SHE DOESN'T WANT TO BE *BTG* FRIENDS.
SHE DOESN'T WANT TO BE ANY KIND OF FRIEND. JUST IGNORE HER.

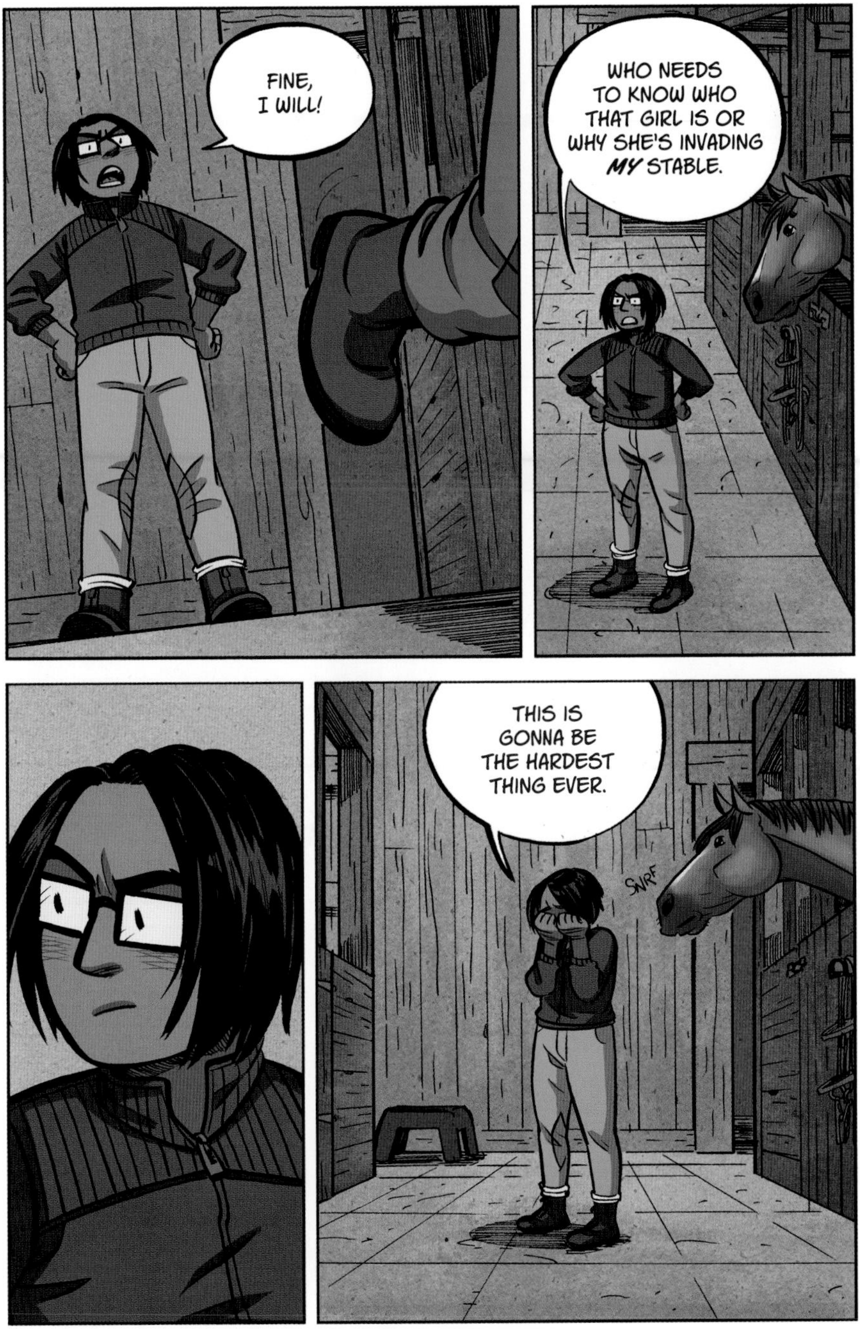
FINE, I WILL!
WHO NEEDS TO KNOW WHO THAT GIRL IS OR WHY SHE'S INVADING MY STABLE.
THIS IS GONNA BE THE HARDEST THING EVER.
SNRF

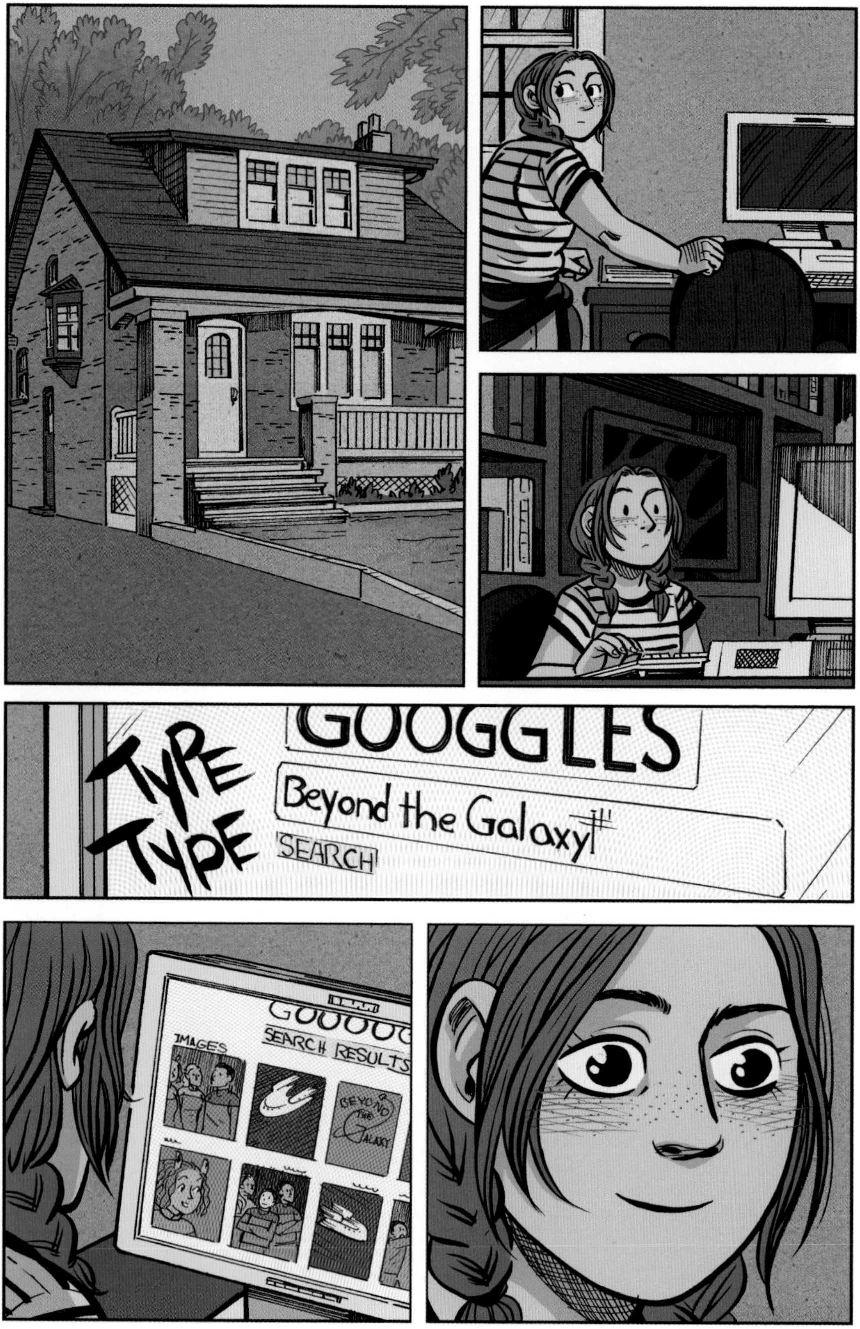

TYPE
TYPE
GOOGGLES
Beyond the Galaxy
SEARCH
SEARCH RESULTS
IMAGES
BEYOND THE GALAXY

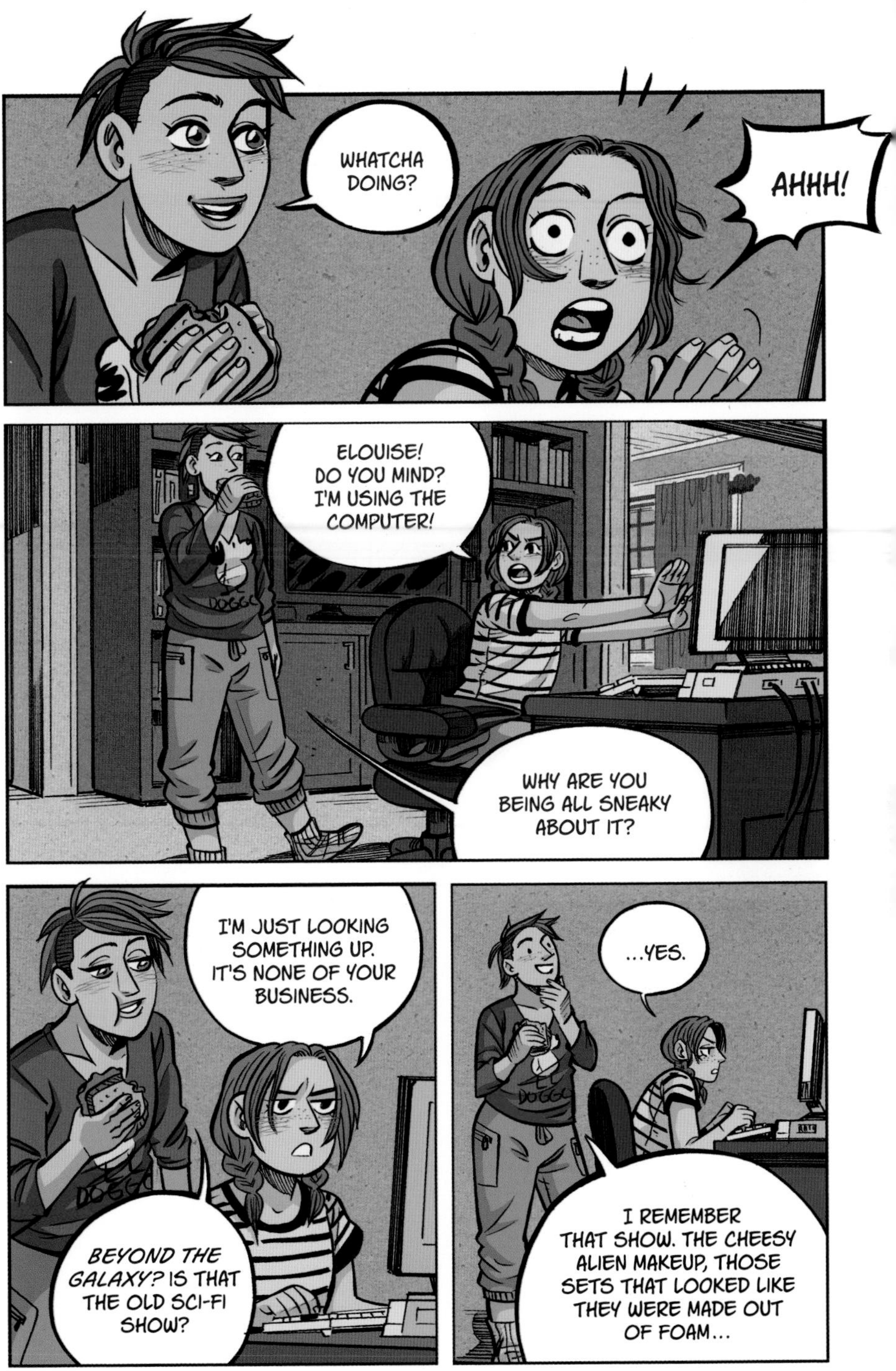
WHATCHA DOING?
AHHH!
ELOUISE! DO YOU MIND? I'M USING THE COMPUTER!
WHY ARE YOU BEING ALL SNEAKY ABOUT IT?
I'M JUST LOOKING SOMETHING UP. IT'S NONE OF YOUR BUSINESS.
BEYOND THE GALAXY? IS THAT THE OLD SCI-FI SHOW?
...YES.
I REMEMBER THAT SHOW. THE CHEESY ALIEN MAKEUP, THOSE SETS THAT LOOKED LIKE THEY WERE MADE OUT OF FOAM...

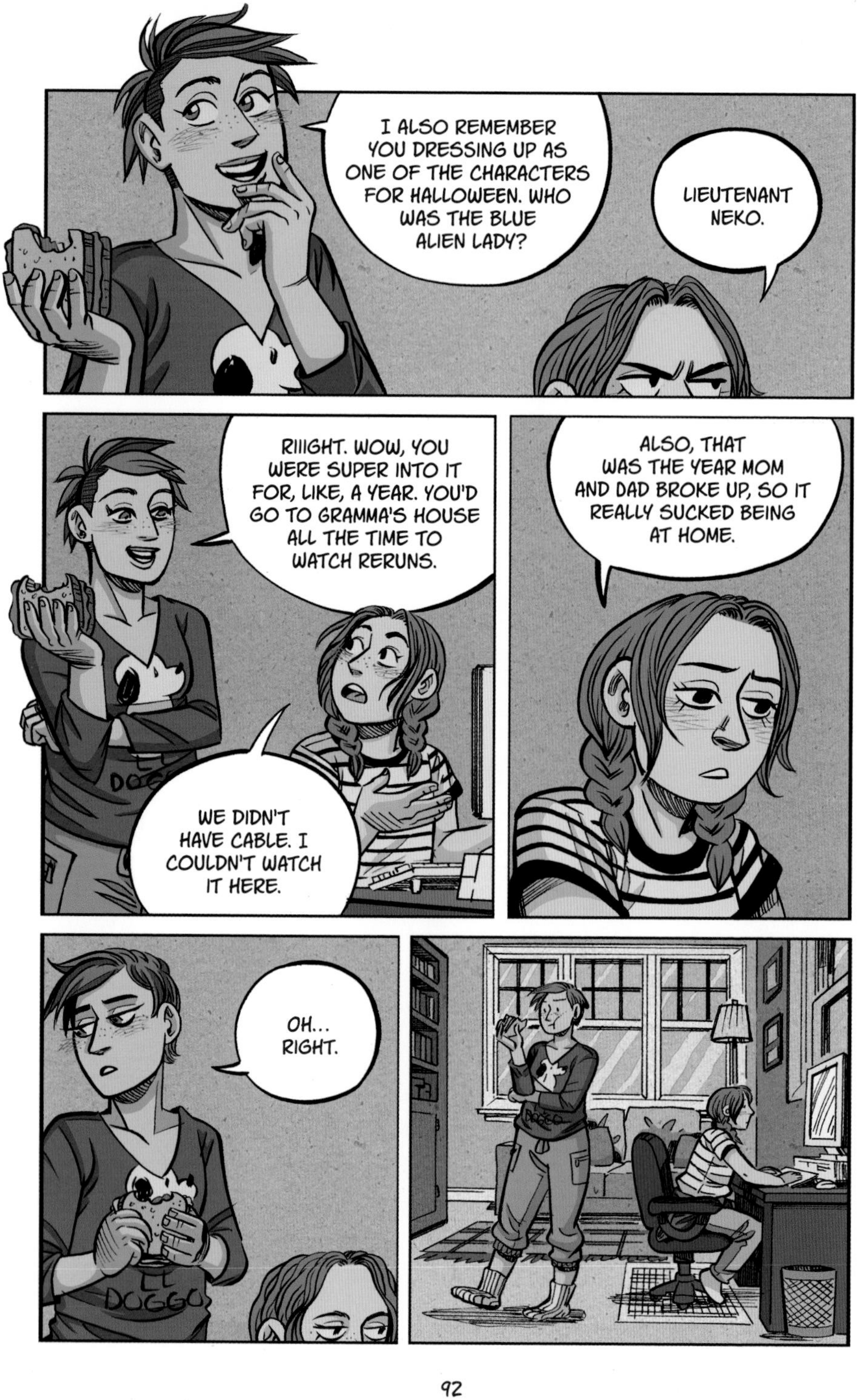
I ALSO REMEMBER YOU DRESSING UP AS ONE OF THE CHARACTERS FOR HALLOWEEN. WHO WAS THE BLUE ALIEN LADY?
LIEUTENANT NEKO.
RIIIGHT. WOW, YOU WERE SUPER INTO IT FOR, LIKE, A YEAR. YOU'D GO TO GRAMMA'S HOUSE ALL THE TIME TO WATCH RERUNS.
WE DIDN'T HAVE CABLE. I COULDN'T WATCH IT HERE.
ALSO, THAT WAS THE YEAR MOM AND DAD BROKE UP, SO IT REALLY SUCKED BEING AT HOME.
OH... RIGHT.

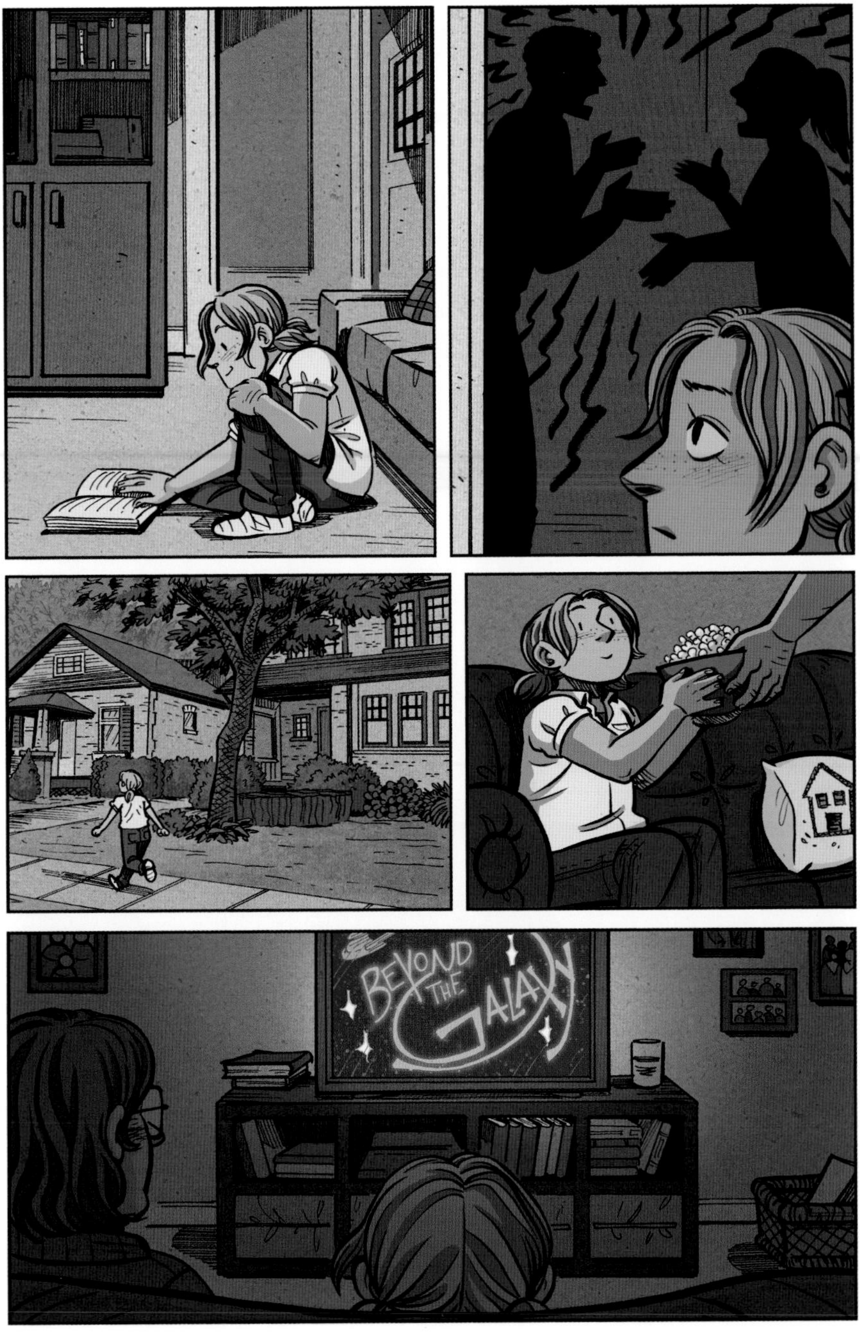

BEYOND THE GALAXY

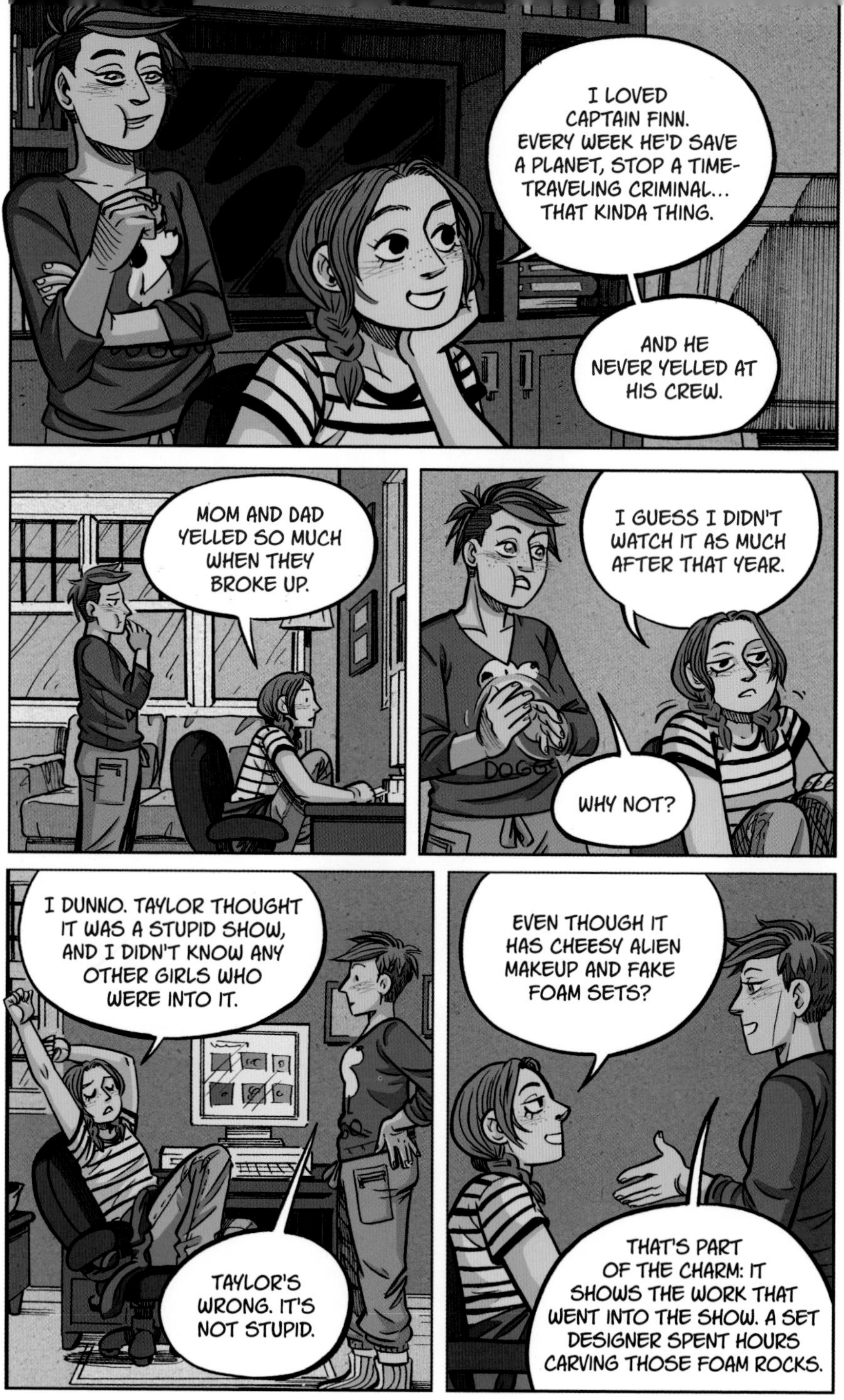
I LOVED CAPTAIN FINN. EVERY WEEK HE'D SAVE A PLANET, STOP A TIME-TRAVELING CRIMINAL... THAT KINDA THING.
AND HE NEVER YELLED AT HIS CREW.
MOM AND DAD YELLED SO MUCH WHEN THEY BROKE UP.
I GUESS I DIDN'T WATCH IT AS MUCH AFTER THAT YEAR.
WHY NOT?
I DUNNO. TAYLOR THOUGHT IT WAS A STUPID SHOW, AND I DIDN'T KNOW ANY OTHER GIRLS WHO WERE INTO IT.
TAYLOR'S WRONG. IT'S NOT STUPID.
EVEN THOUGH IT HAS CHEESY ALIEN MAKEUP AND FAKE FOAM SETS?
THAT'S PART OF THE CHARM: IT SHOWS THE WORK THAT WENT INTO THE SHOW. A SET DESIGNER SPENT HOURS CARVING THOSE FOAM ROCKS.

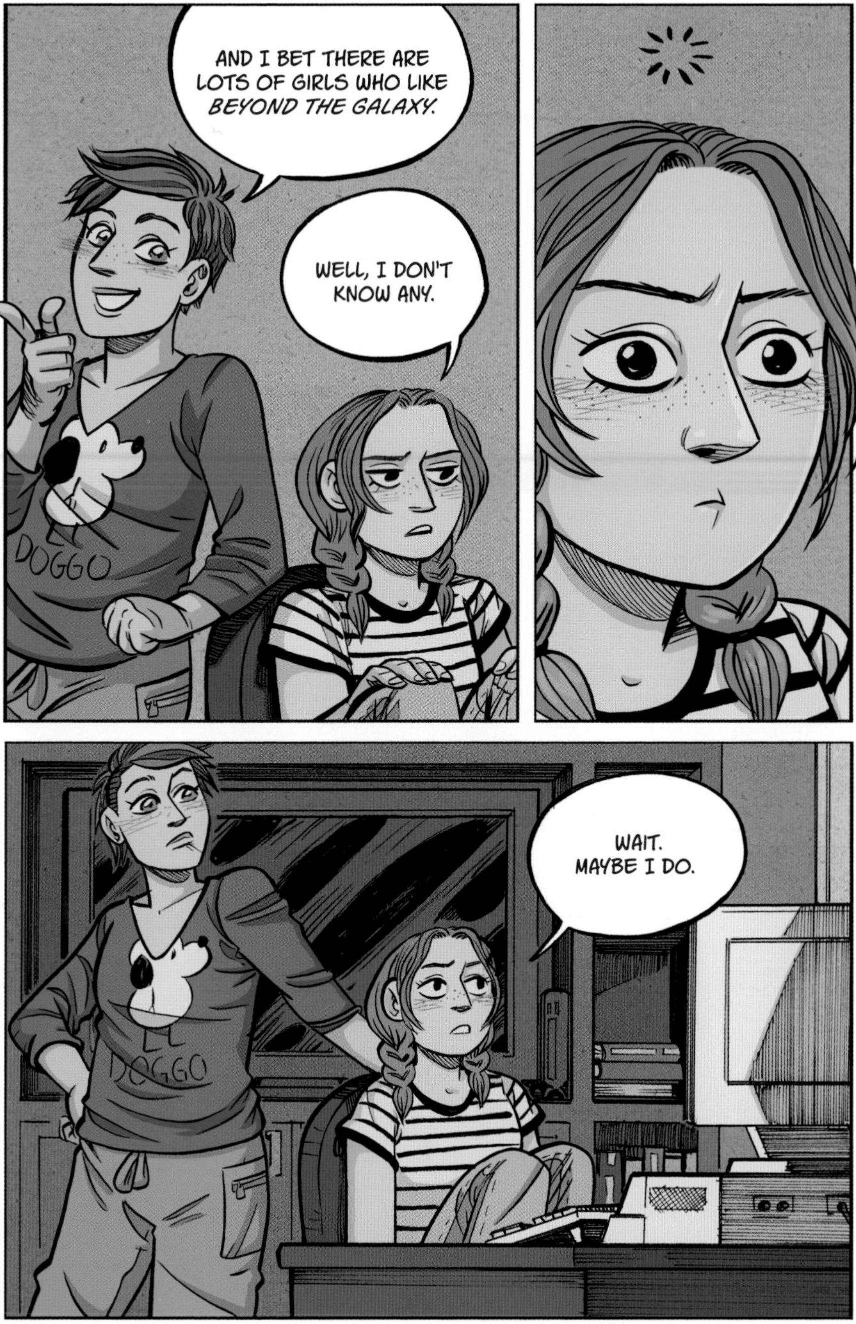
AND I BET THERE ARE LOTS OF GIRLS WHO LIKE *BEYOND THE GALAXY*.
WELL, I DON'T KNOW ANY.
LE DOGGO
WAIT. MAYBE I DO.

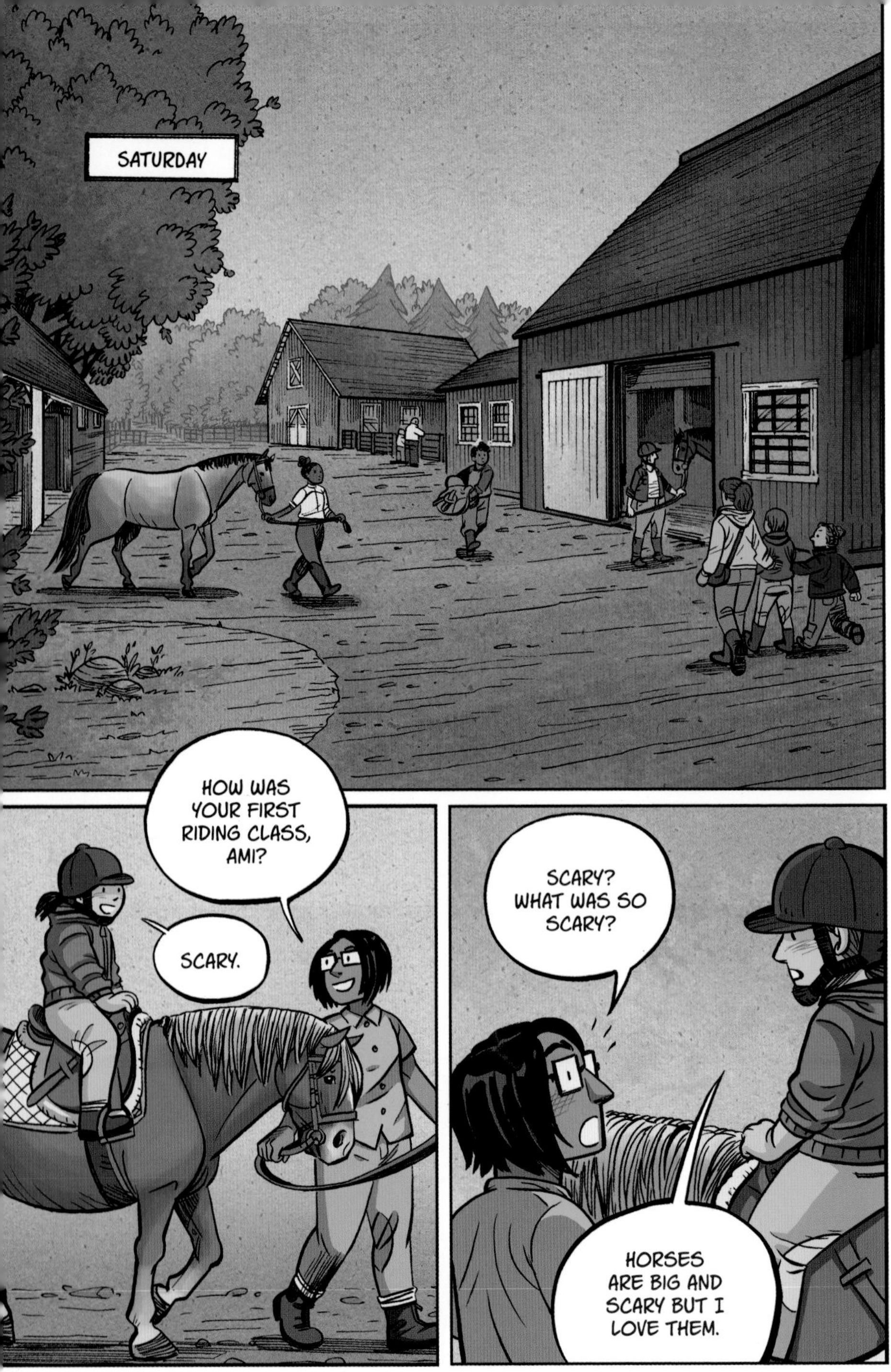
SATURDAY
HOW WAS YOUR FIRST RIDING CLASS, AMI?
SCARY.
SCARY? WHAT WAS SO SCARY?
HORSES ARE BIG AND SCARY BUT I LOVE THEM.

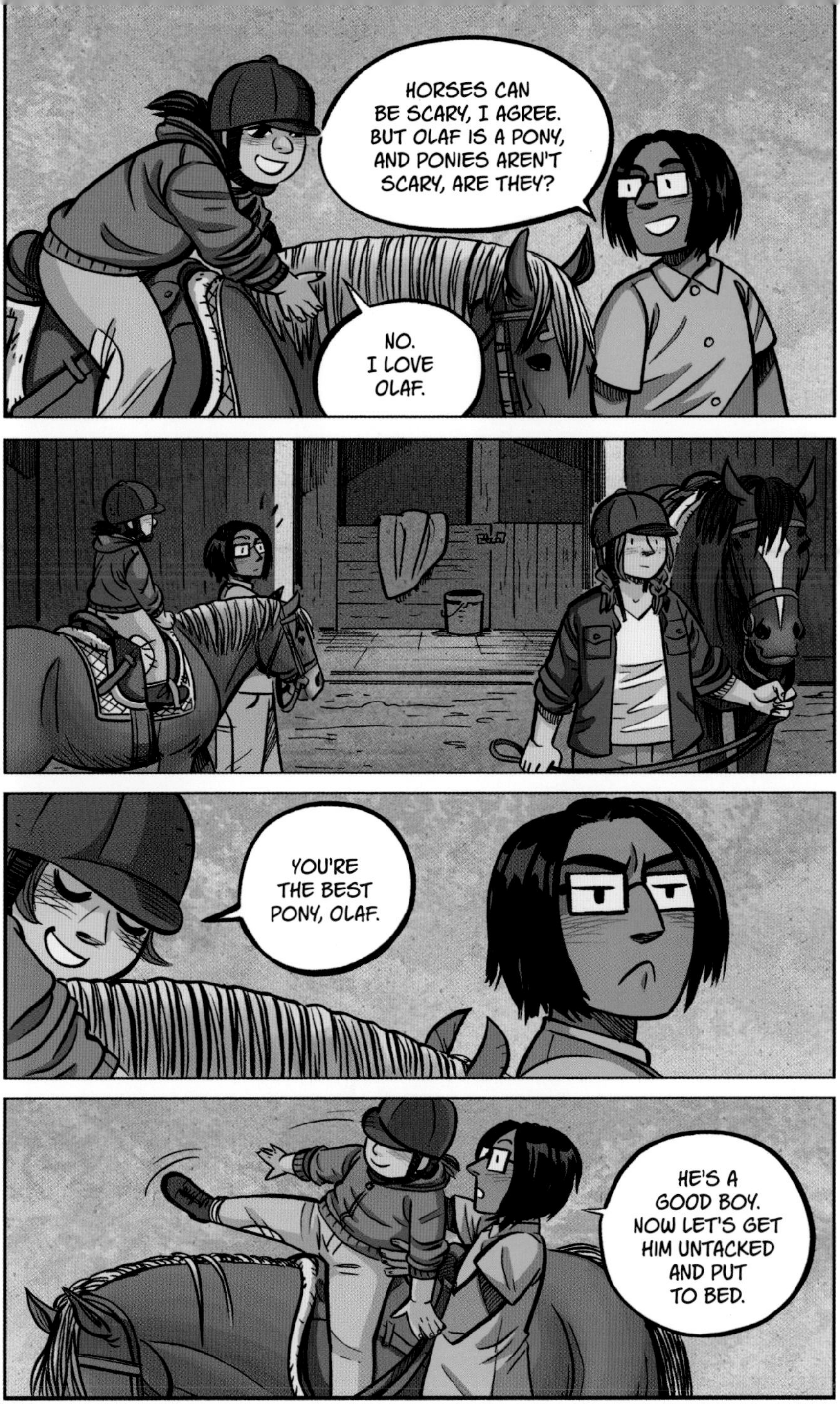
HORSES CAN BE SCARY, I AGREE. BUT OLAF IS A PONY, AND PONIES AREN'T SCARY, ARE THEY?
NO. I LOVE OLAF.
YOU'RE THE BEST PONY, OLAF.
HE'S A GOOD BOY. NOW LET'S GET HIM UNTACKED AND PUT TO BED.

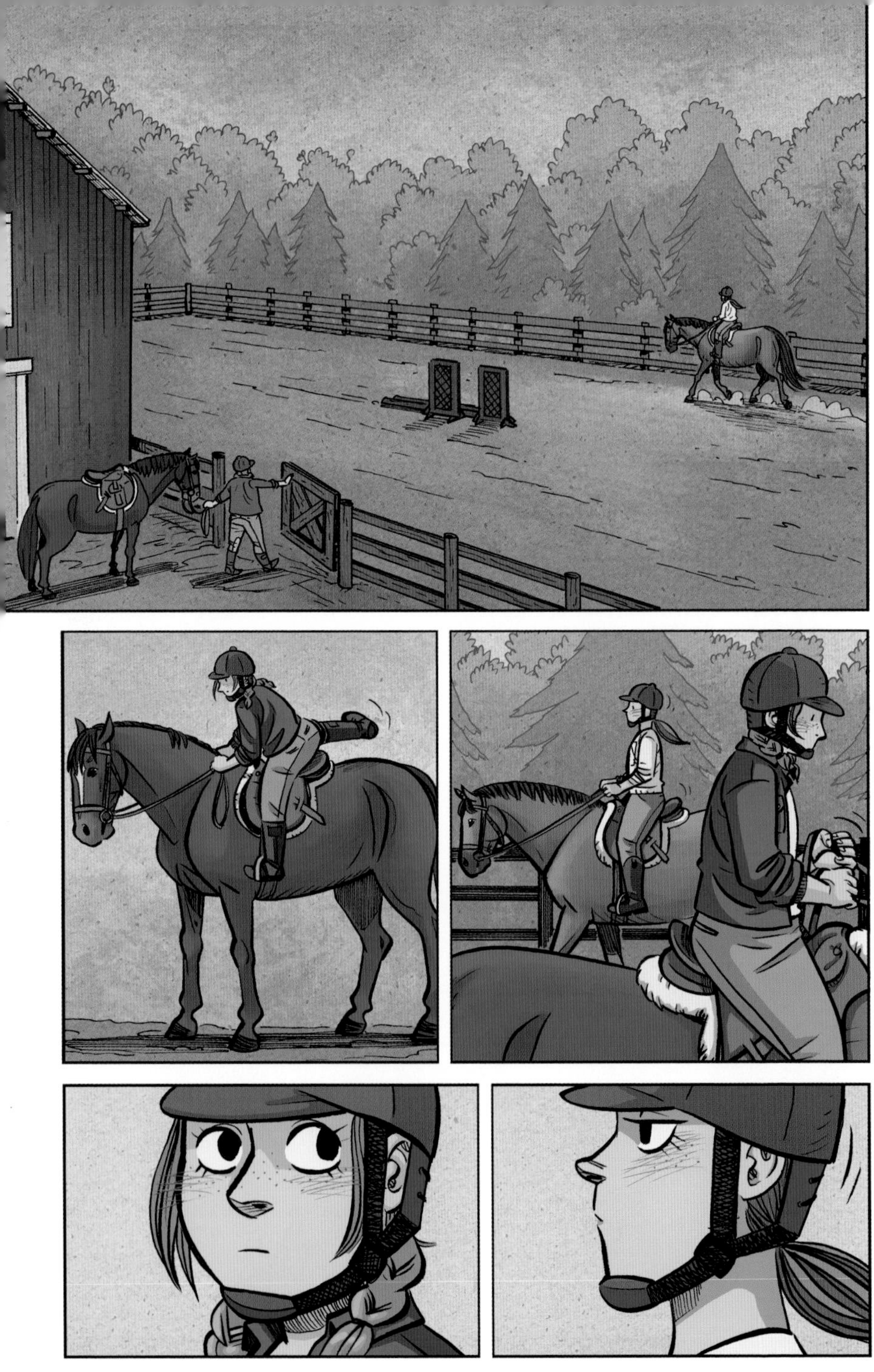

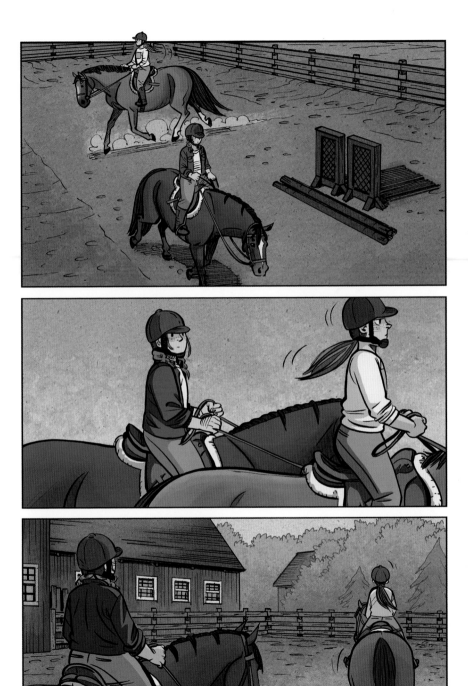

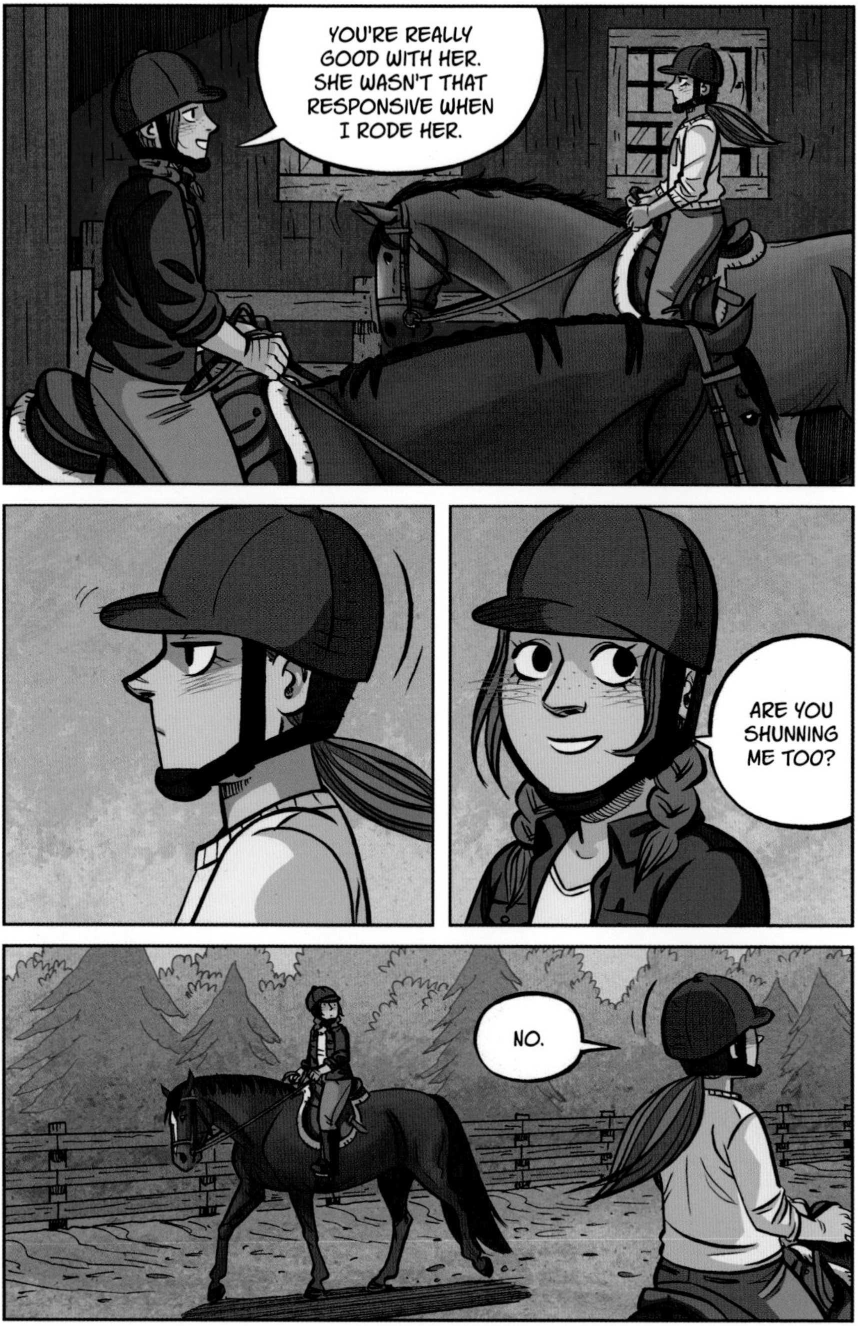
YOU'RE REALLY GOOD WITH HER. SHE WASN'T THAT RESPONSIVE WHEN I RODE HER.
ARE YOU SHUNNING ME TOO?
NO.

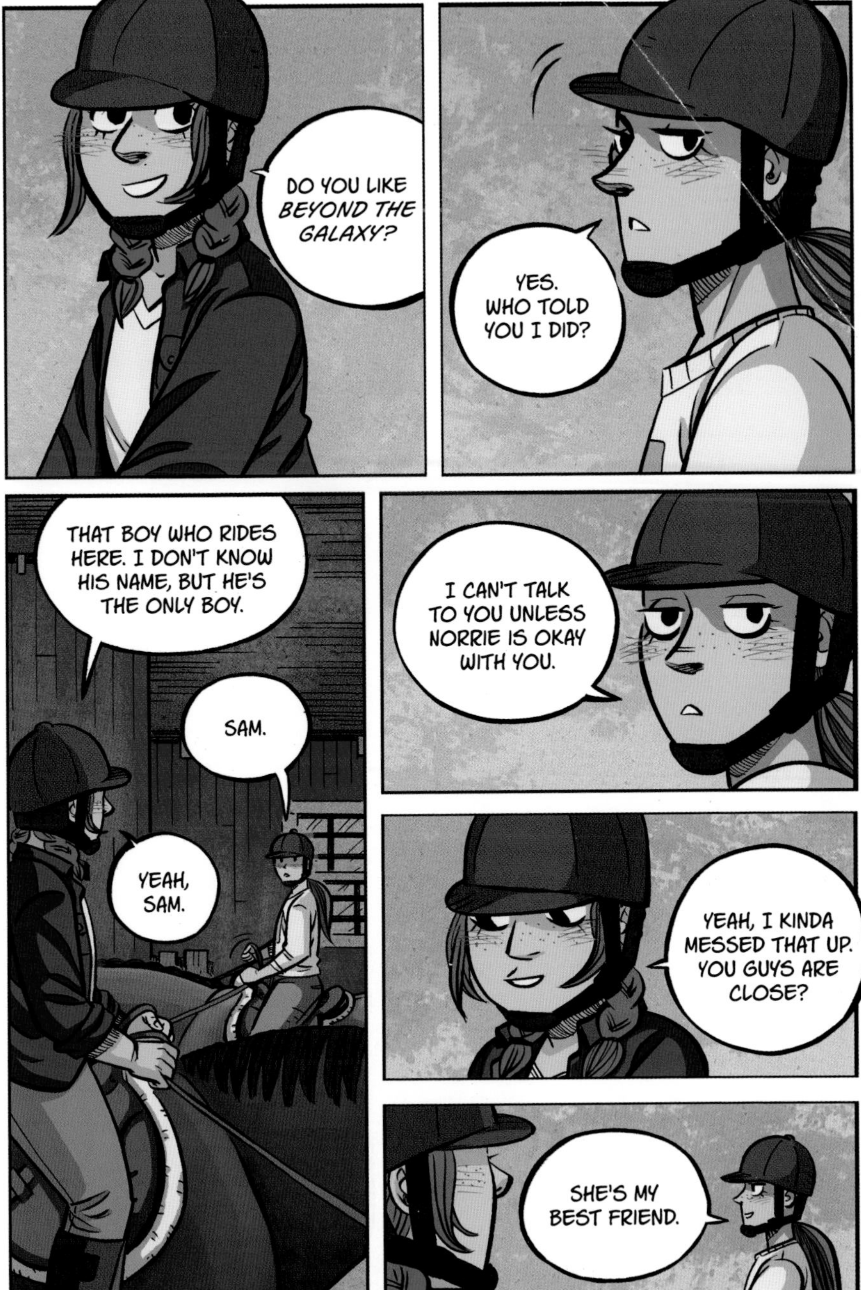
DO YOU LIKE *BEYOND THE GALAXY?*
YES. WHO TOLD YOU I DID?
THAT BOY WHO RIDES HERE. I DON'T KNOW HIS NAME, BUT HE'S THE ONLY BOY.
SAM.
YEAH, SAM.
I CAN'T TALK TO YOU UNLESS NORRIE IS OKAY WITH YOU.
YEAH, I KINDA MESSED THAT UP. YOU GUYS ARE CLOSE?
SHE'S MY BEST FRIEND.

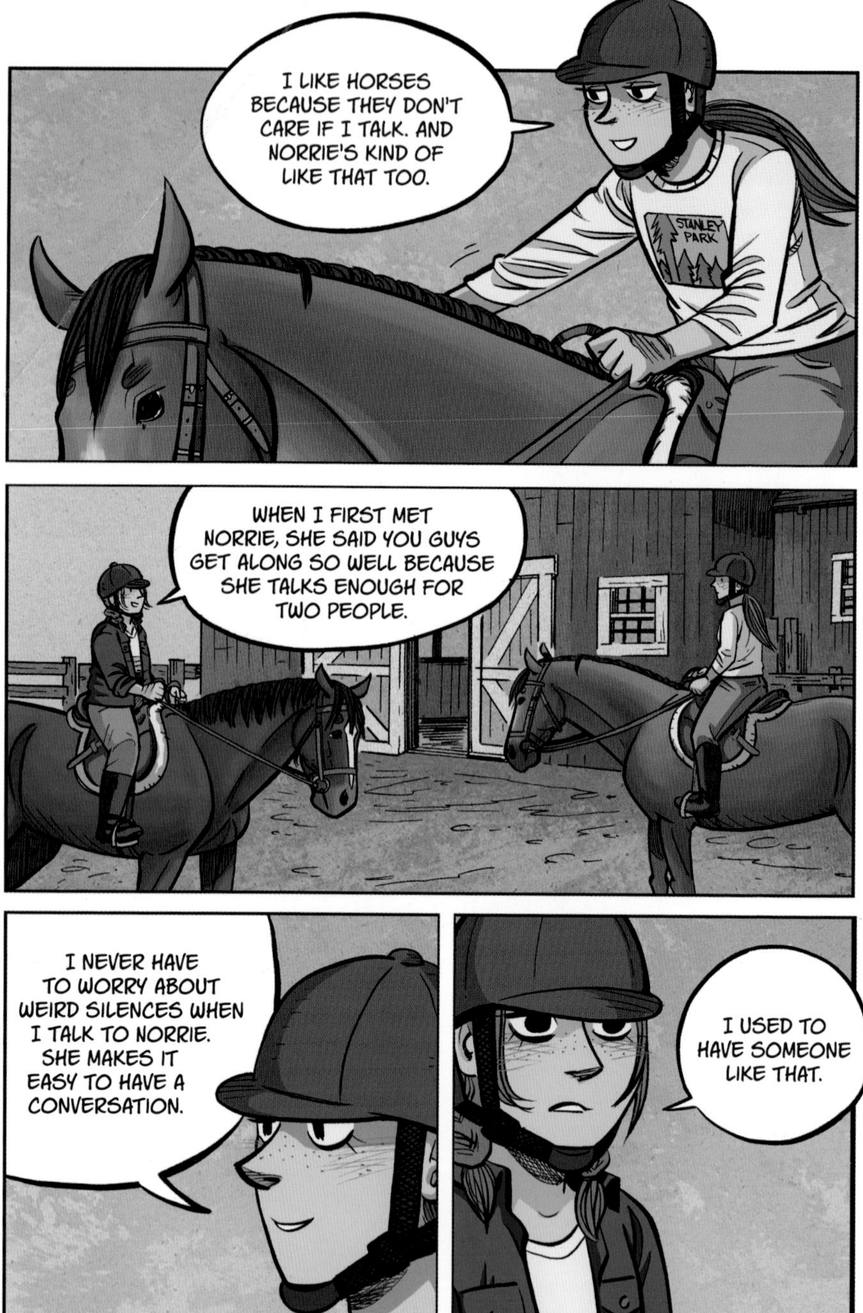
I LIKE HORSES BECAUSE THEY DON'T CARE IF I TALK. AND NORRIE'S KIND OF LIKE THAT TOO.
STANLEY PARK
WHEN I FIRST MET NORRIE, SHE SAID YOU GUYS GET ALONG SO WELL BECAUSE SHE TALKS ENOUGH FOR TWO PEOPLE.
I NEVER HAVE TO WORRY ABOUT WEIRD SILENCES WHEN I TALK TO NORRIE. SHE MAKES IT EASY TO HAVE A CONVERSATION.
I USED TO HAVE SOMEONE LIKE THAT.

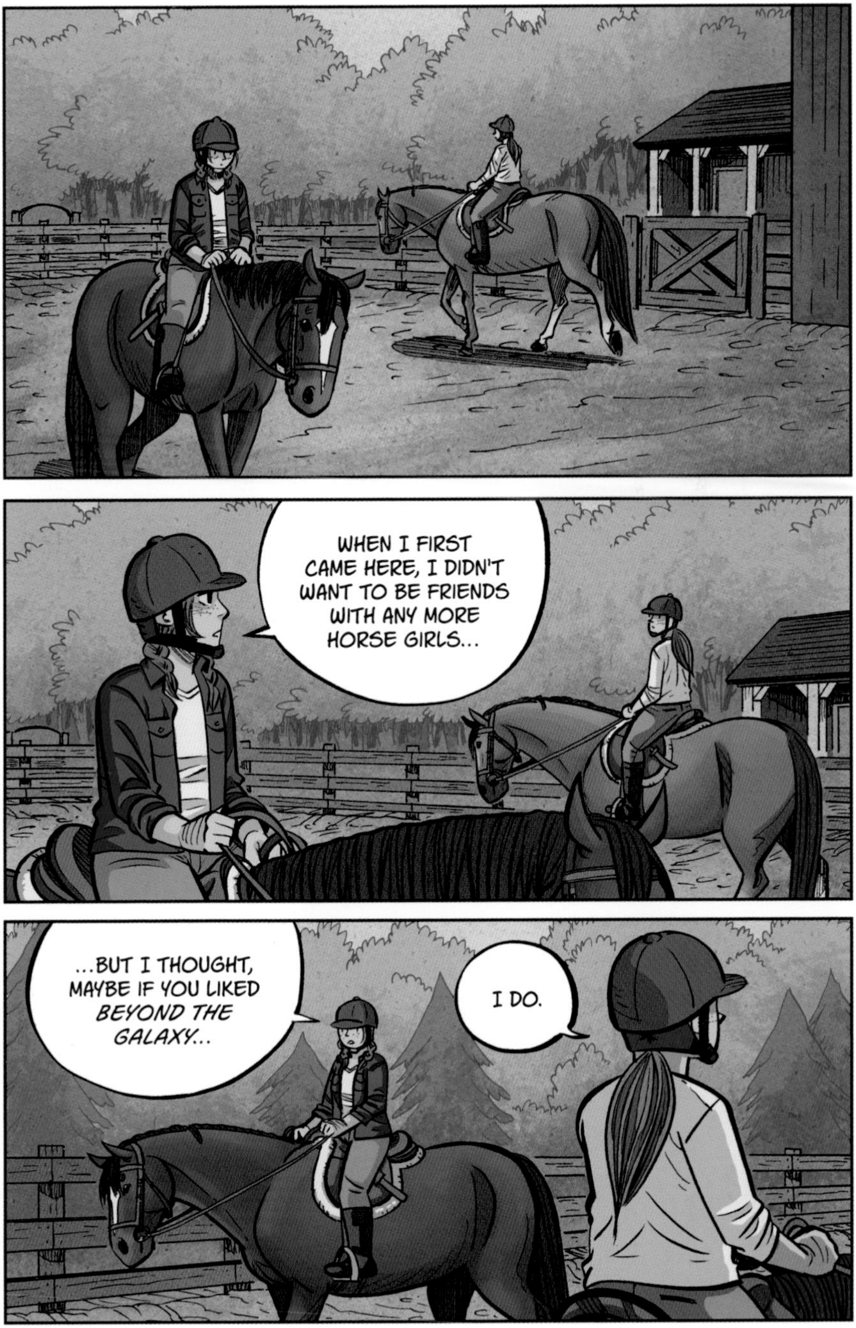
WHEN I FIRST CAME HERE, I DIDN'T WANT TO BE FRIENDS WITH ANY MORE HORSE GIRLS...
...BUT I THOUGHT, MAYBE IF YOU LIKED *BEYOND THE GALAXY*...
I DO.

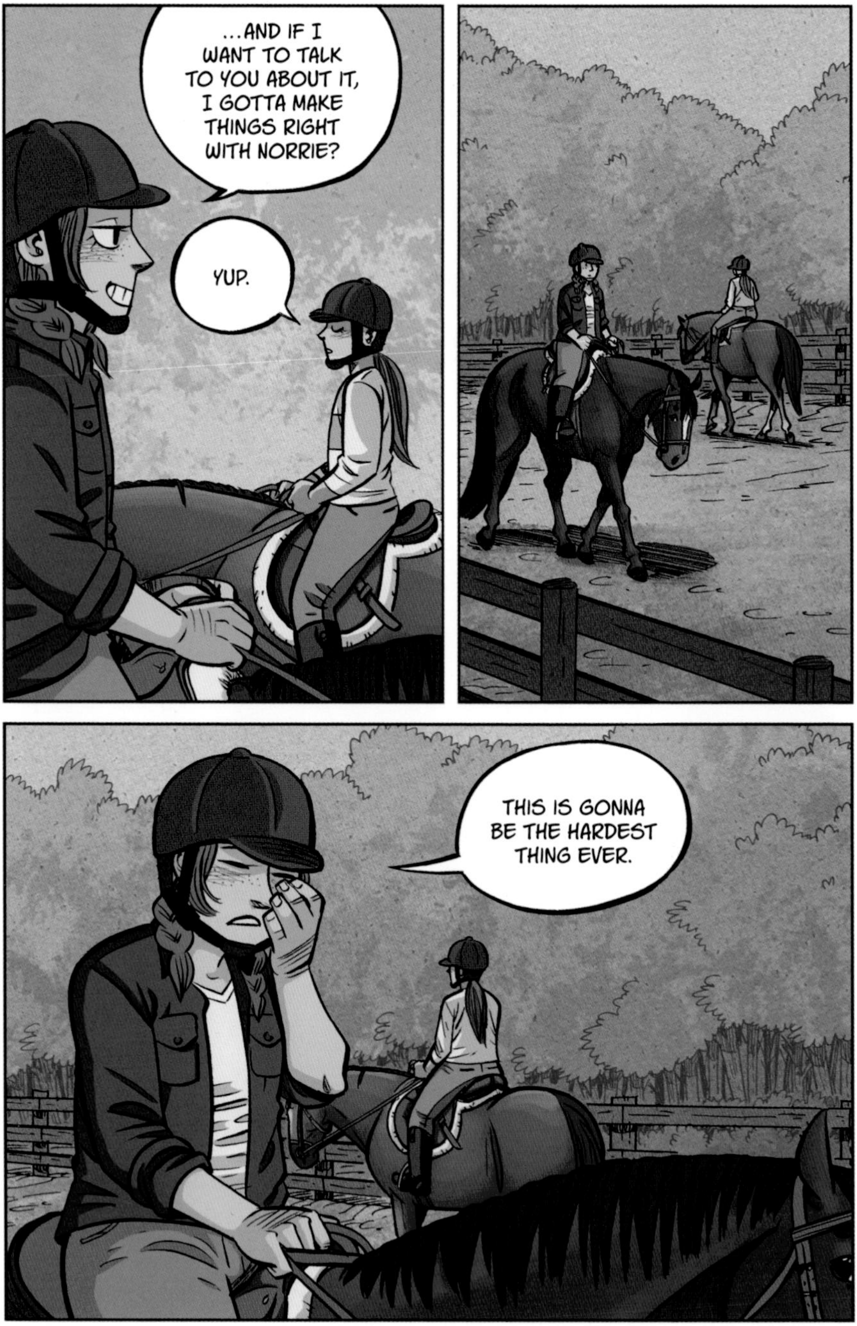
...AND IF I WANT TO TALK TO YOU ABOUT IT, I GOTTA MAKE THINGS RIGHT WITH NORRIE?
YUP.
THIS IS GONNA BE THE HARDEST THING EVER.

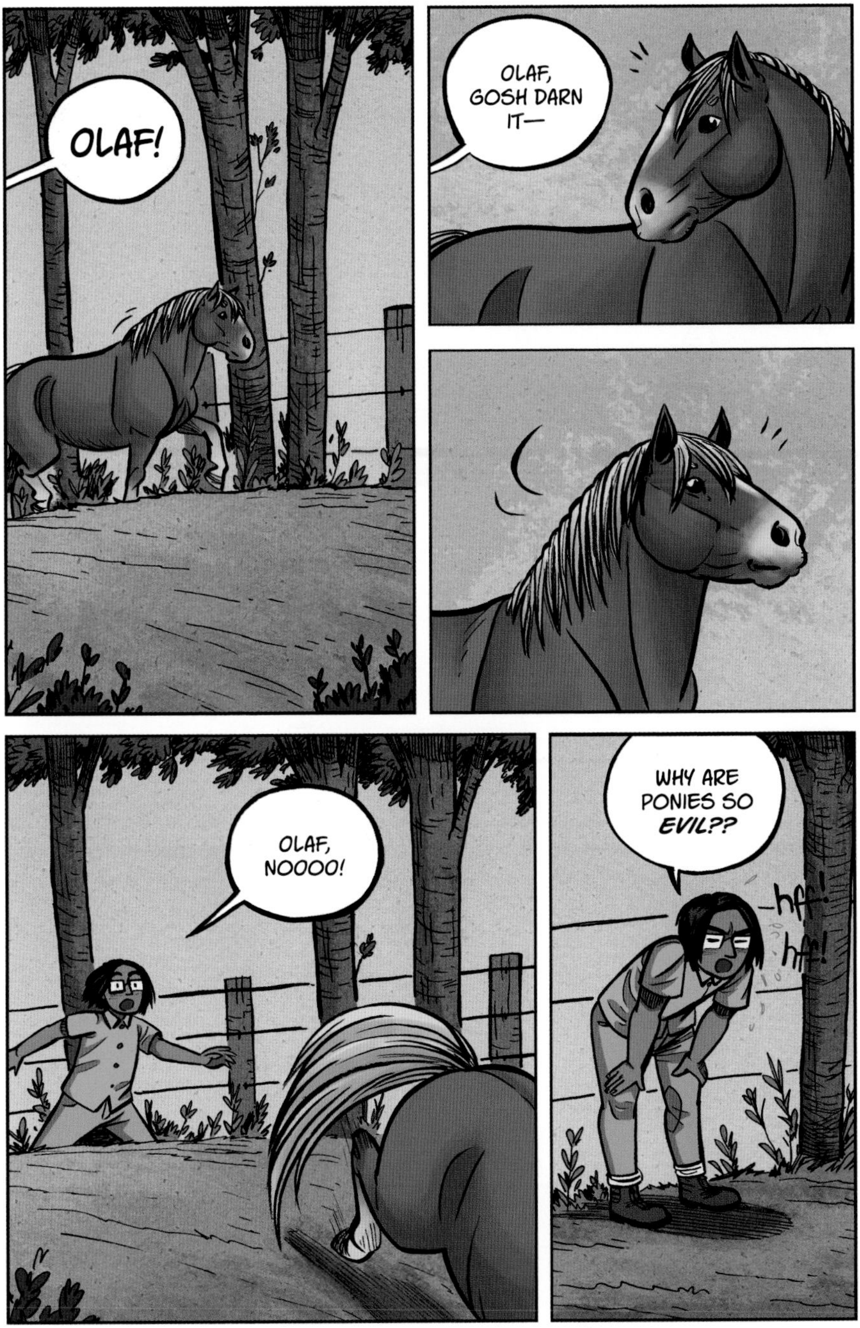
OLAF!
OLAF, GOSH DARN IT—
OLAF, NOOOO!
WHY ARE PONIES SO *EVIL??*
hff!
hff!

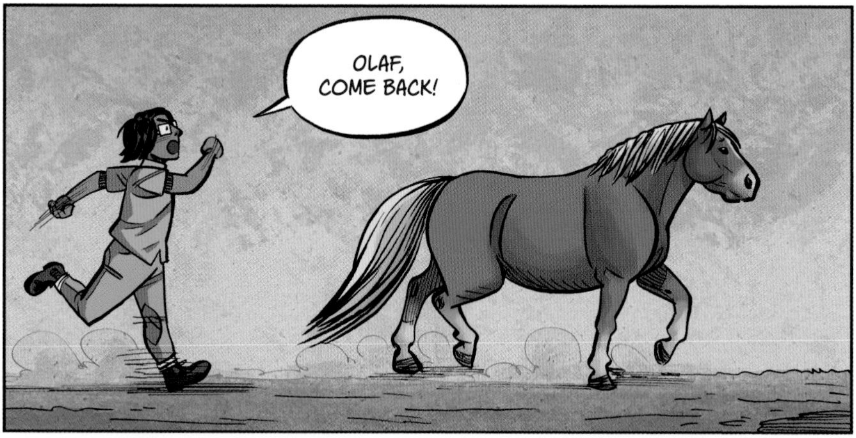
OLAF, COME BACK!

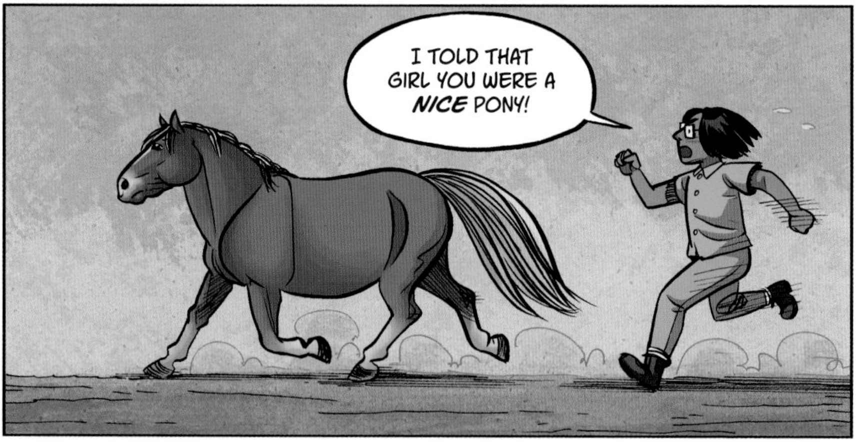
I TOLD THAT GIRL YOU WERE A *NICE* PONY!

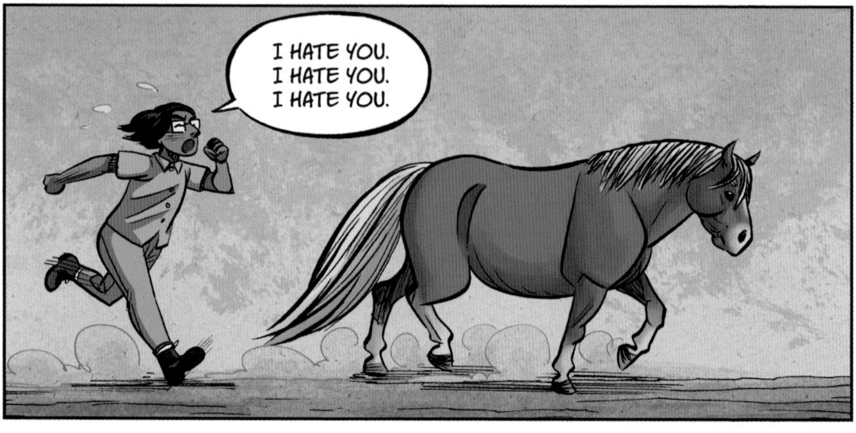
I HATE YOU. I HATE YOU. I HATE YOU.

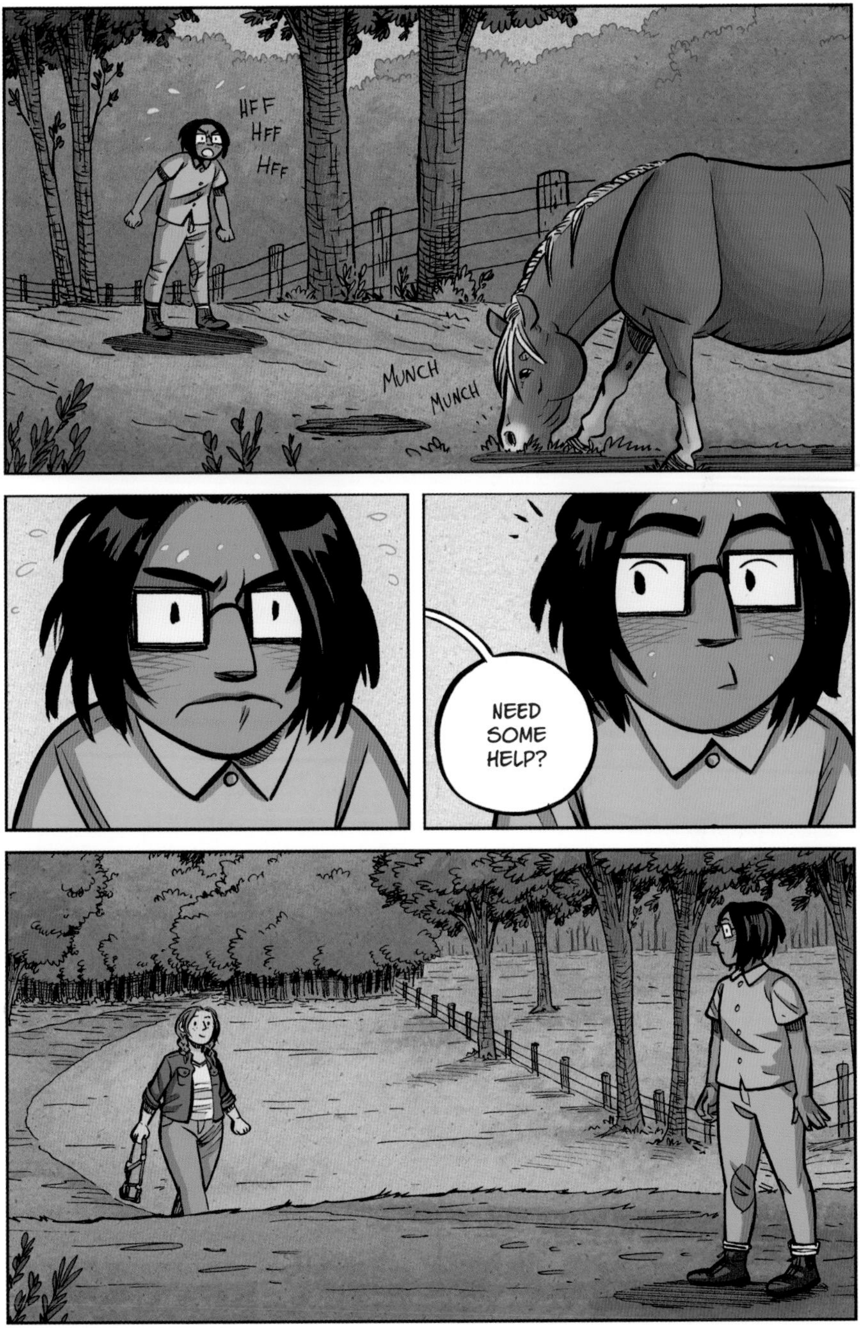
HFF
HFF
HFF
MUNCH
MUNCH
NEED SOME HELP?

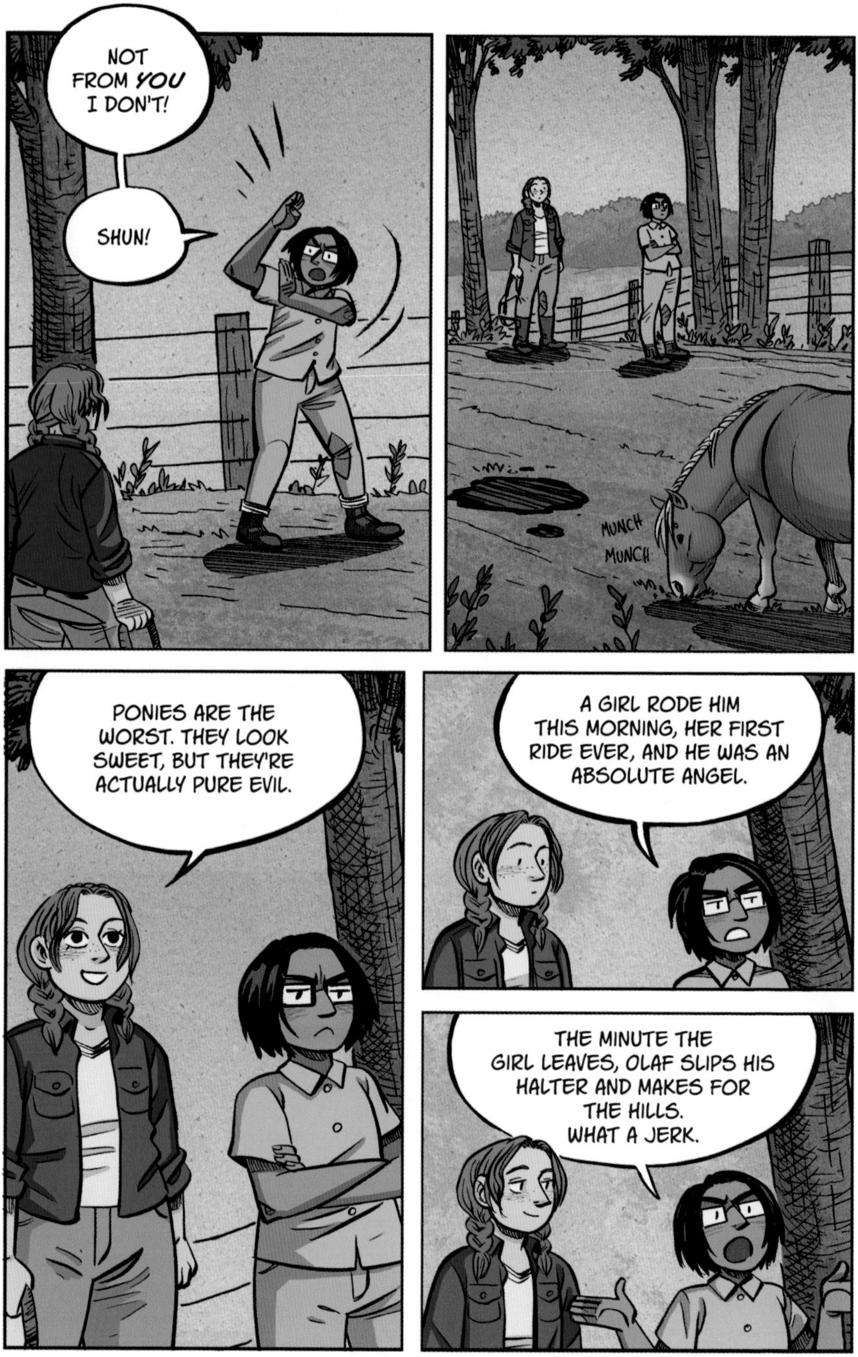
NOT FROM *YOU* I DON'T!
SHUN!
MUNCH
MUNCH
PONIES ARE THE WORST. THEY LOOK SWEET, BUT THEY'RE ACTUALLY PURE EVIL.
A GIRL RODE HIM THIS MORNING, HER FIRST RIDE EVER, AND HE WAS AN ABSOLUTE ANGEL.
THE MINUTE THE GIRL LEAVES, OLAF SLIPS HIS HALTER AND MAKES FOR THE HILLS.
WHAT A JERK.

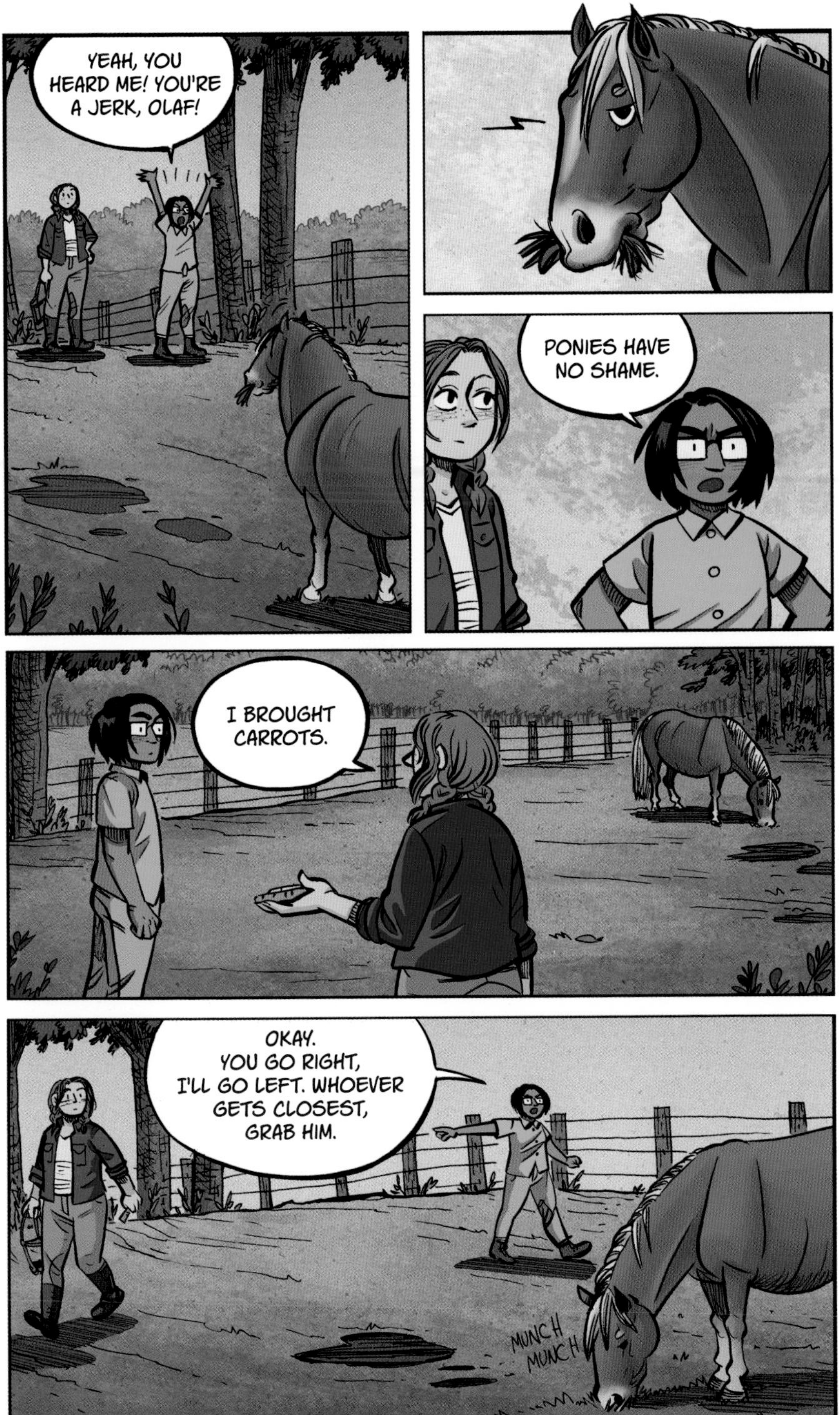
YEAH, YOU HEARD ME! YOU'RE A JERK, OLAF!
PONIES HAVE NO SHAME.
I BROUGHT CARROTS.
OKAY. YOU GO RIGHT, I'LL GO LEFT. WHOEVER GETS CLOSEST, GRAB HIM.
MUNCH MUNCH

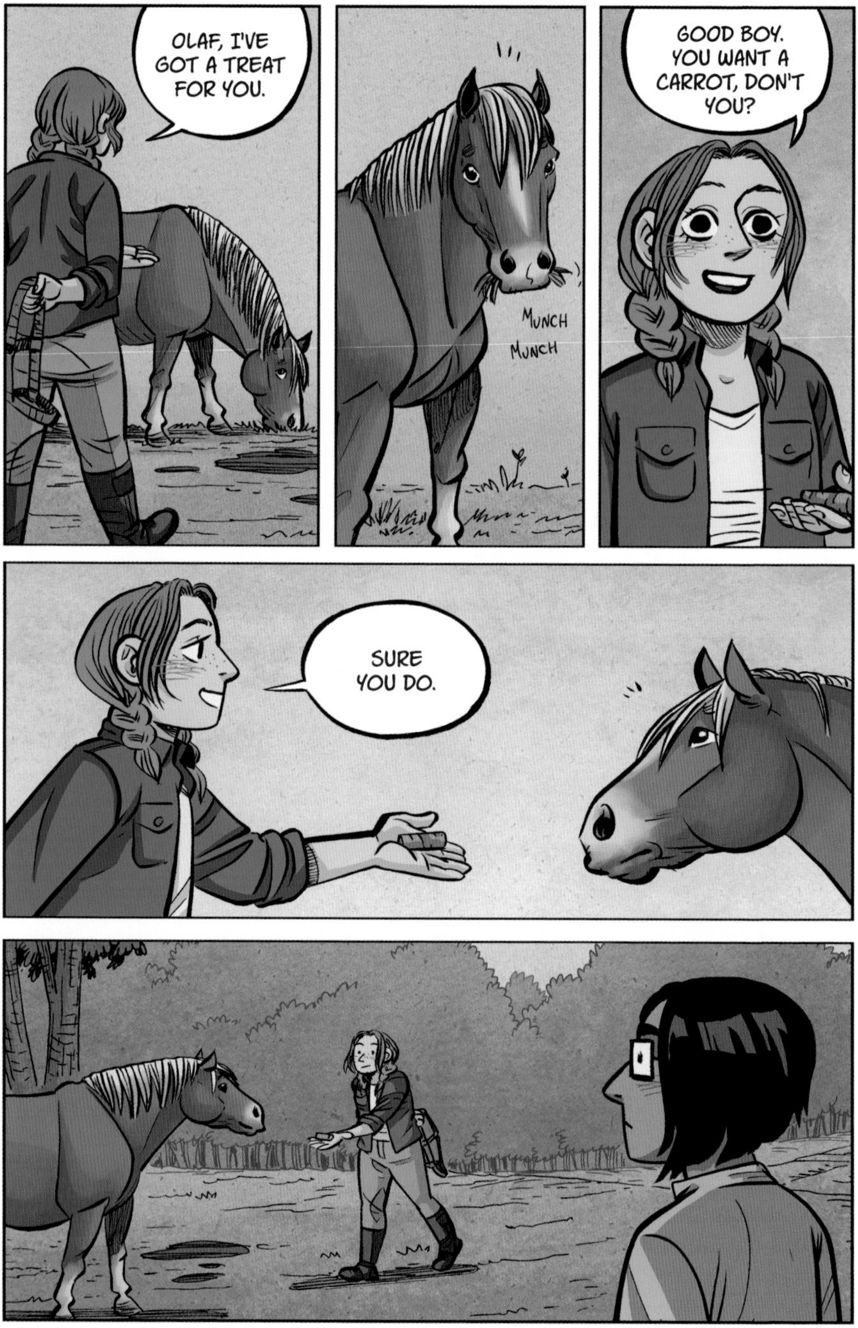
OLAF, I'VE GOT A TREAT FOR YOU.
MUNCH
MUNCH
GOOD BOY. YOU WANT A CARROT, DON'T YOU?
SURE YOU DO.

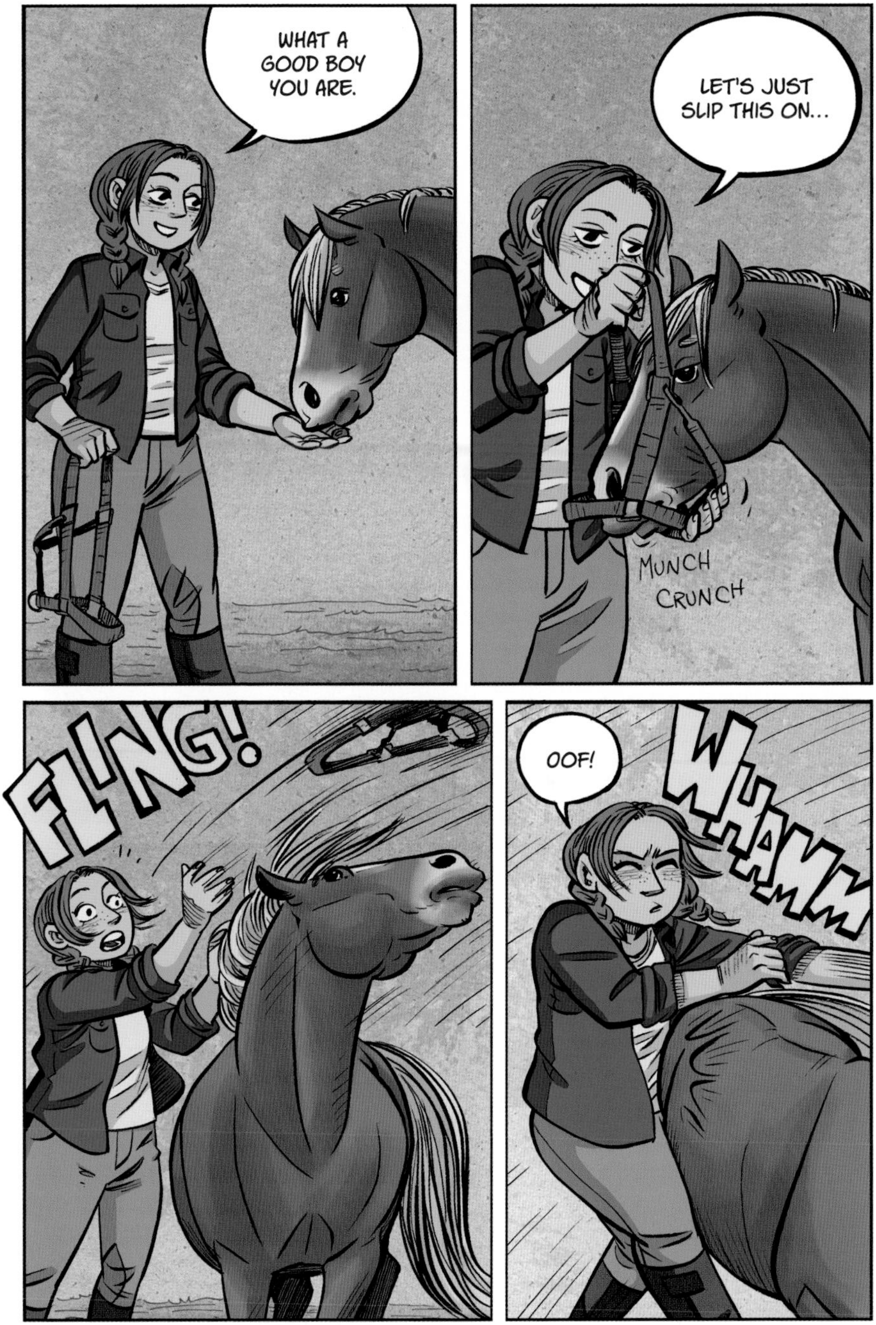
WHAT A GOOD BOY YOU ARE.
LET'S JUST SLIP THIS ON...
MUNCH CRUNCH
FLING!
OOF!
WHAMM

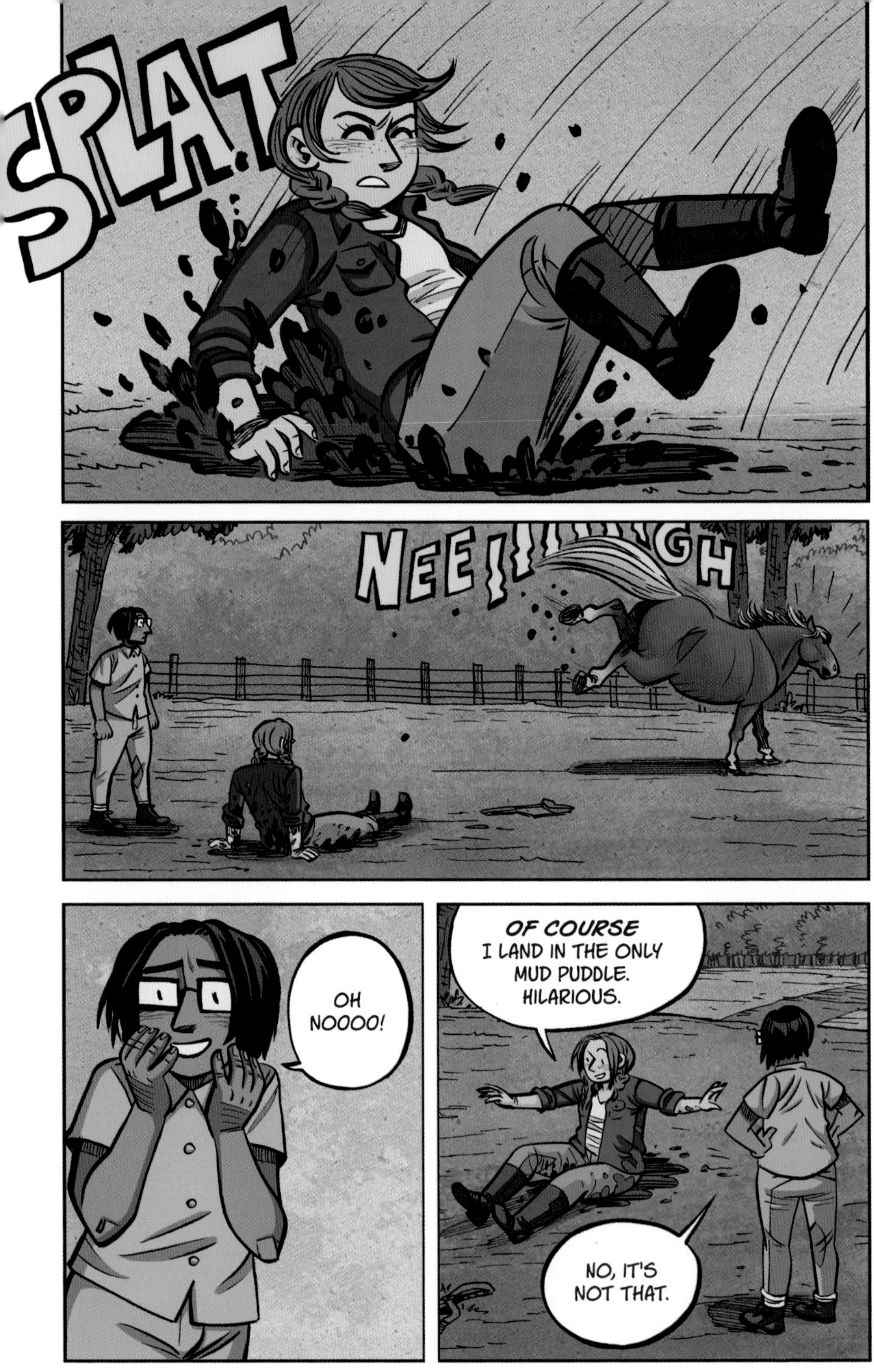
SPLAT
NEEIIIIIIGH
OH NOOOO!
OF COURSE I LAND IN THE ONLY MUD PUDDLE. HILARIOUS.
NO, IT'S NOT THAT.

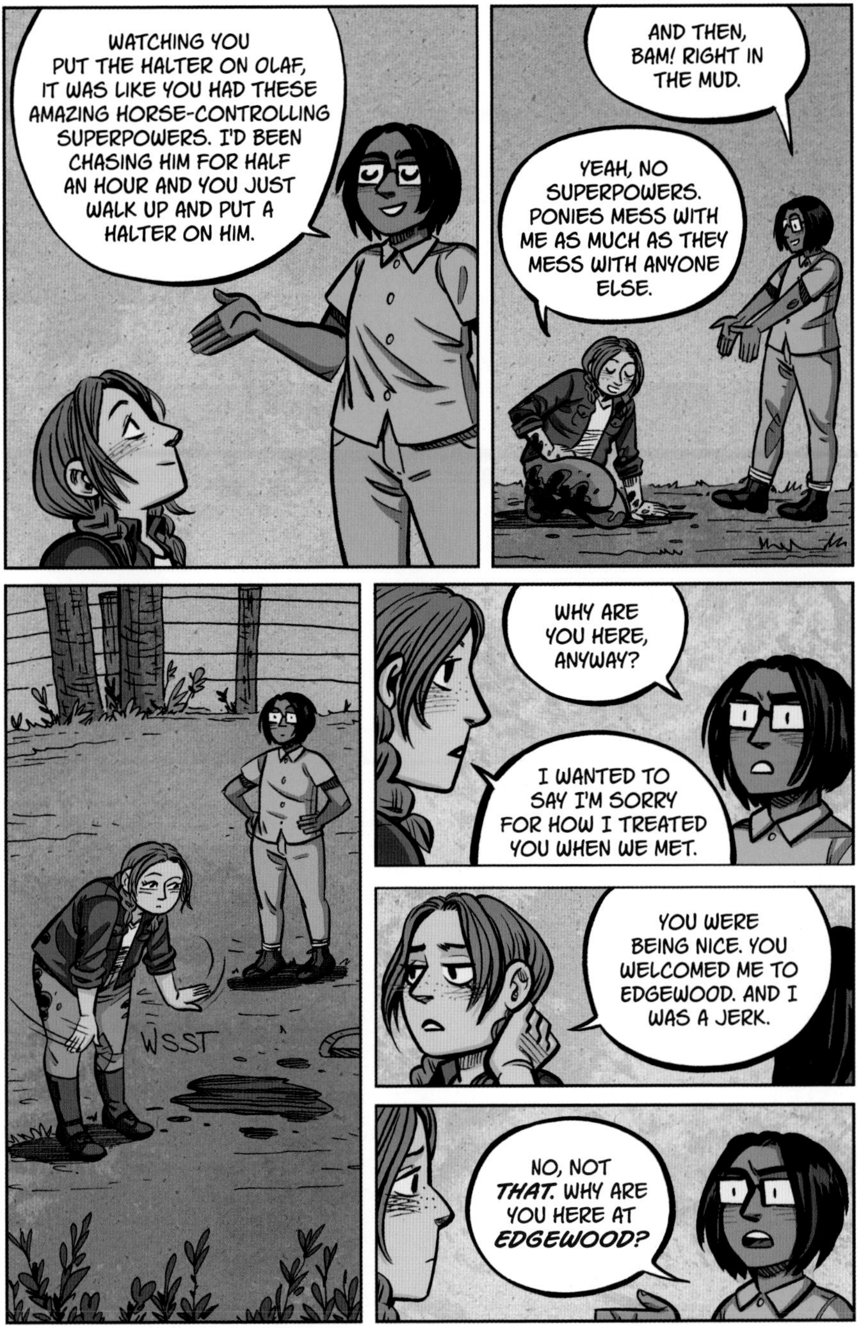
WATCHING YOU PUT THE HALTER ON OLAF, IT WAS LIKE YOU HAD THESE AMAZING HORSE-CONTROLLING SUPERPOWERS. I'D BEEN CHASING HIM FOR HALF AN HOUR AND YOU JUST WALK UP AND PUT A HALTER ON HIM.
AND THEN, BAM! RIGHT IN THE MUD.
YEAH, NO SUPERPOWERS. PONIES MESS WITH ME AS MUCH AS THEY MESS WITH ANYONE ELSE.
WSST
WHY ARE YOU HERE, ANYWAY?
I WANTED TO SAY I'M SORRY FOR HOW I TREATED YOU WHEN WE MET.
YOU WERE BEING NICE. YOU WELCOMED ME TO EDGEWOOD. AND I WAS A JERK.
NO, NOT *THAT.* WHY ARE YOU HERE AT *EDGEWOOD?*

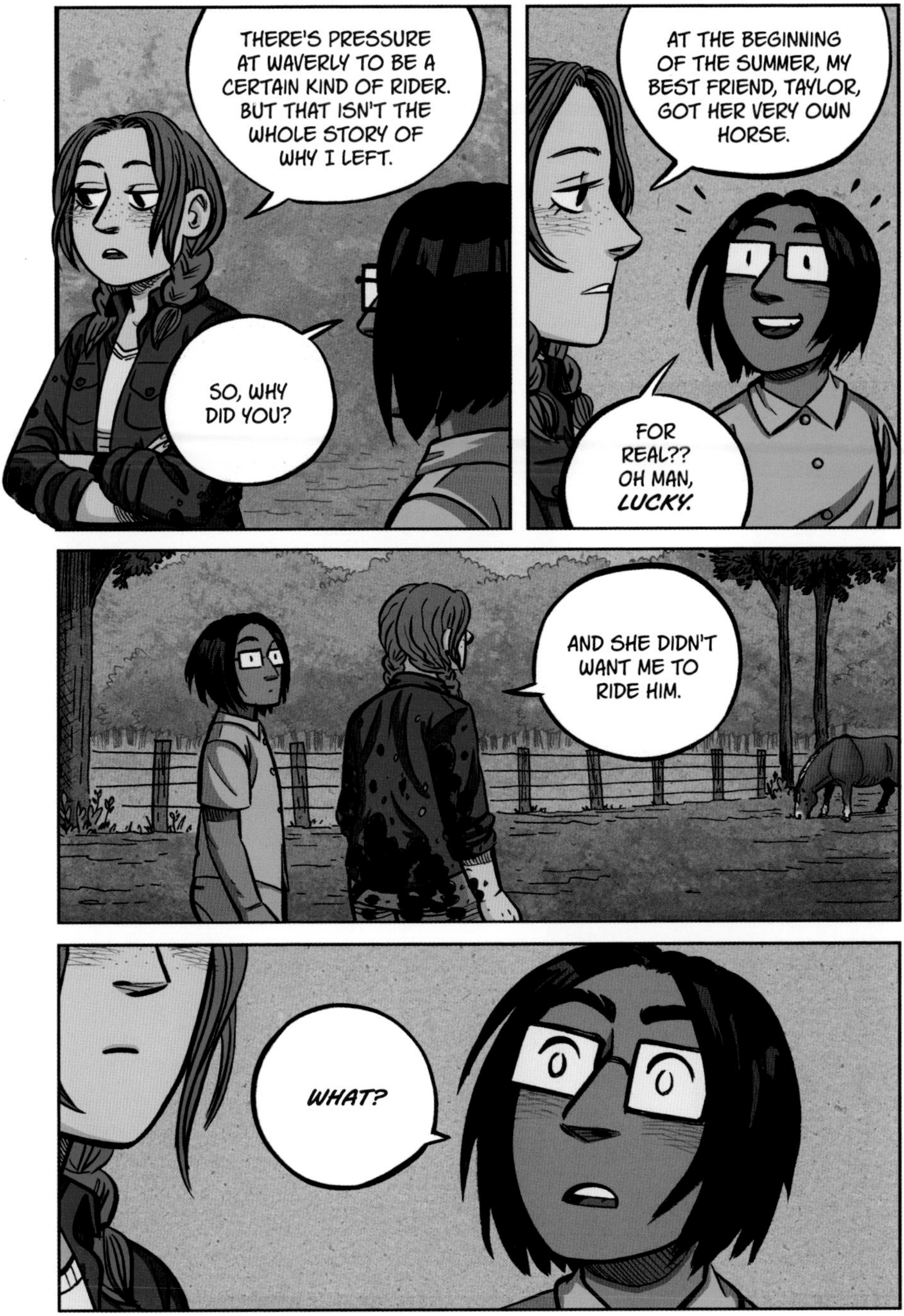

THERE'S PRESSURE AT WAVERLY TO BE A CERTAIN KIND OF RIDER. BUT THAT ISN'T THE WHOLE STORY OF WHY I LEFT.
SO, WHY DID YOU?
AT THE BEGINNING OF THE SUMMER, MY BEST FRIEND, TAYLOR, GOT HER VERY OWN HORSE.
FOR REAL?? OH MAN, LUCKY.
AND SHE DIDN'T WANT ME TO RIDE HIM.
WHAT?

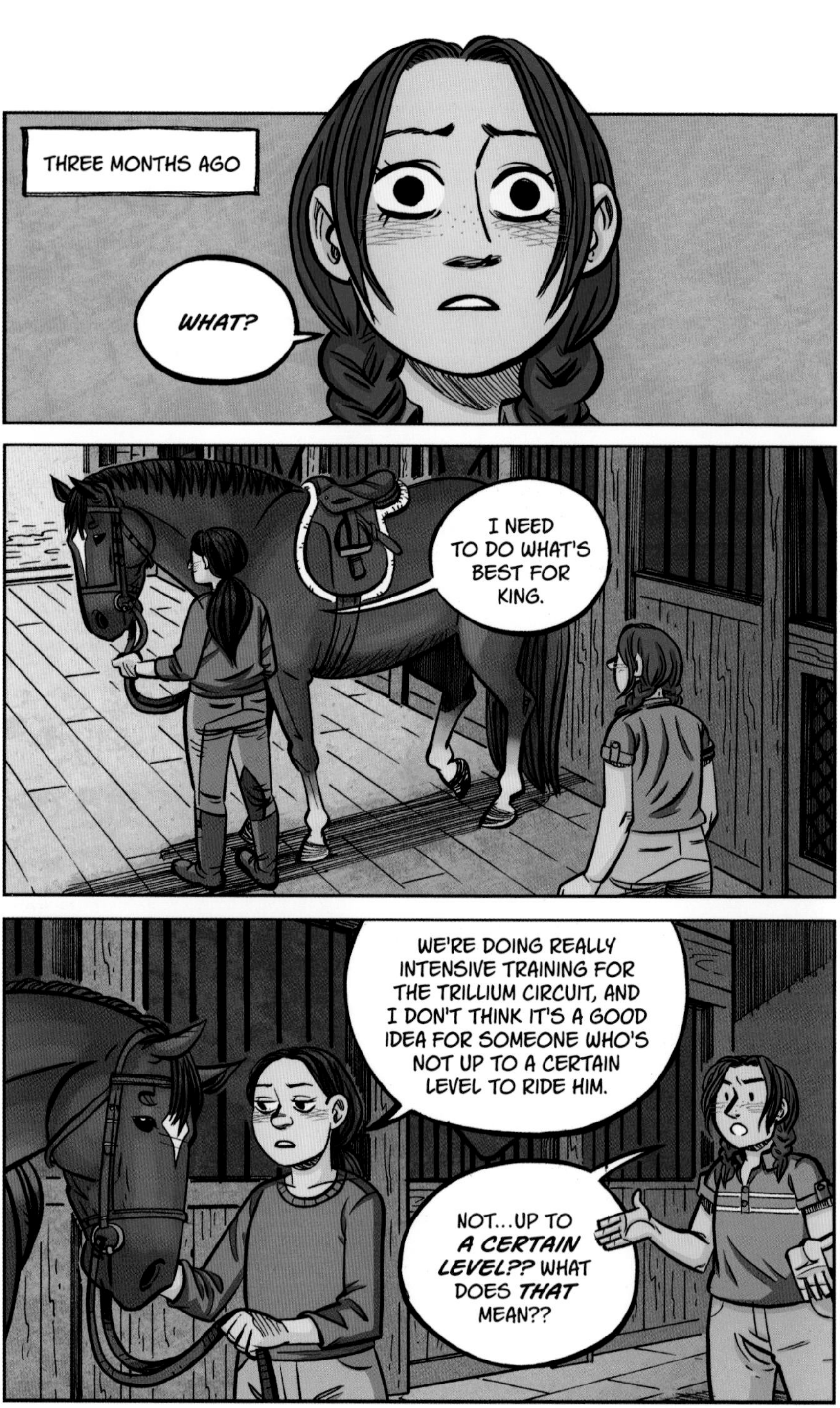
THREE MONTHS AGO
WHAT?
I NEED TO DO WHAT'S BEST FOR KING.
WE'RE DOING REALLY INTENSIVE TRAINING FOR THE TRILLIUM CIRCUIT, AND I DON'T THINK IT'S A GOOD IDEA FOR SOMEONE WHO'S NOT UP TO A CERTAIN LEVEL TO RIDE HIM.
NOT...UP TO ***A CERTAIN LEVEL??*** WHAT DOES ***THAT*** MEAN??

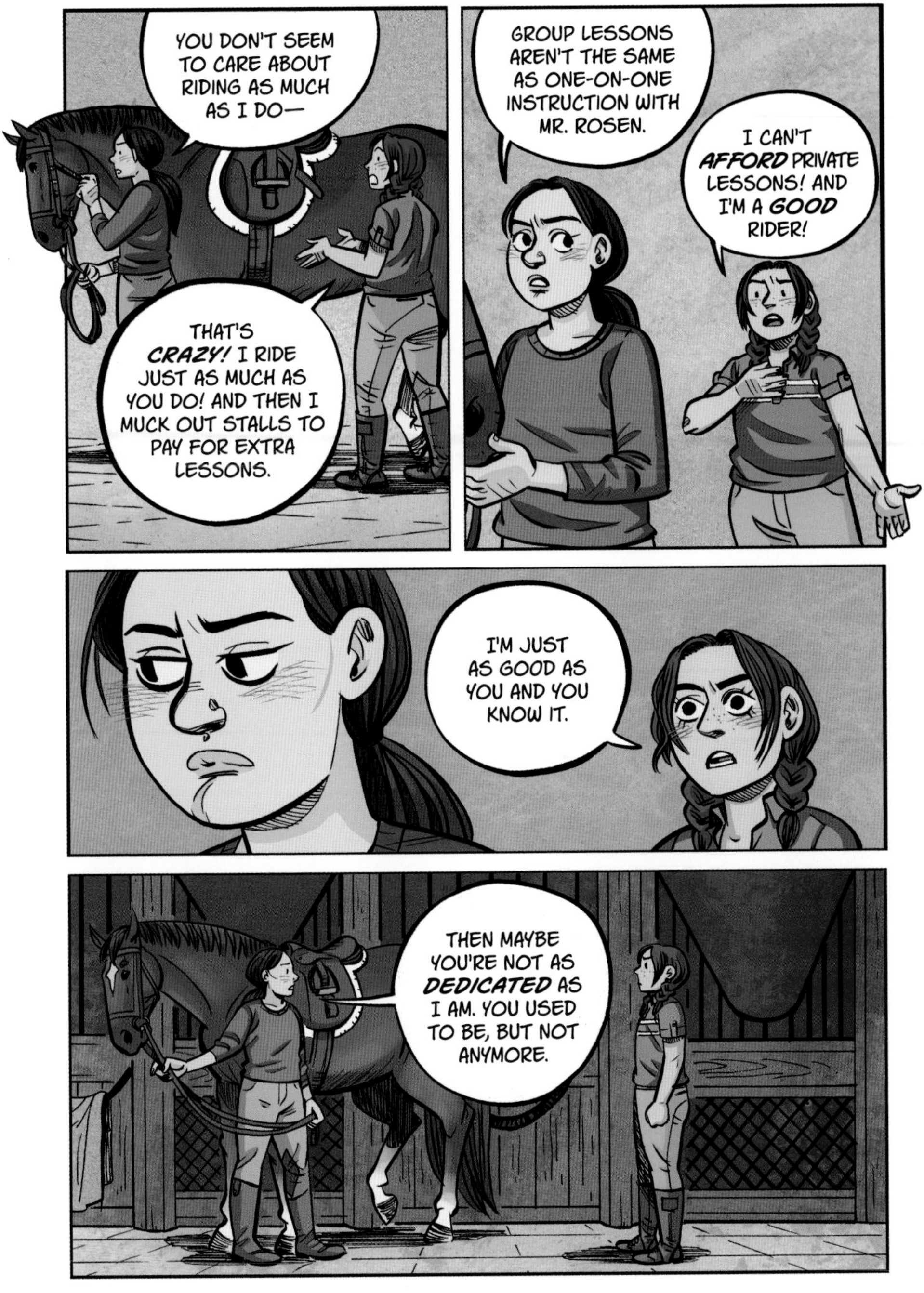
YOU DON'T SEEM TO CARE ABOUT RIDING AS MUCH AS I DO—
THAT'S *CRAZY!* I RIDE JUST AS MUCH AS YOU DO! AND THEN I MUCK OUT STALLS TO PAY FOR EXTRA LESSONS.
GROUP LESSONS AREN'T THE SAME AS ONE-ON-ONE INSTRUCTION WITH MR. ROSEN.
I CAN'T ***AFFORD*** PRIVATE LESSONS! AND I'M A ***GOOD*** RIDER!
I'M JUST AS GOOD AS YOU AND YOU KNOW IT.
THEN MAYBE YOU'RE NOT AS ***DEDICATED*** AS I AM. YOU USED TO BE, BUT NOT ANYMORE.

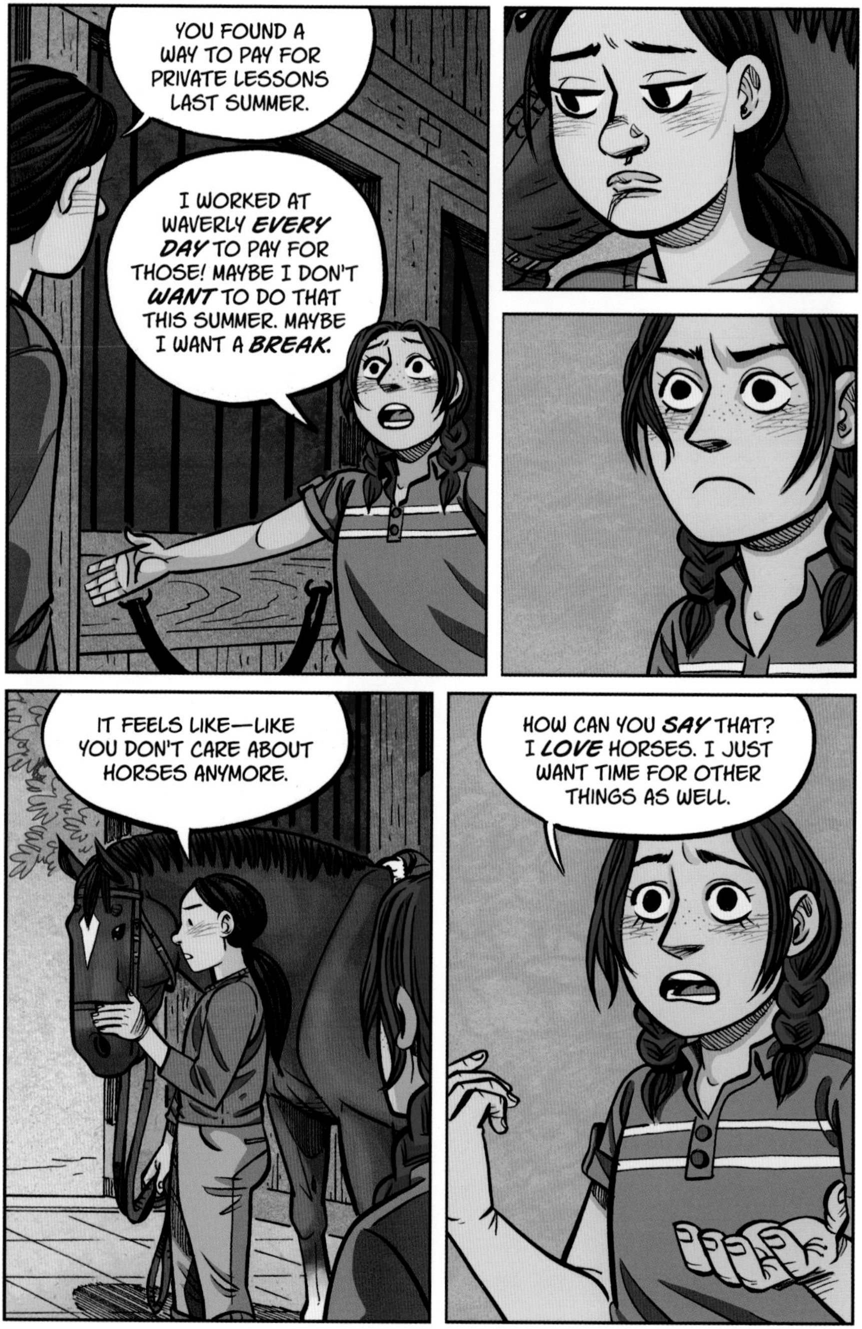
YOU FOUND A WAY TO PAY FOR PRIVATE LESSONS LAST SUMMER.
I WORKED AT WAVERLY *EVERY DAY* TO PAY FOR THOSE! MAYBE I DON'T *WANT* TO DO THAT THIS SUMMER. MAYBE I WANT A *BREAK.*
IT FEELS LIKE—LIKE YOU DON'T CARE ABOUT HORSES ANYMORE.
HOW CAN YOU *SAY* THAT? I *LOVE* HORSES. I JUST WANT TIME FOR OTHER THINGS AS WELL.

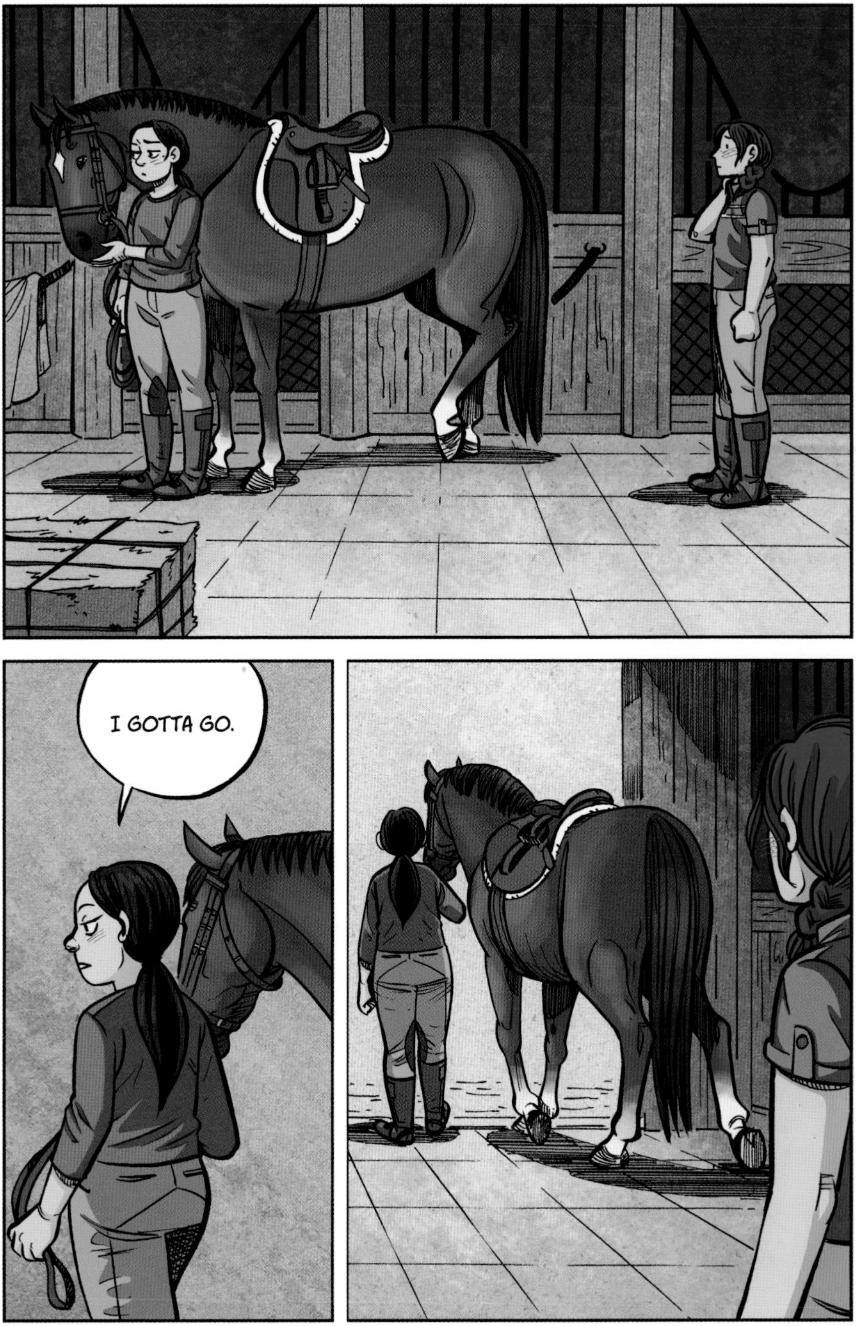
I GOTTA GO.

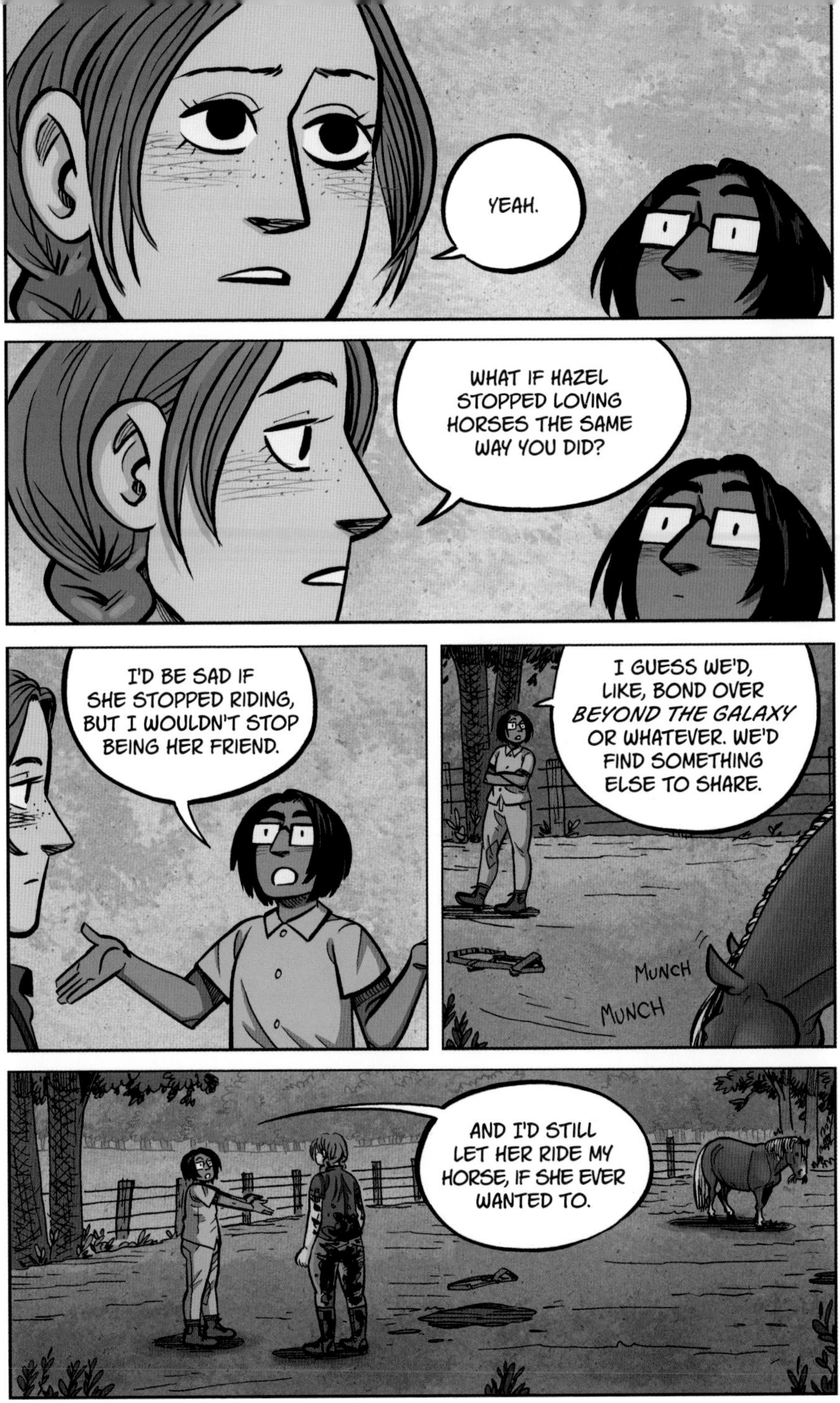
YEAH.
WHAT IF HAZEL STOPPED LOVING HORSES THE SAME WAY YOU DID?
I'D BE SAD IF SHE STOPPED RIDING, BUT I WOULDN'T STOP BEING HER FRIEND.
I GUESS WE'D, LIKE, BOND OVER *BEYOND THE GALAXY* OR WHATEVER. WE'D FIND SOMETHING ELSE TO SHARE.
MUNCH
MUNCH
AND I'D STILL LET HER RIDE MY HORSE, IF SHE EVER WANTED TO.

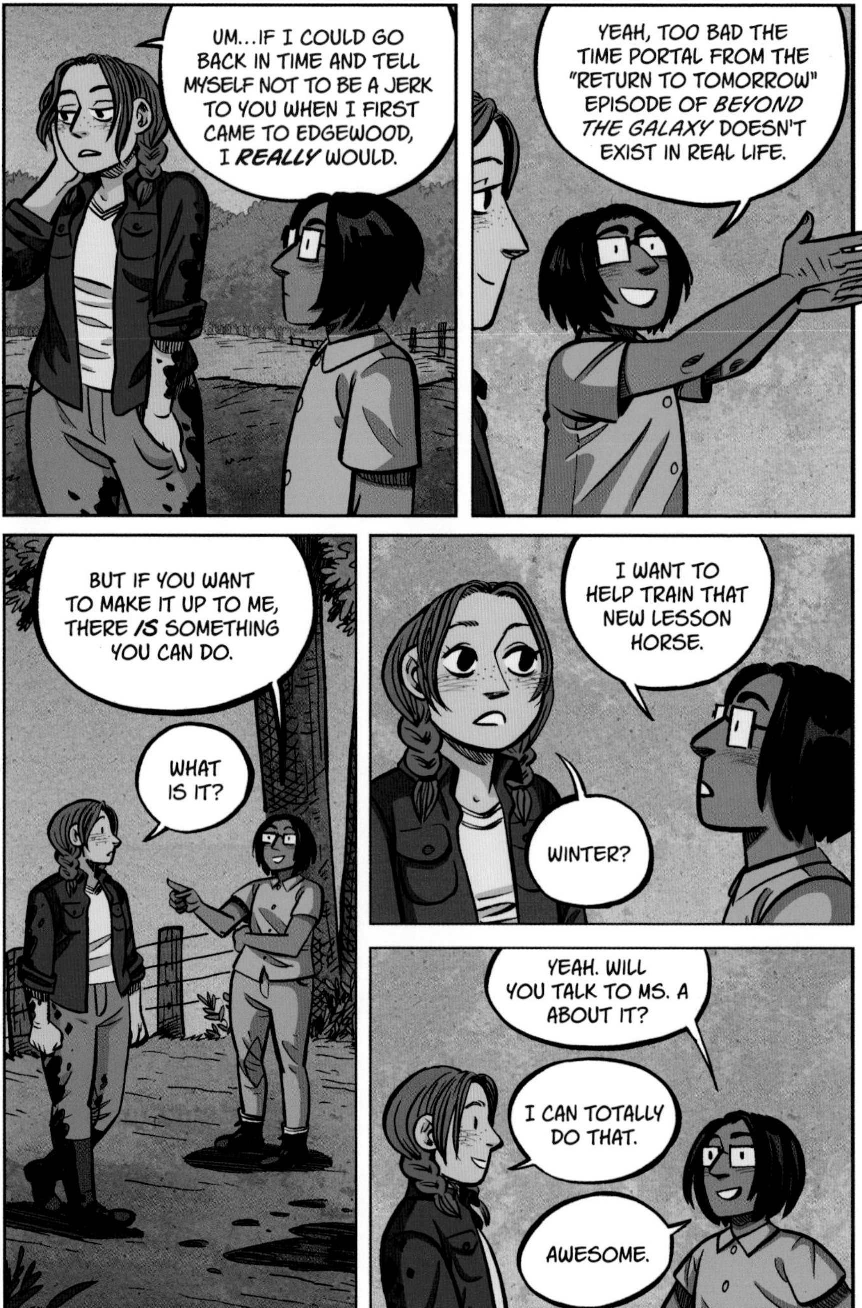
UM...IF I COULD GO BACK IN TIME AND TELL MYSELF NOT TO BE A JERK TO YOU WHEN I FIRST CAME TO EDGEWOOD, I *REALLY* WOULD.
YEAH, TOO BAD THE TIME PORTAL FROM THE "RETURN TO TOMORROW" EPISODE OF *BEYOND THE GALAXY* DOESN'T EXIST IN REAL LIFE.
BUT IF YOU WANT TO MAKE IT UP TO ME, THERE *IS* SOMETHING YOU CAN DO.
WHAT IS IT?
I WANT TO HELP TRAIN THAT NEW LESSON HORSE.
WINTER?
YEAH. WILL YOU TALK TO MS. A ABOUT IT?
I CAN TOTALLY DO THAT.
AWESOME.

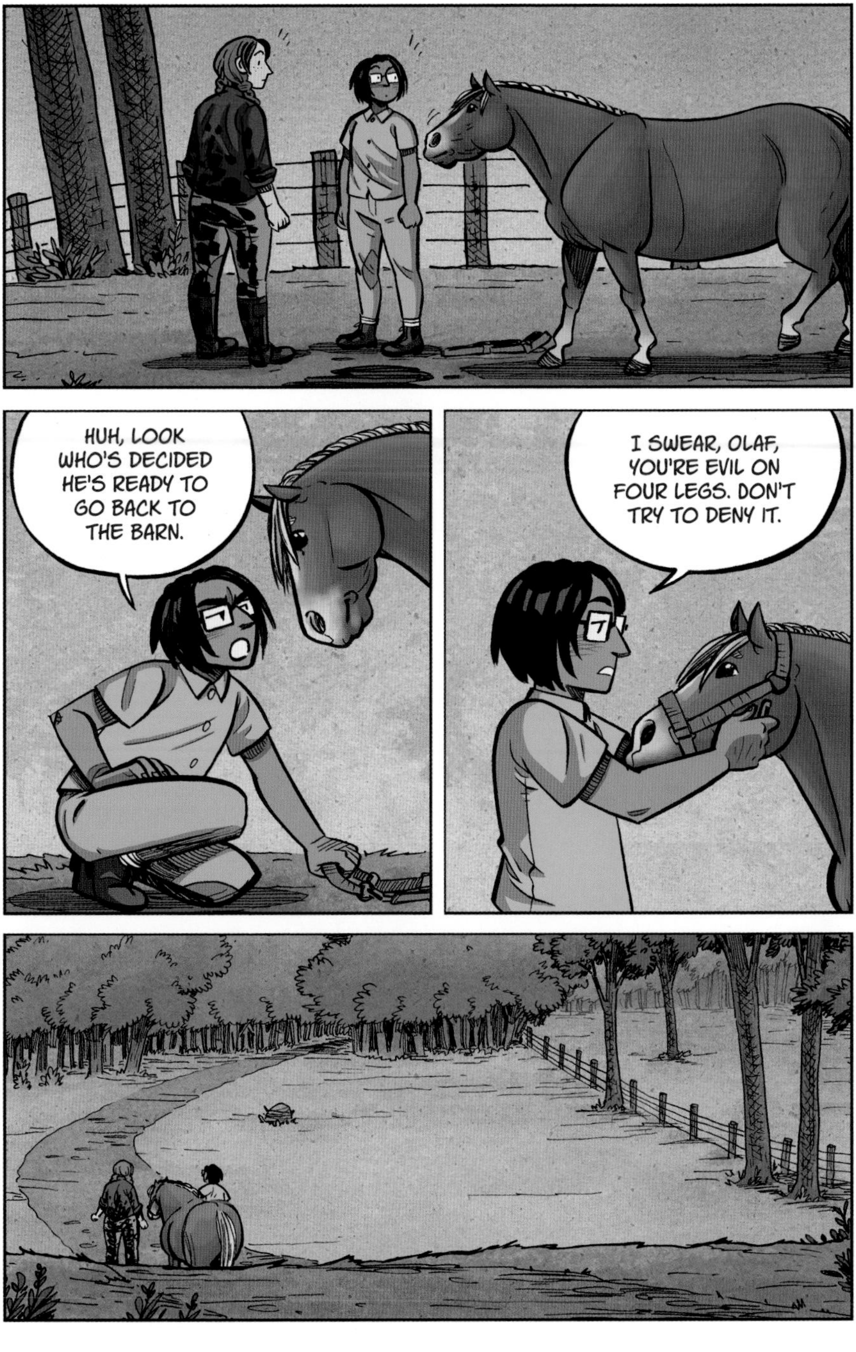
HUH, LOOK WHO'S DECIDED HE'S READY TO GO BACK TO THE BARN.
I SWEAR, OLAF, YOU'RE EVIL ON FOUR LEGS. DON'T TRY TO DENY IT.

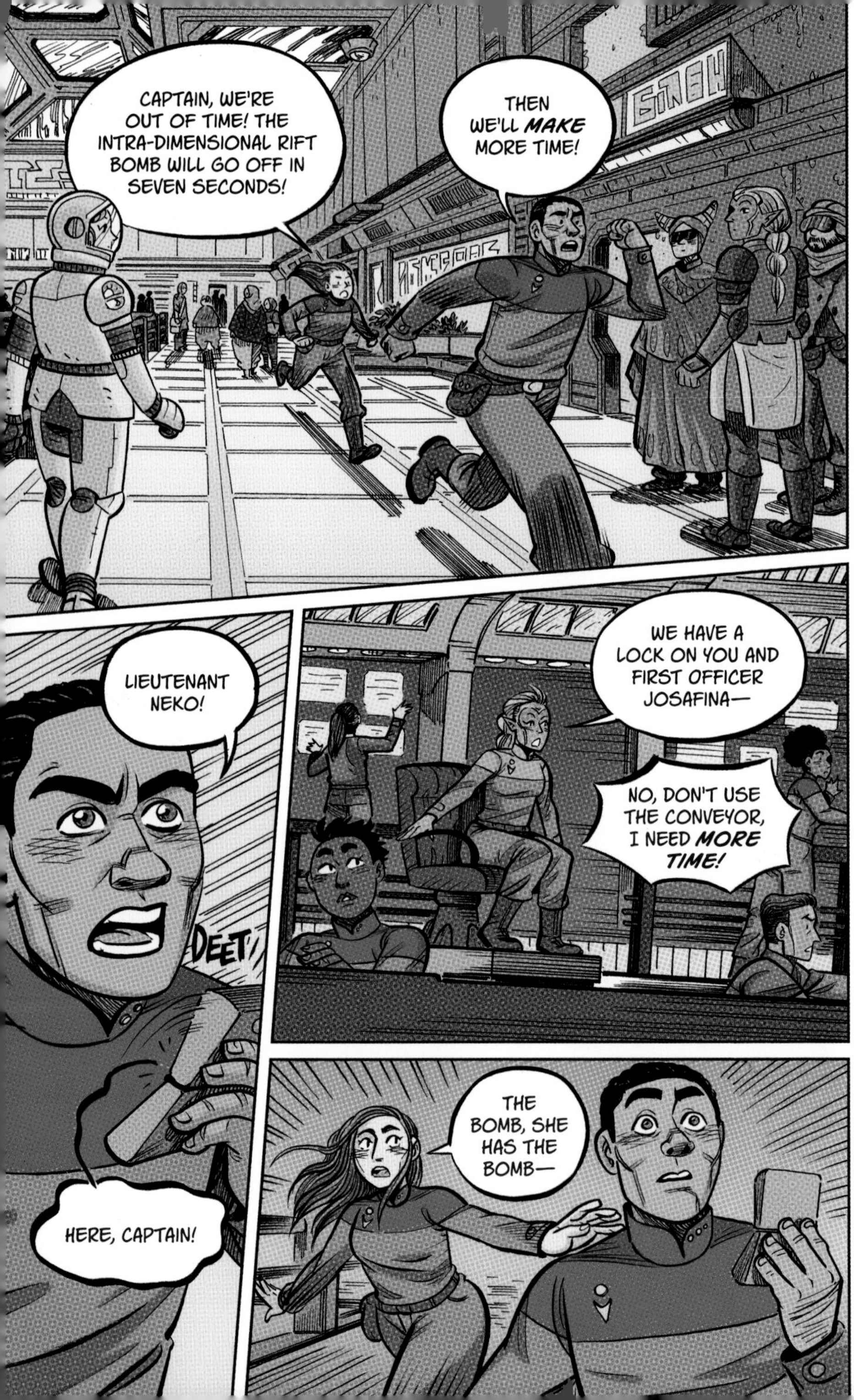
CAPTAIN, WE'RE OUT OF TIME! THE INTRA-DIMENSIONAL RIFT BOMB WILL GO OFF IN SEVEN SECONDS!
THEN WE'LL *MAKE* MORE TIME!
LIEUTENANT NEKO!
DEET
HERE, CAPTAIN!
WE HAVE A LOCK ON YOU AND FIRST OFFICER JOSAFINA—
NO, DON'T USE THE CONVEYOR, I NEED *MORE TIME!*
THE BOMB, SHE HAS THE BOMB—

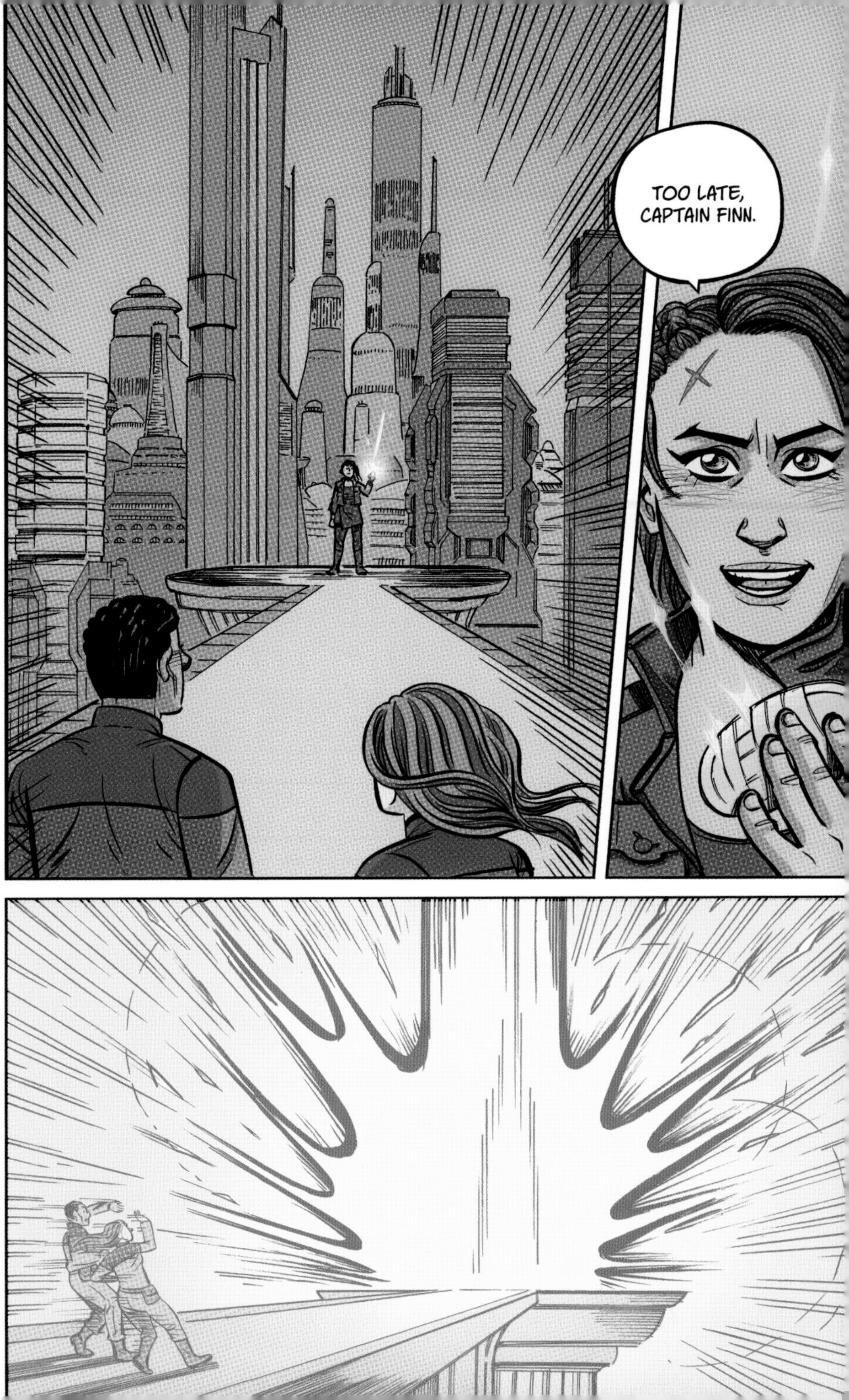
TOO LATE, CAPTAIN FINN.

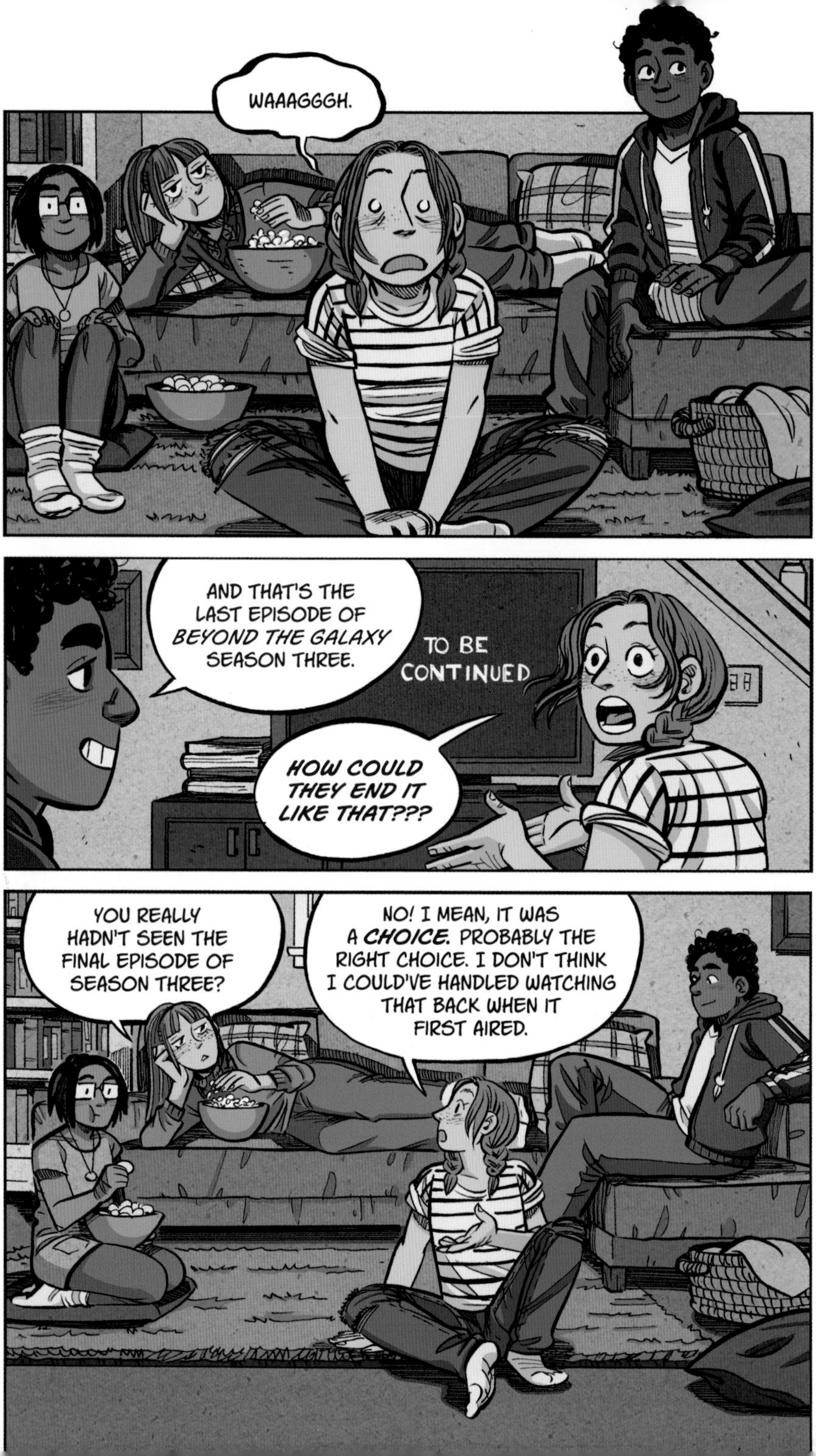
WAAAGGGH.
AND THAT'S THE LAST EPISODE OF *BEYOND THE GALAXY* SEASON THREE.
TO BE CONTINUED
HOW COULD THEY END IT LIKE THAT???
YOU REALLY HADN'T SEEN THE FINAL EPISODE OF SEASON THREE?
NO! I MEAN, IT WAS A ***CHOICE.*** PROBABLY THE RIGHT CHOICE. I DON'T THINK I COULD'VE HANDLED WATCHING THAT BACK WHEN IT FIRST AIRED.

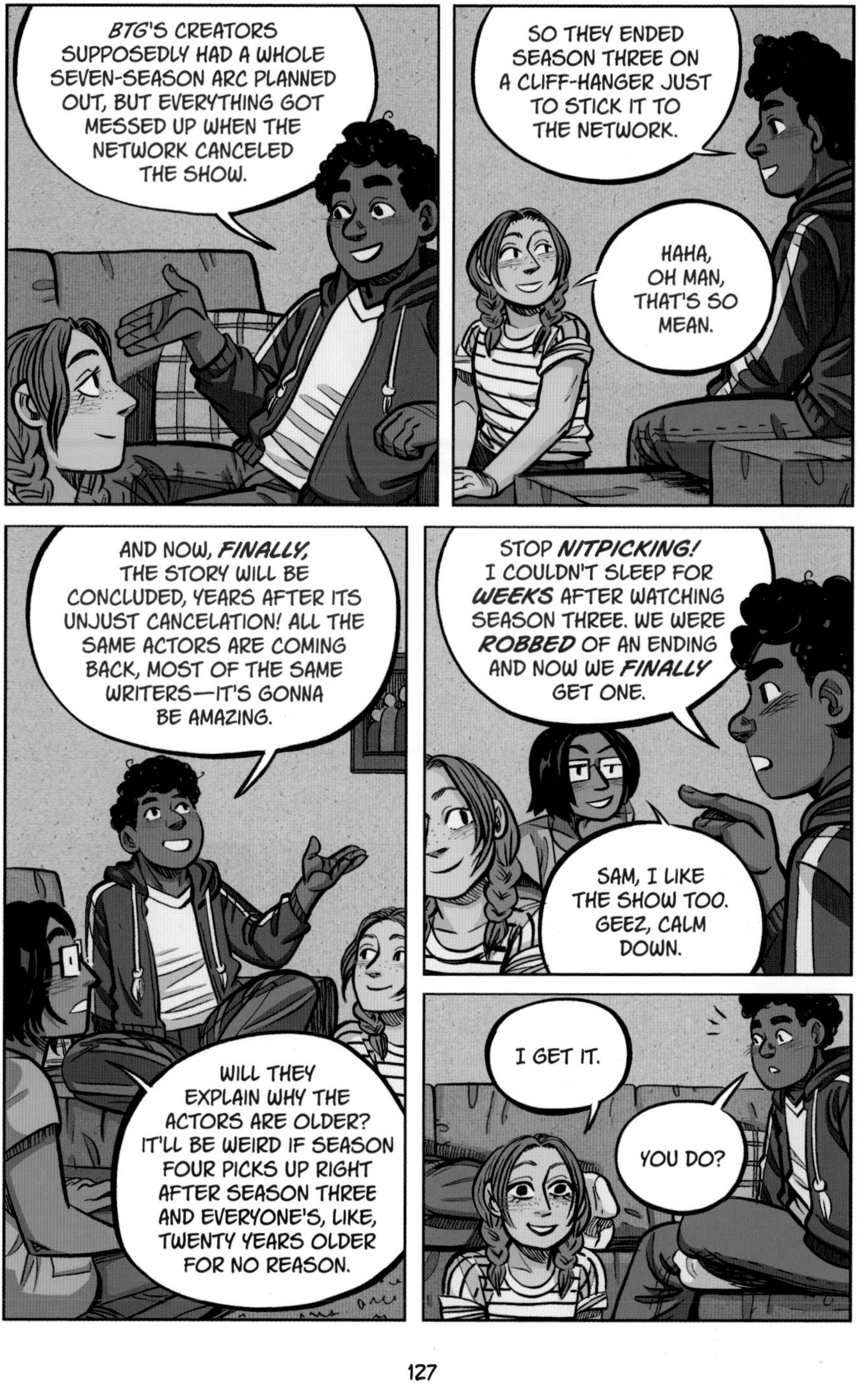
BTG'S CREATORS SUPPOSEDLY HAD A WHOLE SEVEN-SEASON ARC PLANNED OUT, BUT EVERYTHING GOT MESSED UP WHEN THE NETWORK CANCELED THE SHOW.
SO THEY ENDED SEASON THREE ON A CLIFF-HANGER JUST TO STICK IT TO THE NETWORK.
HAHA, OH MAN, THAT'S SO MEAN.
AND NOW, ***FINALLY,*** THE STORY WILL BE CONCLUDED, YEARS AFTER ITS UNJUST CANCELATION! ALL THE SAME ACTORS ARE COMING BACK, MOST OF THE SAME WRITERS—IT'S GONNA BE AMAZING.
WILL THEY EXPLAIN WHY THE ACTORS ARE OLDER? IT'LL BE WEIRD IF SEASON FOUR PICKS UP RIGHT AFTER SEASON THREE AND EVERYONE'S, LIKE, TWENTY YEARS OLDER FOR NO REASON.
STOP ***NITPICKING!*** I COULDN'T SLEEP FOR ***WEEKS*** AFTER WATCHING SEASON THREE. WE WERE ***ROBBED*** OF AN ENDING AND NOW WE ***FINALLY*** GET ONE.
SAM, I LIKE THE SHOW TOO. GEEZ, CALM DOWN.
I GET IT.
YOU DO?

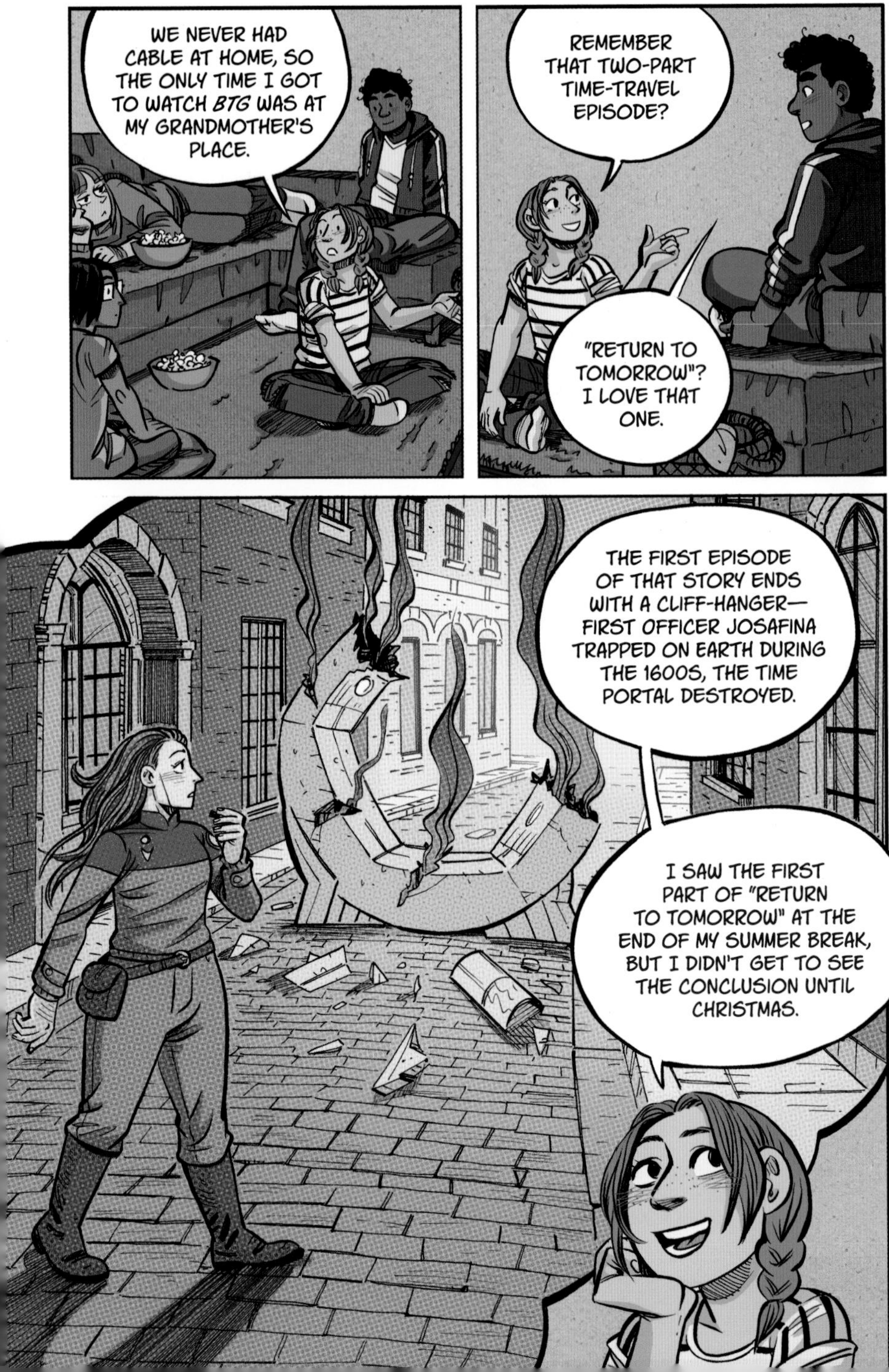
WE NEVER HAD CABLE AT HOME, SO THE ONLY TIME I GOT TO WATCH *BTG* WAS AT MY GRANDMOTHER'S PLACE.
REMEMBER THAT TWO-PART TIME-TRAVEL EPISODE?
"RETURN TO TOMORROW"? I LOVE THAT ONE.
THE FIRST EPISODE OF THAT STORY ENDS WITH A CLIFF-HANGER— FIRST OFFICER JOSAFINA TRAPPED ON EARTH DURING THE 1600S, THE TIME PORTAL DESTROYED.
I SAW THE FIRST PART OF "RETURN TO TOMORROW" AT THE END OF MY SUMMER BREAK, BUT I DIDN'T GET TO SEE THE CONCLUSION UNTIL CHRISTMAS.

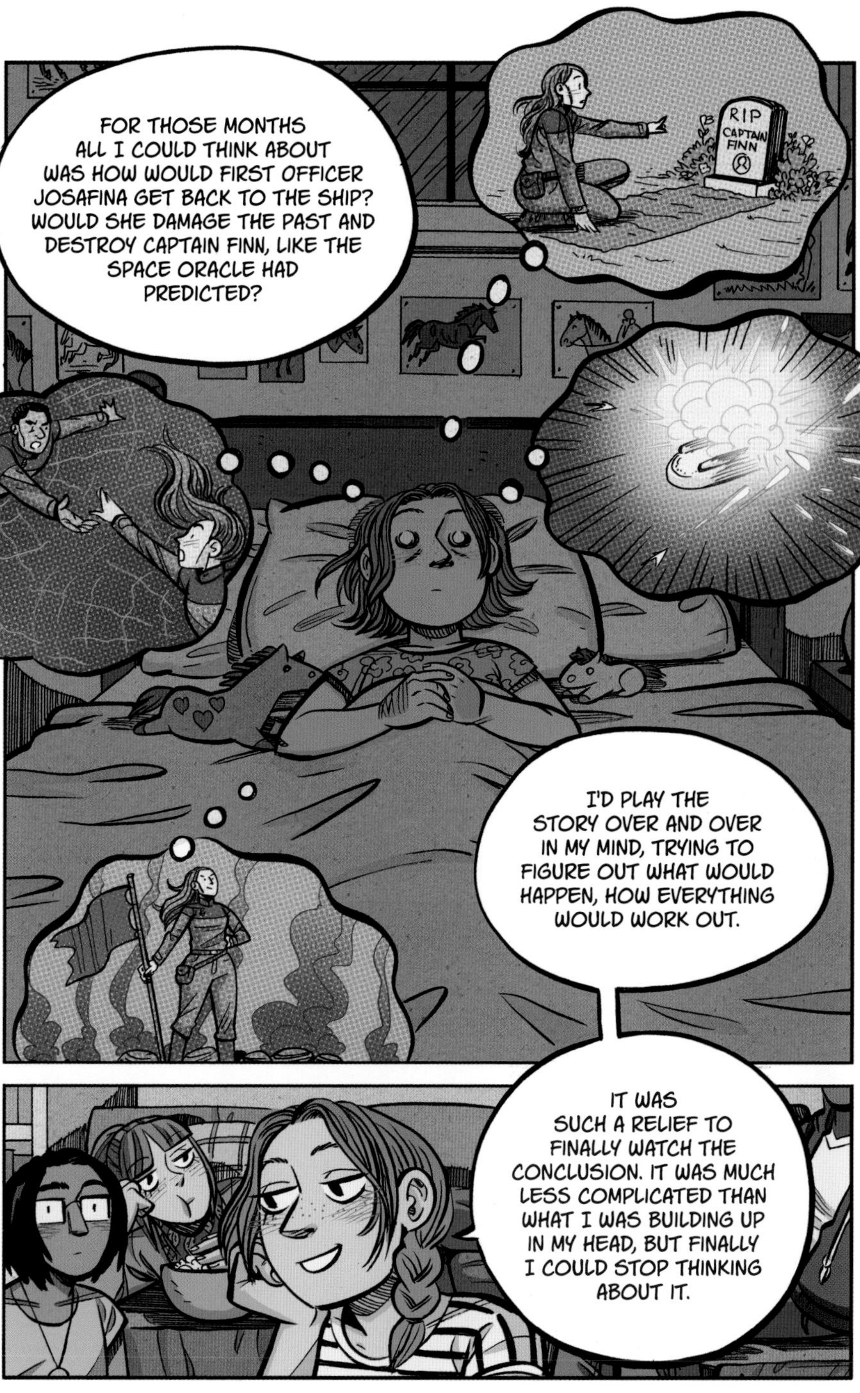

FOR THOSE MONTHS ALL I COULD THINK ABOUT WAS HOW WOULD FIRST OFFICER JOSAFINA GET BACK TO THE SHIP? WOULD SHE DAMAGE THE PAST AND DESTROY CAPTAIN FINN, LIKE THE SPACE ORACLE HAD PREDICTED?
RIP CAPTAIN FINN
I'D PLAY THE STORY OVER AND OVER IN MY MIND, TRYING TO FIGURE OUT WHAT WOULD HAPPEN, HOW EVERYTHING WOULD WORK OUT.
IT WAS SUCH A RELIEF TO FINALLY WATCH THE CONCLUSION. IT WAS MUCH LESS COMPLICATED THAN WHAT I WAS BUILDING UP IN MY HEAD, BUT FINALLY I COULD STOP THINKING ABOUT IT.

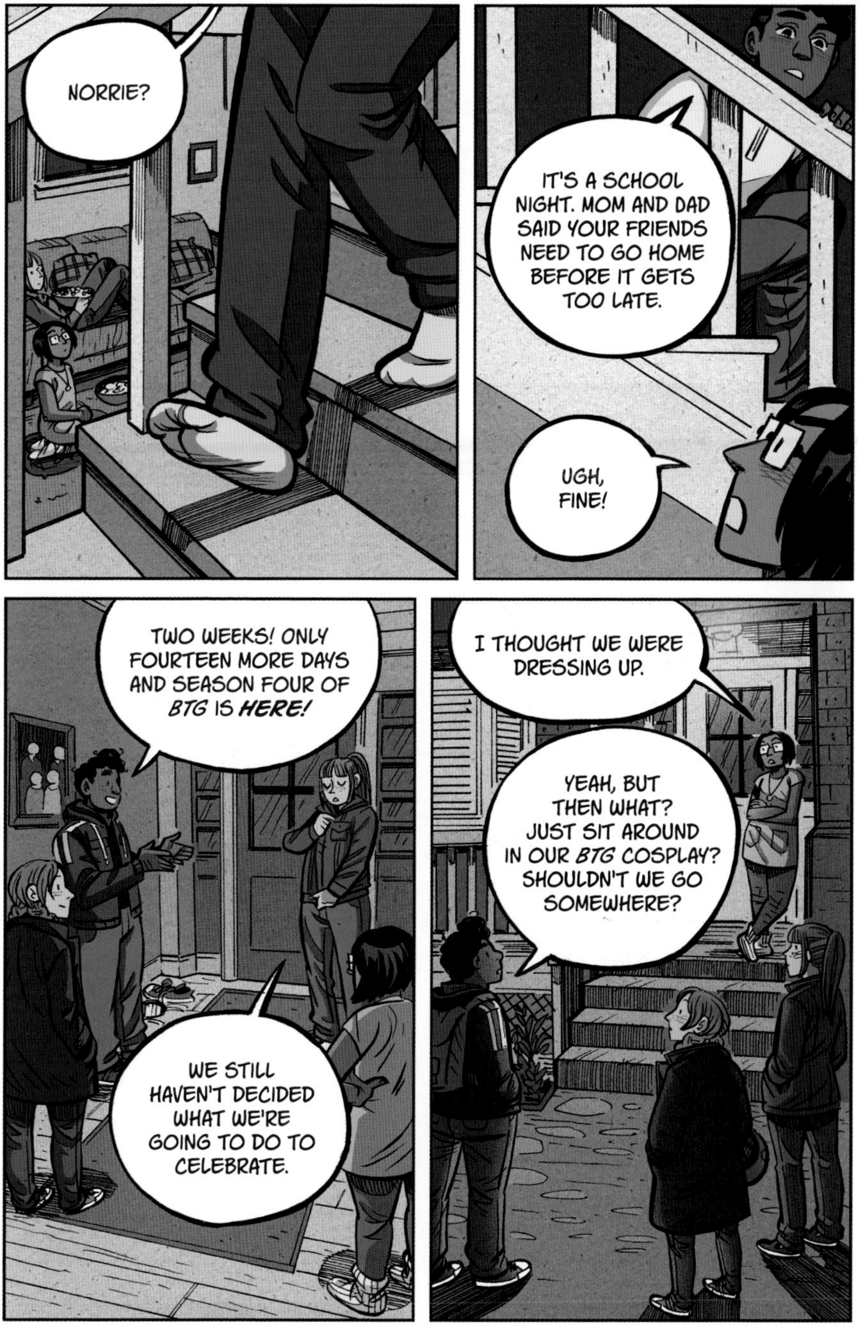
NORRIE?
IT'S A SCHOOL NIGHT. MOM AND DAD SAID YOUR FRIENDS NEED TO GO HOME BEFORE IT GETS TOO LATE.
UGH, FINE!
TWO WEEKS! ONLY FOURTEEN MORE DAYS AND SEASON FOUR OF *BTG* IS ***HERE!***
WE STILL HAVEN'T DECIDED WHAT WE'RE GOING TO DO TO CELEBRATE.
I THOUGHT WE WERE DRESSING UP.
YEAH, BUT THEN WHAT? JUST SIT AROUND IN OUR *BTG* COSPLAY? SHOULDN'T WE GO SOMEWHERE?

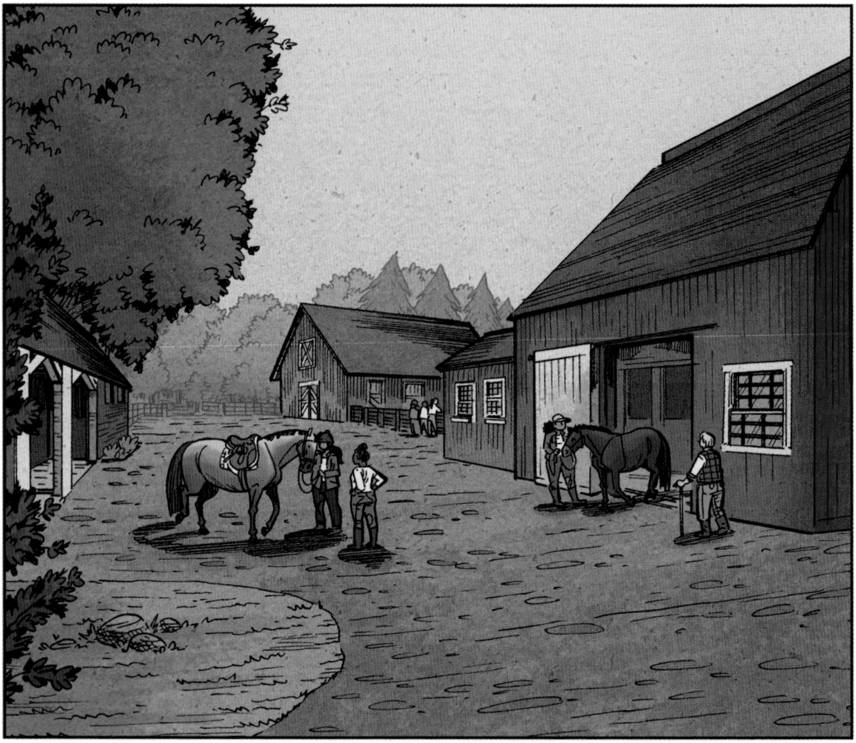

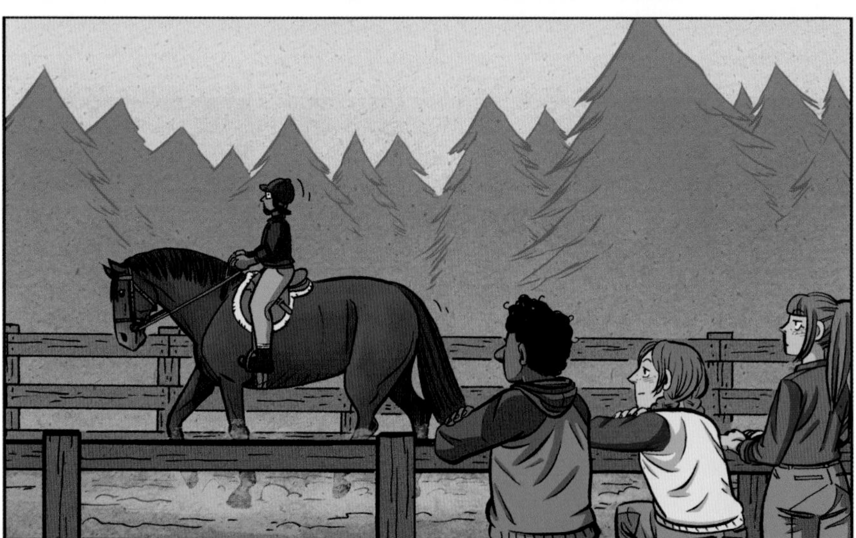

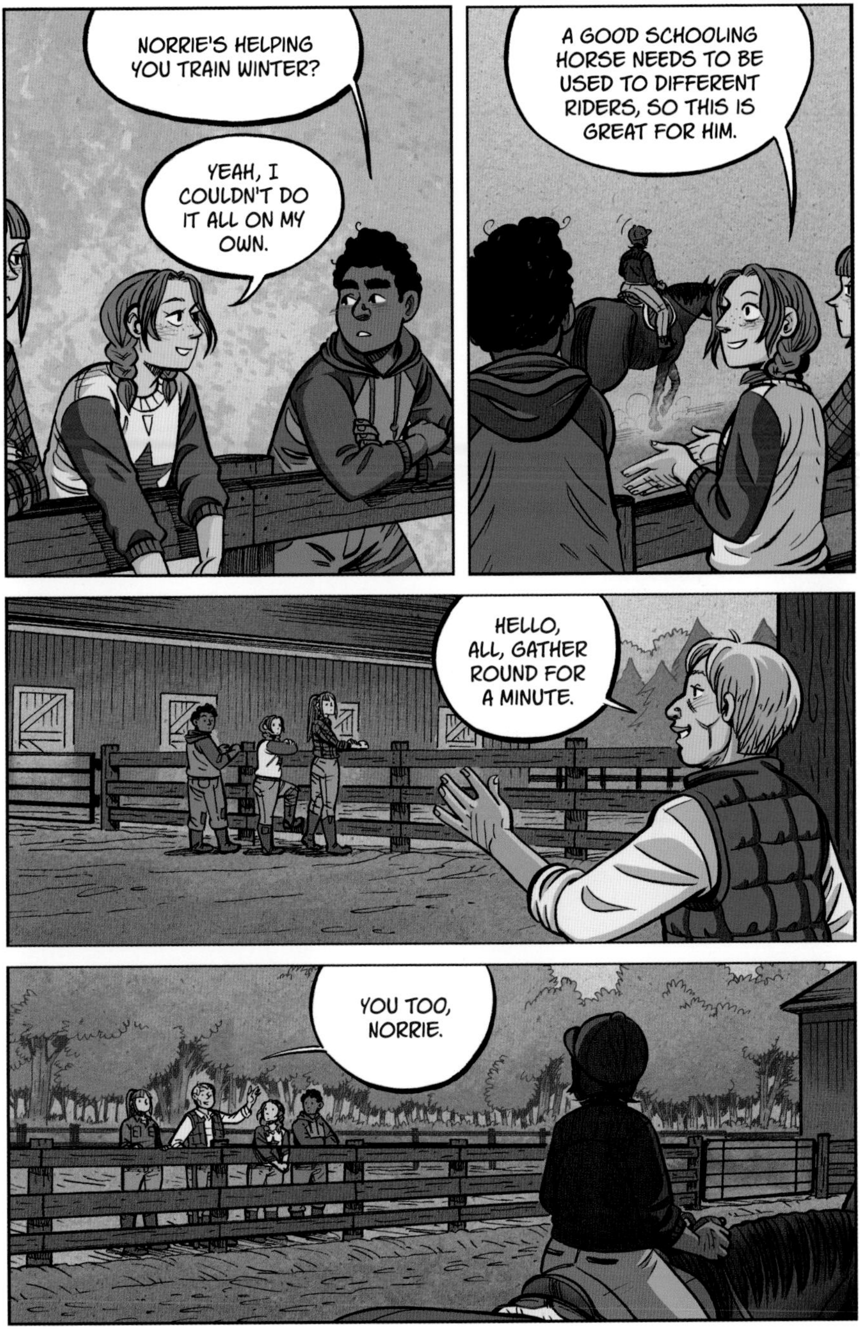
NORRIE'S HELPING YOU TRAIN WINTER?
YEAH, I COULDN'T DO IT ALL ON MY OWN.
A GOOD SCHOOLING HORSE NEEDS TO BE USED TO DIFFERENT RIDERS, SO THIS IS GREAT FOR HIM.
HELLO, ALL, GATHER ROUND FOR A MINUTE.
YOU TOO, NORRIE.

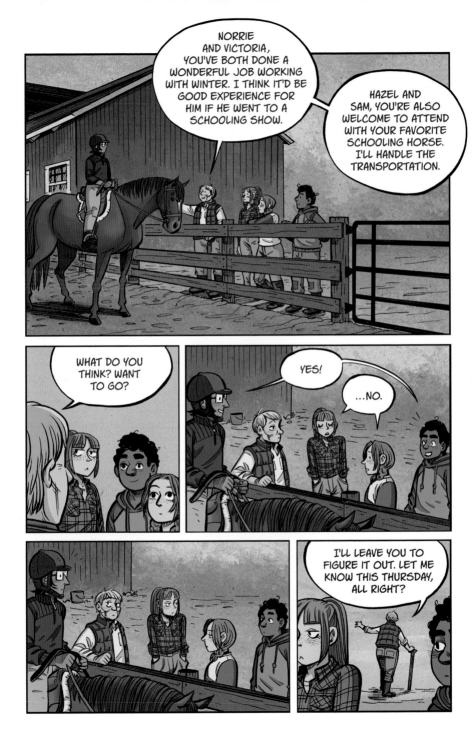

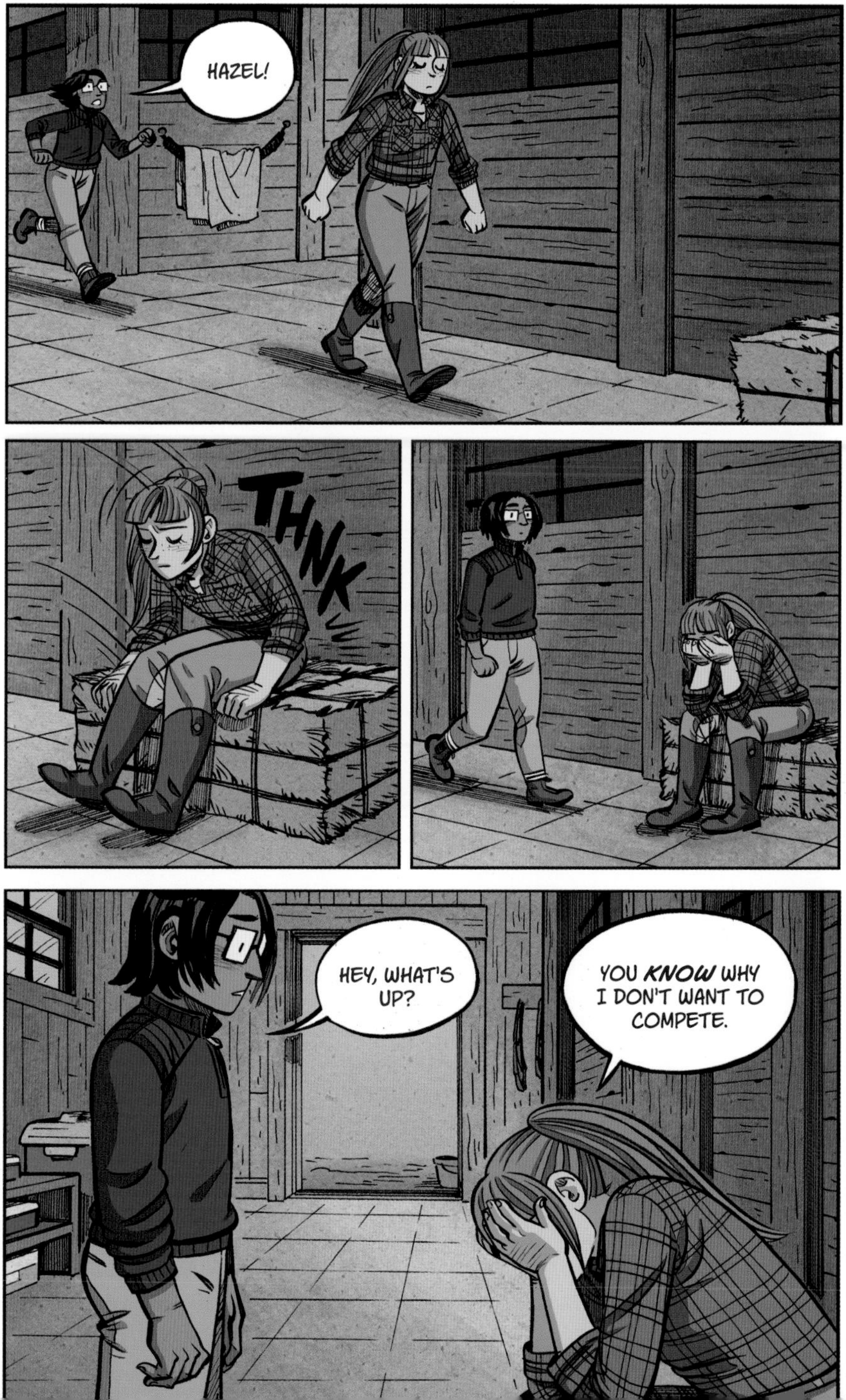
HAZEL!
THNK
HEY, WHAT'S UP?
YOU *KNOW* WHY I DON'T WANT TO COMPETE.

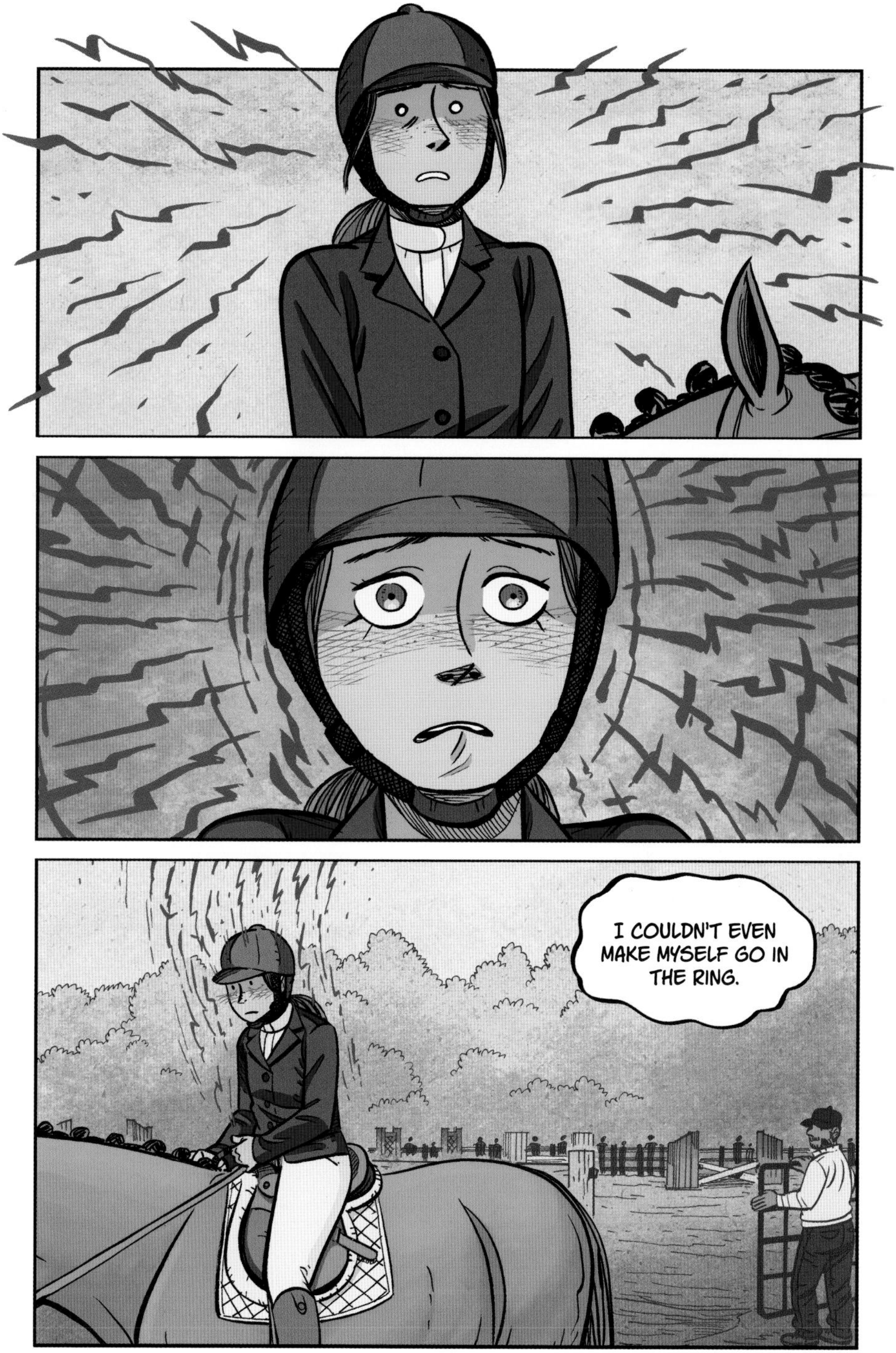
I COULDN'T EVEN MAKE MYSELF GO IN THE RING.

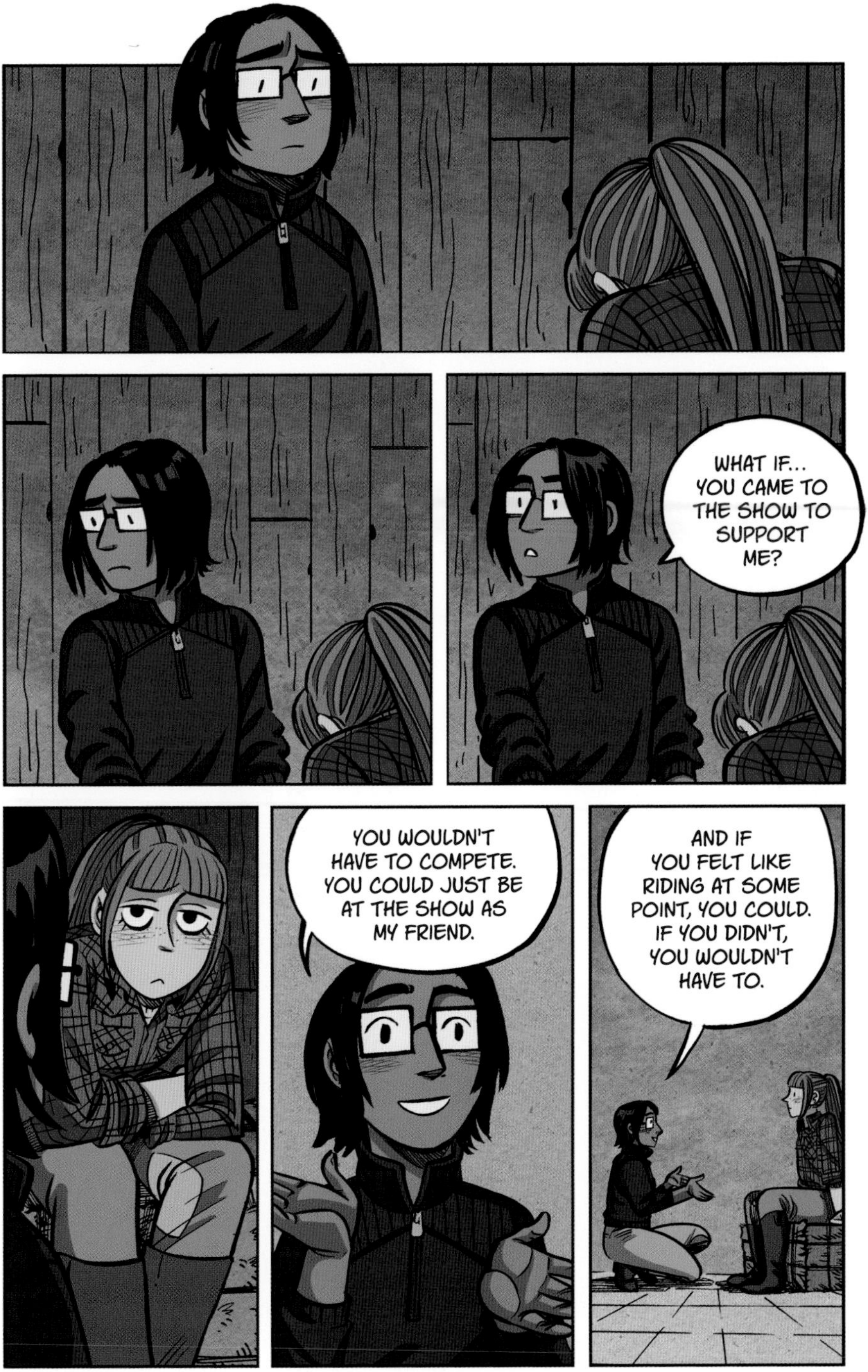
WHAT IF... YOU CAME TO THE SHOW TO SUPPORT ME?
YOU WOULDN'T HAVE TO COMPETE. YOU COULD JUST BE AT THE SHOW AS MY FRIEND.
AND IF YOU FELT LIKE RIDING AT SOME POINT, YOU COULD. IF YOU DIDN'T, YOU WOULDN'T HAVE TO.

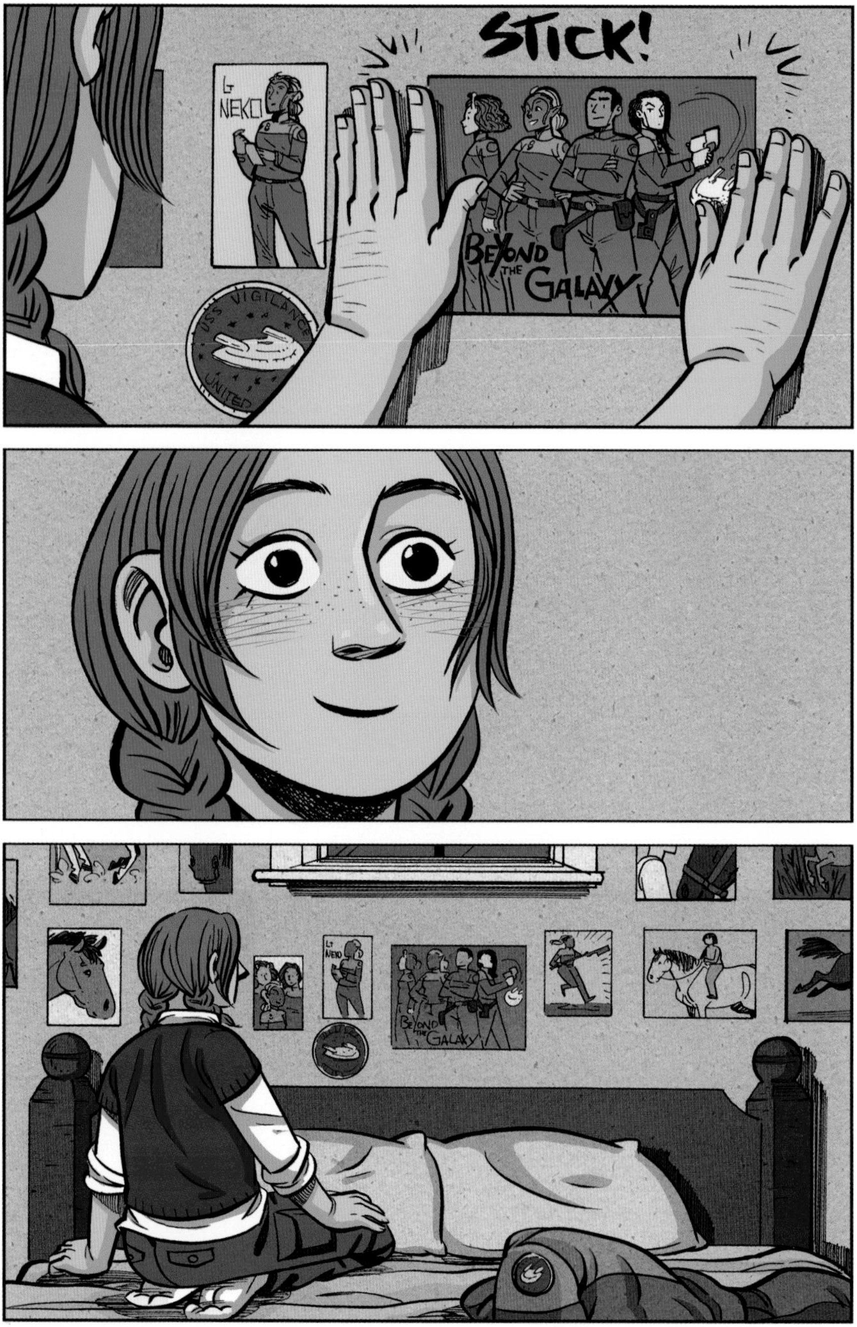
STICK!
LT NEKO
BEYOND THE GALAXY
USS VIGILANCE
UNITED
LT NEKO
BEYOND THE GALAXY

VIC! YOUR FRIENDS ARE HERE!

THE ONLY REASON I GOT TO GO OUT ON A SCHOOL NIGHT IS BECAUSE I TOLD MY PARENTS WE WERE ALL STUDYING TOGETHER.

LITTLE DO THEY KNOW! MUAHAHA!

I STUDIED! I GOT ALL THE GOOD LOUIS RIEL FACTS LOCKED INSIDE MY BRAIN.

OKAY, JUST CHECKING.

BUT YOU DID STUDY FOR THAT TEST WE HAVE TOMORROW, RIGHT?

HERE'S WHAT I'VE BEEN WORKING ON.

153

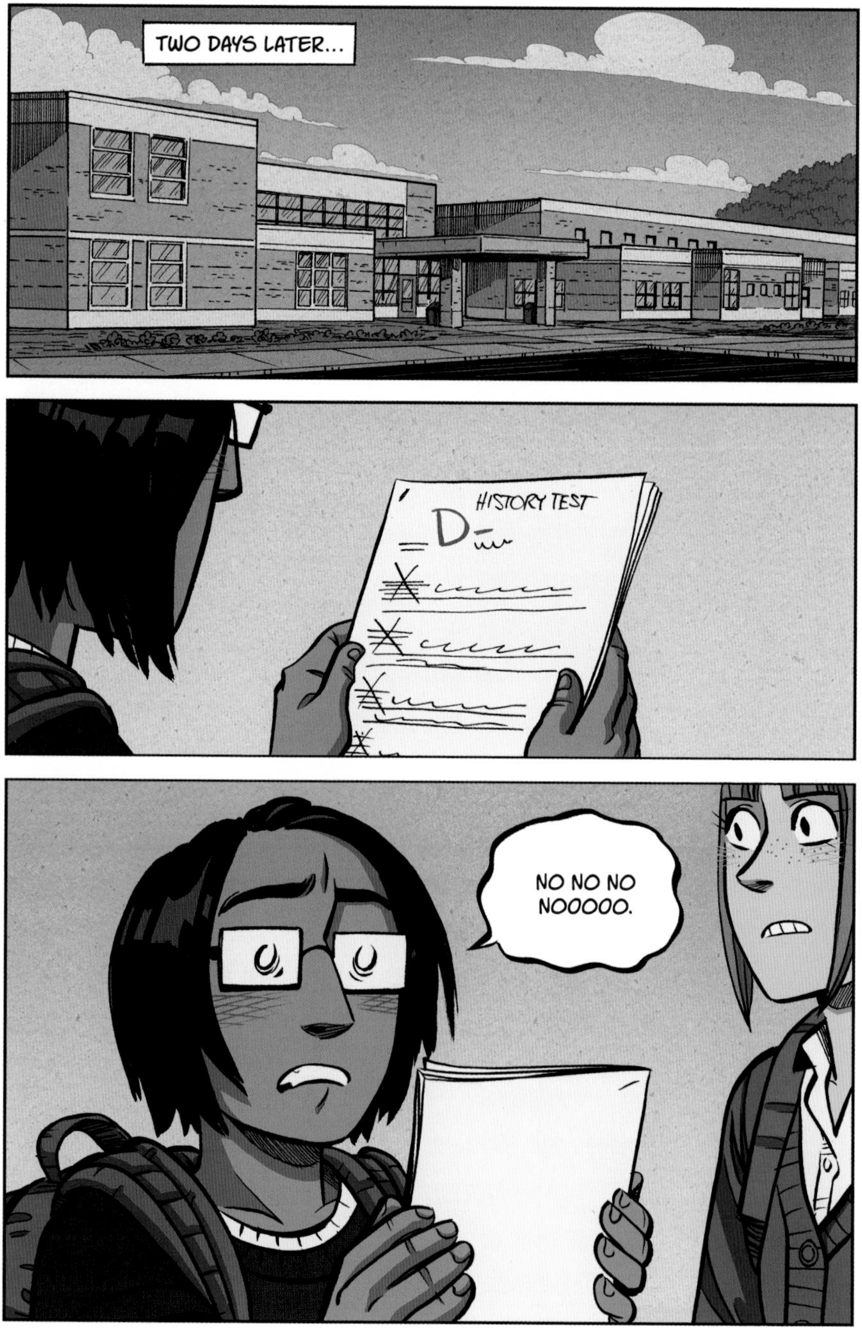
TWO DAYS LATER...
HISTORY TEST
D-
NO NO NO
NOOOOO.

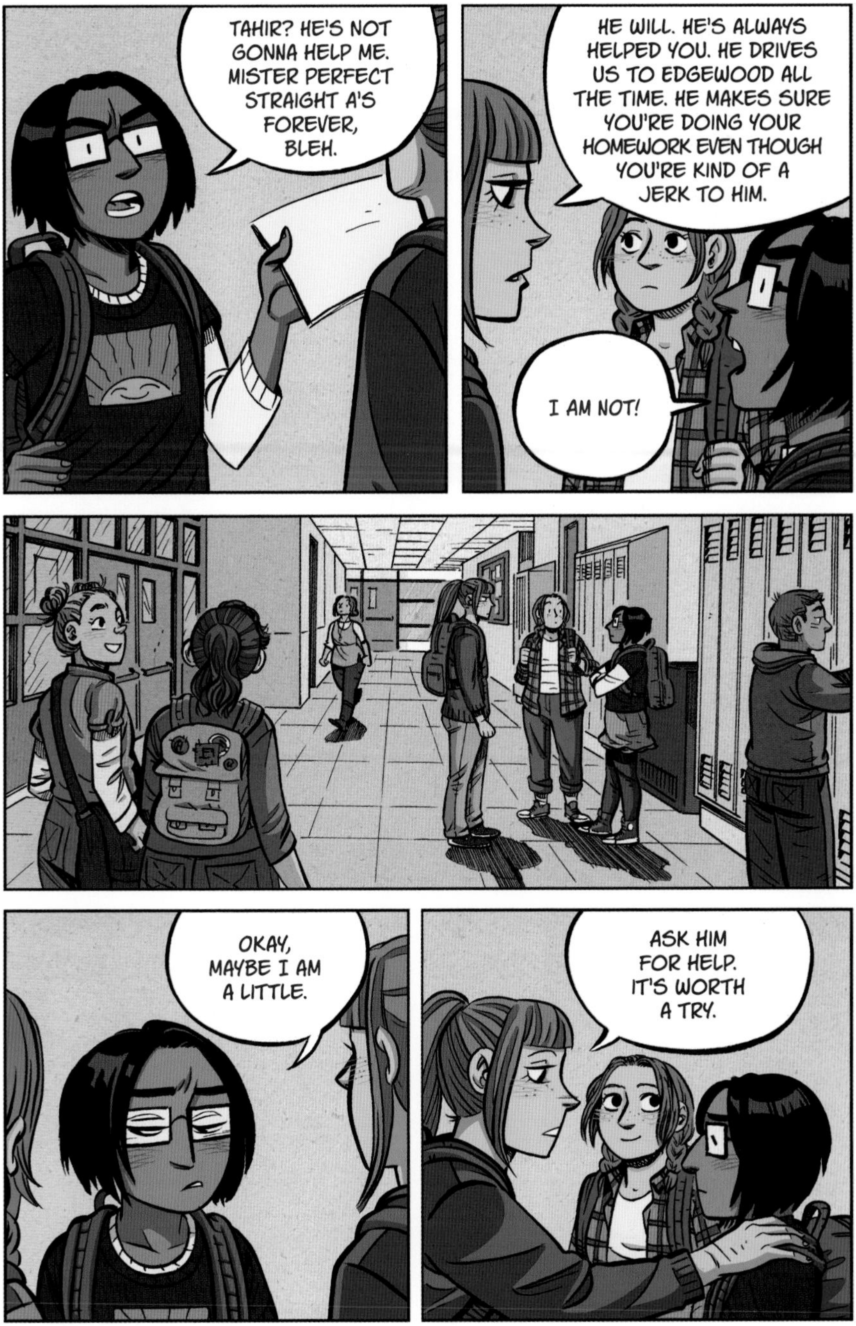

TAHIR? HE'S NOT GONNA HELP ME. MISTER PERFECT STRAIGHT A'S FOREVER, BLEH.
HE WILL. HE'S ALWAYS HELPED YOU. HE DRIVES US TO EDGEWOOD ALL THE TIME. HE MAKES SURE YOU'RE DOING YOUR HOMEWORK EVEN THOUGH YOU'RE KIND OF A JERK TO HIM.
I AM NOT!
OKAY, MAYBE I AM A LITTLE.
ASK HIM FOR HELP. IT'S WORTH A TRY.

SIIIGHH

TAHIR'S ROOM

TAHIR?

YEAH?

UM, MIND IF I TALK TO YOU ABOUT SOMETHING?

SURE.

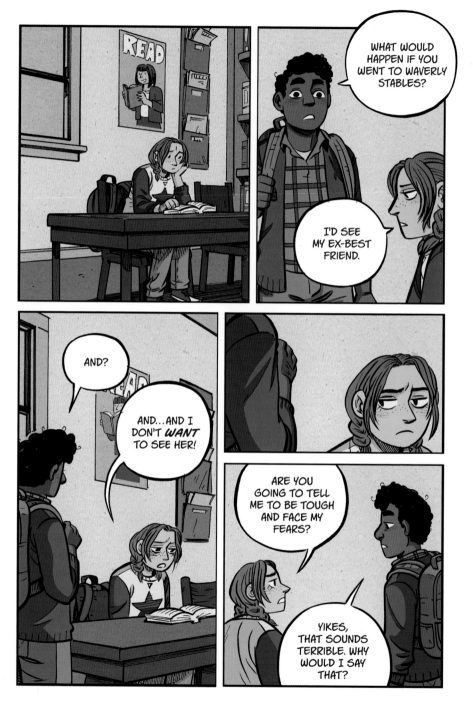

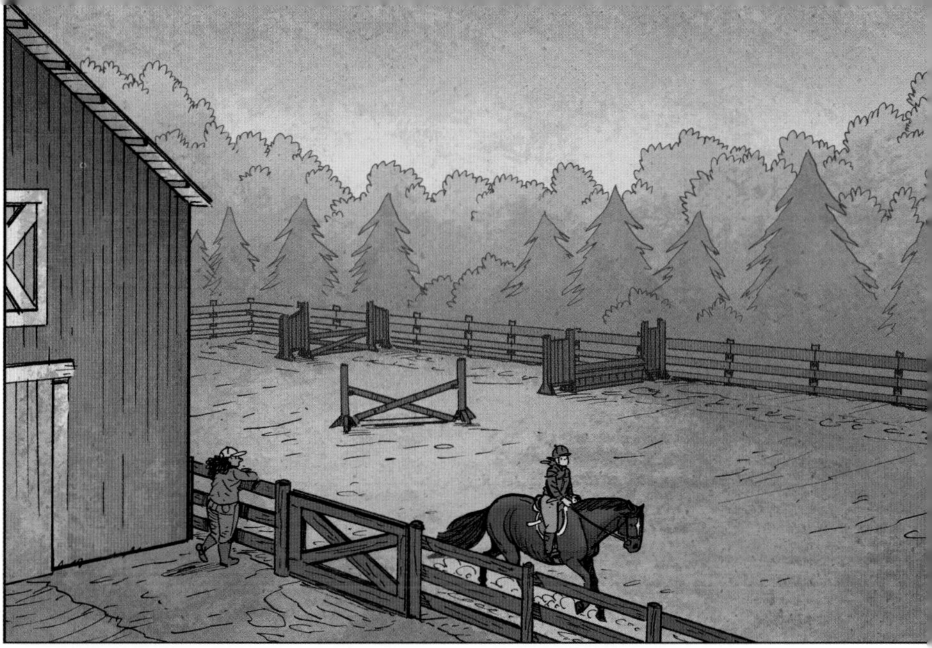

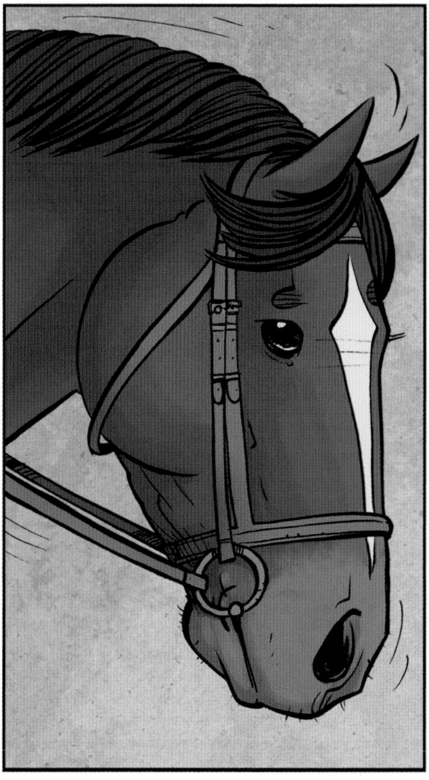

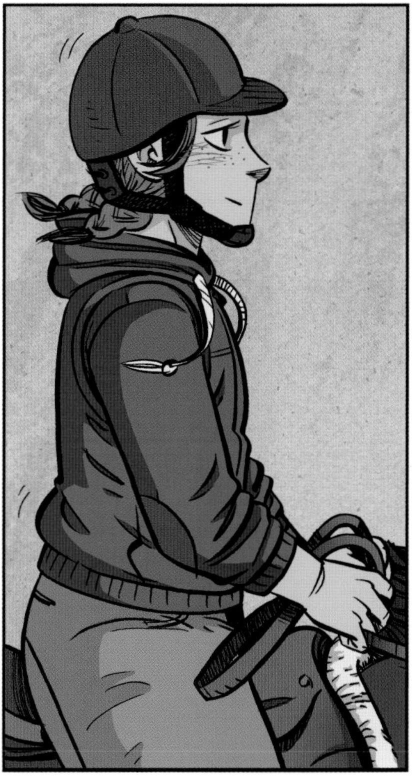

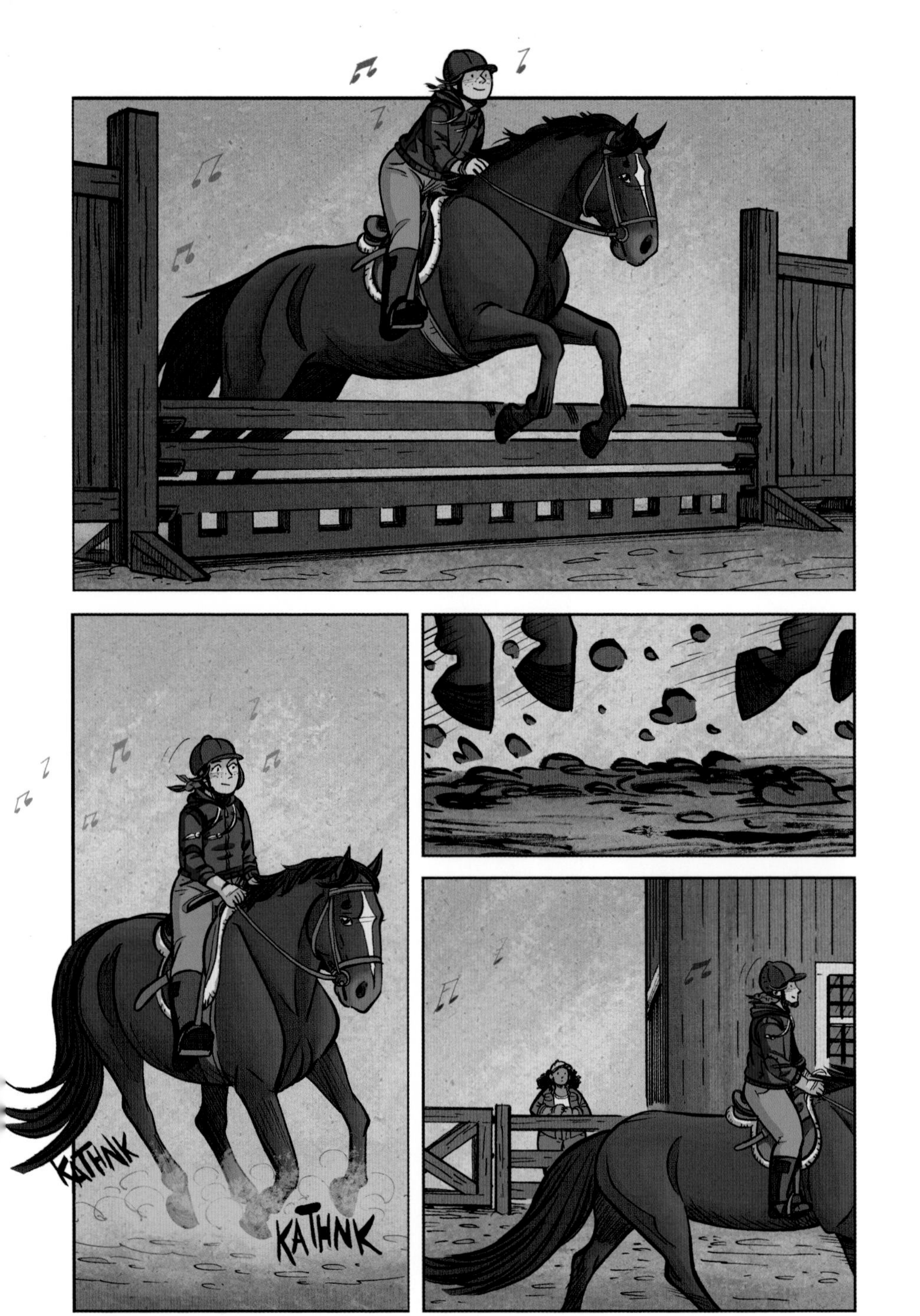
KATHNK
KATHNK

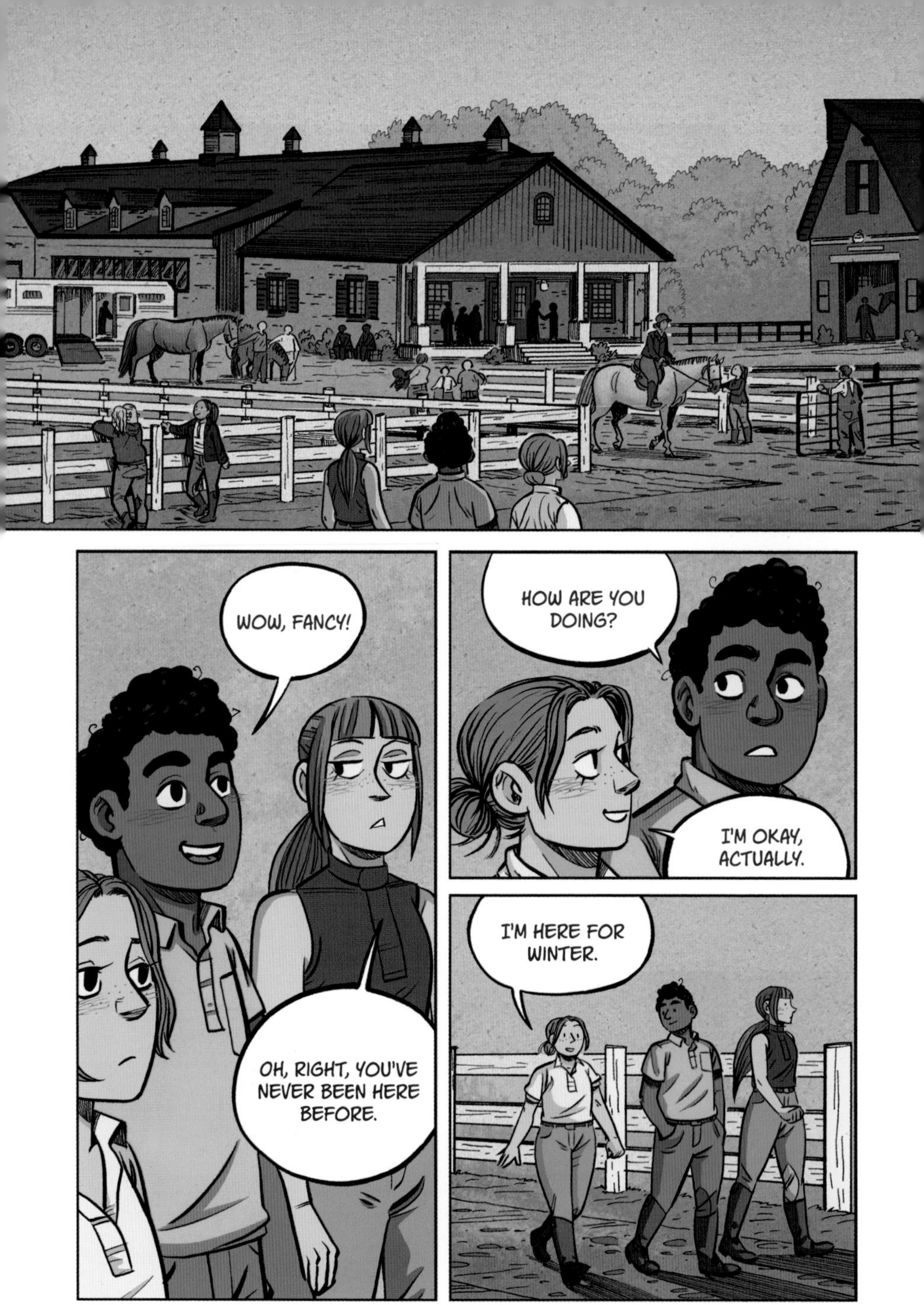
WOW, FANCY!
OH, RIGHT, YOU'VE NEVER BEEN HERE BEFORE.
HOW ARE YOU DOING?
I'M OKAY, ACTUALLY.
I'M HERE FOR WINTER.

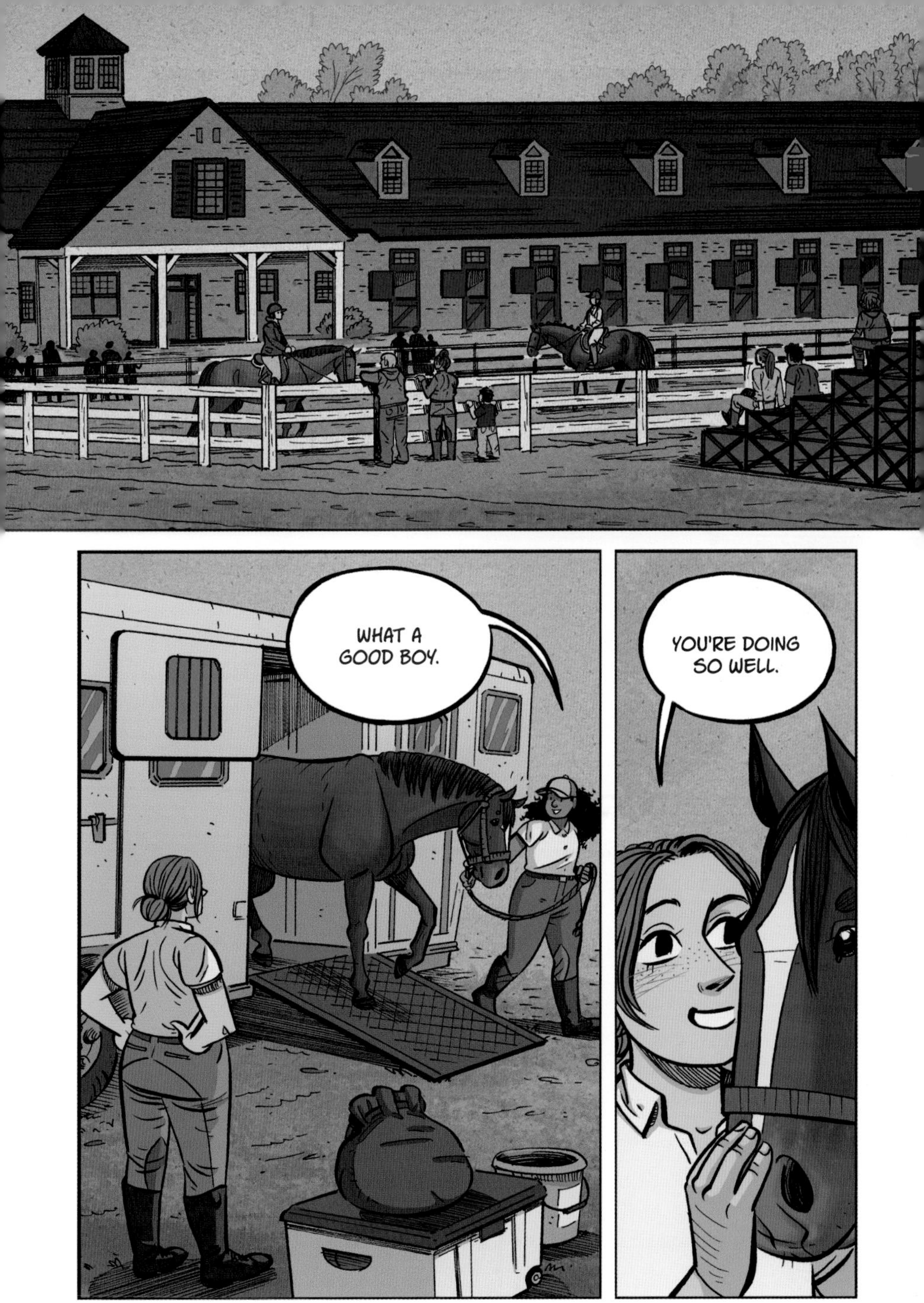
WHAT A GOOD BOY.
YOU'RE DOING SO WELL.

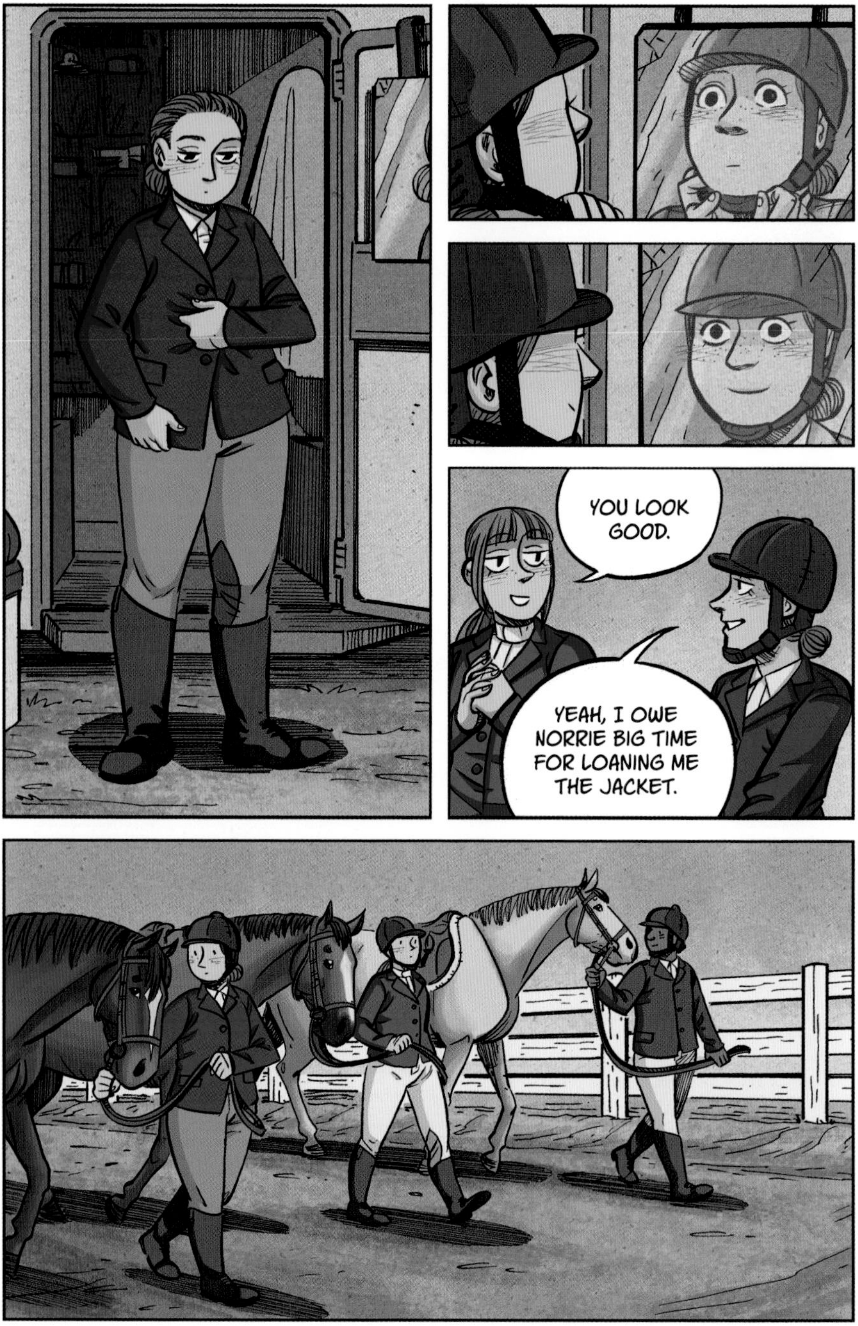
YOU LOOK GOOD.
YEAH, I OWE NORRIE BIG TIME FOR LOANING ME THE JACKET.

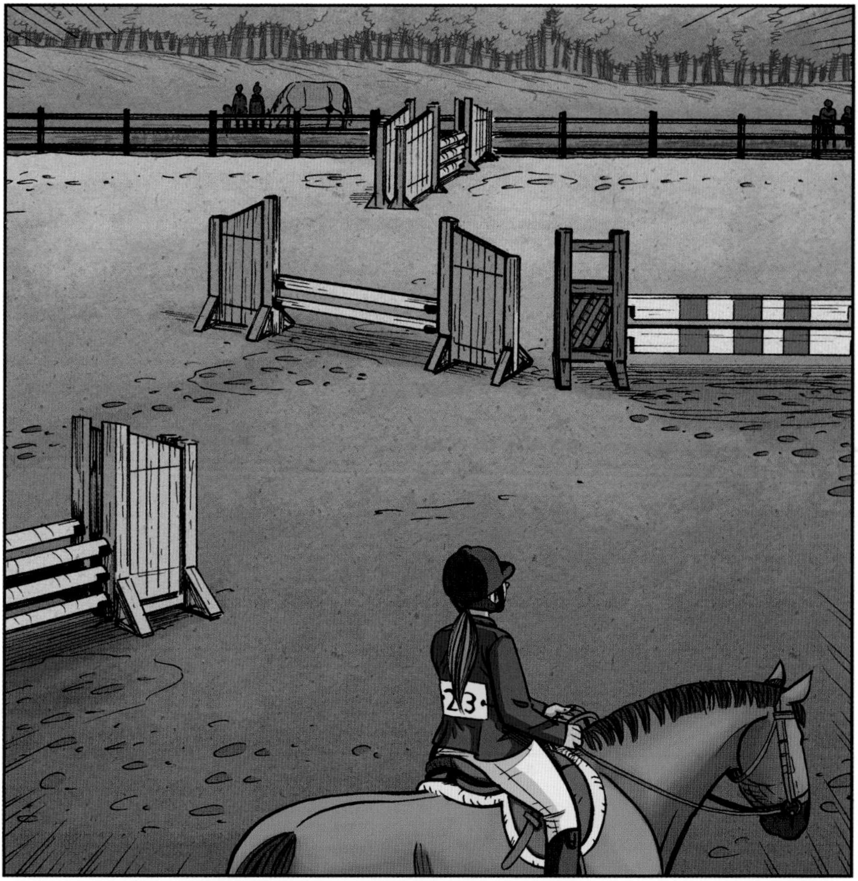
23

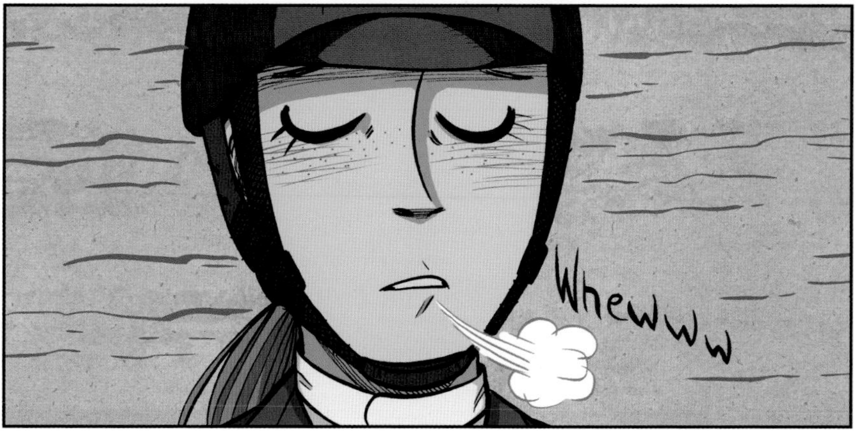
Whewww

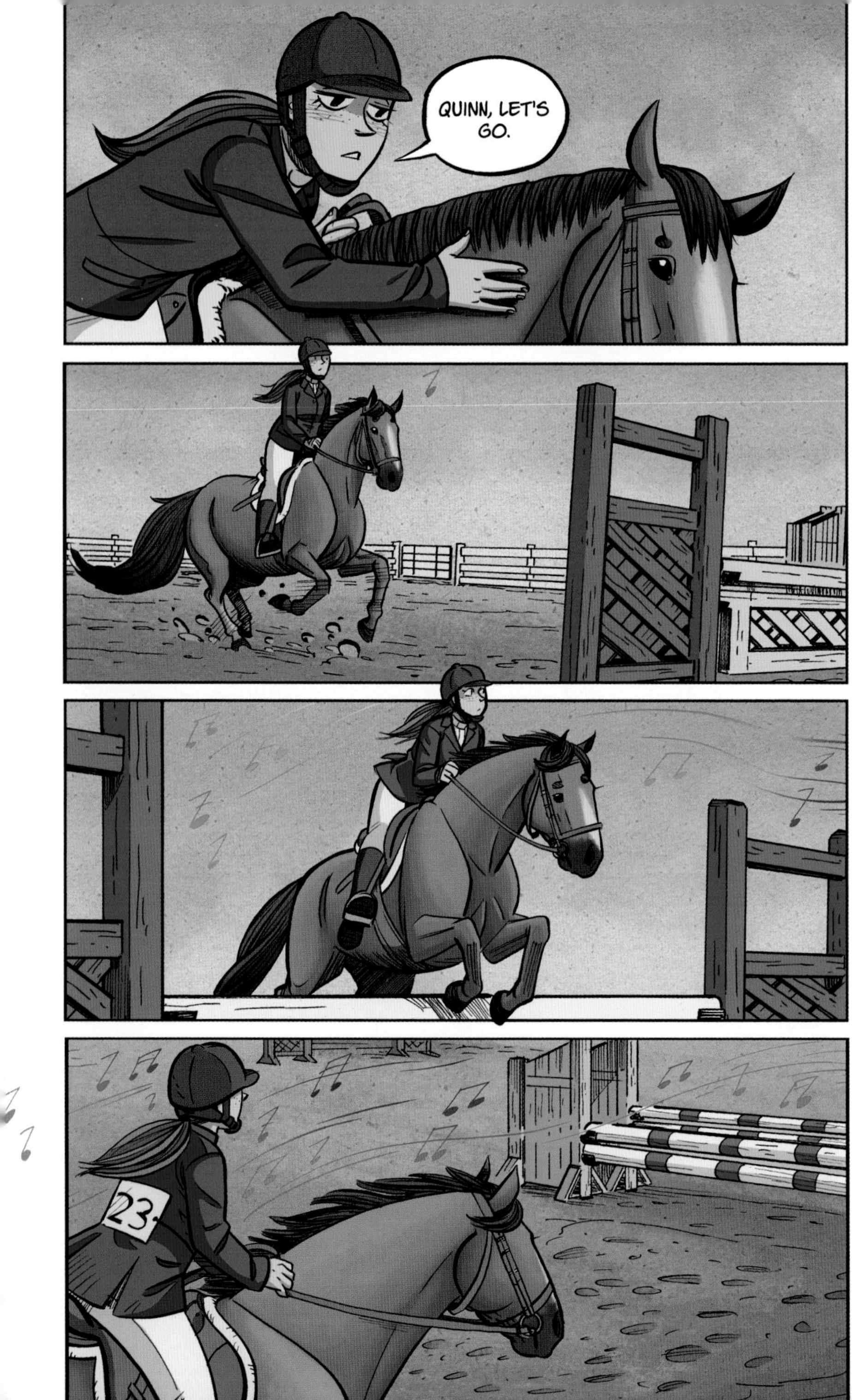
QUINN, LET'S GO.
23

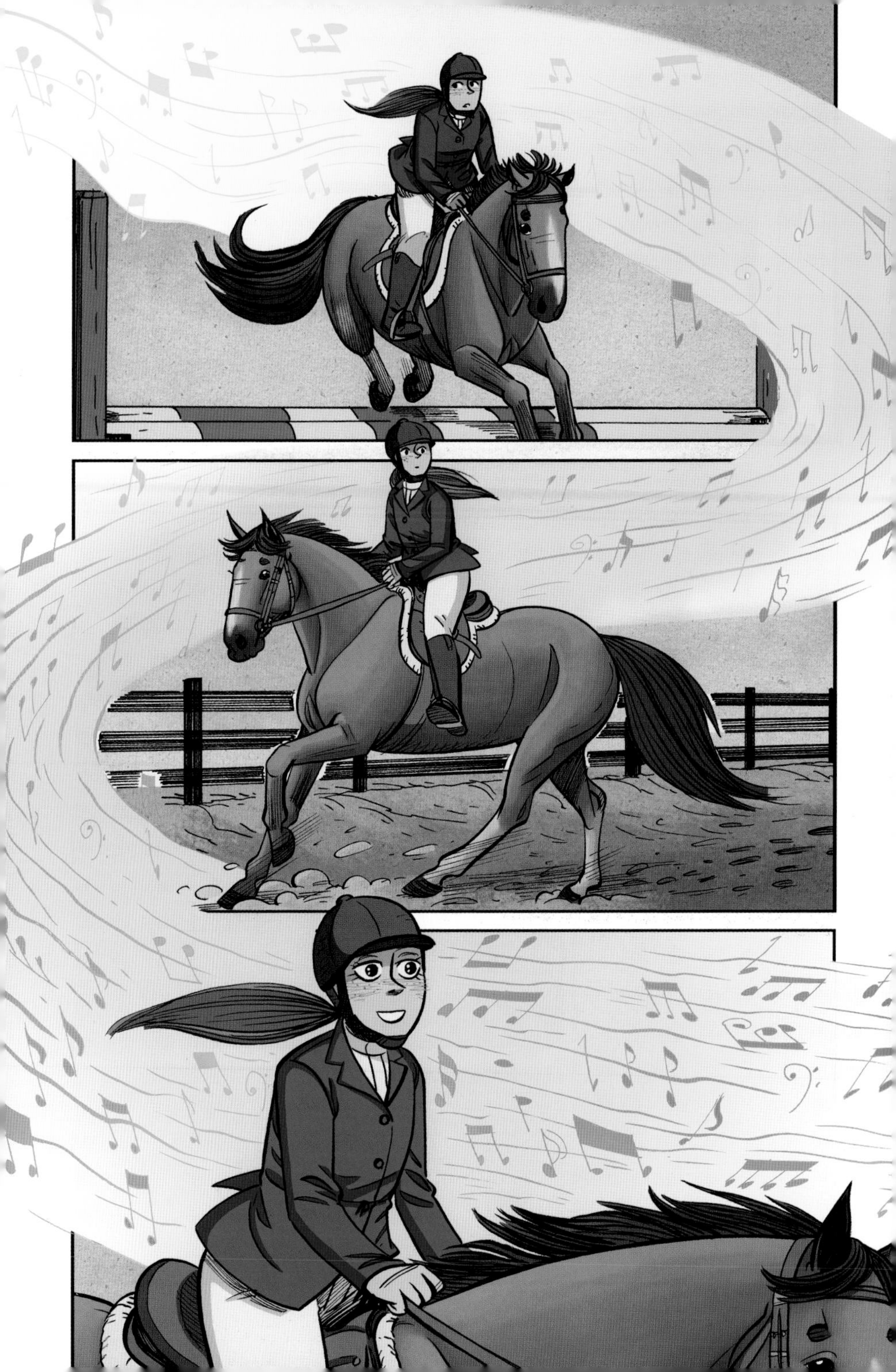

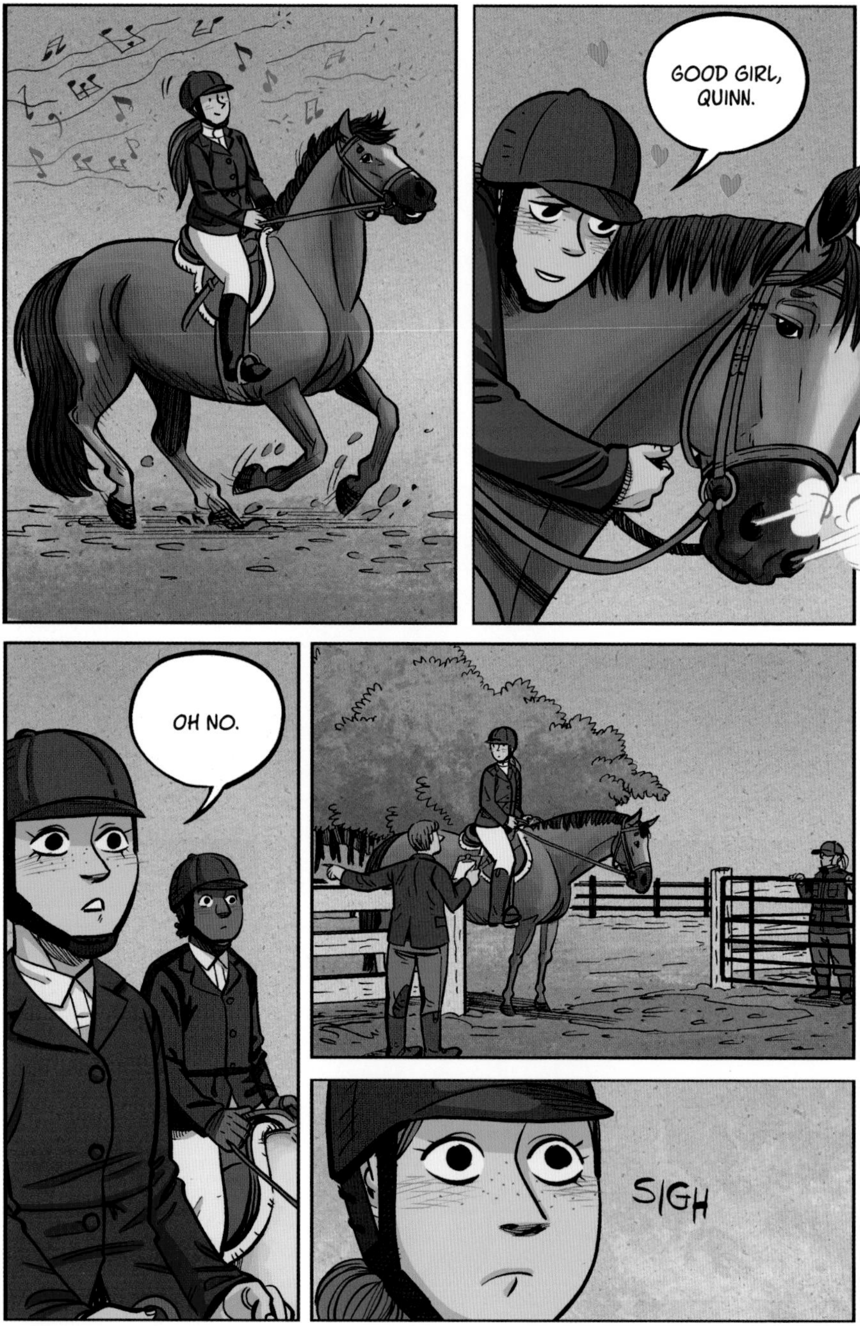
GOOD GIRL,
QUINN.
OH NO.
SIGH

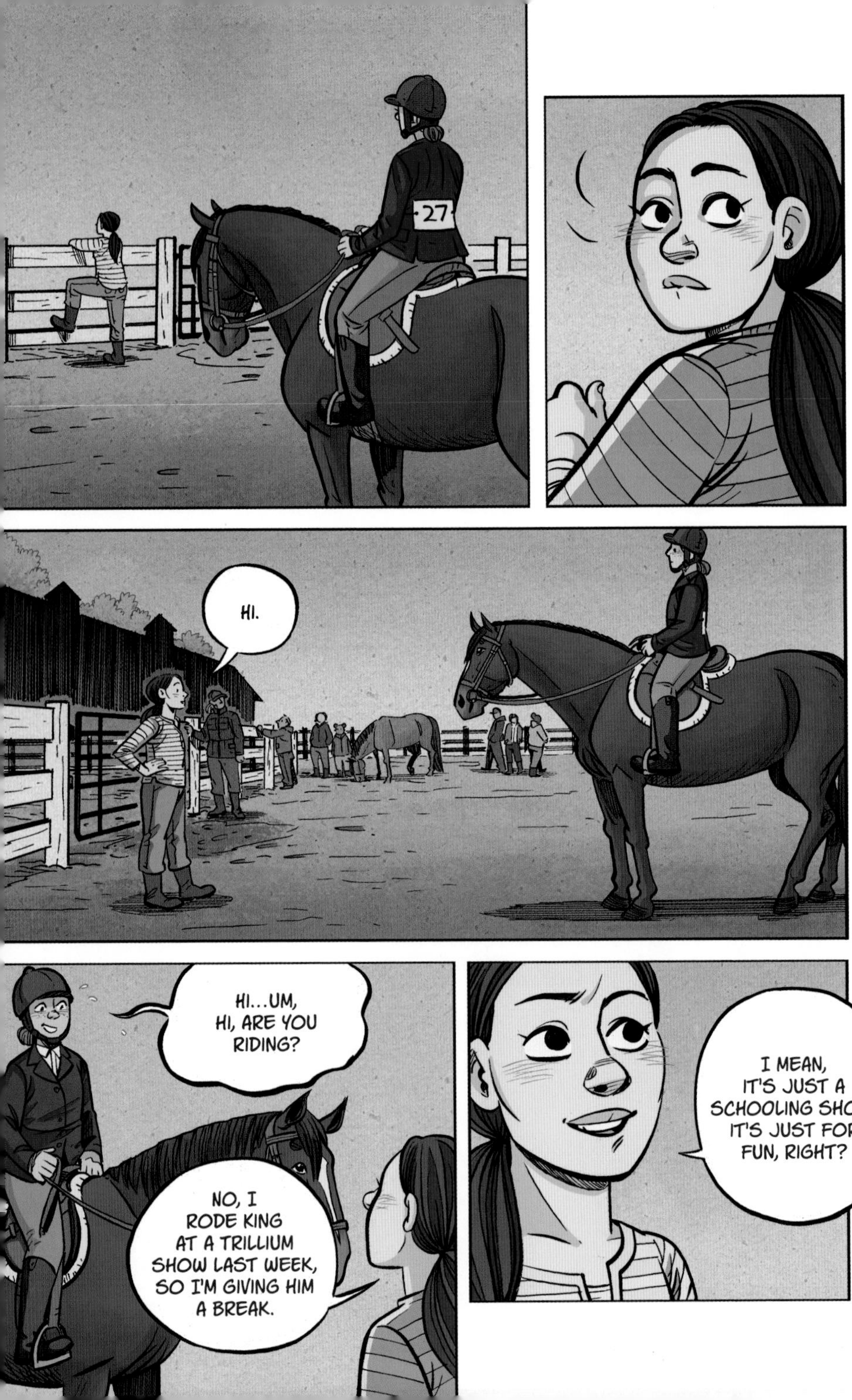
27
HI.
HI...UM, HI, ARE YOU RIDING?
NO, I RODE KING AT A TRILLIUM SHOW LAST WEEK, SO I'M GIVING HIM A BREAK.
I MEAN, IT'S JUST A SCHOOLING SHOW. IT'S JUST FOR FUN, RIGHT?

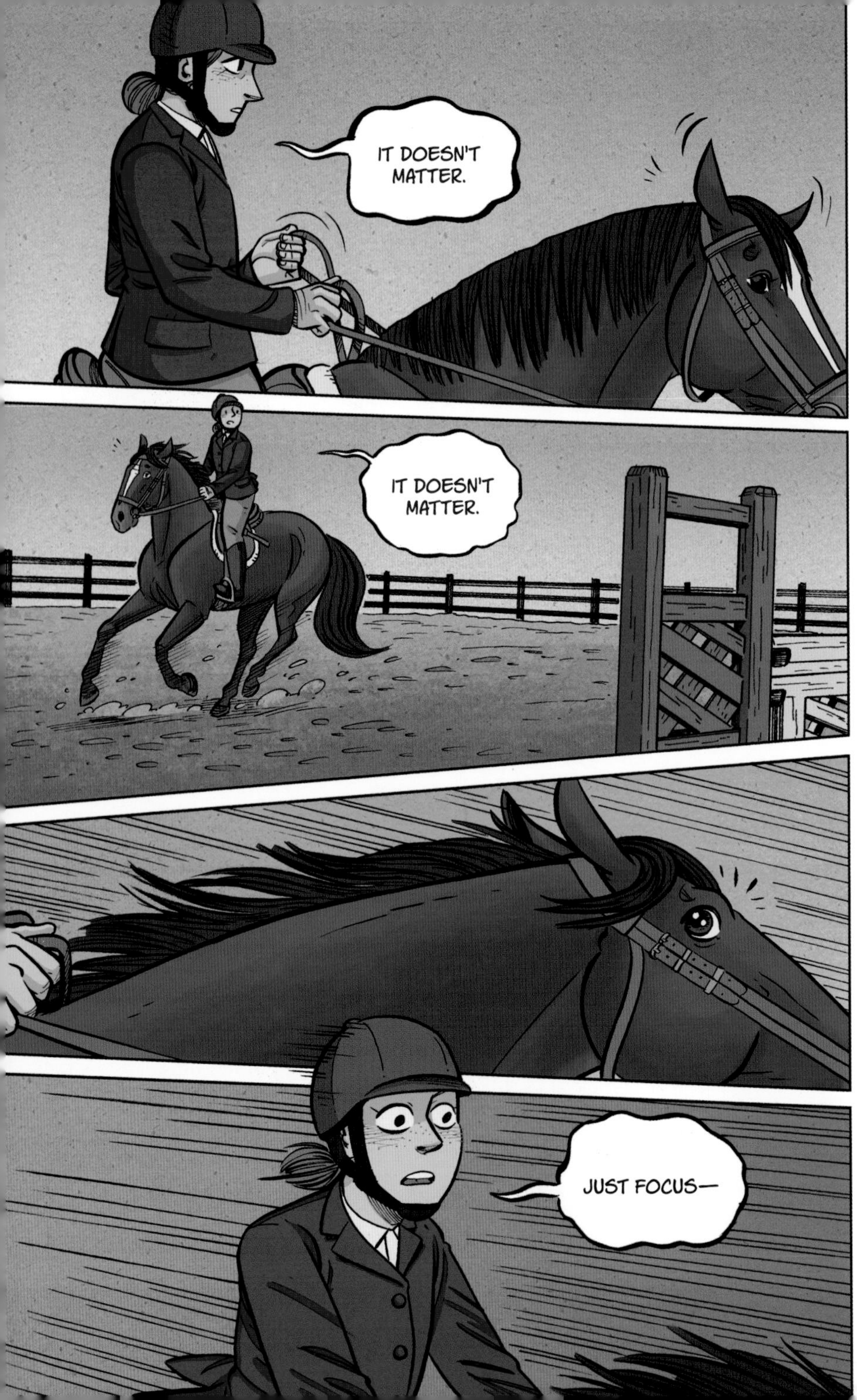
IT DOESN'T MATTER.
IT DOESN'T MATTER.
JUST FOCUS—

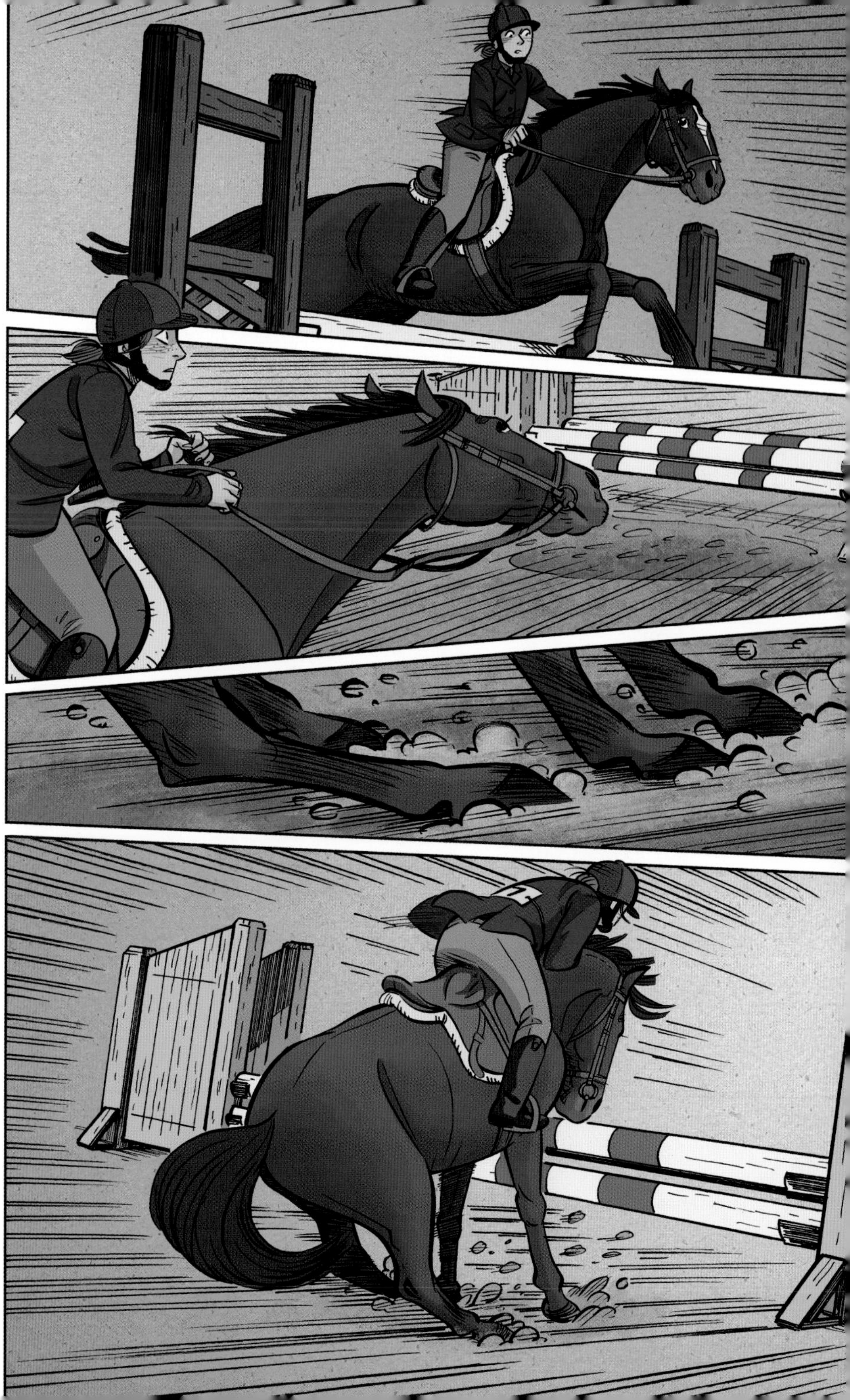

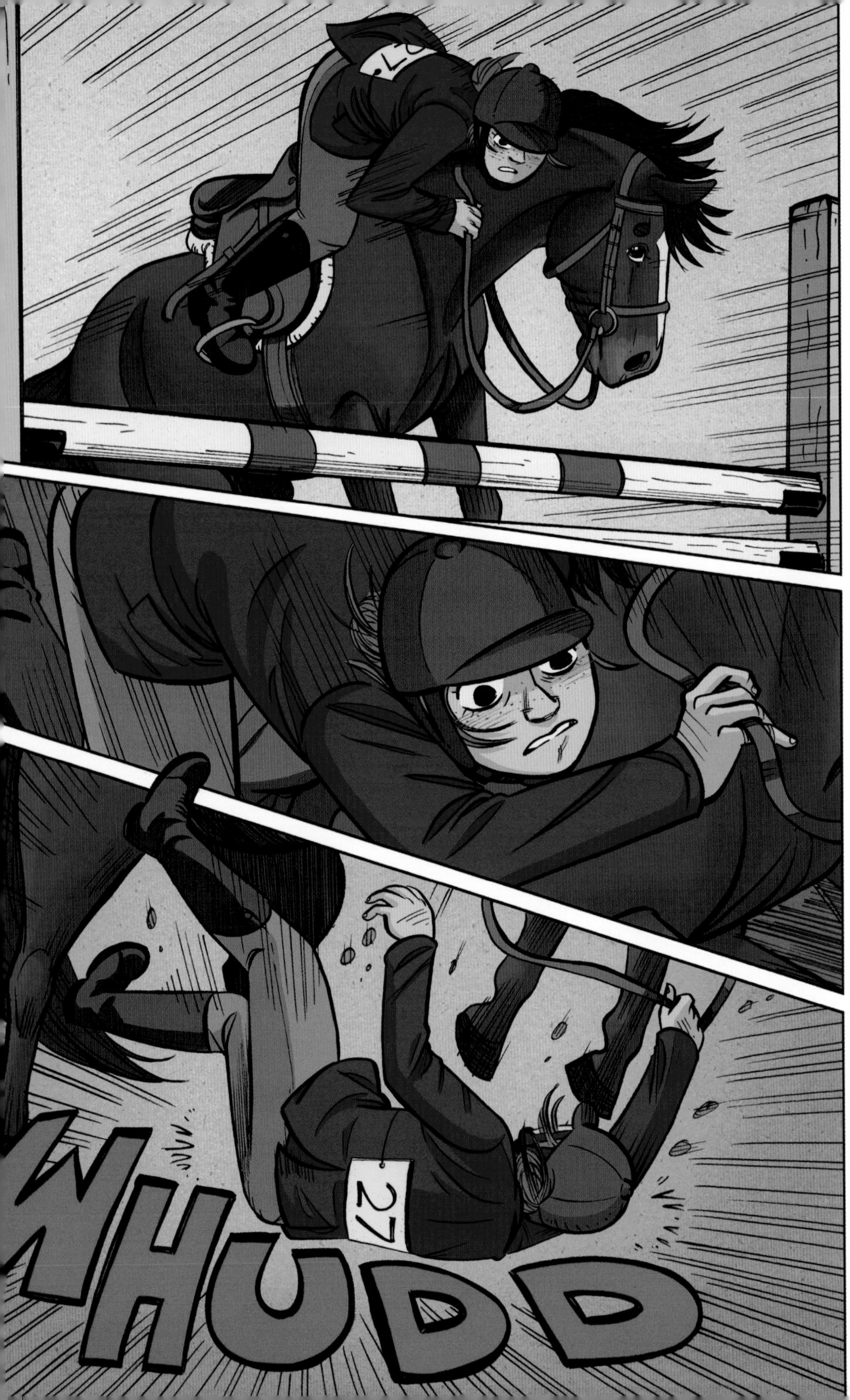
WHUDD

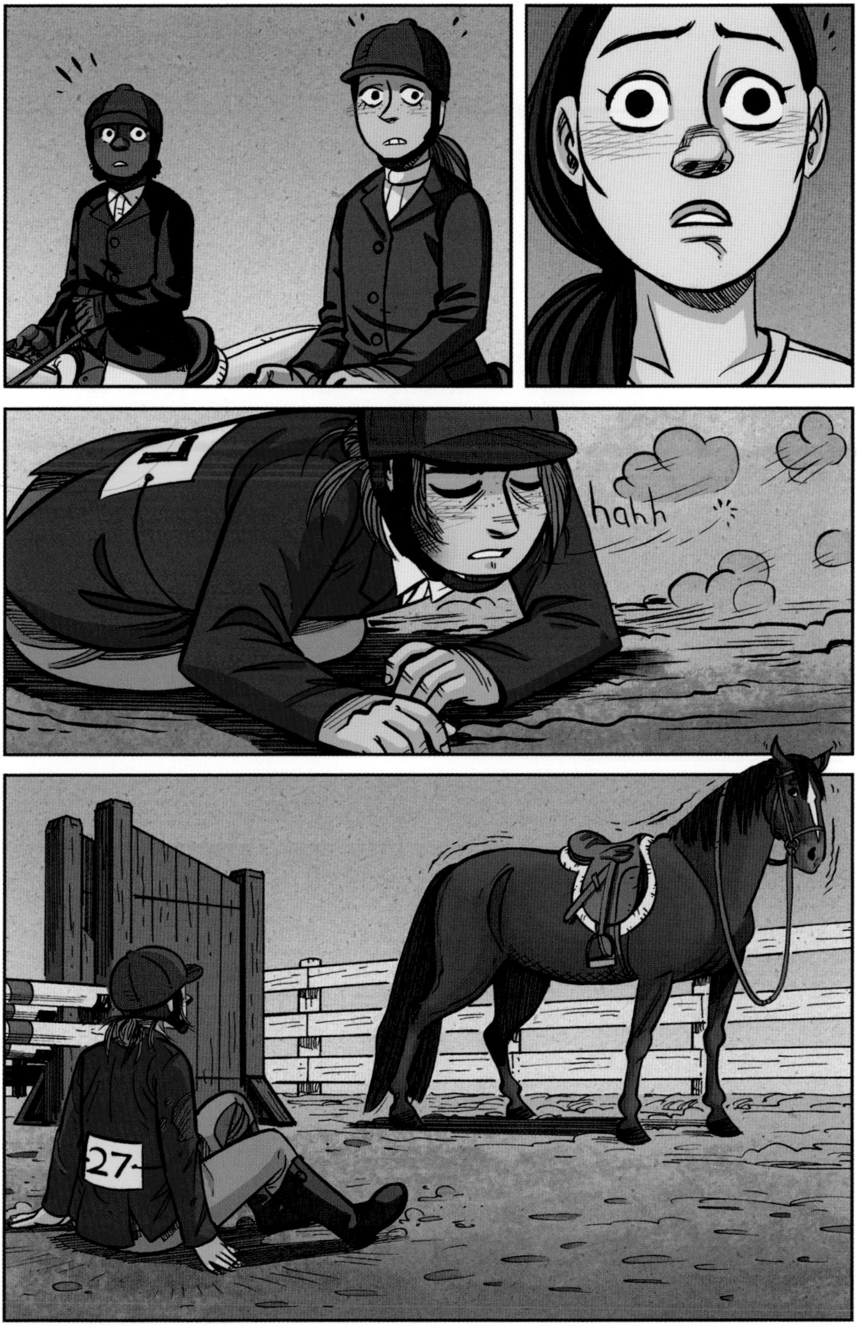
hahh
27

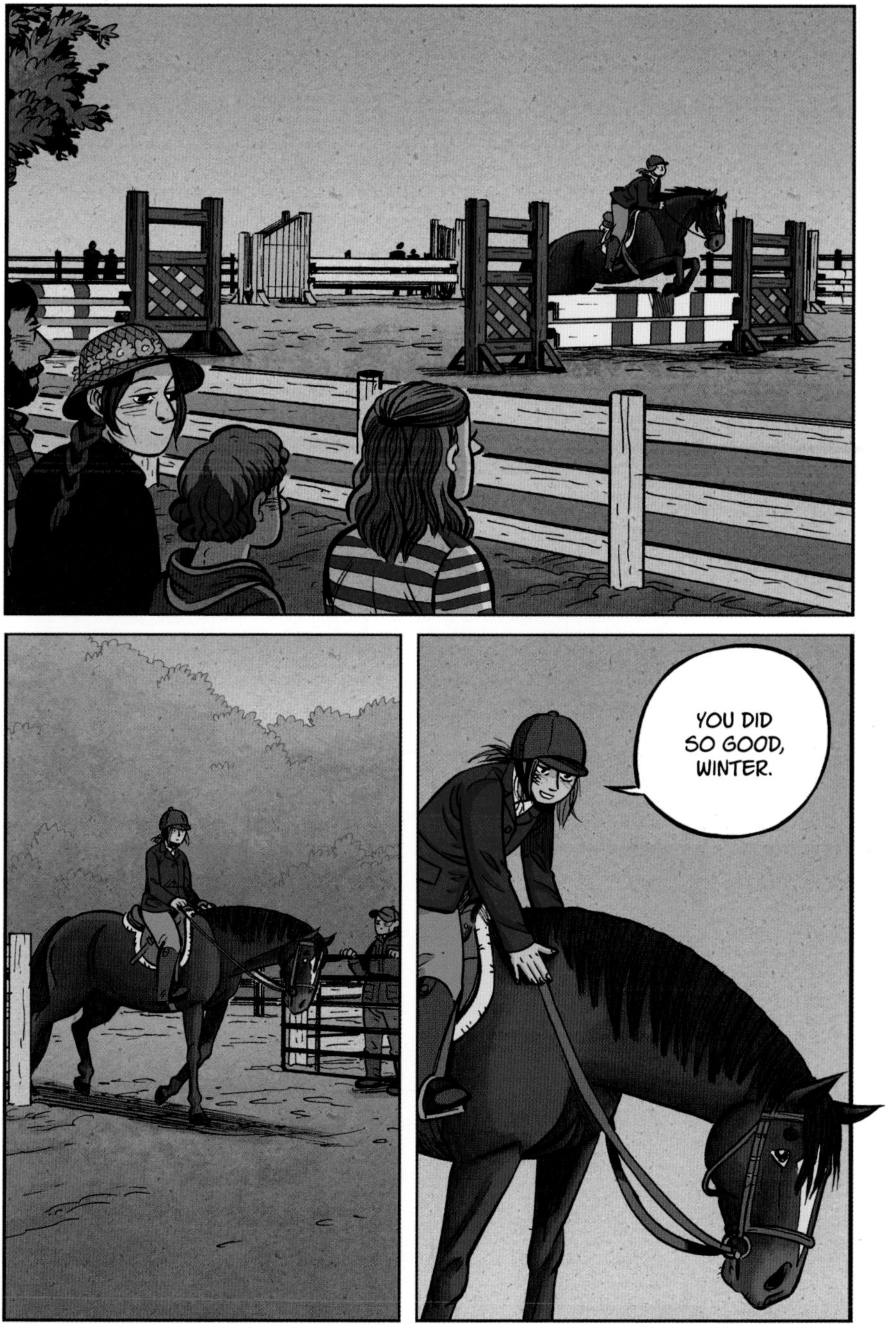
YOU DID SO GOOD, WINTER.

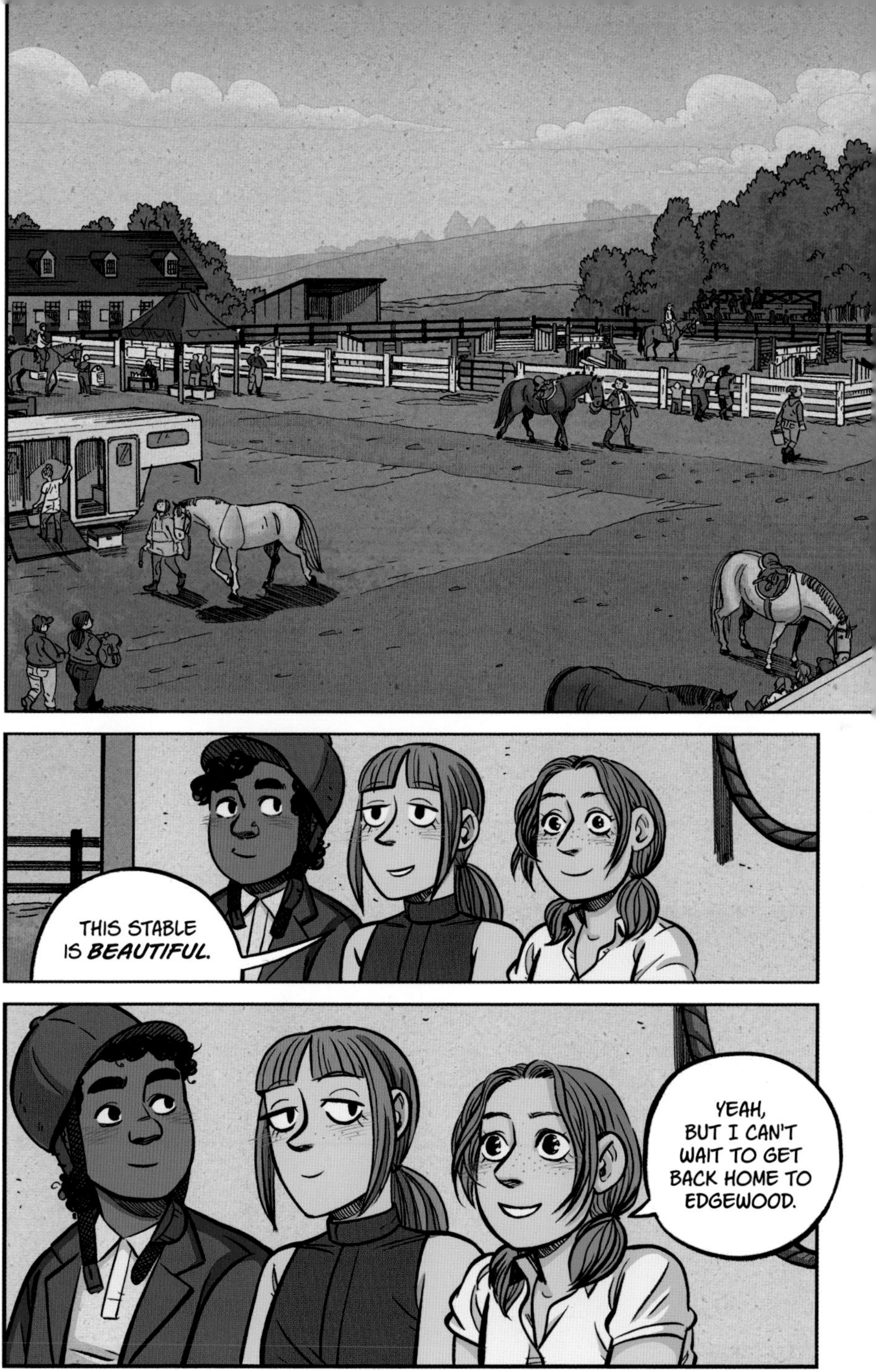
THIS STABLE IS BEAUTIFUL.
YEAH, BUT I CAN'T WAIT TO GET BACK HOME TO EDGEWOOD.

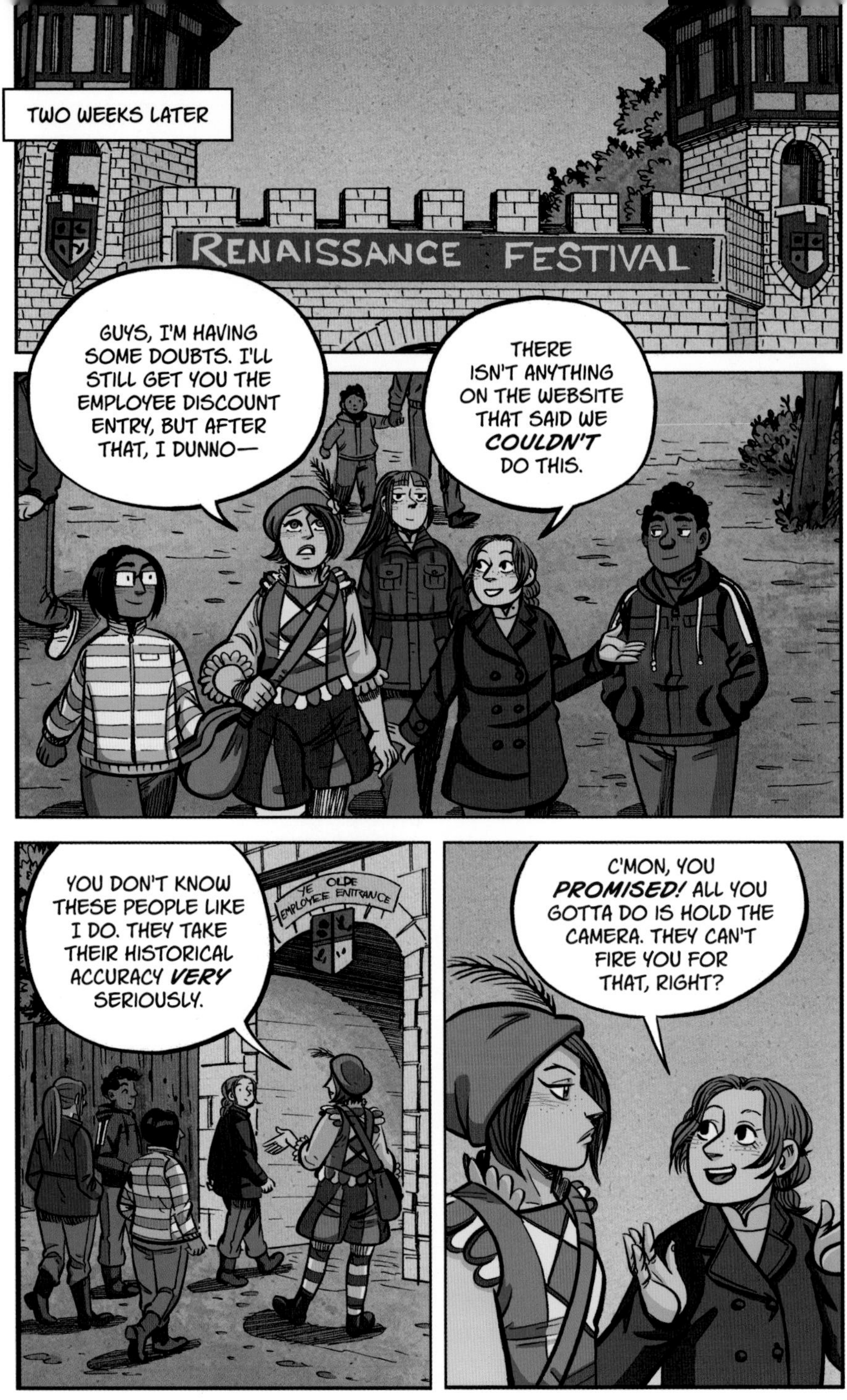
TWO WEEKS LATER
RENAISSANCE FESTIVAL
GUYS, I'M HAVING SOME DOUBTS. I'LL STILL GET YOU THE EMPLOYEE DISCOUNT ENTRY, BUT AFTER THAT, I DUNNO—
THERE ISN'T ANYTHING ON THE WEBSITE THAT SAID WE *COULDN'T* DO THIS.
YE OLDE EMPLOYEE ENTRANCE
YOU DON'T KNOW THESE PEOPLE LIKE I DO. THEY TAKE THEIR HISTORICAL ACCURACY *VERY* SERIOUSLY.
C'MON, YOU *PROMISED!* ALL YOU GOTTA DO IS HOLD THE CAMERA. THEY CAN'T FIRE YOU FOR THAT, RIGHT?

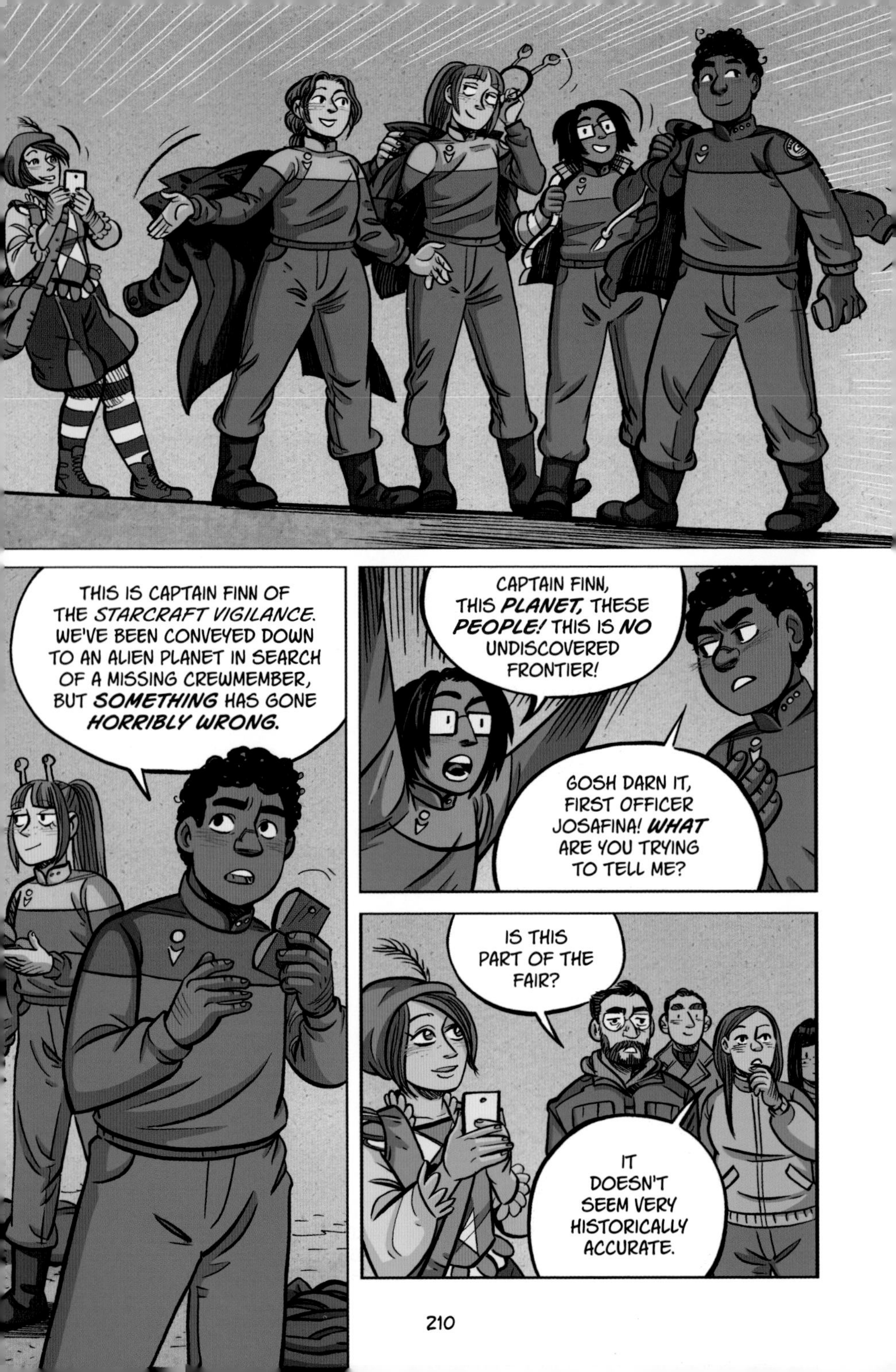

THIS IS CAPTAIN FINN OF THE *STARCRAFT VIGILANCE*. WE'VE BEEN CONVEYED DOWN TO AN ALIEN PLANET IN SEARCH OF A MISSING CREWMEMBER, BUT **SOMETHING** HAS GONE ***HORRIBLY WRONG.***
CAPTAIN FINN, THIS ***PLANET,*** THESE ***PEOPLE!*** THIS IS ***NO*** UNDISCOVERED FRONTIER!
GOSH DARN IT, FIRST OFFICER JOSAFINA! ***WHAT*** ARE YOU TRYING TO TELL ME?
IS THIS PART OF THE FAIR?
IT DOESN'T SEEM VERY HISTORICALLY ACCURATE.

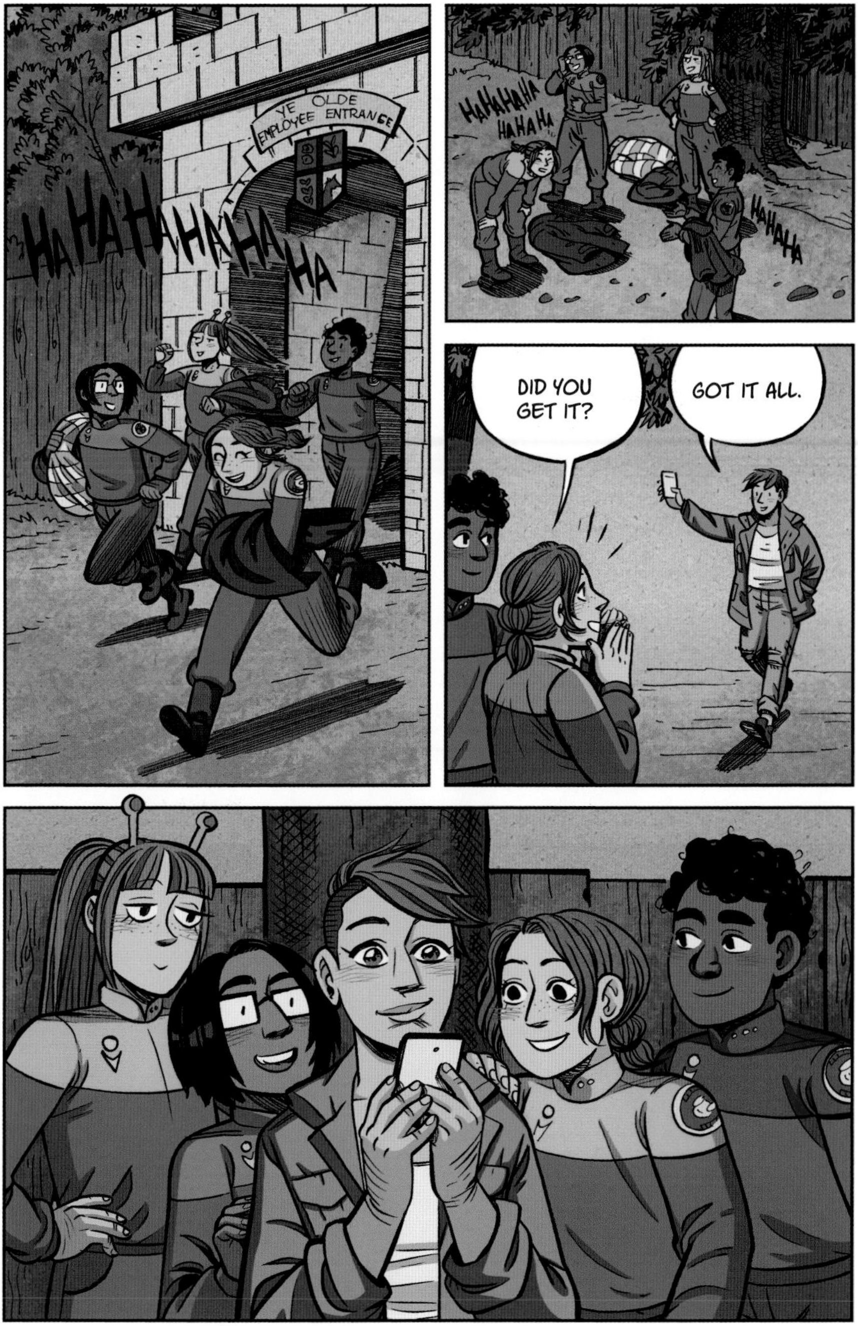
YE OLDE
EMPLOYEE ENTRANCE
HAHAHAHAHAHAHAHA
HAHAHAHA
HAHAHA
HAHAHA
DID YOU GET IT?
GOT IT ALL.

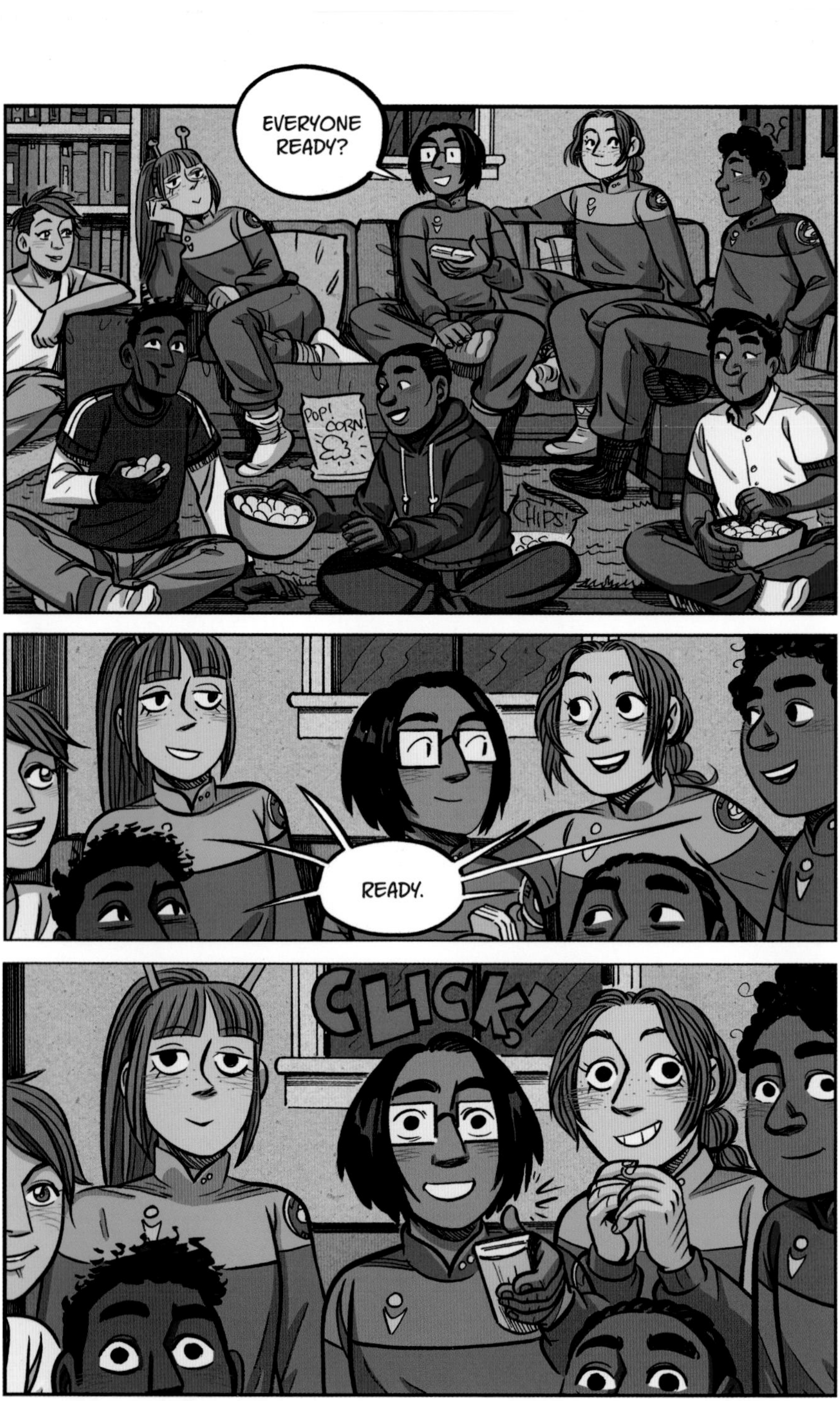
EVERYONE READY?
POP! CORN!
CHIPS!
READY.
CLICK!